MYSTERY *for* CHRISTMAS

MYSTERY for CHRISTMAS

Edited by Richard Dalby

GALLERY BOOKS
An Imprint of W. H. Smith Publishers Inc.
112 Madison Avenue
New York City 10016

First published in the United States in 1990 by Gallery Books, an imprint of
W.H. Smith Publishers, Inc., 112 Madison Avenue, New York,
New York 10016 by arrangement with Michael O'Mara Books, London

Gallery Books are available for bulk purchase for sales
promotions and premium use. For details write or telephone the
Manager of Special Sales, W.H. Smith Publishers, Inc.,
112 Madison Avenue, New York, New York 10016. (212) 532–6600

ISBN 0–8317–6294–2

Manufactured in the United States

CONTENTS

FOREWORD

Christmas has traditionally been associated with the narration of thrilling tales of mystery and the supernatural. *Mystery for Christmas*, like its two companion volumes *Ghosts for Christmas* and *Chillers for Christmas*, ranges over more than 150 years from Dickens to the present day. The first half comprises a varied number of early stories, including classics by Dickens and Hardy, together with several less familiar tales which have not been in print for several decades.

Charles Dickens, who encouraged so many of his great literary contemporaries (including Wilkie Collins, Mrs Gaskell, J.S. Le Fanu, and Amelia B. Edwards) to contribute Christmas mystery and ghost stories to his magazines *Household Words* and *All the Year Round*, is here represented by one of his earliest tales from *Sketches by Boz*.

Other classic Victorian tales of mystery and terror are contributed by Thomas Hardy, Mrs J.H. Riddell, and the popular French collaborators Erckmann-Chatrian.

From the first six decades of the twentieth century, we have a varied and unusual selection of supernatural gems by Edward Lucas White, Marjorie Bowen, Margery Lawrence, and Muriel Spark.

The second half of this volume comprises a dozen completely new, previously unpublished Christmas stories by some of the best short story writers active in Britain today. These range from crime stories by H.R.F. Keating and John S. Glasby to seasonal tales of the supernatural by Derek Stanford and Mary Williams.

M.R. James, who produced a new ghost story annually each Christmas for many years, is himself featured here both early and later in his career respectively in the stories by Ron Weighell and David Rowlands.

Following its two predecessors, I hope this anthology will continue to entertain and popularize the age-old tradition of telling seasonal ghost and mystery stories at Christmas.

Richard Dalby

THE BLACK VEIL

by Charles Dickens

Charles Dickens (1812–70) began his literary
career by contributing short sketches and tales
to the *Monthly Magazine* and the *Evening
Chronicle* in London. These were soon collected
together and published as *Sketches by 'Boz',
Illustrative of Every-Day Life and Every-Day People*
(1836–7). Among these can be found 'The
Black Veil', the earliest in a long line of
Victorian Christmas mystery stories.

One winter's evening, towards the close of the year 1800, or
within a year or two of that time, a young medical practitioner,
recently established in business, was seated by a cheerful fire, in
his little parlour, listening to the wind which was beating the rain in
pattering drops against the window, and rumbling dismally in the
chimney. The night was wet and cold; he had been walking through mud
and water the whole day, and was now comfortably reposing in his
dressing-gown and slippers, more than half-asleep and less than half
awake, revolving a thousand matters in his wandering imagination. First,
he thought how hard the wind was blowing, and how the cold sharp rain
would be at that moment beating in his face, if he were not comfortably
housed at home. Then his mind reverted to his annual Christmas visit to
his native place and dearest friends; he thought how glad they would all
be to see him, and how happy it would make Rose if he could only tell
her that he had found a patient at last, and hoped to have more, and to
come down again, in a few months' time, and marry her, and take her
home to gladden his lonely fireside, and stimulate him to fresh exertions.

Then he began to wonder when his first patient would appear, or whether he was destined by a special dispensation of Providence, never to have any patients at all; and then he thought about Rose again, and dropped to sleep and dreamed about her, till the tones of her sweet merry voice sounded in his ears and her soft tiny hand rested on his shoulder.

There *was* a hand upon his shoulder, but it was neither soft nor tiny; its owner being a corpulent, round-headed boy, who, in consideration of the sum of one shilling per week and his food, was let out by the parish to carry medicine and messages. As there was no demand for the medicine, however, and no necessity for the messages, he usually occupied his unemployed hours—averaging fourteen a day—in abstracting peppermint drops, taking animal nourishment, and going to sleep.

'A lady, sir—a lady!' whispered the boy, rousing his master with a shake.

'What lady?' cried our friend, starting up, not quite certain that his dream was an illusion, and half-expecting that it might be Rose herself. 'What lady? Where?'

'*There*, sir!' replied the boy, pointing to the glass door leading into the surgery, with an expression of alarm which the very unusual apparition of a customer might have tended to excite.

The surgeon looked towards the door, and started himself, for an instant, on beholding the appearance of his unlooked-for visitor.

It was a singularly tall woman, dressed in deep mourning, and standing so close to the door that her face almost touched the glass. The upper part of her figure was carefully muffled in a black shawl, as if for the purpose of concealment; and her face was shrouded by a thick black veil. She stood perfectly erect; her figure was drawn up to its full height, and though the surgeon *felt* that the eyes beneath the veil were fixed on him, she stood perfectly motionless, and evinced, by no gesture whatever, the slightest consciousness of his having turned towards her.

'Do you wish to consult me?' he inquired, with some hesitation, holding open the door. It opened inwards, and therefore the action did not alter the position of the figure, which still remained motionless on the same spot.

She slightly inclined her head in token of acquiescence.

'Pray walk in,' said the surgeon.

The figure moved a step forward; and then, turning its head in the direction of the boy—to his infinite horror—appeared to hesitate.

'Leave the room, Tom,' said the young man, addressing the boy, whose large round eyes had been extended to their utmost width during this brief interview. 'Draw the curtain, and shut the door.'

The boy drew a green curtain across the glass part of the door, retired into the surgery, closed the door after him, and immediately applied one of his large eyes to the keyhole on the other side.

The surgeon drew a chair to the fire, and motioned the visitor to a seat. The mysterious figure slowly moved towards it. As the blaze shone upon the black dress, the surgeon observed that the bottom of it was saturated with mud and rain.

'You are very wet,' he said.

'I am,' said the stranger, in a low, deep voice.

'And you are ill?' added the surgeon compassionately, for the tone was that of a person in pain.

'I am,' was the reply—'very ill: not bodily, but mentally. It is not for myself, or on my own behalf,' continued the stranger, 'that I come to you. If I laboured under bodily disease, I should not be out alone at such an hour, or on such a night as this; and, if I were afflicted with it twenty-four hours hence, God knows how gladly I would lie down and pray to die. It is for another that I beseech your aid, sir. I may be mad to ask it for him—I think I am; but, night after night, through the long dreary hours of watching and weeping, the thought has been ever present to my mind; and though even *I* see the hopelessness of human assistance availing him, the bare thought of laying him to his grave without it makes my blood run cold!' And the shudder, such as the surgeon well knew art could not produce, trembled through the speaker's frame.

There was a desperate earnestness in this woman's manner that went to the young man's heart. He was young in his profession, and had not yet witnessed enough of the miseries which are daily presented before the eyes of its members, to have grown comparatively callous to human suffering.

'If,' he said, rising hastily, 'the person of whom you speak be in so hopeless a condition as you describe, not a moment is to be lost. I will go with you instantly. Why did you not obtain medical advice before?'

'Because it would have been useless before—because it is useless even now,' replied the woman, clasping her hands passionately.

The surgeon gazed for a moment on the black veil, as if to ascertain the expression of the features beneath it; its thickness, however, rendered such a result impossible.

'You *are* ill,' he said gently, 'although you do not know it. The fever which has enabled you to bear, without feeling it, the fatigue you have

[3]

evidently undergone, is burning within you now. Put that to your lips,' he continued, pouring out a glass of water—'compose yourself for a few moments, and then tell me, as calmly as you can, what the disease of the patient is, and how long he has been ill. When I know what it is necessary I should know, to render my visit serviceable to him, I am ready to accompany you.'

The stranger lifted the glass of water to her mouth without raising the veil; put it down again untasted; and burst into tears.

'I know,' she said, sobbing aloud, 'that what I say to you now seems like the ravings of a fever. I have been told so before, less kindly than by you. I am not a young woman; and they do say that, as life steals on towards its final close, the last short remnant, worthless as it may seem to all beside, is dearer to its possessor than all the years that have gone before, connected though they be with the recollection of old friends long since dead, and young ones—children, perhaps—who have fallen off from and forgotten one as completely as if they had died too. My natural term of life cannot be many years longer, and should be dear on that account; but I would lay it down without a sigh—with cheerfulness—with joy—if what I tell you now were only false or imaginary. Tomorrow morning, he of whom I speak will be, I *know*, though I would fain think otherwise, beyond the reach of human aid; and yet tonight, though he is in deadly peril, you must not see, and could not serve him.'

'I am unwilling to increase your distress,' said the surgeon, after a short pause, 'by making any comment on what you have just said, or appearing desirous to investigate a subject you are so anxious to conceal; but there is an inconsistency in your statement which I cannot reconcile with probability. This person is dying tonight, and I cannot see him when my assistance might possibly avail; you apprehend it will be useless tomorrow, and yet you would have me see him then! If he be indeed as dear to you as your words and manner would imply, why not try to save his life before delay and the progress of his disease render it impracticable?'

'God help me!' exclaimed the woman, weeping bitterly, 'how can I hope strangers will believe what appears incredible even to myself? You will *not* see him, then, sir?' she added, rising suddenly.

'I did not say that I declined to see him,' replied the surgeon; 'but I warn you, that if you persist in this extraordinary procrastination, and the individual dies, a fearful responsibility rests with you.'

'The responsibility will rest heavily somewhere,' replied the stranger bitterly. 'Whatever responsibility rests with me, I am content to bear, and ready to answer.'

'As I incur none,' continued the surgeon, 'by acceding to your request, I will see him in the morning, if you leave me the address. And what hour can he be seen?'

'Nine,' replied the stranger.

'You must excuse my pressing these inquiries,' said the surgeon, 'but is he in your charge now?'

'He is not,' was her rejoinder.

'Then, if I gave you instructions for his treatment through the night you could not assist him?'

The woman wept bitterly as she replied, 'I could not.'

Finding that there was but little prospect of obtaining more information by prolonging the interview, and anxious to spare the woman's feelings, which, subdued at first by a violent effort, were now irrepressible and most painful to witness, the surgeon repeated his promise of calling in the morning at the appointed hour. His visitor, after giving him a direction to an obscure part of Walworth, left the house in the same mysterious manner in which she had entered it.

It will be readily believed that so extraordinary a visit produced a considerable impression on the mind of the young surgeon; and that he speculated a great deal, and to very little purpose, on the possible circumstances of the case. In common with the generality of people, he had often heard and read of singular instances, in which a presentiment of death, at a particular day, or even minute, had been entertained and realised. At one moment, he was inclined to think that the present might be such a case; but then it occurred to him that all the anecdotes of the kind he had ever heard were of persons who had been troubled with a foreboding of their own death. This woman, however, spoke of another person—a man; and it was impossible to suppose that a mere dream or delusion of fancy would induce her to speak of his approaching dissolution with such terrible certainty as she had spoken. It could not be that the man was to be murdered in the morning, and that the woman, originally a consenting party, and bound to secrecy by an oath, had relented, and though unable to prevent the commission of some outrage on the victim, had determined to prevent his death, if possible, by the timely interposition of medical aid? The idea of such things happening within two miles of the metropolis appeared too wild and preposterous to be entertained beyond the instant. Then his original impression, that the woman's intellects were disordered, recurred; and, as it was the only mode of solving the difficulty with any degree of satisfaction, he obstinately made up his mind to believe that she was mad. Certain misgivings upon this point, however, stole upon his thoughts at the time, and presented themselves again and again through the long, dull course of a sleepless night; during which, in spite of all his efforts to the contrary, he was unable to banish the black veil from his disturbed imagination.

The back part of Walworth, at its greatest distance from town, is a straggling, miserable place enough, even in these days; but, five-and-thirty years ago the greater portion of it was little better than a dreary waste, inhabited by a few scattered people of questionable character, whose poverty prevented their living in any better neighbourhood, or whose pursuits and mode of life rendered its solitude desirable. Very many of the houses which have since sprung up on all sides were not built until some years afterwards; and the great majority even of those which were sprinkled about, at irregular intervals, were of the rudest and most miserable description.

The appearance of the place through which he walked in the morning was not calculated to raise the spirits of the young surgeon, or to dispel any feeling of anxiety or depression which the singular kind of visit he was about to make had awakened. Striking off from the high-road, his way lay across a marshy common, through irregular lanes, with here and there a ruinous and dismantled cottage fast falling to pieces with decay and neglect. A stunted tree, or pool of stagnant water, roused into a sluggish action by the heavy rain of the preceding night, skirted the path occasionally; and now and then a miserable patch of garden ground, with a few old boards knocked together for a summer-house, and old palings imperfectly mended with stakes pilfered from the neighbouring hedges, bore testimony at once to the poverty of the inhabitants and the little scruple they entertained in appropriating the property of other people to their own use. Occasionally a filthy-looking woman would make her appearance from the door of a dirty house, to empty the contents of some cooking utensil into the gutter in front, or to scream after a little slip-shod girl who had contrived to stagger a few yards from the door under the weight of a sallow infant almost as big as herself; but scarcely anything was stirring around; and so much of the prospect as could be faintly traced through the cold damp mist which hung heavily over it, presented a lonely and dreary appearance, perfectly in keeping with the objects we have described.

After plodding wearily through the mud and mire; making many inquiries for the place to which he had been directed; and receiving as many contradictory and unsatisfactory replies in return; the young man at length arrived before the house which had been pointed out to him as the object of his destination. It was a small, low building, one storey above the ground, with even a more desolate and unpromising exterior than any he had yet passed. An old yellow curtain was closely drawn across the window upstairs, and the parlour shutters were closed, but not fastened. The house was detached from any other, and, as it stood at an angle of a narrow lane, there was no other habitation in sight.

When we say that the surgeon hesitated, and walked a few paces beyond the house, before he could prevail upon himself to lift the knocker, we say nothing that need raise a smile upon the face of the boldest reader. The police of London were a very different body in that day; the isolated position of the suburbs, when the rage for building and the progress of improvement had not yet begun to connect them with the main body of the city and its environs, rendered many of them (and this in particular) a place of resort for the worst and most depraved characters. Even the streets in the gayest parts of London were imperfectly lighted at that time; and such places as these were left entirely to the mercy of the moon and stars. The chances of detecting desperate characters, or of tracing them to their haunts, were thus rendered very few, and their offences naturally increased in boldness, as the consciousness of comparative security became the more impressed upon them by daily experience. Added to these considerations, it must be remembered that the young man had spent some time in the public hospitals of the metropolis; and, although neither Burke nor Bishop had then gained a horrible notoriety, his own observation might have suggested to him how easily the atrocities to which the former has since given his name might be committed. Be this as it may, whatever reflection made him hesitate, he *did* hesitate; but, being a young man of strong mind and great personal courage, it was only for an instant. He stepped briskly back and knocked gently at the door.

A low whispering was audible immediately afterwards, as if some person at the end of the passage were conversing stealthily with another on the landing above. It was succeeded by the noise of a pair of heavy boots upon the bare floor. The door-chain was softly unfastened; the door opened; and a tall, ill-favoured man, with black hair and a face, as the surgeon often declared afterwards, as pale and haggard as the countenance of any dead man he ever saw, presented himself.

'Walk in, sir,' he said, in a low tone.

The surgeon did so, and the man, having secured the door again by the chain, led the way to a small back-parlour at the extremity of the passage.

'Am I in time?'

'Too soon!' replied the man. The surgeon turned hastily round, with a gesture of astonishment not unmixed with alarm, which he found it impossible to repress.

'If you'll step in here, sir,' said the man, who had evidently noticed the action—'if you'll step in here, sir, you won't be detained five minutes, I assure you.'

The surgeon at once walked into the room. The man closed the door, and left him alone.

It was a little cold room, with no other furniture than two deal chairs, and a table of the same material. A handful of fire, unguarded by any fender, was burning in the grate, which brought out the damp, if it served no more comfortable purpose, for the unwholesome moisture was stealing down the walls in long, slug-like tracks. The window, which was broken and patched in many places, looked into a small enclosed piece of ground, almost covered with water. Not a sound was to be heard, either within the house or without. The young surgeon sat down by the fire-place, to await the result of his first professional visit.

He had not remained in this position many minutes when the noise of some approaching vehicle struck his ear. It stopped; the street-door was opened; a low talking succeeded, accompanied with a shuffling noise of footsteps along the passage and on the stairs, as if two or three men were engaged in carrying some heavy body to the room above. The creaking of the stairs, a few seconds afterwards, announced that the newcomers, having completed their task, whatever it was, were leaving the house. The door was again closed, and the former silence was restored.

Another five minutes elapsed; and the surgeon had resolved to explore the house, in search of some one to whom he might make his errand known, when the room door opened, and his last night's visitor, dressed in exactly the same manner, with the veil lowered as before, motioned him to advance. The singular height of her form, coupled with the circumstance of her not speaking, caused the idea to pass across his brain, for an instant, that it might be a man disguised in woman's attire. The hysteric sobs which issued from beneath the veil, and the convulsive attitude of grief of the whole figure, however, at once exposed the absurdity of the suspicion; and he hastily followed.

The woman led the way upstairs to the front room, and paused at the door, to let him enter first. It was scantily furnished with an old deal box, a few chairs, and a tent bedstead, without hangings or cross-rails, which was covered with a patchwork counterpane. The dim light admitted through the curtain which he had noticed from the outside, rendered the objects in the room so indistinct, and communicated to all of them so uniform a hue, that he did not at first perceive the object on which his eye at once rested when the woman rushed frantically past him, and flung herself on her knees by the bedside.

Stretched upon the bed, closely enveloped in a linen wrapper, and covered with blankets, lay a human form, stiff and motionless. The head and face, which were those of a man, were uncovered, save for a bandage which passed over the head and under the chin. The eyes were closed. The left arm lay heavily across the bed, and the woman held the passive hand.

The surgeon gently pushed the woman aside, and took the hand in his.

'My God!' he exclaimed, letting it fall involuntarily—'the man is dead!'

The woman started to her feet, and beat her hands together. 'Oh, don't say so, sir!' she exclaimed, with a burst of passion amounting almost to frenzy. 'Oh, don't say so, sir! I can't bear it! Men have been brought to life before, when unskilful people have given them up for lost; and men have died, who might have been restored if proper means had been resorted to. Don't let him lie here, sir, without one effort to save him! This very moment life may be passing away. Do try, sir—do, for Heaven's sake!' And, while speaking, she hurriedly chafed, first the forehead, and then the breast of the senseless form before her; and then wildly beat the cold hands, which, when she ceased to hold them, fell listlessly and heavily back on the coverlet.

'It is of no use, my good woman,' said the surgeon soothingly, as he withdrew his hand from the man's breast. 'Stay—undraw that curtain!'

'Why?' said the woman, starting up.

'Undraw that curtain!' repeated the surgeon, in an agitated tone.

'I darkened the room on purpose,' said the woman, throwing herself before him as he rose to withdraw it. 'Oh, sir, have pity on me! If it can be of no use, and he is really dead, do not expose that form to other eyes than mine!'

'This man died no natural or easy death,' said the surgeon. 'I *must* see the body!' With a motion so sudden that the woman hardly knew that he had slipped from beside her, he tore open the curtain, admitted the full light of day, and returned to the bedside.

'There has been violence here,' he said, pointing towards the body, and gazing intently on the face, from which the black veil was now, for the first time, removed. In the excitement of a minute before, the female had thrown off the bonnet and veil, and now stood with her eyes fixed upon him. Her features were those of a woman of about fifty, who had once been handsome. Sorrow and weeping had left traces upon them which not time itself would ever have produced without their aid; her face was deadly pale; and there was a nervous contortion of the lip, and an unnatural fire in her eye, which showed too plainly that her bodily and mental powers had nearly sunk beneath an accumulation of misery.

'There has been violence here,' said the surgeon, preserving his searching glance.

'There has!' replied the woman.

'This man has been murdered.'

'That I call God to witness he has,' said the woman passionately; 'pitilessly, inhumanly murdered!'

'By whom?' said the surgeon, seizing the woman by the arm.

'Look at the butchers' marks, and then ask me!' she replied.

The surgeon turned his face towards the bed, and bent over the body which now lay full in the light of the window. The throat was swollen, and a livid mark encircled it. The truth flashed suddenly upon him.

'That is one of the men who were hanged this morning!' he exclaimed, turning away with a shudder.

'It is,' replied the woman, with a cold, unmeaning stare.

'Who was he?' inquired the surgeon.

'My son,' rejoined the woman; and fell senseless at his feet.

It was true. A companion, equally guilty with himself, had been acquitted for want of evidence; and this man had been left for death, and executed. To recount the circumstances of the case, at this distant period, must be unnecessary, and might give pain to some persons still alive. The history was an everyday one. The mother was a widow without friends or money, and had denied herself necessaries to bestow them on her orphan boy. That boy, unmindful of her prayers, and forgetful of the sufferings she had endured for him—incessant anxiety of mind, and voluntarily starvation of body—had plunged into a career of dissipation and crime. And this was the result; his own death by the hangman's hands, and his mother's shame and incurable insanity.

For many years after this occurrence, and when profitable and arduous avocations would have led many men to forget that such a miserable being existed, the young surgeon was a daily visitor at the side of the harmless mad-woman; not only soothing her by his presence and kindness, but alleviating the rigour of her condition by pecuniary donations for her comfort and support, bestowed with no sparing hand. In the transient gleam of recollection and consciousness which preceded her death, a prayer for his welfare and protection, as fervent as mortal ever breathed, rose from the lips of this poor, friendless creature. That prayer flew to heaven, and was heard. The blessings he was instrumental in conferring have been repaid to him a thousand-fold: but, amid all the honours of rank and station which have since been heaped upon him, and which he has so well earned, he can have no reminiscence more gratifying to his heart than that connected with The Black Veil.

THE BANSHEE'S
WARNING

by Mrs J.H. Riddell

Mrs J.H. Riddell (née Charlotte Cowan,
1832–1906) was, in the company of other
leading female novelists like Amelia Edwards
and Margaret Oliphant, one of the finest writers
of ghost stories in the Victorian era. She penned
many excellent Christmas tales including 'Fairy
Water', 'The Old House in Vauxhall Walk', 'A
Strange Christmas Game', and 'The Haunted
River'. The following story is taken from her
collection *The Banshee's Warning, and other tales*
(1894). A memorable Christmas 'miracle story'
in the tradition established by *A Christmas
Carol*, it originally appeared under the title
'Hertford O'Donnell's Warning' in the
Christmas Number of *London Society*, 1867.

Many a year ago, before chloroform was thought of, there lived
in an old rambling house in Gerrard Street, Soho, a young
Irishman called Hertford O'Donnell.

After Hertford O'Donnell he was entitled to write M.R.C.S., for he
had studied hard to gain this distinction, and the elder surgeons at Guy's
(his hospital) considered him, in their secret hearts, one of the most
rising operators of the day.

Having said chloroform was unknown at the time this story opens, it
will strike my readers that, if Hertford O'Donnell were a rising and
successful operator in those days, of necessity he combined within

himself a larger number of striking qualities than are by any means necessary to form a successful operator in these.

There was more than mere hand skill, more than even thorough knowledge of his profession, needful for the man who, dealing with conscious subjects, essayed to rid them of some of the diseases to which flesh is heir. There was greater courage required in the manipulator of old than is altogether essential now. Then, as now, a thorough mastery of his instruments—a steady hand—a keen eye—a quick dexterity, were indispensable to a good operator; but, added to all these things, there were formerly required a pulse which knew no quickening—a mental strength which never faltered—a ready power of adaptation in unexpected circumstances—fertility of resource in difficult cases, and a brave front under all emergencies.

If I refrain from adding that a hard as well as a courageous heart was an important item in the programme, it is only out of deference to general opinion, which, amongst other delusions, clings to the belief that courage and hardness are antagonistic qualities.

Hertford O'Donnell, however, was hard as steel. He understood his work, and he did it thoroughly; but he cared no more for quivering nerves and contracting muscles, for screams of agony, for faces white with pain, and teeth clenched in the extremity of anguish, than he did for a stony countenance of the dead, which sometimes in the dissecting room appalled younger and less experienced men.

He had no sentiment, and he had no sympathy. The human body was to him an ingenious piece of mechanism, which it was at once a pleasure and a profit to understand. Precisely as Brunel loved the Thames Tunnel, or any other singular engineering feat, so O'Donnell loved a patient on whom he operated successfully, more especially if the ailment possessed by the patient were of a rare and difficult character.

And for this reason he was much liked by all who came under his hands, for patients are apt to mistake a surgeon's interest in their cases for interest in themselves; and it was gratifying to John Dicks, plasterer, and Timothy Regan, labourer, to be the happy possessors of remarkable diseases, which produced a cordial understanding between them and the handsome Irishman.

If he were hard and cool at the moment of hewing them to pieces, that was all forgotten, or remembered only as a virtue, when, after being discharged from hospital like soldiers who have served in a severe campaign, they met Mr O'Donnell in the street, and were accosted by that rising individual, just as though he considered himself nobody.

He had a royal memory, this stranger in a strange land, both for faces and cases; and, like the rest of his countrymen, he never felt it beneath his dignity to talk cordially to corduroy and fustian.

In London, as at Calgillan, he never held back his tongue from speaking a cheery or a kindly word. His manners were pliable enough, if his heart were not; and the porters, and the patients, and the nurses, and the students at Guy's all were pleased to see Hertford O'Donnell.

Rain, hail, sunshine, it was all the same; there was a life, and a brightness about the man which communicated itself to those with whom he came in contact. Let the mud out in Smithfield be a foot deep, or the London fog thick as pea-soup, Mr O'Donnell never lost his temper, never uttered a surly reply to the gatekeeper's salutation, but spoke out blithely and cheerfully to his pupils and his patients, to the sick and to the well, to those below and to those above him.

And yet, spite of all these good qualities—spite of his handsome face, his fine figure, his easy address and his unquestionable skill as an operator, the dons, who acknowledged his talent, shook their heads gravely when two or three of them, in private and solemn conclave, talked confidentially of their younger brother.

If there were many things in his favour, there were more in his disfavour. He was Irish—not merely by the accident of birth, which might have been forgiven, since a man cannot be held accountable for such caprices of Nature, but by every other accident and design which is objectionable to the orthodox and respectable and representative English mind.

In speech, appearance, manner, habits, modes of expression, habits of life, Hertford O'Donnell was Irish. To the core of his heart he loved the island which he, nevertheless, declared he never meant to revisit; and amongst the English he moved, to all intents and purposes, a foreigner who was resolved, so said the great prophets at Guy's, to go to destruction as fast as he could and let no man hinder him.

'He means to go the whole length of his tether,' observed one of the ancient wiseacres to another; which speech implied a conviction that Hertford O'Donnell, having sold himself to the Evil One, had determined to dive the full length of his rope into wickedness before being pulled to the shore where even wickedness is negative—where there are no mad carouses, no wild, sinful excitement, nothing but impotent wailing and gnashing of teeth.

A reckless, graceless, clever, wicked devil—going to his natural home as fast as in London a man can possibly progress thither: this was the opinion his superiors held of the man who lived all alone with a housekeeper and her husband (who acted as butler) in his big house near Soho.

Gerrard Street was not then an utterly shady and forgotten locality: carriage patients found their way to the rising young surgeon—some great personages thought it not beneath them to fee an individual whose consulting rooms were situated on what was even then the wrong side of Regent Street. He was making money; and he was spending it; he was over head and ears in debt—useless, vulgar debt—senselessly con-tracted, never bravely faced. He had lived at an awful pace ever since he came to London, at a pace which only a man who hopes and expects to die young can ever travel.

Life! what good was it? Death! was he a child, or a woman, or a coward, to be afraid of that hereafter? God knew all about the trifle which had upset his coach better than the dons at Guy's; and he did not dread facing his Maker, and giving an account to Him, even of the disreputable existence he had led since he came to London.

Hertford O'Donnell knew the world pretty well, and the ways thereof were to him as roads often traversed; therefore, when he said that at the day of judgment he felt certain he should come off better than many of those who censured him, it may be assumed that, although his views of post-mortem punishment were vague, unsatisfactory, and infidel, still his information as to the peccadilloes of his neighbours was such as consoled himself.

And yet, living all alone in the old house near Soho Square, grave thoughts would intrude frequently into the surgeon's mind—thoughts which were, so to say, italicized by peremptory letters, and still more peremptory visits from people who wanted money.

Although he had many acquaintances, he had no single friend, and accordingly these thoughts were received and brooded over in solitude, in those hours when, after returning from dinner or supper, or congenial carouse, he sat in his dreary room smoking his pipe and considering means and ways, chances and certainties.

In good truth he had started in London with some vague idea that as his life in it would not be of long continuance, the pace at which he elected to travel could be of little consequence; but the years since his first entry into the metropolis were now piled one on the top of another, his youth was behind him, his chances of longevity, spite of the way he had striven to injure his constitution, quite as good as ever. He had come to that time in existence, to that narrow strip of table land whence the ascent of youth and the descent of age are equally discernible—when, simply because he has lived for so many years, it strikes a man as possible he may have to live for just as many more, with the ability for hard work gone, with the boon companions scattered abroad, with the capacity for enjoying convivial meetings a mere memory, with small means, perhaps, with no bright hopes, with the pomp and the equipage, and the fairy carriages, and the glamour which youth flings over earthly objects, faded away like the pageant of yesterday, while the dreary ceremony of living has to be gone through today and tomorrow and the morrow after, as though the gay cavalcade and the martial music, and the glittering helmets and the prancing steeds were still accompanying the wayfarer to his journey's end.

Ah! my friends, there comes a moment when we must all leave the coach with its four bright bays, its pleasant freight, its cheery company, its guard who blows the horn so merrily through villages and along lonely country roads.

Long before we reach that final stage, where the black business claims us for its own especial property, we have to bid good-bye to all easy thoughtless journeying, and betake ourselves, with what zest we will, to traversing the common of Reality. There is no royal road across it that ever I heard of. From the king on his throne to the labourer who vaguely imagines what manner of being a king is, we have all to tramp across that desert at one period of our lives, at all events, and that period usually is when, as I have said, a man starts to find the hopes and the strength and the buoyancy of youth left behind, while years and years of life lie stretching out before him.

Even supposing a man's spring-time to have been a cold and ungenial one, with bitter easterly winds and nipping frosts, biting the buds and retarding the blossom, still it was spring for all that—spring, with the young green leaves sprouting forth, with the flowers unfolding tenderly, with the songs of birds and the rush of waters, with the summer before and the autumn afar off, and winter remote as death and eternity; but when once the trees have donned their summer foliage, when the pure white blossoms have disappeared, and a gorgeous red and orange, and purple blaze of many-coloured flowers fills the gardens; then, if there comes a wet, dreary day, the idea of autumn and winter is not so difficult to realise. When once twelve o'clock is reached, the evening and night become facts, not possibilities; and it was of the afternoon and the evening and the night, Hertford O'Donnell sat thinking on the Christmas Eve when I crave permission to introduce him to my readers.

A good-looking man, ladies considered him. A tall, dark-complexioned, black-haired, straight-limbed, deeply, divinely blue-eyed fellow, with a soft voice, with a pleasant brogue, who had ridden like a Centaur over the loose stone walls in Connemara, who had danced all night at the Dublin balls, who had walked over the Bennebeola mountains, gun in hand, day after day without weariness: who had led a mad, wild life while 'studying for a doctor'—as the Irish phrase goes—in Dublin, and who, after the death of his eldest brother left him free to return to Calgillan and pursue the usual utterly useless, utterly purposeless, utterly pleasant life of an Irish gentleman possessed of health, birth, and expectations, suddenly kicked over the paternal traces, bade adieu to Calgillan Castle and the blandishments of a certain beautiful Miss Clifden, beloved of his mother, and laid out to be his wife, walked down the avenue without even so much company as a gossoon to carry his carpet-bag, shook the dust from his feet at the lodge-gates, and took his seat on the coach, never once looking back at Calgillan, where his favourite mare was standing in the stable, his greyhounds chasing one another round the home paddock, his gun at half-cock in his dressing-room, and his fishing-tackle all in order and ready for use.

He had not kissed his mother nor asked for his father's blessing; he left Miss Clifden arrayed in her bran-new-riding-habit, without a word of affection or regret; he had spoken no syllable of farewell to any servant about the place; only when the old woman at the lodge bade him good morning and God-blessed his handsome face, he recommended her bitterly to look well at it, for she would never see it more.

Twelve years and a half had passed since then without either Nancy Black or any other one of the Calgillan people having set eyes on Master Hertford's handsome face. He had kept his vow to himself—he had not written home; he had not been indebted to mother or father for even a tenpenny-piece during the whole of that time; he had lived without God—so far as God ever lets a man live without him—and his own private conviction was that he could get on very well without either. One thing only he felt to be needful—money; money to keep him when the evil days of sickness, or age, or loss of practice came upon him. Though a spendthrift, he was not a simpleton. Around him he saw men, who, having started with fairer prospects than his own, were nevertheless reduced to indigence; and he knew that what had happened to others might happen to himself.

An unlucky cut, slipping on a bit of orange-peel in the street, the merest accident imaginable, is sufficient to change opulence to beggary in the life's programme of an individual whose income depends on eye, on nerve, on hand; and besides the consciousness of this fact, Hertford O'Donnell knew that beyond a certain point in his profession progress was not easy.

It did not depend quite on the strength of his own bow or shield whether he counted his earnings by hundreds of thousands. Work may achieve competence; but mere work cannot, in a profession at all events, compass wealth.

He looked around him, and he perceived that the majority of great men—great and wealthy—had been indebted for their elevation more to the accidents of birth, patronage, connection or marriage than to personal ability.

Personal ability, no doubt, they possessed; but then, little Jones, who lived in Frith Street, and who could barely keep himself and his wife and family, had ability, too, only he lacked the concomitants of success.

He wanted something or some one to puff him into notoriety—a brother at court—a lord's leg to mend—a rich wife to give him prestige in society; and, lacking this something or someone, he had grown grey-haired and faint-hearted in the service of that world which utterly despises its most obsequious servants.

'Clatter along the streets with a pair of hired horses, snub the middle classes, and drive over the commonality—that is the way to compass wealth and popularity in England,' said Hertford O'Donnell bitterly; and, as the man desired wealth and popularity, he sat before his fire, with a foot on each hob, and a short pipe in his mouth, considering how he might best obtain the means to clatter along the streets in his carriage, and splash plebeians with mud from his wheels like the best.

In Dublin he could, by means of his name and connection, have done well; but then he was not in Dublin, neither did he want to be. The bitterest memories of his life were inseparable from the name of the Green Island, and he had no desire to return to it.

Besides, in Dublin, heiresses are not quite so plentiful as in London; and an heiress, Hertford O'Donnell had decided, would do more for him than years of steady work.

A rich wife could clear him of debt, introduce him to fashionable practice, afford him that measure of social respectability which a medical bachelor invariably lacks; deliver him from the loneliness of Gerrard Street, and the domination of Mr and Mrs Coles.

To most men, deliberately bartering away their dependence for money seems so prosaic a business that they strive to gloss it over even to themselves, and to assign every reason for their choice, save that which is really the influencing one.

Not so, however, with Hertford O'Donnell. He sat beside the fire scoffing over his proposed bargain—thinking of the lady's age—her money-bags—her desirable house in town—her seat in the country—her snobbishness—her folly.

'It would be a fitting ending,' he sneered; 'and why I did not settle the matter tonight passes my comprehension. I am not a fool, to be frightened with old women's tales; and yet I must have turned white. I felt I did, and she asked me whether I was ill. And then to think of my being such an idiot as to ask her if she had heard anything like a cry, as though she would be likely to hear *that*—she, with her poor *parvenu* blood, which, I often imagine, must have been mixed with some of her father's strong pickling vinegar. What the deuce could I have been dreaming about? I wonder what it really was?' and Hertford O'Donnell pushed his hair back from his forehead and took another draught from the too familiar tumbler, which was placed conveniently on the chimney piece.

'After expressly making up my mind to propose, too!' he mentally continued. 'Could it have been conscience—that myth, which somebody, who knew nothing of the matter, said "makes cowards of us all"? I don't believe in conscience; and even it there be such a thing capable of being developed by sentiment and cultivation, why should it trouble me? I have no intention of wronging Miss Janet Price Ingot—not the least. Honestly and fairly I shall marry her; honestly and fairly I shall act by her. An old wife is not exactly an ornamental article of furniture in a man's house; and I do not know that the fact of her being well gilded makes her look any more ornamental. But she shall have no cause for complaint; and I will go and dine with her tomorrow and settle the matter.'

Having arrived at which resolution, Mr O'Donnell arose, kicked down the fire—burning hollow—with the heel of his boot, knocked the ashes out of his pipe, emptied his tumbler, and bethought him it was time to go to bed. He was not in the habit of taking rest so early as a quarter to twelve o'clock; but he felt unusually weary—tired mentally and bodily—and lonely beyond all power of expression.

'The fair Janet would be better than this,' he said, half aloud; and then, with a start and a shiver and a blanched face, he turned sharply round, whilst a low, sobbing, wailing cry echoed mournfully through the room. No form of words could give an idea of the sound. The plaintiveness of the Eolian harp—that plaintiveness which so soon affects and lowers the highest spirits—would have seemed wildly gay in comparison to the sadness of the cry which seemed floating in the air. As the summer wind comes and goes amongst the trees, so that mournful wail came and went—came and went. It came in a rush of sound, like a gradual crescendo managed by a skilful musician, and it died away like a lingering note, so that the listener could scarcely tell the exact moment when it faded away into silence.

I say faded away, for it disappeared as the coast line disappears in the twilight, and there was utter stillness in the apartment.

Then for the first time, Hertford O'Donnell looked at his dog, and, beholding the creature crouched into a corner beside the fireplace, called upon him to come out.

His voice sounded strange, even to himself, and apparently the dog thought so too, for he made no effort to obey the summons.

'Come out, sir,' his master repeated, and then the animal came crawling reluctantly forward, with his hair on end, his eyes almost starting from his head, trembling violently, as the surgeon, who caressed him, felt.

'So you heard it, Brian?' he said to the dog. 'And so your ears are sharper than hers, old fellow? It's a mighty queer thing to think of, being favoured with a visit from a banshee in Gerrard Street; and as the lady has travelled so far, I only wish I knew whether there is any sort of refreshment she would like to take after her long journey.'

He spoke loudly and with a certain mocking defiance, seeming to think the phantom he addressed would reply; but when he stopped at the end of his sentence, no sound came through the stillness. There was utter silence in the room—silence broken only by the falling of the cinders on the hearth, and the breathing of the dog.

'If my visitor would tell me,' he proceeded, 'for whom this lamentation is being made, whether for myself, or for some member of my illustrious family, I should feel immensely obliged. It seems too much honour for a poor surgeon to have such attention paid him. Good heavens! What is that?' he exclaimed, as a ring, loud and peremptory, woke all the echoes in the house, and brought his housekeeper, in a state of distressing dishabille, 'out of her warm bed,' as she subsequently stated, to the head of the staircase.

Across the hall Hertford O'Donnell strode, relieved at the prospect of speaking to any living being. He took no precaution of putting up the chain, but flung the door wide. A dozen burglars would have proved welcome in comparison to that ghostly intruder; and, as I have said, he threw the door open, admitting a rush of wet, cold air, which made poor Mrs Coles' few remaining teeth chatter in her head.

'Who is there?—what do you want?' asked the surgeon, seeing no person, and hearing no voice. 'Who is there?—why the devil can't you speak?'

But when even this polite exhortation failed to elicit an answer, he passed out into the night, and looked up the street, and down the street, to see nothing but the drizzling rain and the blinking lights.

'If this goes on much longer, I shall soon think I must be either mad or drunk,' he muttered, as he re-entered the house and locked and bolted the door once more.

'Lord's sake! what is the matter, sir?' asked Mrs Coles, from the upper flight, careful only to reveal the borders of her nightcap to Mr O'Donnell's admiring gaze. 'Is anybody killed?—have you to go out, sir?'

'It was only a runaway ring,' he answered, trying to reassure himself with an explanation he did not in his heart believe.

'Runaway!—I'd runaway them,' murmured Mrs Coles, as she retired to the conjugal couch, where Coles was, to quote her own expression, 'snoring like a pig through it all.' Almost immediately afterwards she heard her master ascend the stairs and close his bedroom door.

'Madam will surely be too much of a gentlewoman to intrude here,' thought the surgeon, scoffing even at his own fears; but when he lay down he did not put out his light, and he made Brian leap up and crouch on the coverlet beside him.

The man was fairly frightened, and would have thought it no discredit to his manhood to acknowledge as much. He was not afraid of death, he was not afraid of trouble, he was not afraid of danger; but he was afraid of the banshee; and as he lay with his hand on the dog's head, he thought over all the stories he had ever heard about this family retainer in the days of his youth. He had not thought about her for years and years. Never before had he heard her voice himself. When his brother died, she had not thought it necessary to travel up to Dublin and give him notice of the impending catastrophe. 'If she had, I would have gone down to Calgillan, and perhaps saved his life,' considered the surgeon. 'I wonder who this is for! If for me, that will settle my debts and my marriage. If I could be quite certain it was either of the old people I would start for Ireland tomorrow.' And then vaguely his mind wandered on to think of every banshee story he had ever heard in his life. About the beautiful lady with the wreath of flowers, who sat on the rocks below Red Castle, in the County Antrim, crying till one of the sons died for love of her; about the

Round Chamber at Dunluce, which was swept clean by the banshee every night; about the bed in a certain great house in Ireland, which was slept in constantly, although no human being passed ever in or out after dark; about that general officer who, the night before Waterloo, said to a friend, 'I have heard the banshee, and shall not come off the field alive tomorrow; break the news gently to poor Carry'; and who, nevertheless, coming safe off the field, had subsequently news about poor Carry broken tenderly and pitifully to him; about the lad who, aloft in the rigging, hearing through the night a sobbing and wailing coming over the waters, went down to the captain and told him he was afraid they were somehow out of their reckoning, just in time to save the ship, which when morning broke, they found, but for his warning, would have been on the rocks. It was blowing great guns, and the sea was all fret and turmoil, and they could sometimes see in the trough of the waves, as down a valley, the cruel black reefs they had escaped.

On deck the captain stood speaking to the boy who had saved them, and asking how he knew of their danger; and when the lad told him, the captain laughed, and said her ladyship had been outwitted that time.

But the boy answered, with a grave shake of his head, that the warning was either for him or his, and that if he got safe to port there would be bad tidings waiting for him from home; whereupon the captain bade him go below, and get some brandy and lie down.

He got the brandy, and he laid down, but he never rose again; and when the storm abated—when a great calm succeeded to the previous tempest—there was a very solemn funeral at sea; and on their arrival at Liverpool the captain took a journey to Ireland to tell a widowed mother how her only son died, and to bear his few effects to the poor, desolate soul.

And Hertford O'Donnell thought again about his own father, riding full-chase across country, and hearing, as he galloped by a clump of plantation, something like a sobbing and wailing. The hounds were in full cry; but he still felt, as he afterwards expressed it, that there was something among those trees he could not pass; and so he jumped off his horse, and hung the reins over the branch of a fir and beat the cover well, but not a thing could he find in it.

Then, for the first time in his life, Miles O'Donnell turned his horse's head *from* the hunt, and, within a mile of Calgillan, met a man running to tell him Mr Martin's gun had burst and hurt him badly.

And he remembered the story, also, of how Mary O'Donnell, his great-aunt, being married to a young Englishman, heard the banshee as she sat one evening waiting for his return; and of how she, thinking the bridge by which he often came home unsafe for horse and man, went out in a great panic, to meet and entreat him go round by the main road for her sake. Sir Everard was riding alone in the moonlight, making straight for the bridge, when he beheld a figure dressed all in white upon it. Then there was a crash, and the figure disappeared.

The lady was rescued and brought back to the hall; but next morning there were two dead bodies within its walls—those of Lady Eyreton and her still-born son.

Quicker than I write them, these memories chased one another through Hertford O'Donnell's brain; and there was one more terrible memory than any, which would recur to him, concerning an Irish nobleman who, seated alone in his great town-house in London, heard the banshee, and rushed out to get rid of the phantom, which wailed in his ear, nevertheless, as he strode down Piccadilly. And then the surgeon remembered how he went with a friend to the opera, feeling sure that there no banshee, unless she had a box, could find admittance, until suddenly he heard her singing up amongst the highest part of the scenery, with a terrible mournfulness, with a pathos which made the prima donna's tenderest notes seem harsh by comparison.

As he came out, some quarrel arose between him and a famous fire-eater, against whom he stumbled; and the result was that the next afternoon there was a new Lord—, *vice* Lord—, killed in a duel with Captain Bravo.

Memories like these are not the most enlivening possible; they are apt to make a man fanciful, and nervous, and wakeful; but as time ran on, Hertford O'Donnell fell asleep, with his candle still burning and Brian's cold nose pressed against his hand.

He dreamt of his mother's family—the Hertfords, of Artingbury, Yorkshire, far-off relatives of Lord Hertford—so far off that even Mrs O'Donnell held no clue to the genealogical maze.

He thought he was at Artingbury, fishing; that it was a misty summer's morning and the fish rising beautifully. In his dream he hooked one after another, and the boy who was with him threw them into the basket.

At last there was one more difficult to land than the others; and the boy, in his eagerness to watch the sport, drew nearer and nearer to the brink, while the fisher, intent on his prey, failed to notice his companion's danger.

Suddenly there was a cry, a splash, and the boy disappeared from sight.

Next instant he rose again, however, and then, for the first time, Hertford O'Donnell saw his face.

It was one he knew well.

In a moment he plunged into the water, and struck out for the lad. He had him by the hair, he was turning to bring him back to land, when the stream suddenly changed into a wide, wild, shoreless sea, where the billows were chasing one another with a mad, demoniac mirth.

For a while O'Donnell kept the land and himself afloat. They were swept under the waves, and came forth again, only to see larger waves rushing towards them; but through all the surgeon never loosened his hold until a tremendous billow engulfing them both, tore the boy from him.

With the horror of that he awoke, to hear a voice saying quite distinctly: 'Go to the hospital!—go at once!'

The surgeon started up in bed, rubbed his eyes and looked about him. The candle was flickering faintly in its socket. Brian, with his ears pricked forward, had raised his head at his master's sudden jump.

Everything was quiet, but still those words were ringing in his ear— 'Go to the hospital!—go at once!'

The tremendous peal of the bell overnight, and this sentence, seemed to be simultaneous.

That he was wanted at Guy's—wanted imperatively—came to O'Donnell like an inspiration.

Neither sense nor reason had anything to do with the conviction that roused him out of bed, and made him dress as speedily as possible and grope his way down the staircase, Brian following.

He opened the front door and passed out into the darkness. The rain was over, and the stars were shining as he pursued his way down Newport Market, and thence, winding in and out in a south-east direction, through Lincoln's Inn Fields and Old Square to Chancery Lane, whence he proceeded to St Paul's.

Along the deserted streets he resolutely continued his walk. He did not know what he was going to Guy's for. Some instinct was urging him on, and he neither strove to combat nor control it. Only once had the thought of turning back occurred, and that was at the archway leading into Old Square. There he had paused for a moment, asking himself whether he were not gone stark, staring mad; but Guy's seemed preferable to the haunted house in Gerrard Street, and he walked resolutely on, determining to say, if any surprise were expressed at his appearance, that he had been sent for.

On, thinking of many things: of his wild life in London; of the terrible cry he had heard overnight—that terrible wail which he could not drive away from his memory, even as he entered Guy's, and confronted the porter, who said:

'You have just been sent for, sir; did you meet the messenger?'

Like one in a dream, Hertford O'Donnell heard him; like one in a dream, also, he asked what was the matter.

'Bad accident, sir: fire; fall of a balcony—unsafe—old building. Mother and child—a son; child with compound fracture of thigh.' This, the joint information of porter and house-surgeon, mingled together, and made a roar in Mr O'Donnell's ears like the sound of the sea breaking on a shingly shore.

Only one sentence he understood perfectly—'Immediate amputation necessary.' At this point he grew cool; he was the careful, cautious, successful surgeon in a moment.

'The child, you say?' he answered; 'let me see him.'

In the days of which I am writing, the two surgeons had to pass a staircase leading to the upper stories. On the lower step of this staircase, partially in shadow, Hertford O'Donnell beheld as he came forward, an old woman seated.

An old woman with streaming grey hair, with attenuated arms, with head bowed forward, with scanty clothing, with bare feet; who never looked up at their approach, but sat unnoticing, shaking her head and wringing her hands in an extremity of grief.

'Who is that?' asked Mr O'Donnell, almost involuntarily.

'Who is what?' demanded his companion.

'That—that woman,' was the reply.

'What woman?'

'There—are you blind?—seated on the bottom step of the staircase. What is she doing?' persisted Mr O'Donnell.

'There is no woman near us,' his companion answered, looking at the rising surgeon very much as though he suspected him of seeing double.

'No woman!' scoffed Hertford. 'Do you expect me to disbelieve the evidence of my own eyes?' and he walked up to the figure, meaning to touch it.

But as he essayed to do so, the woman seemed to rise in the air and float away, with her arms stretched high up over her head, uttering such a wail of pain, and agony, and distress, as caused the Irishman's blood to curdle.

'My God! did you hear that?' he said to his companion.

[25]

'What?' was the reply.

Then, although he knew the sound had fallen on deaf ears, he answered—

'The wail of the banshee! Some of my people are doomed!'

'I trust not,' answered the house-surgeon.

With nerves utterly shaken, Mr O'Donnell walked forward to the accident ward. There, with his face shaded from the light, lay his patient—a young boy, with a compound fracture of the thigh.

In that ward, in the face of actual pain or danger capable of relief, the surgeon had never known faltering nor fear; and now he carefully examined the injury, felt the pulse, inquired as to the treatment pursued, and ordered the sufferer to be carried to the operating room.

While he was laying out his instruments he heard the boy lying on the table murmur faintly—

'Tell her not to cry so—tell her not to cry.'

'What is he talking about?' Hertford O'Donnell inquired.

'The nurse says he had been speaking about some woman crying ever since he came in—his mother, most likely,' answered one of the attendants.

'He is delirious, then?' observed the surgeon.

'No, sir,' pleaded the boy excitedly. 'No; it is that woman–that woman with the grey hair. I saw her looking from the upper window before the balcony gave way. She has never left me since, and she won't be quiet, wringing her hands and crying.'

'Can you see her now?' Hertford O'Donnell inquired, stepping to the side of the table. 'Point out where she stands.'

Then the lad stretched forth a feeble finger in the direction of the door, where clearly, as he had seen her seated on the stairs, the surgeon saw a woman standing—a woman with grey hair and scanty clothing, and upstretched arms and bare feet.

'A word with you, sir,' O'Donnell said to the house surgeon, drawing him back from the table. 'I cannot perform this operation: send for some other person. I am ill; I am incapable.'

'But,' pleaded the other, 'there is no time to get anyone else. We sent for Mr— before we troubled you, but he was out of town, and all the rest of the surgeons live so far away. Mortification may set in at any moment, and—' Then Hertford O'Donnell fell fainting on the floor.

How long he lay in that dead-like swoon I cannot say: but when he returned to consciousness, the principal physician of Guy's was standing beside him in the cold grey light of the Christmas morning.

'The boy?' murmured O'Donnell faintly.

'Now, my dear fellow, keep yourself quiet,' was the reply.

'The boy?' he repeated irritably. 'Who operated?'

'No one,' Dr— answered. 'It would have been useless cruelty. Mortification had set in, and—'

Hertford O'Donnell turned his face to the wall, and his friend could not see it.

'Do not distress yourself,' went on the physician kindly. 'Allington says he could not have survived the operation in any case. He was quite delirious from the first, raving about a woman with grey hair, and—'

'Yes, I know,' Hertford O'Donnell interrupted; 'and the boy had a mother, they told me, or I dreamt it.'

'Yes; bruised and shaken, but not seriously injured.'

'Has she blue eyes and fair hair—fair hair rippling and wavy? Is she white as a lily, with just a faint flush of colour in her cheeks? Is she young, and trusting, and innocent? No; I am wandering. She must be nearly thirty now. Go, for God's sake, and tell me if you can find a woman that you could imagine having been as a girl such as I describe.'

'Irish?' asked the doctor; and O'Donnell made a gesture of assent.

'It is she then,' was the reply; 'a woman with the face of an angel.'

'A woman who should have been my wife,' the surgeon answered; 'whose child was my son.'

'Lord help you!' ejaculated the doctor. Then Hertford O'Donnell raised himself from the sofa where they had laid him, and told his companion the story of his life—how there had been bitter feud between his people and her people—how they were divided by old animosities and by difference of religion—how they had met by stealth, and exchanged rings and vows, all for nought—how his family had insulted hers, so that her father, wishful for her to marry a kinsman of his own, bore her off to a far-away land, and made her write him a letter of eternal farewell—how his own parents had kept all knowledge of the quarrel from him till she was utterly beyond his reach—how they had vowed to discard him unless he agreed to marry according to their wishes—how he left home, and came to London, and pushed his fortune. All this Hertford O'Donnell repeated; and when he had finished, the bells were ringing for morning service—ringing loudly—ringing joyfully: 'Peace on earth, good will towards men.'

But there was little peace that morning for Hertford O'Donnell. He had to look on the face of his dead son, wherein he beheld, as though reflected, the face of the boy in his dream.

Stealthily he followed his friend, and beheld, with her eyes closed, her cheeks pale and pinched, her hair thinner, but still falling like a veil over her, the love of his youth, the only woman he had ever loved devotedly and unselfishly.

There is little space left here to tell of how the two met at last—of how the stone of the years seemed suddenly rolled away from the tomb of their past, and their youth arose and returned to them, amid their tears.

She had been true to him, through persecution, through contumely, through kindness, which was more trying; through shame, and grief, and poverty, she had been loyal to the lover of her youth; and before the new year dawned there came a letter from Calgillan, saying that the banshee had been heard there, and praying Hertford, if he was still alive, to let bygones be bygones, in consideration of the long years of estrangement—the anguish and remorse of his afflicted parents.

More than that, Hertford O'Donnell, if a reckless man, was an honourable one; and so, on the Christmas Day, when he was to have proposed for Miss Ingot, he went to that lady and told her how he had wooed and won in the years of his youth one who, after many days, was miraculously restored to him. And from the hour in which he took her into his confidence he never thought her either vulgar or foolish, but rather he paid homage to the woman who, when she had heard the whole tale repeated, said simply, 'Ask her to come to me till you claim her—and God bless you both.'

THE CITIZEN'S WATCH

by Erckmann-Chatrian

'Erckmann-Chatrian' was the collaborative name
of the most successful and popular writing team
in France during the latter half of the nineteenth
century: Emile Erckmann (1822–1899) and
Alexandre Chatrian (1826–1890). Their most
famous work, *The Polish Jew*, was adapted for
the London stage by Sir Henry Irving as *The
Bells*; and many of their historical tales became
accepted reading texts in British schools. 'The
Citizen's Watch' is one of a large number of
Erckmann-Chatrian's thrilling mystery stories
originally gathered together as *Histoires et Contes
Fantastiques*.

I

The day before the Christmas of 1832, my friend Wilfred with his
counter-bass slung behind him, and I with my violin under my
arm, set out from the Black Forest to Heidelberg. There had been
a deep fall of snow, so that looking over the wide expanse of deserted
country we could discover no trace of the way along which we should go,
no road, no path. The bitter wind whistled around with monotonous
perseverance, and Wilfred, with his knapsack upon his meagre
shoulders, his long legs wide-stretched, the peak of his hat drawn down
over his nose, marched on in front of me humming a merry tune from
Ondine. Once he looked round with a strange smile, and said—

'Comrade, play me the Robin waltz. I should like to dance.'

A laugh followed these words, and the brave fellow again continued his way. I trod in his steps, the snow being nearly up to our knees, and as I went on I found myself becoming by degrees very melancholy.

At length the steeples of Heidelberg peeped up in the distance, and we began to hope that we should arrive there before nightfall. As we pressed on we heard the galloping of a horse behind us. It was about five o'clock in the evening, and big flakes of snow were floating down in the grey light. When the horseman came near to us he pulled in his steed, looking at us out of the corner of his eye. For our part we also looked at him.

Picture to yourself a strongly built man with red whiskers and hair, wearing a fine three-cornered hat, in a brown riding-cloak, and a loose fox-skin pelisse, his hands thrust into furred gloves reaching up to his elbows—an alderman or burgomaster with portly stomach, with a fine valise strapped on the croup of his powerful thick-set horse. Truly a character.

'Hullo, my friends,' said he, disengaging one of his hands from the mittens which hung to his trunk-hose, 'you are going to Heidelberg to play, I suppose.'

Wilfred looked at the stranger, and said shortly—

'What is that to you?'

'Ah, certainly. I have some good advice to give you.'

'Good advice!'

'Yes. If you want it.'

Wilfred took long strides without making any reply, and I, stealing a sidelong glance, thought that the stranger looked just like a great cat, his ears standing up, his eyelids half closed, his moustache bristling, and his air tender and paternal.

'My dear friend,' said he to me, frankly, 'you would do best to return by the way you have come.'

'Why, sir?'

'The illustrious Master Pimenti of Novara is about to give a grand Christmas concert at Heidelberg; all the town will be there, you will not take a kreutzer.'

Wilfred, looking round in a bad temper, said—

'We laugh at your master Pimenti and all his like. Look at that young man; look at him well. You see he has not yet got a single hair on his chin; he has only played in the little cabins in the Black Forest for the *bourengredel* and the charcoal-burners to dance. Well, this little fellow, with his long fair hair and his big blue eyes, defies all your Italian impostors. His left hand holds in it melodious treasures—treasures of grace and suppleness. His right hand is gifted with the most wonderful command over the fiddlestick, that heaven in its most bounteous mood ever bestowed on man.'

'Ah, ah,' said the other. 'Is that so?'

'It is as I tell you,' cried Wilfred, setting off at his full speed, and blowing on his red fingers.

I thought he was only making fun of the stranger, who kept up with us at a gentle trot.

So we went on for about half a league in silence. All of a sudden the stranger said to us, sharply—

'Whatever may be your ability, go back again to the Black Forest. We have enough vagabonds at Heidelberg without your coming to increase the number. I give you good advice, especially under the present circumstances. Take it.'

Wilfred was about to make a sharp reply, but the stranger, putting his horse to the gallop, was already going down the Elector's Avenue. As he rode on, a company of ravens flew over the plain, seeming as if they were accompanying him, and filling the air with their clamour.

We came to Heidelberg at seven o'clock, and we there found on every wall the big placards of Pimenti.

'Grand Concert, Solo, &c.'

The same evening while visiting the taverns we met many musicians from the Black Forest—old comrades, who invited us to join them. There was old Brêmer, the violincellist; his two sons, Ludwig and Karl, two good second violins; Henry Siebel, the clarionet player; the famous Bertha, with her harp; lastly, Wilfred, with his counter-bass, and myself as first violin.

It was resolved that we should go together, and that after Christmas we should share like brothers. Wilfred had already taken for us two a room on the sixth floor of a little inn called the Pied-de-Mouton, in the middle of the Holdergrasse, for four kreutzers a night. It was in truth nothing more than a garret, but luckily there was an iron stove in it, and so we lighted a fire there in order to dry our clothes.

While we were sitting down enjoying ourselves eating chestnuts and drinking a flask of wine, behold Annette, the servant, in a little red petticoat, hat of black velvet, her cheeks red, her lips rosy as cherries—

Annette comes creeping up the stair, knocks at the door, enters, and throws herself into my arms overjoyed.

I had known the dear girl for a long time, for we came from the same village, and I may tell you that her bright eyes and her pretty ways had completely captivated me.

'I have come to talk with you for a minute,' said she, sitting down upon a stool. 'I saw you come an hour ago, and so here I am.'

Then she commenced to chatter, asking me news about this person and that, till she had asked after all the village, hardly giving me time to reply to her. At length she stopped and looked at me with her sweet expression. We should have sat there till morning if Mother Gredel Dick had not commenced to call out at the foot of the stairs—

'Annette! Annette! Where are you?'

'I am coming, I am coming,' cried the poor child, jumping up.

She gave me a little tap on the cheek and ran to the door, but before going she stopped.

'Ah,' she cried, coming back again, 'I forgot to tell you. Do you know of it?'

'Of what?'

'Of the death of our pro-rector, Zâhn?'

'Well, what is that to us?'

'Oh, take care, take care, if your papers are not in order. They will be here tomorrow at eight o'clock to see them. They have been stopping every one, all the world, during the last five days. The pro-rector was murdered in the library of St Christopher's cloister yesterday evening. Last week some one murdered, in a like manner, the old sacristan, Ulmet Elias, of the Rue des Juifs. Some days before, some one killed the old wise woman Christina Haas, and the agate merchant, Seligmann, of the Rue Durlach. Do look well after yourself, my poor Kaspar,' said she tenderly, 'and see that your papers are all right.'

While she was speaking the voice on the stairs kept on crying—

'Annette, Annette, are you coming? Ah, the baggage! to leave me all alone.'

We could also hear the voices of the drinkers as they called for wine, for beer, for ham, for sausages. It was necessary she should go, and Annette ran away as she had come, and we heard her sweet voice—

'Heavens, madam, why do you call so? One would think that the house was on fire!'

Wilfred shut the door, and having sat down again, we looked at one another with some uneasiness.

'That is strange news,' said he. 'Are your papers all right?'

'No doubt they are,' and I handed mine to him.

'Good! Mine are there. I had them looked over before I left. For all that, these murders may be unpleasant for us. I am afraid we shall do no good here, so many families will be in mourning, and, besides, the distraction of the others, the worrying vigilance of the police, the disturbance—'

'Nonsense,' said I. 'You see only the dark side of things.'

We continued to talk of these strange events till it was past midnight. The fire in our little stove lit up every cranny in the roof, the square window with its three cracked panes, the straw mattress spread out near the eaves where the sloping roof met the floor, the black cross beams, and threw a dancing shadow of the little fir table on the worm-eaten floor. From time to time a mouse, attracted by the warmth, would dart like an arrow along the floor. We heard the wind moaning in the high chimneys, and sweeping the powdered snow off the roofs. I thought of Annette. All was silence.

All of a sudden Wilfred, taking off his waistcoat, said—'It is time we went to sleep. Let us put some wood on the fire and go to bed!'

'Yes. It is the best thing we can do.'

Saying so, I took off my boots, and in a couple of minutes we were on the pallet, the coverlet drawn up to our chins, a piece of wood under our heads for a pillow. Wilfred was quickly asleep. The light from the stove came and went. The wind grew fiercer, and I at length slept, in my turn, like one of the blessed.

Towards two o'clock in the morning I was roused by a strange noise. I thought at first that it must be a cat upon the roof, but, placing my ear against the rafters, I was not long in uncertainty. Some one was passing over the roof. I nudged Wilfred with my elbow to wake him.

'Be quiet,' said he, taking my hand. He had heard the noise as well as I. The fire threw around its last gleams, which flickered on the old walls. I was about to get up, when, with one blow of a stone, the fastening of the little window was broken and the casement was thrown open. A white face, with red whiskers, gleaming eyes, and twitching cheeks, appeared, and looked into the room. Our terror was such that we could not even cry out. The man put one leg and then another through the window, and at last jumped into the loft, so lightly, however, that his footsteps made not a sound.

This man, round-shouldered, short, thick-set, his face distorted like that of a tiger on the spring, was none other than the good natured fellow who had given us advice on our road to Heidelberg. But how changed he was! In spite of the terrible cold he was in his shirt sleeves. He had on a plain pair of breeches. His stockings were of wool, and in his shoes were silver buckles. A long knife, stained with blood, glistened in his hand.

Wilfred and I thought we were lost. He did not seem, however, to see us as we lay in the shadow of the garret, although the flame of the fire was rekindled by the cold air which came in at the window. The man sat down on a stool, and shivered in a strange manner. Suddenly his green yellowish eyes rested on me. His nostrils dilated. He looked towards me for a minute. The blood froze in my veins. Then he turned away towards the fire, coughed huskily, like a cat, not a muscle of his face moving. At length he took out of his trouser-pocket a large watch, looked at it like one seeking the time, and either not knowing what he was doing or designedly, laid the watch upon the table. Then he rose as if uncertain what to do, looked at the window, appeared to hesitate, and went out at the door, leaving it wide open.

I rose to bolt the door, and I could hear the steps of the man as he went down two flights of stairs. A great curiosity overcame my fear, and when I heard him open a window looking into the yard, I turned to an opening in a little turret on the stairs which looked out on the same side. The yard, from this height, looked like a well. A wall fifteen or sixteen feet high divided it in two. To the right of this wall was the yard of a pork-butcher; on the left was that of the inn, the Pied-de-Mouton. It was covered with damp moss and such vegetation as grows in dark corners. The top of the wall could be reached from the window which the man had opened, and from there the wall ran straight on till it reached the roof of a big solemn-looking building at the back of the Bergstrasse. As the moon shone between big snow-clouds, I saw all this in an instant, and I trembled as my eye fell upon the man on the wall, his head bent down, his long knife in his hand, while the wind sighed mournfully around.

He reached the roof in front, and disappeared in at a window.

I thought I was dreaming. For some moments I stood there, my mouth open, my breast bare, my hair flying, the rime from off the roof falling about my head. At last, recovering myself, I went back to our garret, where I found Wilfred, haggard-looking and murmuring a prayer in a low voice. I hastened to put some wood in the stove, and to bolt the door.

'Well?' asked my friend, rising.

'Well,' said I, 'we have escaped. If that man did not see us it is because heaven did not will our death.'

'Yes,' said he. 'Yes. It was one of the murderers whom Annette spoke about. Good heavens! What a figure, and what a knife!'

He fell back upon the bed. I drained the wine that remained in the flask, and as the fire burnt up and the heat spread itself through the room, and since the bolt on the door seemed strong enough, I took fresh courage.

But the watch was there, and the man might come back for it. The idea made us cold with fear.

'What had we better do?' asked Wilfred. 'It seems to me that our best way would be to go back as quickly as we can to the Black Forest.'

'Why?'

'I do not much care now for double-bass. Do as you wish.'

'But why should we return? What necessity is there for us to leave? We have committed no crime.'

'Hush, hush,' said he. 'That simple word "crime" would suffice to hang us if any one heard us talking. Poor devils like us are made examples of for the benefit of others. People don't care whether they are guilty or not. It will be enough if they find that watch here.'

'Listen, Wilfred,' said I. 'It will do us no good to lose our heads. I certainly believe that a crime has been committed near at hand this night. Yes, I believe it, it is most probable; but in such a case, what ought an honest man to do? Instead of flying he ought to assist in discovering the guilty; he ought—'

'And how—how can we assist?'

'The best way will be to take the watch, give it up to the magistrate, and tell him all that has occurred.'

'Never—never. I could not dare to touch that watch.'

'Very well, then, I will go. Let us lie down now and see if we can get some sleep.'

'I cannot sleep.'

'Well then, let us talk. Light your pipe and let us wait for daybreak. I daresay there may be some one up in the inn. If you like, we will go down.'

'I like to remain here better.'

'All right.'

And we sat down beside the fire.

As soon as it was light I went to take up the watch that lay upon the table. It was a very handsome one, with two dials, the one showing the hours and the other the minutes. Wilfred seemed in better spirits.

'Kaspar,' said he, 'after considering the matter over, I think it might be better for me to go to the magistrate. You are too young to manage such matters. You would not be able to explain yourself.'

'As you wish,' said I.

'Yes, it might seem strange that a fellow of my age should send a lad on such an errand.'

'All right. I understand, Wilfred.'

He took the watch, and I could see that his vanity alone urged him on. He would have blushed, no doubt, among his friends at the idea that he was less courageous than myself.

We descended from our garret wrapt in deep thought. As we went along the alley which leads to the Rue Saint Christopher, we heard the clinking of glasses and forks. I recognised the voices of old Brêmer and his two sons, Ludwig and Karl.

'Would it not be well,' I said to Wilfred, 'before going out, to have something to drink?'

At the same time I pushed open the door of the inn. All our friends were there, the violins, the hunting-horns hung up upon the walls, the harp in a corner. We were welcomed with joyful cries, and were pressed to place ourselves at the table.

'Ha,' said old Brêmer, 'good luck to you, comrades. More wind! more snow! All the inns are full of folk, and every flake that falls is a florin in our pockets.'

I saw Annette fresh, beaming, laughing at me with her eyes and lips. The sight did me good. The best cuts of meat were for me, and every time that she came to lay a dish on my right her sweet hand was laid upon my shoulder.

My heart bounded as I thought of the chestnuts we had eaten together. Then the ghastly figure of the murderer passed from time to time before my eyes, and made me tremble. I looked at Wilfred. He was in deep thought. As it struck eight o'clock we were about to part, when the door of the room opened and three tall fellows, with livid faces, with eyes shining like those of rats, with misshapen hats, followed by several others, appeared on the threshold. One of them, with a long nose, formed, as they say, to scent good dishes, a big baton attached to his wrist, approached, and exclaimed—

'Your papers, gentlemen.'

Everyone hastened to comply with this command. Wilfred, however, who stood beside the stove, was seized with an unfortunate fit of trembling, and when the police-officer lifted his eye from the paper in order to take a side glance at him, he discovered him in the act of slipping the watch into his boot. The officer struck his comrade on the thigh, and said to him in a joking tone—

'Ha, it seems that we trouble this gentleman!'

At these words Wilfred, to the surprise of all, fell fainting. He sank into a chair, white as death, and Madoc, the chief of the police, coolly drew forth the watch, with a harsh laugh. When he had looked at it, however, he became grave, and turning to his followers—

'Let no one leave,' he cried, in a terrible voice. 'We will take all of them. This is the watch of the citizen, Daniel van den Berg. Attention! Bring the handcuffs.'

The word made our blood run cold, and terror seized on us all. As for me, I slipped under a bench near the wall, and as the officers were engaged in securing poor old Brêmer, his sons, Henry, and Wilfred, who sobbed and entreated, I felt a little hand rest on my neck. It was the pretty hand of Annette, and I pressed it to my lips in a farewell kiss. She took hold of of me by the ear, and led me gently, gently. At the bottom of the table I saw the flap of the cellar open. I slipped through it, and the flap closed above me.

All this took but a moment, while all around was in an uproar.

In my retreat I heard a great stamping, then all was still. My poor friends had gone. Mother Gredel Dick, left standing alone upon the threshold, was uttering some peacock-like cries, declaring that the Pied-de-Mouton had lost its good name.

I leave you to imagine what were my reflections during that day, squatted down behind a cask, cross-legged, my feet under me, thinking that if a dog should come down, or if the innkeeper should take it into her head to come to fill a flask of wine, if a cask should run out and it was necessary to tap another—that any one of these things might ruin me.

All these thoughts and a thousand others passed through my brain. In my mind's eye I already saw old Brêmer, Wilfred, Karl, Ludwig, and Bertha hanging from a gibbet, surrounded by a crowd of ravens, who glutted themselves on them. My hair stood on end at the picture.

Annette, no less anxious than myself, in her fear took care to close the cellar-flap every time she went in and out, and I heard the old dame say to her—

'Leave that flap alone. Are you foolish, that you bother so much about it?'

So the door remained half-open, and from the deep shadow in which I was I saw fresh revellers gather around the tables. I heard their cries, their disputes, and no end of accounts of the terrible band of criminals.

'The scoundrels!' said one. 'Thank heaven, they are caught. What a pest have they been to Heidelberg! One dared not walk in the streets after six o'clock. Business was interrupted. However, it is all over now. In five days everything will be put in order again.'

'You see those musicians from the Black Forest,' cried another, 'are all a lot of scoundrels. They make their way into houses pretending that they come to play. They look around, examine the locks, the chests, the cupboards, the ins and outs, and some fine morning the master of the house is found in his bed with his throat cut, his wife has been murdered, his children strangled, the whole place ransacked from top to bottom, the barn burnt down or something of that kind. What wretches they are! They ought to be put to death without any mercy, and then we should have some peace.'

'All the town will go to see them hanged,' said Mother Gredel. 'It will be one of the best days in my life.'

'Do you know, if it had not been for the watch of the citizen Daniel they would never have been discovered. The watch disappeared last night, and this morning Daniel gave notice of its loss to the police. In one hour after, Madoc laid his hand on the whole gang—ha! ha! ha!' and all the room rang with their laughter, while I trembled with shame, rage, and fear by turns.

At last night came, and only a few drinkers sat at the table. The people of the inn had been up late the night before, and I heard the fat mistress gape and say—

'Ah, heavens! when shall we be able to go to bed?'

Only one light remained in the room.

'Go to sleep, mistress,' said the sweet voice of Annette. 'I can see very well to all that is wanted until these gentlemen go.'

The topers took the hint, and all left save one, who remained drowsily before his glass.

The watchman at length came round, looked in, woke the man up, and I heard him go out grumbling and reeling till he came to the door.

'Now,' said I to myself, 'that is the last. Things have gone well. Mother Gredel will go to sleep, and little Annette will come to let me out.'

While this pleasant thought passed through my mind I stretched my cramped limbs, when I heard the old innkeeper say—

'Annette, shut up, and do not forget to bar the door. I am going into the cellar.'

It seemed that such was her custom, in order to see all was right.

'The cask is not empty,' stammered Annette, 'there is no necessity for you to go down.'

'Look after your own business,' said the old woman, and I saw the light of her candle as the she began to descend.

I had only time to place myself again behind the barrel. The woman, bent down under the low roof of the cellar, went about from one cask to another, and I heard her say—

'Ah, the jade! How she lets the wine drip from the taps! Look! look! I must teach her how to turn a tap better. Did one ever see such a thing! Did one ever see the like!'

Her light threw deep shadows on the damp wall. I drew myself closer and closer.

All of a sudden, when I was imagining that the woman's visit was ended, I heard her sigh—a sigh so deep, so mournful, that I thought something extraordinary must have happened. I raised my head just the least bit, and what did I see? Dame Gredel Dick, her mouth open, her eyes almost out of her head, looking at the foot of the barrel behind which I lay still as a mouse. She had seen one of my feet under the woodwork on which the barrel rested, and she imagined, no doubt, that she had discovered the very chief of the assassins lying hid there in order to throttle her in the night. I at once resolved what to do. Standing up, I said to her—

'Madam, in heaven's name, have pity on me. I am—'

But then, without looking at me, without listening to me, she began to utter her peacock-like cries, cries to stun you, while she began to rush out of the cellar as fast as her extreme stoutness would let her. I was seized with terror, and taking hold of her dress, I threw myself on my knees. That seemed to make matters worse.

'Help! Murder! Oh, heaven! let me go. Take my money. Oh, oh!'

It was terrible.

'Madam,' said I, 'look at me. I am not what you take me for.'

Bah! she was foolish with fright. She raved and bawled in such a shrill voice that if she had been under the earth all the neighbourhood must have been aroused. In such a strait, becoming angry, I pulled her back, jumped before her to the door and shut it in her face with a noise like thunder, fastening the bolt. During the struggle her light had gone out. Dame Gredel remained in the dark, and her voice was now only heard feebly as if far off.

Exhausted, breathless, I looked at Annette, whose trouble equalled mine. We could not speak, and we listened to the cries as they died away. The poor woman had fainted.

'Oh, Kaspar!' said Annette then, taking my hands in hers, 'what shall we do? Save yourself, save yourself. Someone has perhaps heard the noise. Have you killed her?'

'Killed? Me?'

'Ah well. Run. I will open the door.'

She drew the bolt, and I ran off down the street without so much as even waiting to thank her. How ungrateful! But I was so afraid. The danger was so near.

The sky was black. It was an abominable night, not a star to be seen, not a ray of light, and the wind, and the snow! I ran on for at least half an hour before I stopped to take breath, and then imagine how surprised I was when, on lifting up my eyes, I saw, just in front of me, the Pied-de-Mouton. In my fright I must have run round the neighbourhood; perhaps I had gone round and round. My legs felt heavy, were covered with mud, and my knees shook.

The inn, which had been deserted an hour before, was now as lively as a bee-hive. Lights gleamed from every window. No doubt the place was full of police-officers. Wretched as I was, worn out with cold and hunger, desperate, not knowing where to hide my head, I took the strangest course of all.

'Well,' said I, 'one can but die after all, and one may as well be hanged as leave one's bones in the fields on the way to the Black Forest.' And I went into the inn to give myself up.

Besides the sour-looking fellows in battered hats, whom I had seen in the morning, and who went and came, ferreted about, and looked everywhere, before a table sat the chief magistrate Zimmer, clothed in black, solemn, with a piercing eye, and by him was his secretary Roth, with his brown periwig, his wise look, and his great eyes big as oyster-shells. No one paid any attention to me, a circumstance which changed my resolution. I sat down in one of the corners of the room, by the great oven, in company with two or three neighbours who had come to see what was going on, and asked in a calm voice for half-a-pint of wine and for something to eat.

Annette was near ruining me.

'Heavens,' she cried, 'is it possible!'

But an exclamation or two amidst such a clatter did not signify. No one noticed it. Having eaten with a good appetite, I listened to the examination of Mother Gredel, who sat in a large chair, her hair all ruffled, and her eyes still wide open with fright.

'What age did the man appear to be?' asked the magistrate.

'About forty or fifty. He was a tremendous man, with black or brown whiskers, I cannot say exactly which. He had a big nose and green eyes.'

'Was there nothing peculiar about his appearance—any blotches or wounds on his face?'

'No. I do not remember any. He had a big mallet and pistols.'

'Very well, and what did he say?'

'He took hold of me by the throat. Happily I cried out so loudly that I frightened him, and then I defended myself with my nails. Ah! when one is about to be murdered, how one can defend oneself?'

'Nothing is more natural, madam, nothing more legitimate. Write that down, M. Roth. The coolness of this good woman has been really wonderful.'

So the deposition went on.

After that they examined Annette, who simply said that she had been so frightened that she really did not notice anything.

'That is enough,' said the magistrate. 'If we require further information we will come again tomorrow.'

All went away, and I asked Mother Gredel to let me have a room for the night. She had not the slightest recollection of me—so much had fear distracted her brain.

'Annette,' she said, 'show the gentleman to the little green room on the third floor. For me, I cannot stand on my feet. Oh heaven! What strange things happen in this world!'

Annette, having lit a candle, led me to the room, and when we were alone together she said to me—

'Ah Kaspar, Kaspar! I should never have believed it of you! I shall never forgive myself for having loved a robber!'

'What, Annette,' cried I, sitting down, despairingly, 'you too! Ah, you have given me the last blow!'

I could have burst into tears, but she saw the wrong she had done me, and, putting her arms around me, said—

'No, no! You do not belong to them. You are too gentle for that, my dear Kaspar. But it is strange—you must have a daring spirit to come here again!'

I explained to her that I was near dying of cold outside, and that that had decided me. We remained some minutes in deep thought, and then she went off for fear Mother Gredel would be after her. When I was alone, having looked out to see that no wall ran near my window, and having examined the bolt on my door, I gave thanks to heaven for having delivered me from so many perils. Then I got into bed, and fell into a deep sleep.

II

The next morning I was up at eight o'clock. The day was dull and misty. When I drew my bedcurtains, I saw that the snow was heaped up upon the window-sill, and that the panes were all frosted. I began to think sorrowfully about my friends. Had they suffered from the cold? How would Bertha and old Brêmer get on? The thought of their trouble grieved me at my heart.

As I was thinking, a strange noise rose outside. It approached the inn, and it was not without some fear that I took my place at a window in order to see what it was.

They were bringing the band of supposed robbers to the inn, in order that they might be confronted with Mother Gredel, who was too unwell, after her terrible fright, to go out. My poor comrades came down the muddy street between two files of police-officers, followed by a crowd of lads, howling and whistling like very savages. I can even now see that picture. Poor Brêmer, handcuffed to his son Ludwig; then Karl and Wilfred together; lastly, Bertha, who came by herself, crying in a pitiable manner—

'In heaven's name, gentlemen, in heaven's name, have pity on a poor innocent player on the harp! Fancy me killing, robbing! Oh, heaven, can it be!'

She wrung her hands. The others were sad, their heads bowed down, their hair hanging over their faces.

All the folk in the place congregated in the alley around the inn. The police put all strangers out of it, and shut the door, and the crowd waited eagerly without, standing in the mud, flattening noses against the window-panes.

The greatest stillness reigned in the house, and having dressed myself I opened the door of my room to listen, and to see if I could not learn how matters were going. I heard voices of men as they went and came on the lower landings, which assured me that all the passages were guarded. My door opened on the landing just opposite to the window through which the murderer had fled. I had not before noticed it, but as I stood there, all of a sudden, I perceived that the window was open, that there was no snow upon the sill, and when I came near I saw new traces upon the wall. I shivered when I saw them. The man had been there again! Did he come every night? The cat, the polecat, the ferret, all preying animals, have their one path on which they prey. What a discovery! A mysterious light seemed to illumine my soul.

'Ah,' I thought, 'if I had but a chance to point out the real murderer, my comrades would be saved.'

With my eyes I followed the tracks, which stretched out so clearly to the wall of the neighbouring house.

At that moment I heard some one putting questions. They had opened the door in order to get fresh air. I listened.

'Do you acknowledge having taken part in the murder of the sacristan Ulmet Elias, on the twentieth of this month?'

Then followed some indistinct words.

'Close the door, Madoc,' said the magistrate; 'close the door, madam is unwell.'

I heard no more.

As I leant my head upon the banister, a great conflict took place within me.

'I am able to save my friends,' said I. 'God has pointed out to me the way to render them back to their families. If I fail to do my duty I shall be their murderer—my peace, my honour, will be for ever lost. I shall always look upon myself as the most cowardly, the vilest of mankind!'

For a long time, however, I hesitated, but all of a sudden I resolved. Going down the stairs, I went into the kitchen.

'Have you ever seen that watch?' asked the magistrate of Mother Gredel. 'Remember yourself, madam.'

Without waiting for her to reply, I advanced into the room, and in a firm voice, said—

'That watch, M. Magistrate, I myself have seen in the very hands of the murderer. I identify it. As to the man himself, I can deliver him to you, if you will listen to me.'

There was complete silence around. The police-officers looked at one another astounded. My poor comrades seemed to take courage.

'Who are you, sir?' asked the magistrate.

'I am the friend of these unfortunate prisoners, and I am not ashamed to say it, for all of them, M. Magistrate, all of them, are honest folk, not one of whom is capable of committing such a crime as is laid to their charge.'

Again there was silence. Bertha began to weep. The magistrate appeared to collect himself. Then looking fixedly at me, he said—

'Where do you say we can find the murderer?'

'Here, here, M. Magistrate, in this very house. In order to convince you of the truth of what I say, I only beg a minute's private conversation.'

'Very well,' he said, rising.

He made a sign to Madoc, the chief of the police, to follow us, and for the rest to stay behind. We went out.

I rapidly ascended the stairs and they followed me closely. On the third landing I stopped before the window and showed them the tracks of the man in the snow.

'Those are the assassin's tracks,' I said. 'He comes along there each night. He went along there at two o'clock yesterday morning. He returned last night, and without doubt he will come again tonight.'

The magistrate and Madoc looked at the marks for some minutes without uttering a word.

'And what grounds have you for saying that those are the tracks of the murderer?' asked the magistrate incredulously.

I told them all about the apparition of the man in our garret, I showed them the window from which I had seen him as he fled in the moonlight, which Wilfred had not witnessed as he had remained in bed, and I confessed to them that it was fear alone which had restrained me from telling them all this on the previous night.

'It is strange,' muttered the magistrate. 'This modifies the position of the prisoners very much. But how do you account for the murderer being hidden in the cellar of the inn?'

'That man was myself.'

And I told him all that had passed on the preceding day, from the time my comrades were arrested to the moment of my flight.

'That is enough,' he said.

Turning towards the chief of the police—

'I confess, Madoc,' said he, 'the declarations of these musicians never appeared to me to be conclusive, they were far from satisfying me that they were guilty. Then their papers, at least those of some of them, would establish an alibi such as it would be very difficult to overcome. In the meantime, young man, notwithstanding the apparent truth of your statement, you must remain in our custody until the truth is established. Do not let him out of your sight, Madoc, and take such measures as you think fit.'

The magistrate descended the stairs very thoughtfully, and folded up his papers, without asking another question.

'Conduct the accused back to their prison,' said he, and throwing a contemptuous glance on the fat old innkeeper, he went away, followed by his secretary.

Madoc alone remained with two officers.

'Madam,' said Madoc, 'you must be silent respecting all that has occurred. For the rest, let this young fellow have the room he had yesterday.'

Madoc's look, and the tone in which he spoke, did not admit of reply. Mother Gredel declared she would do whatever he required, so long as he preserved her from the robbers.

'Do not trouble yourself about robbers,' said Madoc. 'We shall remain here all day and all night to keep you safe. Look after your affairs without fear, and to begin with, let us have something to eat. Young man, may I have the pleasure of your company to dinner?'

My position did not admit of my declining his offer, so I accepted the invitation.

We seated ourselves before a ham and a flask of Rhine wine. Some people came in as usual, and tried to obtain information from Mother Gredel and Annette, but they took good care not to speak in our presence, and were very reserved, a matter in them which was very meritorious.

We spent the afternoon in smoking our pipes and in drinking. No one paid us any attention.

The chief of the police, in spite of his extremely upright figure, his piercing eye, his pale lips, and his great eagle nose, was not a bad fellow when he had had something to drink. He told us some tales with much happiness and fluency. He wanted to kiss Annette in the passage. At every joke of his his followers burst out in loud laughter, but as for myself, I was sad and silent.

'Well, young man,' said he to me, laughing, 'cannot you forget the death of your worthy grandmother? What the deuce! We are all mortal. Empty your glass and drive off these miserable thoughts.'

The others joined in, and time passed on amidst a cloud of tobacco smoke, the clinking of glasses, and the tinkling of pewter pots.

At nine o'clock, however, when the watchman had been round, a sudden change came over the scene. Madoc rose and said—

'Ah, then, let us see to our little business; close the door and put the shutters to. Be brisk. As for you, madam and mademoiselle, you had better go to bed.'

These three men, so abominably shabby, looked more like robbers themselves than the preservers of peace and justice. They drew out of their pockets iron bars, at the end of which was a leaden ball, and Madoc, tapping on the pocket of his riding-coat, assured himself that his pistol was there. The next minute he drew it out to put a cap under the hammer.

All this they did with the greatest calmness, and then the chief ordered me to lead them to my garret.

We went up. When we arrived there we found that Annette had taken the trouble to light a fire there. Madoc, muttering curses between his teeth, hastened to throw water over it and extinguish it. Then pointing to the pallet, he said—

'If you have the heart, you may sleep!'

He sat down with his men at the end of the room near to the wall, and one of them blew out the light.

And I lay there praying to heaven to send the murderer to us.

After a minute or two the silence was so profound that no one could have imagined that there were three men in the room, watching, listening to the slightest noise, like hunters on the track of some timorous beast. I could not sleep, for a thousand horrible thoughts occurred to me. I listened to the clock striking one, two. Nothing happened; no one came.

At three o'clock one of the police-officers moved, and then I thought my man must have come, but all became quiet again. Then I began to think that Madoc must regard me as an impostor; to think how put out he would be, and how he would revenge himself on me the next day; how, wishing to assist my comrades, I had myself run into the toils.

When three o'clock had struck, the time seemed to me to go very quickly. I should have liked the night to have been much longer; time might afford me a loophole of escape.

As I was thinking thus for the hundredth time, all of a sudden, without the least noise, the window opened, and two eyes shone in at the aperture. All was still in the garret.

'The others have gone to sleep,' I thought.

The face stopped there for a moment. Did he suspect something? How my heart beat! The blood ran fast through my veins, but my brow, nevertheless, was cold with fear. I could not breathe.

The face remained there for some seconds, and then he seemed suddenly to make up his mind, and glided into the garret as quietly as of old.

A terrible cry, sharp, ringing, broke the stillness.

'Seize him!'

All the house seemed to ring with the noise of cries, of stamping feet, of husky exclamations, making me shiver with dread. The man shouted, the others panted with the struggle. Then I heard a crash which made the floor creak, the grinding of teeth, the clinking of handcuffs.

'Light,' cried Madoc.

When the light was in, throwing around a blue glare, I could dimly see the police-officers bent over a man in his shirt sleeves. One held him by the throat, the other knelt on his breast. Madoc held his handcuffed hands with a grip which seemed to crush the very bones. The man seemed insensible, save that one of his feet from time to time lifted itself and fell upon the floor again with a convulsive motion. His eyes were almost out of his head, and the froth was on his lips. Hardly had I lighted the candle when the police-officers exclaimed, astonished—

'The citizen!'

All three rose, and I saw them look at one another pale with fright.

The man's eye turned itself to Madoc. He seemed about to speak. In a little while I heard him murmur—

'What a dream! Oh heaven! what a dream!'

Then he drew a long breath, and remained quite still.

I drew near to look on him. It was certainly he, the man who had given us good advice as we were on our way to Heidelberg. Did he know that we should be his ruin; had he some terrible presentiment? He remained perfectly still. The blood trickled from his side over the white floor, and Madoc, recovering himself, bent down beside him and tore his shirt aside from his breast. Then we saw that he had stabbed himself to the heart.

'Ah,' said Madoc, with a sour smile, 'the citizen has cheated the gibbet. He did not let the opportunity slip. You others, stop here while I go and fetch the magistrate.'

He put on his hat, which had fallen off in the struggle, and went out without saying another word.

I remained in the room with the man and the two officers

At eight o'clock the next day all Heidelberg was acquainted with the wonderful news. It was a strange event in its history. Who would have suspected Daniel van den Berg, the chief woollen-draper, a man of wealth position, had these tastes for blood?

The affair was discussed in a thousand different styles. Some said that the rich citizen must have been a somnambulist and irresponsible for his actions—others that he murdered from a mere love of it, for he could not intend to gain anything by his crimes. Perhaps he was both a somnambulist and an assassin also. It is an incontestable fact that the moral being, the will, the soul, whatever you like to name it, does not dominate the somnambulist, but the animal nature, abandoned to itself in such a state, follows naturally the impulse of its instincts whether they be peaceful or sanguinary, and the appearance of Daniel van den Berg, his flat head bulging out behind the ears, his long bristling moustaches, his yellow eyes, all seemed to say that he belonged to the cat tribe—a terrible race, killing for the sake of killing.

However that might be, my comrades were freed.

For five days Annette was famous as a model of devotedness. The son of the burgomaster, Trungott, the plague of his family, even came and asked her to marry him. As for me, I hastened to get back again to the Black Forest, where since that time I have filled the position of leader of the orchestra in the tavern of the Sabre-Vert, on the Tubingian road. If you should happen to pass that way, and if my story has interested you, look in and see me. We will have a bottle or two together, and I will tell you a story which will make your hair stand on end.

WHAT THE
SHEPHERD SAW

by Thomas Hardy

This atmospheric tale of murder and mystery by
the master storyteller Thomas Hardy
(1840–1928) was first published in the
Christmas Number of *The Illustrated London
News* in 1881.

FIRST NIGHT

The genial Justice of the Peace—now, alas, no more—who made himself responsible for the facts of this story, used to begin in the good old-fashioned way with a bright moonlight night and a mysterious figure, an excellent stroke for an opening, even to this day, if well followed up.

The Christmas moon (he would say) was showing her cold face to the upland, the upland reflecting the radiance in frost-sparkles so minute as only to be discernible by an eye near at hand. This eye, he said, was the eye of a shepherd lad, young for his occupation, who stood within a wheeled hut of the kind commonly in use among sheep-keepers during the early lambing season, and was abstractedly looking through the loophole at the scene without.

The spot was called Lambing Corner, and it was a sheltered portion of that wide expanse of rough pastureland known as the Marlbury Downs, which you directly traverse when following the turnpike-road across

Mid-Wessex from London, through Aldbrickham, in the direction of Bath and Bristol. Here, where the hut stood, the land was high and dry, open, except to the north, and commanding an undulating view for miles. On the north side grew a tall belt of coarse furze, with enormous stalks, a clump of the same standing detached in front of the general mass. The clump was hollow, and the interior had been ingeniously taken advantage of as a position for the before-mentioned hut, which was thus completely screened from winds, and almost invisible, except through the narrow approach. But the furze twigs had been cut away from the two little windows of the hut, that the occupier might keep his eye on his sheep.

In the rear, the shelter afforded by the belt of furze bushes was artificially improved by an enclosure of upright stakes, interwoven with boughs of the same prickly vegetation, and within the enclosure lay a renowned Marlbury-Down breeding flock of eight hundred ewes.

To the south, in the direction of the young shepherd's idle gaze, there rose one conspicuous object above the uniform moonlit plateau, and only one. It was a Druidical trilithon, consisting of three oblong stones in the form of a doorway, two on end, and one across as a lintel. Each stone had been worn, scratched, washed, nibbled, split, and otherwise attacked by ten thousand different weathers; but now the blocks looked shapely and little the worse for wear, so beautifully were they silvered over by the light of the moon. The ruin was locally called the Devil's Door.

An old shepherd presently entered the hut from the direction of the ewes, and looked around in the gloom.

'Be ye sleepy?' he asked in cross accents of the boy.

The lad replied rather timidly in the negative.

'Then,' said the shepherd, 'I'll get me home-along, and rest for a few hours. There's nothing to be done here now as I can see. The ewes can want no more tending till daybreak—'tis beyond the bounds of reason that they can. But as the order is that one of us must bide, I'll leave 'ee, d'ye hear. You can sleep by day, and I can't. And you can be down to my house in ten minutes if anything should happen. I can't afford 'ee candle; but, as 'tis Christmas week, and the time that folks have hollerdays, you can enjoy yerself by falling asleep a bit in the chair instead of biding awake all the time. But mind, not longer at once than while the shade of the Devil's Door moves a couple of spans, for you must keep an eye upon the ewes.'

The boy made no definite reply, and the old man, stirring the fire in the stove with his crook-stem, closed the door upon his companion and vanished.

As this had been more or less the course of events every night since the season's lambing had set in, the boy was not at all surprised at the charge, and amused himself for some time by lighting straws at the stove. He then went out to the ewes and new-born lambs, re-entered, sat down, and finally fell asleep. This was his customary manner of performing his watch, for though special permission for naps had this week been accorded, he had, as a matter of fact, done the same thing on every preceding night, sleeping often till awakened by a smack on the shoulder at three or four in the morning from the crook-stem of the old man.

It might have been about eleven o'clock when he awoke. He was so surprised at awaking without, apparently, being called or struck, that on second thoughts he assumed that somebody must have called him in spite of appearances, and looked out of the hut window towards the sheep. They all lay as quiet as when he had visited them, very little bleating being audible, and no human soul disturbing the scene. He next looked from the opposite window, and here the case was different. The frost-facets glistened under the moon as before; an occasional furze bush showed as a dark spot on the same; and in the foreground stood the ghostly form of the trilithon. But in front of the trilithon stood a man.

That he was not the shepherd or any one of the farm labourers was apparent in a moment's observation, his dress being a dark suit, and his figure of slender build and graceful carriage. He walked backwards and forwards in front of the trilithon.

The shepherd lad had hardly done speculating on the strangeness of the unknown's presence here at such an hour, when he saw a second figure crossing the open sward towards the locality of the trilithon and furze clump that screened the hut. This second personage was a woman; and immediately on sight of her the male stranger hastened forward, meeting her just in front of the hut window. Before she seemed to be aware of his intention he clasped her in his arms.

The lady released herself and drew back with some dignity

'You have come, Harriet—bless you for it!' he exclaimed fervently.

'But not for this,' she answered, in offended accents. And then, more good-naturedly, 'I have come, Fred, because you entreated me so! What can have been the object of your writing such a letter? I feared I might be doing you grievous ill by staying away. How did you come here?'

'I walked all the way from my father's.'

'Well, what is it? How have you lived since we last met?'

'But roughly; you might have known that without asking. I have seen many lands and many faces since I last walked these downs, but I have only thought of you.'

'Is it only to tell me this that you have summoned me so strangely?'

A passing breeze blew away the murmur of the reply and several succeeding sentences, till the man's voice again became audible in the words, 'Harriet—truth between us two! I have heard the the Duke does not treat you too well.'

'He is warm-tempered, but he is a good husband.'

'He speaks roughly to you, and sometimes even threatens to lock you out of doors.'

'Only once, Fred! On my honour, only once. The Duke is a fairly good husband, I repeat. But you deserve punishment for this night's trick of drawing me out. What does it mean?'

'Harriet, dearest, is this fair or honest? Is it not notorious that your life with him is a sad one—that, in spite of the sweetness of your temper, the sourness of his embitters your days? I have come to know if I can help you. You are a Duchess, and I am Fred Ogbourne; but it is not impossible that I may be able to help you. . . . By God! the sweetness of that tongue ought to keep him civil, especially when there is added to it the sweetness of that face!'

'Captain Ogbourne!' she exclaimed, with an emphasis of playful fear. 'How can such a comrade of my youth behave to me as you do? Don't speak so, and stare at me so! Is this really all you have to say? I see I ought not to have come.'Twas thoughtlessly done.'

Another breeze broke the thread of discourse for a time.

'Very well. I perceive you are dead and lost to me,' he could next be heard to say; '"Captain Ogborne" proves that. As I once loved you I love you now, Harriet, without one jot of abatement; but you are not the woman you were—you once were honest towards me; and now you conceal your heart in made-up speeches. Let it be; I can never see you again.'

'You need not say that in such a tragedy tone, you silly. You may see me in an ordinary way—why should you not? But, of course, not in such a way as this. I should not have come now, if it had not happened that the Duke is away from home, so that there is nobody to check my erratic impulses.'

'When does he return?'

'The day after tomorrow, or the day after that.'

'Then meet me again tomorrow night.'

'No, Fred, I cannot.'

'If you cannot tomorrow night, you can the night after; one of the two before he comes please bestow on me. Now, your hand upon it! Tomorrow or next night you will see me to bid me farewell!' He seized the Duchess's hand.

'No, but Fred—let go my hand! What do you mean by holding me so? If it be love to forget all respect to a woman's present position in thinking of her past, then yours may be so, Frederick. It is not kind and gentle of you to induce me to come to this place for pity of you, and then to hold me tight here.'

'But see me once more! I have come two thousand miles to ask it.'

'O, I must not! There will be slanders—Heaven knows what! I cannot meet you. For the sake of old times don't ask it.'

'Then own two things to me; that you did love me once, and that your husband is unkind to you often enough now to make you think of the time when you cared for me.'

'Yes—I own them both,' she answered faintly. 'But owning such as that tells against me; and I swear the inference is not true.'

'Don't say that; for you have come—let me think the reason of your coming what I like to think it. It can do you no harm. Come once more!'

He still held her hand and waist. 'Very well, then,' she said. 'Thus far you shall persuade me. I will meet you tomorrow night or the night after. Now let me go.'

He released her, and they parted. The Duchess ran rapidly down the hill towards the outlying mansion of Shakeforest Towers, and when he had watched her out of sight, he turned and strode off in the opposite direction. All then was silent and empty as before.

Yet it was only for a moment. When they had quite departed, another shape appeared upon the scene. He came from behind the trilithon. He was a man of stouter build than the first, and wore the boots and spurs of a horseman. Two things were at once obvious from this phenomenon: that he had watched the interview between the Captain and the Duchess; and that, though he probably had seen every movement of the couple, including the embrace, he had been too remote to hear the reluctant words of the lady's conversation—or, indeed, any words at all—so that the meeting must have exhibited itself to his eye as the assignation of a pair of well-agreed lovers. But it was necessary that several years should elapse before the shepherd-boy was old enough to reason this out.

The third individual stood still for a moment, as if deep in meditation. He crossed over to where the lady and gentleman had stood, and looked at the ground; then he too turned and went away in a third direction as widely divergent as possible from those taken by the two interlocutors. His course was towards the highway; and a few minutes afterwards the trot of a horse might have been heard upon its frosty surface, lessening till it died away upon the ear.

The boy remained in the hut, confronting the trilithon as if he expected yet more actors on the scene, but nobody else appeared. How long he stood with his little face against the loophole he hardly knew; but he was rudely awakened from his reverie by a punch in his back, and in the feel of it he familiarly recognized the stem of the old shepherd's crook.

'Blame thy young eyes and limbs, Bill Mills—now you have let the fire out, and you know I want it kept in! I thought something would go wrong with 'ee up here, and I couldn't bide in bed no more than thistledown on the wind, that I could not! Well, what's happened, fie upon 'ee?'

'Nothing.'

'Ewes all as I left 'em?'

'Yes.'

'Any lambs want bringing in?'

'No.'

The shepherd relit the fire, and went out among the sheep with a lantern, for the moon was getting low. Soon he came in again.

'Blame it all—thou'st say that nothing have happened; when one ewe have twinned and is like to go off, and another is dying for want of half an eye of looking to! I told 'ee, Bill Mills, if anything went wrong to come down and call me; and this is how you have done it.'

'You said I could go to sleep for a hollerday, and I did.'

'Don't you speak to your betters like that, young man, or you'll come to the gallows-tree! You didn't sleep all the time, or you wouldn't have been peeping out of that there hole! Now you can go home, and be up here again by breakfast-time. I be an old man, and there's old men that deserve well of the world; but no—I must rest how I can!'

The elder shepherd then lay down inside the hut, and the boy went down the hill to the hamlet where he dwelt.

SECOND NIGHT

When the next night drew on the actions of the boy were almost enough to show that he was thinking of the meeting he had witnessed, and of the promise wrung from the lady that she would come there again. As far as the sheep-tending arrangements were concerned, tonight was but a repetition of the foregoing one. Between ten and eleven o'clock the old shepherd withdrew as usual for what sleep at home he might chance to get without interruption, making up the other necessary hours of rest at some time during the day: the boy was left alone.

The frost was the same as on the night before, except perhaps that it was a little more severe. The moon shone as usual, except that it was three-quarters of an hour later in its course; and the boy's condition was much the same, except that he felt no sleepiness whatever. He felt, too, rather afraid; but upon the whole he preferred witnessing an assignation of strangers to running the risk of being discovered absent by the old shepherd.

It was before the distant clock of Shakeforest Towers had struck eleven that he observed the opening of the second act of this midnight drama. It consisted in the appearance of neither lover nor Duchess, but of the third figure—the stout man, booted and spurred—who came up from the easterly direction in which he had retreated the night before. He walked once round the trilithon, and next advanced towards the clump concealing the hut, the moonlight shining full upon his face and revealing him to be the Duke. Fear seized upon the shepherd-boy: the Duke was Jove himself to the rural population, whom to offend was starvation, homelessness, and death, and whom to look at was to be mentally scathed and dumbfoundered. He closed the stove, so that not a spark of light appeared, and hastily buried himself in the straw that lay in a corner.

The Duke came close to the clump of furze and stood by the spot where his wife and the Captain had held their dialogue; he examined the furze as if searching for a hiding-place, and in doing so discovered the hut. The latter he walked round and then looked inside; finding it to all seeming empty, he entered, closing the door behind him and taking his place at the little circular window against which the boy's face had been pressed just before.

The Duke had not adopted his measures too rapidly, if his object were concealment. Almost as soon as he had stationed himself there eleven o'clock struck, and the slender young man who had previously graced the scene promptly reappeared from the north quarter of the down. The spot of assignation having, by the accident of his running forward on the foregoing night, removed itself from the Devil's Door to the clump of furze, he instinctively came thither, and waited for the Duchess where he had met her before.

But a fearful surprise was in store for him tonight, as well as for the trembling juvenile. At his appearance the Duke breathed more and more quickly, his breathings being distinctly audible to the crouching boy. The young man had hardly paused when the alert nobleman softly opened the door of the hut, and, stepping round the furze, came full upon Captain Fred.

'You have dishonoured her, and you shall die the death you deserve!' came to the shepherd's ears, in a harsh, hollow whisper through the boarding of the hut.

The apathetic and taciturn boy was excited enough to run the risk of rising and looking from the window, but he could see nothing for the intervening furze boughs, both the men having gone round to the side. What took place in the few following moments he never exactly knew. He discerned portion of a shadow in quick muscular movement; then there was the fall of something on the grass; then there was stillness.

Two or three minutes later the Duke became visible round the corner of the hut, dragging by the collar the now inert body of the second man. The Duke dragged him across the open space towards the trilithon. Behind this ruin was a hollow, irregular spot, overgrown with furze and stunted thorns, and riddled by the old holes of badgers, its former inhabitants, who had now died out or departed. The Duke vanished into this depression with his burden, reappearing after the lapse of a few seconds. When he came forth he dragged nothing behind him.

He returned to the side of the hut, cleansed something on the grass, and again put himself on the watch, though not as before, inside the hut, but without, on the shady side. 'Now for the second!' he said.

It was plain, even to the unsophisticated boy, that he now awaited the other person of the appointment—his wife, the Duchess—for what pupose it was terrible to think. He seemed to be a man of such determined temper that he would scarcely hesitate in carrying out a course of revenge to the bitter end. Moreover—though it was what the shepherd did not perceive—this was all the more probable, in that the moody Duke was labouring under the exaggerated impression which the sight of the meeting in dumb show had conveyed.

The jealous watcher waited long, but he waited in vain. From within the hut the boy could hear his occasional exclamations of surprise, as if he were almost disappointed at the failure of his assumption that his guilty Duchess would surely keep the tryst. Sometimes he stepped from the shade of the furze into the moonlight, and held up his watch to learn the time.

About half-past eleven he seemed to give up expecting her. He then went a second time to the hollow behind the trilithon, remaining there nearly a quarter of an hour. From this place he proceeded quickly over a shoulder of the declivity, a little to the left, presently returning on horseback, which proved that his horse had been tethered in some secret place down there. Crossing anew the down between the hut and the trilithon, and scanning the precincts as if finally to assure himself that she had not come, he rode slowly downwards in the direction of Shakeforest Towers.

The juvenile shepherd thought of what lay in the hollow yonder; and no fear of the crook-stem of his superior officer was potent enough to detain him longer on that hill alone. Any live company, even the most terrible, was better than the company of the dead; so, running with the speed of a hare in the direction pursued by the horseman, he overtook the revengeful Duke at the second descent (where the great western road crossed before you came to the old park entrance on that side—now closed up and the lodge cleared away, though at the time it was wondered why, being considered the most convenient gate of all).

Once within the sound of the horse's footsteps, Bill Mills felt comparatively comfortable; for, though in awe of the Duke because of his position, he had no moral repugnance to his companionship on account of the grisly deed he had committed, considering that powerful nobleman to have a right to do what he chose on his own lands. The Duke rode steadily on beneath his ancestral trees, the hoofs of his horse sending up a smart sound now that he had reached the hard road of the drive, and soon drew near the front door of his house, surmounted by parapets with square-cut battlements that cast a notched shade upon the gravelled terrace. These outlines were quite familiar to little Bill Mills, though nothing within their boundary had ever been seen by him.

When the rider approached the mansion a small turret door was quickly opened and a woman came out. As soon as she saw the horseman's outlines she ran forward into the moonlight to meet him.

'Ah dear—and are you come!' she said. 'I heard Hero's tread just when you rode over the hill, and I knew it in a moment. I would have come further if I had been aware—'

'Glad to see me, eh?'

'How can you ask that?'

'Well; it is a lovely night for meetings.'

'Yes, it is a lovely night.'

[57]

The Duke dismounted and stood by her side. 'Why should you have been listening at this time of night, and yet not expecting me?' he asked.

'Why, indeed! There is a strange story attached to that, which I must tell you at once. But why did you come a night sooner than you said you would come? I am rather sorry—I really am!' (shaking her head playfully) 'for as a surprise to you I had ordered a bonfire to be built, which was to be lighted on your arrival tomorrow; and now it is wasted. You can see the outline of it just out there.'

The Duke looked across to a spot of rising glade, and saw the faggots in a heap. He then bent his eyes with a bland and puzzled air on the ground, 'What is this strange story you have to tell me that kept you awake?' he murmured.

'It is this—and it is really rather serious. My cousin Fred Ogbourne—Captain Ogbourne as he is now—was in his boyhood a great admirer of mine, as I think I have told you, though I was six years his senior. In strict truth, he was absurdly fond of me.'

'You have never told me of that before.'

'Then it is your sister I told—yes, it was. Well, you know I have not seen him for many years, and naturally I had quite forgotten his admiration of me in old times. But guess my surprise when the day before yesterday, I received a mysterious note bearing no address, and found on opening it that it came from him. The contents frightened me out of my wits. He had returned from Canada to his father's house, and conjured me by all he could think of to meet him at once. But I think I can repeat the exact words, though I will show it to you when we get indoors.'

'My DEAR COUSIN HARRIET,' the note said, 'After this long absence you will be surprised at my sudden reappearance, and more by what I am going to ask. But if my life and future are of any concern to you at all, I beg that you will grant my request. What I require of you, is, dear Harriet, that you meet me about eleven tonight by the Druid stones on Marlbury Downs, about a mile or more from your house. I cannot say more, except to entreat you to come. I will explain all when you are there. The one thing is, I want to see you. Come alone. Believe me, I would not ask this if my happiness did not hang upon it—God knows how entirely! I am too agitated to say more—Yours.   FRED.'

'That was all of it. Now, of course, I ought not to have gone, as it turned out, but that I did not think of then. I remembered his impetuous temper, and feared that something grievous was impending over his head, while he had not a friend in the world to help him, or any one except myself to whom he would care to make his trouble known. So I wrapped myself up and went to Marlbury Downs at the time he had named. Don't you think I was courageous?'

'Very.'

'When I got there—but shall we not walk on; it is getting cold?' The Duke, however, did not move. 'When I got there he came, of course, as a full grown man and officer, and not as the lad that I had known him. When I saw him I was sorry I had come. I can hardly tell you how he behaved. What he wanted I don't know even now; it seemed to be no more than the mere meeting with me. He held me by the hand and waist—O so tight— and would not let me go till I had promised to meet him again. His manner was so strange and passionate that I was afraid of him in such a lonely place, and I promised to come. Then I escaped— then I ran home—and that's all. When the time drew on this evening for the appointment—which of course, I never intended to keep—I felt uneasy, lest when he found I meant to disappoint him he would come on to the house; and that's why I could not sleep. But you are so silent!'

'I have had a long journey.'

'Then let us get into the house. Why did you come alone and unattended like this?'

'It was my humour.'

After a moment's silence, during which they moved on, she said, 'I have thought of something which I hardly like to suggest to you. He said that if I failed to come tonight he would wait again tomorrow night. Now, shall we tomorrow night go to the hill together—just to see if he is there; and if he is, read him a lesson on his foolishness in nourishing this old passion, and sending for me so oddly, instead of coming to the house?'

'Why should we see if he's there?' said her husband moodily.

'Because I think we ought to do something in it. Poor Fred! He would listen to you if you reasoned with him, and set our positions in their true light before him. It would be no more than Christian kindness to a man who unquestionably is very miserable from some cause or other. His head seems quite turned.'

By this time they had reached the door, rung the bell, and waited. All the house seemed to be asleep; but soon a man came to them, the horse was taken away, and the Duke and Duchess went in.

THIRD NIGHT

There was no help for it. Bill Mills was obliged to stay on duty, in the old shepherd's absence, this evening as before, or give up his post and living. He thought as bravely as he could of what lay behind the Devil's Door, but with no great success, and was therefore in a measure relieved, even if awe-stricken, when he saw the forms of the Duke and Duchess strolling across the frosted greensward. The Duchess was a few yards in front of her husband and tripped on lightly.

'I tell you he has not thought it worth while to come again!' the Duke insisted, as he stood still, reluctant to walk further.

'He is more likely to come and wait all night; and it would be harsh treatment to let him do it a second time.'

'He is not here; so turn and come home.'

'He seems not to be here, certainly; I wonder if anything has happened to him. If it has. I shall never forgive myself!'

The Duke, uneasily, 'O, no. He has some other engagement.'

'That is very unlikely.'

'Or perhaps he has found the distance too far.'

'Nor is that probable.'

'Then he may have thought better of it.'

'Yes, he may have thought better of it; if, indeed, he is not here all the time—somewhere in the hollow behind the Devil's Door. Let us go and see; it will serve him right to surprise him.'

'O, he's not there.'

'He may be lying very quiet because of you,' she said archly.

'O, no—not because of me!'

'Come, then. I declare, dearest, you lag like an unwilling schoolboy tonight, and there's no responsiveness in you! You are jealous of that poor lad, and it is quite absurd of you.'

'I'll come! I'll come! Say no more, Harriet!'

And they crossed over the green.

Wondering what they would do, the young shepherd left the hut, and doubled behind the belt of furze, intending to stand near the trilithon unperceived. But, in crossing the few yards of open ground he was for a moment exposed to view.

'Ah, I see him at last!' said the Duchess.

'See him!' said the Duke. 'Where?'

'By the Devil's Door; don't you notice a figure there? Ah, my poor lover-cousin, won't you catch it now?' and she laughed half-pityingly. 'But what's the matter?' she asked, turning to her husband.

'It is not he!' said the Duke hoarsely. 'It can't be he!'

'No, it is not he. It is too small for him. It is a boy.'

'Ah, I thought so! Boy, come here.'

The youthful shepherd advanced with apprehension.

'What are you doing here?'

'Keeping sheep, your Grace.'

'Ah, you know me! Do you keep sheep here every night?'

'Off and on, my Lord Duke.'

'And what have you seen here tonight or last night?' inquired the Duchess. 'Any person waiting or walking about?'

The boy was silent.

'He has seen nothing,' interrupted her husband, his eyes so forbiddingly fixed on the boy that they seemed to shine like points of fire. 'Come, let us go. The air is too keen to stand in long.'

When they were gone the boy retreated to the hut and sheep, less fearful now than at first—familiarity with the situation having gradually overpowered his thoughts of the buried man. But he was not to be left alone long. When an interval had elapsed of about sufficient length for walking to and from Shakeforest Towers, there appeared from that direction the heavy form of the Duke. He now came alone.

The nobleman, on his part, seemed to have eyes no less sharp than the boy's for he instantly recognized the latter among the ewes, and came straight towards him.

'Are you the shepherd lad I spoke to a short time ago?'

'I be, my Lord Duke.'

'Now listen to me. Her Grace asked you what you had seen this last night or two up here, and you made no reply. I now ask the same thing, and you need not be afraid to answer. Have you seen anything strange these nights you have been watching here?'

'My Lord Duke, I be a poor heedless boy, and what I see I don't bear in mind.'

'I ask you again,' said the Duke, coming nearer, 'have you seen anything strange these nights you have been watching here?'

'O, my Lord Duke! I be but the under-shepherd boy, and my father he was but your humble Grace's hedger, and my mother only the cinder-woman in the back-yard! I fall asleep when left alone, and I see nothing at all!'

The Duke grasped the boy by the shoulder, and, directly impending over him, stared down into his face, 'Did you see anything strange done here last night, I say?'

'O, my Lord Duke, have mercy, and don't stab me!' cried the shepherd, falling on his knees. 'I have never seen you walking here, or riding here, or lying-in-wait for a man, or dragging a heavy load!'

'H'm!' said his interrogator, grimly, relaxing his hold. 'It is well to know that you have never seen those things. Now, which would you rather—*see me do those things now*, or keep a secret all your life?'

'Keep a secret, my Lord Duke!'

'Sure you are able?'

'O, your Grace, try me!'

'Very well. And now, how do you like sheepkeeping?'

'Not at all. 'Tis lonely work for them that think of spirits, and I'm badly used.'

'I believe you. You are too young for it. I must do something to make you more comfortable. You shall change this smock-frock for a real cloth jacket, and your thick boots for polished shoes. And you shall be taught what you have never yet heard of, and be put to school, and have bats and balls for the holidays, and be made a man of. But you must never say you have been a shepherd boy, and watched on the hills at night, for shepherd boys are not liked in good company.'

'Trust me, my Lord Duke.'

'The very moment you forget yourself, and speak of your shepherd days—this year, next year, in school, out of school, or riding in your carriage twenty years hence—at that moment my help will be withdrawn, and smash down you come to shepherding forthwith. You have parents, I think you say?'

'A widowed mother only, my Lord Duke.'

'I'll provide for her, and make a comfortable woman of her, until you speak of—what?'

'Of my shepherd days, and what I saw here.'

'Good. If you do speak of it?'

'Smash down she comes to widowing forthwith!'

'That's well—very well. But it's not enough. Come here.' He took the boy across to the trilithon, and made him kneel down.

'Now, this was once a holy place,' resumed the Duke. 'An altar stood here, erected to a venerable family of gods, who were known and talked of long before the God we know now. So that an oath sworn here is doubly an oath. Say this after me: "May all the host above—angels and archangels, and principalities and powers—punish me; may I be

[62]

tormented wherever I am—in the house or in the garden, in the fields or in the roads, in church or in chapel, at home or abroad, on land or at sea; may I be afflicted in eating and in drinking, in growing up and in growing old, in living and dying, inwardly and outwardly, and for always, if I ever speak of my life as a shepherd-boy, or of what I have seen done on this Marlbury Down. So be it, and so let it be. Amen and amen." Now kiss the stone.'

The trembling boy repeated the words, and kissed the stone, as desired.

The Duke led him off by the hand. That night the junior shepherd slept in Shakeforest Towers, and the next day he was sent away for tuition to a remote village. Thence he went to a preparatory establishment, and in due course to a public school.

FOURTH NIGHT

On a winter evening many years subsequent to the above-mentioned occurrences, the *ci-devant* shepherd sat in a well-furnished office in the north wing of Shakeforest Towers in the guise of an ordinary educated man of business. He appeared at this time as a person of thirty-eight or forty, though actually he was several years younger. A worn and restless glance of the eye now and then, when he lifted his head to search for some letter or paper which had been mislaid, seemed to denote that his was not a mind so thoroughly at ease as his surroundings might have led an observer to expect. His pallor, too, was remarkable for a countryman. He was professedly engaged in writing, but he shaped not a word. He had sat there only a few minutes, when, laying down his pen and pushing back his chair, he rested a hand uneasily on each of the chair-arms and looked on the floor.

Soon he arose and left the room. His course was along a passage which ended in a central octagonal hall; crossing this he knocked at a door. A faint, though deep, voice told him to come in. The room he entered was a library, and it was tenanted by a single person only—his patron the Duke.

During this long interval of years the Duke had lost all his heaviness of build. He was, indeed, almost a skeleton; his white hair was thin, and his hands were nearly transparent. 'Oh—Mills?' he murmured. 'Sit down. What is it?'

'Nothing new, your Grace. Nobody to speak of has written, and nobody has called.'

'Ah—what then? You look concerned.'

'Old times have come to life, owing to something waking them.'

'Old times be cursed—which old times are they?'

'That Christmas week twenty-two years ago, when the late Duchess's cousin Frederick implored her to meet him on Marlbury Downs. I saw the meeting—it was just such a night as this—and I, as you know, saw more. She met him once, but not the second time.'

'Mills, shall I recall some words to you—the words of an oath taken on that hill by a shepherd-boy?'

'It is unnecessary. He has strenuously kept that oath and promise. Since that night no sound of his shepherd life has crossed his lips—even to yourself. But do you wish to hear more, or do you not, your Grace?'

'I wish to hear no more,' said the Duke sullenly.

'Very well; let it be so. But a time seems coming—may be quite near at hand—when, in spite of my lips, that episode will allow itself to go undivulged no longer.'

'I wish to hear no more!' repeated the Duke.

'You need be under no fear of treachery from me,' said the steward, somewhat bitterly. 'I am a man to whom you have been kind—no patron could have been kinder. You have clothed and educated me; have installed me here; and I am not unmindful. But what of it—has your Grace gained much by my staunchness? I think not. There was great excitement about Captain Ogbourne's disappearance, but I spoke not a word. And his body has never been found. For twenty-two years I have wondered what you did with him. Now I know. A circumstance that occurred this afternoon recalled the time to me most forcibly. To make it certain to myself that all was not a dream, I went up there with a spade; I searched, and saw enough to know that something decays there in a closed badger's hole.'

'Mills, do you think the Duchess guessed?'

'She never did, I am sure, to the day of her death.'

'Did you leave all as you found it on the hill?'

'I did.'

'What made you think of going up there this particular afternoon?'

'What your Grace says you don't wish to be told.'

The Duke was silent; and the stillness of the evening was so marked that there reached their ears from the outer air the sound of a tolling bell.

'What is that bell tolling for?' asked the nobleman.

'For what I came to tell you of, your Grace.'

'You torment me—it is your way!' said the Duke querulously. 'Who's dead in the village?'

'The oldest man—the old shepherd.'

'Dead at last—how old is he?'

'Ninety-four.'

'And I am only seventy. I have four-and-twenty years to the good!'

'I served under that old man when I kept sheep on Marlbury Downs. And he was on the hill that second night, when I first exchanged words with your Grace. He was on the hill *all the time*; but I did not know he was there—nor did you.'

'Ah!' said the Duke, starting up. 'Go on—I yield the point—you may tell!'

'I heard this afternoon that he was at the point of death. It was that which set me thinking of that past time—and induced me to search on the hill for what I have told you. Coming back I heard that he wished to see the Vicar to confess to him a secret he had kept for more than twenty years—"out of respect to my Lord the Duke"—something that he had seen committed on Marlbury Downs when returning to the flock on a December night twenty-two years ago. I have thought it over. He had left me in charge that evening; but he was in the habit of coming back suddenly, lest I should have fallen asleep. That night I saw nothing of him, though he had promised to return. He must have returned, and—found reason to keep in hiding. It is all plain. The next thing is that the Vicar went to him two hours ago. Further than that I have not heard.'

'It is quite enough. I will see the Vicar at daybreak tomorrow.'

'What to do?'

'Stop his tongue for four-and-twenty years—till I am dead at ninety-four, like the shepherd.'

'Your Grace—while you impose silence on me, I will not speak, even though my neck should pay the penalty. I promised to be yours, and I am yours. But is this persistence of any avail?'

'I'll stop his tongue, I say!' cried the Duke with some of his old rugged force. 'Now, you go home to bed, Mills, and leave me to manage him.'

The interview ended, and the steward withdrew. The night, as he had said, was just such an one as the night of twenty-two years before, and the events of the evening destroyed in him all regard for the season as one of cheerfulness and goodwill. He went off to his own house on the further verge of the park, where he led a lonely life, scarcely calling any man friend. At eleven he prepared to retire to bed—but did not retire. He sat down and reflected. Twelve o'clock struck; he looked out at the colourless moon, and, prompted by he knew not what, put on his hat and emerged into the air. Here William Mills strolled on and on, till he reached the top of Marlbury Downs, a spot he had not visited at this hour of the night during the whole score-and-odd years.

He placed himself, as nearly as he could guess, on the spot where the shepherd's hut had stood. No lambing was in progress there now, and the old shepherd who had used him so roughly had ceased from his labours that very day. But the trilithon stood up white as ever; and, crossing the intervening sward, the steward fancifully placed his mouth against the stone. Restless and self-reproachful as he was, he could not resist a smile as he thought of the terrifying oath of compact, sealed by a kiss upon the stones of a Pagan temple. But he had kept his word, rather as a promise than as a formal vow, with much worldly advantage to himself, though not much happiness; till increase of years had bred reactionary feelings which led him to receive the news of tonight with emotions akin to relief.

While leaning against the Devil's Door and thinking on these things, he became conscious that he was not the only inhabitant of the down. A figure in white was moving across his front with long, noiseless strides. Mills stood motionless, and when the form drew quite near he perceived it to be that of the Duke himself in his nightshirt—apparently walking in his sleep. Not to alarm the old man, Mills clung close to the shadow of the stone. The Duke went straight on into the hollow. There he knelt down, and began scratching the earth with his hands like a badger. After a few minutes he arose, sighed heavily, and retraced his steps as he had come.

Fearing that he might harm himself, yet unwilling to arouse him, the steward followed noiselessly. The Duke kept on his path unerringly, entered the park, and made for the house, where he let himself in by a window that stood open—the one probably by which he had come out. Mills softly closed the window behind his patron, and then retired homeward to await the revelations of the morning, deeming it unnecessary to alarm the house.

However, he felt uneasy during the remainder of the night, no less on account of the Duke's personal condition than because of that which was imminent next day. Early in the morning he called at Shakeforest Towers. The blinds were down, and there was something singular upon the porter's face when he opened the door. The steward inquired for the Duke.

The man's voice was subdued as he replied: 'Sir, I am sorry to say that his Grace is dead! He left his room sometime in the night, and wandered about nobody knows where. On returning to the upper floor he lost his balance and fell downstairs.'

The steward told the tale of the Down before the Vicar had spoken. Mills had always intended to do so after the death of the Duke. The consequences to himself he underwent cheerfully; but his life was not prolonged. He died, a farmer at the Cape, when still somewhat under forty-nine years of age.

The splendid Marlbury breeding flock is as renowned as ever, and, to the eye, seems the same in every particular that it was in earlier times; but the animals which composed it on the occasion of the events gathered from the Justice are divided by many ovine generations from its members now. Lambing Corner has long since ceased to be used for lambing purposes, though the name still lingers on as the appellation of the spot. This abandonment of site may be partly owing to the removal of the high furze bushes which lent such convenient shelter at that date. Partly, too, it may be due to another circumstance. For it is said by present shepherds in that district that during the nights of Christmas week flitting shapes are seen in the open space around the trilithon, together with the gleam of a weapon, and the shadow of a man dragging a burden into the hollow. But of these things there is no certain testimony.

THE PICTURE
PUZZLE

by *Edward Lucas White*

Edward Lucas White (1866–1934) was an
American writer who achieved his greatest
success with novels set in ancient Greece; but he
is now chiefly remembered for his short fantasy
tales (often based on vivid dreams) especially
'The House of the Nightmare' (1905),
'Lukundoo' (1907), and 'The Picture Puzzle'
(1909).

I

O f course the instinct of the police and detectives was to run
down their game. That was natural. They seemed astonished
and contemptuous when I urged that all I wanted was my baby;
whether the kidnappers were ever caught or not made no difference to
me. They kept arguing that unless precautions were taken the criminals
would escape and I kept arguing that if they became suspicious of a trap
they would keep away and my only chance to recover our little girl would
be gone forever. They finally agreed and I believe they kept their promise
to me. Helen always felt the other way and maintained that their watchers
frightened off whoever was to meet me. Anyhow I waited in vain, waited
for hours, waited again the next day and the next and the next. We put
advertisements in countless papers, offering rewards and immunity, but
never heard anything more.

I pulled myself together in a sort of a way and tried to do my work. My partner and clerks were very kind. I don't believe I ever did anything properly in those days, but no one ever brought any blunder to my attention. If they came across any they set it right for me. And at the office it was not so bad. Trying to work was good for me. It was worse at home and worse at night. I slept hardly at all.

Helen, if possible, slept less than I. And she had terrible spasms of sobs that shook the bed. She would try to choke them down, thinking I was asleep and she might wake me. But she never went through a night without at least one frightful paroxysm of tears.

In the daylight she controlled herself better, made a heart-breaking and yet heart-warming effort at her normal cheeriness over the breakfast things, and greeted me beautifully when I came home. But the moment we were alone for the evening she would break down.

I don't know how many days that sort of thing kept up. I sympathized in silence. It was Helen herself who suggested that we must force ourselves to be diverted, somehow. The theatre was out of the question. Not merely the sight of a four-year-old girl with yellow locks threw Helen into a passion of uncontrollable sobbing, but all sorts of unexpected trifles reminded her of Amy and affected her almost as much. Confined to our home we tried cards, chess and everything else we could think of. They helped her as little as they helped me.

Then one afternoon Helen did not come to greet me. Instead I came in I heard her call, quite in her natural voice.

'Oh, I'm so glad that is you. Come and help me.'

I found her seated at the library table, her back to the door. She had on a pink wrapper and her shoulders had no despondent droop, but a girlish alertness. She barely turned her head as I entered, but her profile showed no signs of recent weeping. Her face was its natural colour.

'Come and help me,' she repeated. 'I can't find the other piece of the boat.'

She was absorbed, positively absorbed in a picture puzzle.

In forty seconds I was absorbed too. It must have been six minutes before we identified the last piece of the boat. And then we went on with the sky and were still at it when the butler announced dinner.

'Where did you get it?' I asked, over the soup, which Helen really ate.

'Mrs Allstone brought it,' Helen replied, 'just before lunch.'

I blessed Mrs Allstone.

Really it seems absurd, but those idiotic jig-saw puzzles were our salvation. They actually took our minds off everything else. At first I dreaded finishing one. No sooner was the last piece in place than I felt a sudden revulsion, a booming of blood in my ears, and the sense of loss and misery rushed over me like a wave of scalding water. And I knew it was worse for Helen.

But after some days each seemed not merely a respite from pain, but a sedative as well. After a two hours' struggle with a fascinating tangle of shapes and colours, we seemed numb to our bereavement and the bitterness of the smart seemed blunted.

We grew fastidious as to manufacture and finish; learned to avoid crude and clumsy products as bores; developed a pronounced taste for pictures neither too soft nor too plain in colour masses; and became connoisseurs as to cutting, utterly above the obvious and entirely disenchanted with the painfully difficult. We evolved into adepts, quick to recoil from fragments barren of any clue of shape or markings and equally prompt to reject those whose meaning was too definite and insistent. We trod delicately the middle way among segments not one of which was without some clue of outline or tint, and not one of which imparted its message without interrogation, inference and reflection.

Helen used to time herself and try the same puzzle over and over on successive days until she could do it in less than half an hour. She declared that a really good puzzle was interesting the fourth or fifth time and that an especially fine puzzle was diverting if turned face down and put together from the shapes merely, after it had been well learned the other way. I did not enter into the craze to that extent, but sometimes tried her methods for variety.

We really slept, and Helen, though worn and thin, was not abject, not agonized. Her nights passed, if not wholly without tears, yet with only those soft and silent tears, which are more a relief than suffering. With me she was nearly her old self and very brave and patient. She greeted me naturally and we seemed able to go on living.

Then one day she was not at the door to welcome me. I had hardly shut it before I heard her sobbing. I found her again at the library table and over a puzzle. But this time she had just finished it and was bowed over it on the table, shaken all over by her grief.

She lifted her head from her crossed arms, pointed and buried her face in her hands. I understood. The picture I remembered from a magazine of the year before: a Christmas tree with a bevy of children about it and one (we had remarked it at the time) a perfect likeness of our Amy.

As she rocked back and forth, her hands over her eyes, I swept the pieces into their box and put on the lid.

Presently Helen dried her eyes and looked at the table.

'Oh! why did you touch it,' she wailed. 'It was such a comfort to me.'

'You did not seem comforted,' I retorted. 'I thought the contrast . . .' I stopped.

'You mean the contrast between the Christmas we expected and the Christmas we are going to have?' she queried. 'You mean you thought that was too much for me?'

I nodded.

'It wasn't that at all,' she averred. 'I was crying for joy. That picture was a sign.'

'A sign?' I repeated.

'Yes,' she declared, 'a sign that we shall get her back in time for Christmas. I'm going to start and get ready right away.'

At first I was glad of the diversion. Helen had the nursery put in order as if she expected Amy the next day, hauled over all the child's clothes and was in a bustling state of happy expectancy. She went vigorously about her preparation for a Christmas celebration, planned a Christmas Eve dinner for our brothers and sisters and their husbands and wives, and a children's party afterwards with a big tree and a profusion of goodies and gifts.

'You see,' she explained, 'everyone will want their own Christmas at home. So shall we, for we'll just want to gloat over Amy all day. We won't want them on Christmas any more than they'll want us. But this way we can all be together and celebrate and rejoice over our good luck.'

She was as elated and convinced as if it was a certainty. For a while her occupation with preparations was good for her, but she was so forehanded that she was ready a week ahead of time and had not a detail left to arrange. I dreaded a reaction, but her artificial exaltation continued unabated. All the more I feared the inevitable disappointment and was genuinely concerned for her reason. The fixed idea that that accidental coincidence was a prophecy and a guarantee dominated her totally. I was really afraid that the shock of the reality might kill her. I did not want to dissipate her happy delusion, but I could not but try to prepare her for a certain blow. I talked cautiously in wide circles around what I wanted and I did not want to say.

II

On December 22nd, I came home early, just after lunch, in fact. Helen met me, at the door, with such a demeanour of suppressed high spirits, happy secrecy and tingling anticipation that for one moment I was certain Amy had been found and was then in the house.

'I've something wonderful to show you,' Helen declared, and led me to the library.

There on the table was a picture-puzzle fitted together.

She stood and pointed to it with the air of exhibiting a marvel.

I looked at it but could not conjecture the cause of her excitement. The pieces seemed too large, too clumsy and too uniform in outline. It looked a crude and clumsy puzzle, beneath her notice.

'Why did you buy it?' I asked.

'I met a peddler on the street,' she answered, 'and he was so wretched-looking, I was sorry for him. He was young and thin and looked haggard and consumptive. I looked at him and I suppose I showed my feelings. He said:

"Lady, buy a puzzle. It will help you to your heart's desire."

'His words were so odd I bought it, and now just look at what it is.'

I was groping for some foothold upon which to rally my thoughts.

'Let me see the box in which it came,' I asked.

She produced it and I read on the top:

'GUGGENHEIM'S DOUBLE PICTURE
PUZZLE.
TWO IN ONE.
MOST FOR THE MONEY.
ASK FOR GUGGENHEIM'S'

And on the end—

'ASTRAY.
A BREATH OF AIR.
50 CENTS.'

'It's queer,' Helen remarked. 'But it is not a double puzzle at all, though the pieces have the same paper on both sides. One side is blank. I suppose this is ASTRAY. Don't you think so?'

'Astray?' I queried, puzzled.

'Oh,' she cried, in a disappointed, disheartened, almost querulous tone. 'I thought you would be so much struck with the resemblance. You don't seem to notice it at all. Why even the dress is identical!'

'The dress?' I repeated. 'how many times have you done this?'

'Only this once,' she said. 'I had just finished it when I heard your key in the lock.'

'I should have thought,' I commented, 'that it would have been more interesting to do it face up first.'

'Face up!' she cried. 'It is face up.'

Her air of scornful superiority completely shook me out of my sedulous consideration of a moment before.

'Nonsense,' I said, 'that's the back of the puzzle. There are no colours there. It's all pink.'

'Pink!' she exclaimed pointing. 'Do you call that pink!'

'Certainly it's pink,' I asserted.

'Don't you see there the white of the old man's beard?' she queried, pointing again. 'And there the black of his boots? And there the red of the little girl's dress?'

'No,' I declared. 'I don't see anything of the kind. It's all pink. There isn't any picture there at all.'

'No picture!' she cried. 'Don't you see the old man leading the child by the hand?'

'No,' I said harshly, 'I don't see any picture and you know I don't. There isn't any picture there. I can't make out what you are driving at. It seems a senseless joke.'

'Joke! I joke!' Helen half whispered. The tears came into her eyes.

'You are cruel,' she said, 'and I thought you would be struck by the resemblance.'

I was overwhelmed by a pang of self-reproach, solicitude and terror.

'Resemblance to what?' I asked gently.

'Can't you see it?' she insisted.

'Tell me,' I pleaded. 'Show me just what you want me to notice most.'

'The child,' she said pointing, 'is just exactly Amy and the dress is the very red suit she had on when—'

'Dear,' I said, 'try to collect yourself. Indeed you only imagine what you tell me. There is no picture on this side of the sections. The whole thing is pink. That is the back of the puzzle.'

'I don't see how you can say such a thing,' she raged at me. 'I can't make out why you should. What sort of a test are you putting me through? What does it all mean?'

'Will you let me prove to you that this is the back of the puzzle?' I asked.

'If you can,' she said shortly.

[73]

I turned the pieces of the puzzle over, keeping them together as much as possible. I succeeded pretty well with the outer pieces and soon had the rectangle in place. The inner pieces were a good deal mixed up, but even before I had fitted them I exclaimed:

'There look at that!'

'Well,' she asked. 'What do you expect me to see?'

'What do you see?' I asked in turn.

'I see the back of a puzzle,' she answered.

'Don't you see those front steps?' I demanded, pointing.

'I don't see anything,' she asserted, 'except green.'

'Do you call that green?' I queried, pointing.

'I do,' she declared.

'Don't you see the brickwork front of the house,' I insisted, 'and the lower part of a window and part of a door? Yes, and those front-steps in the corner?'

'I don't see anything of the kind,' she declared. 'Any more than you do. What I see is just what you see. It's the back of the puzzle, all pale green.'

I had been feverishly putting together the last pieces as she spoke. I could not believe my eyes and, as the last piece fitted in, was struck with amazement.

The picture showed an old red-brick house, with brown blinds, all open. The top of the front steps was included in the lower right hand corner, most of the front door above them, all of one window on its level, and the side of another. Above appeared all of one of the second floor windows, and parts of those to right and left of it. The other windows were closed, but the sash of the middle one was raised and from it leaned a little girl, a child with frowzy hair, a dirty face and wearing a blue and white check frock. The child was a perfect likeness of our lost Amy, supposing she had been starved and neglected. I was so affected that I was afraid I should faint. I was positively husky when I asked:

'Don't you see that?'

'I see Nile green,' she maintained. 'The same as you see.'

I swept the pieces into the box.

'We are neither of us well,' I said.

'I should think you must be deranged to behave so,' she snapped, 'and it is no wonder I am not well the way you treat me.'

'How could I know what you wanted me to see?' I began.

'Wanted you to see!' she cried. 'You keep it up? You pretend you didn't see it, after all? Oh! I have no patience with you.'

She burst into tears, fled upstairs and I heard her slam and lock our bedroom door.

I put that puzzle together again and the likeness of that hungry, filthy child in the picture to our Amy made my heart ache.

I found a stout box, cut two pieces of straw-board just the shape of the puzzle and a trifle larger, laid one on top of it and slid the other under it. Then I tied it together with string and wrapped it in paper and tied the whole.

I put the box in my overcoat pocket and went out carrying the flat parcel.

I walked round to MacIntyre's.

I told him the whole story and showed him the puzzle.

'Do you want the truth?' he asked.

'Just that,' I said.

'Well,' he reported. 'You are as overstrung as she is and the same way. There is absolutely no picture on either side of this. One side is solid green and the other solid pink.'

'How about the coincidence of the names on the box?' I interjected. 'One suited what I saw, one what she said she saw.'

'Let's look at the box,' he suggested.

He looked at it on all sides.

'There's not a letter on it,' he announced. 'Except "picture puzzle" on top and "50 cents" on the end.'

'I don't feel insane,' I declared.

'You aren't,' he reassured me. 'Nor in any danger of being insane. Let me look you over.'

He felt my pulse, looked at my tongue, examined both eyes with his ophthalmoscope, and took a drop of my blood.

'I'll report further,' he said, 'in confirmation tomorrow. You're all right, or nearly so, and you'll soon be really all right. All you need is a little rest. Don't worry about this idea of your wife's, humour her. There won't be any terrible consequences. After Christmas go to Florida or somewhere for a week or so. And don't exert yourself from now till after that change.'

When I reached home, I went down into the cellar, threw that puzzle and its box into the furnace and stood and watched it burn to ashes.

III

When I came upstairs from the furnace Helen met me as if nothing had happened. By one of her sudden revulsions of mood she was even more gracious than usual, and was at dinner altogether charming. She did not refer to our quarrel or to the puzzle.

The next morning over our breakfast we were both opening our mail. I had told her that I should not go to the office until after Christmas and that I wanted her to arrange for a little tour that would please her. I had phoned to the office not to expect me until after New Year's.

My mail contained nothing of moment.

Helen looked up from hers with an expression curiously mingled of disappointment, concern and a pleased smile.

'It is so fortunate you have nothing to do,' she said. 'I spent four whole days choosing toys and found most of those I selected at Bleich's. They were to have been delivered day before yesterday but they did not come. I telephoned yesterday and they said they would try to trace them. Here is a letter saying that the whole lot was missent out to Roundwood. You noticed that Roundwood station burned Monday night. They were all burnt up. Now I'll have to go and find more like them. You can go with me.'

I went.

The two days were a strange mixture of sensations and emotions.

Helen had picked over Bleich's stock pretty carefully and could duplicate from it few of the burned articles, could find acceptable substitutes for fewer. There followed an exhausting pursuit of the unattainable through a bewildering series of toy-shops and department-stores. We spent most of our time at counters and much of the remainder in a taxicab.

In a way it was very trying. I did not mind the smells and bad air and other mere physical discomforts. But the mental strain continually intensified. Helen's confidence that Amy would be restored to us was steadily waning and her outward exhibition of it was becoming more and more artificial, and consciously sustained, and more and more of an effort. She was coming to foresee, in spite of herself, that our Christmas celebration would be a most terrible mockery of our bereavement. She was forcing herself not to confess it to herself and not to show it to me. The strain told on her. It told on me to watch it, to see the inevitable crash coming nearer and nearer and to try to put away from myself the pictures of her collapse, of her probable loss of reason, of her possible death, which my imagination kept thrusting before me.

On the other hand Helen was to all appearance, if one had no prevision by which to read her, her most charming self. Her manner to shop-girls and other sales-people was a delight to watch. Her little speeches to me were full of her girlish whimsicality and unexpectedness. Her good will towards all the world, her resolution that everything must come right and would come right haloed her in a sort of aureole of romance. Our lunches were ideal hours, full of the atmosphere of courtship, of lovemaking, of exquisite companionship. In spite of my forebodings, I caught the contagion of the Christmas shopping crowds; in spite of her self-deception, Helen revelled in it. The purpose to make as many people as possible as happy as might be irradiated Helen with the light of fairyland; her resolve to be happy herself in spite of everything made her a sort of fairy queen. I found myself less and less anxious and more and more almost expectant. I knew Helen was looking for Amy every instant. I found myself in the same state of mind.

Our lunch on Christmas Eve was a strange blend of artificiality and genuine exhilaration. After it we had but one purchase to make.

'We are in no hurry,' Helen said, 'Let's take a horse-hansom for old sake's sake.'

In it we were like boy and girl together until the jeweller's was reached.

There gloom, in spite of us, settled down over our hopes and feelings. Helen walked to the hansom like a grey ghost. Like the whisper of some far-off stranger I heard myself order the driver to take us home.

In the hansom we sat silent, looking straight in front of us at nothing. I stole a glance at Helen and saw a tear in the corner of her eye. I sat choking.

All at once she seized my hand.

'Look!' she exclaimed, 'Look!'

I looked where she pointed, but discerned nothing to account for her excitement.

'What is it?' I queried.

'The old man!' she exclaimed.

'What old man?' I asked bewildered.

'The old man on the puzzle,' she told me. 'The old man who was leading Amy.'

Then I was sure she was demented. To humour her I asked:

'The old man with the brown coat?'

[77]

'Yes,' she said eagerly. 'The old man with the long grey hair over his collar.'

'With the walking stick?' I inquired.

'Yes,' she answered. 'With the crooked walking stick.'

I saw him too! This was no figment of Helen's imagination.

It was absurd of course, but my eagerness caught fire from hers. I credited the absurdity. In what sort of vision it mattered not she had seen an old man like this leading our lost Amy.

I spoke to the driver, pointed out to him the old man, told him to follow him without attracting his attention and offered him anything he asked to keep him in sight.

Helen became possessed with the idea that we should lose sight of the old man in the crowds. Nothing would do but we must get out and follow him on foot. I remonstrated that we were much more likely to lose sight of him that way, and still more likely to attract his notice, which would be worse than losing him. She insisted and I told the man to keep us in view.

A weary walk we had, though most of it was mere strolling after a tottering figure or loitering about shops he entered.

It was near dusk and full time for us to be at home when he began to walk fast. So fast he drew away from us in spite of us. He turned a corner a half a square ahead of us. When we turned into that street he was nowhere to be seen.

Helen was ready to faint with disappointment. With no hope of helping her, but some instinctive idea of postponing the evil moment I urged her to walk on, saying that perhaps we might see him. About the middle of the square I suddenly stood still.

'What is the matter?' Helen asked.

'The house!' I said.

'What house?' she queried.

'The house in the puzzle picture,' I explained. 'The house where I saw Amy at the window.'

Of course she had not seen any house on the puzzle, but she caught at the last straw of hope.

It was a poor neighbourhood of crowded tenements, not quite a slum, yet dirty and unkempt and full of poor folks.

The house door was shut, I could find no sign of any bell. I knocked. No one answered. I tried the door. It was not fastened and we entered a dirty hallway, cold and damp and smelling repulsively. A fat woman stuck her head out of a door and jabbered at us in an unknown tongue.

A man with a fez on his greasy black hair came from the back of the hallway and was equally unintelligible.

'Does nobody here speak English?' I asked.

The answer was as incomprehensible as before.

I made to go up the stairs.

The man, and the woman, who was now standing before her door, both chattered at once, but neither made any attempt to stop me. They waved vaguely explanatory, deprecating hands towards the blackness of the stairway. We went up.

On the second floor landing we saw just the old man we had been following.

He stared at us when I spoke to him.

'Son-in-law,' he said, 'son-in-law.'

He called and a door opened. An oldish woman answered him in apparently the same jargon. Behind was a young woman holding a baby.

'What is it?' she asked with a great deal of accent but intelligibly.

Three or four children held on by her skirts.

Behind her I saw a little girl in a blue-check dress.

Helen screamed.

IV

The people turned out to be refugees from the settlement about the sacked German Mission at Dehkhargan near Tabriz, Christianized Persians, such stupid villagers that they had never thought or had been incapable of reporting their find to the police, so ignorant that they knew nothing of rewards or advertisements, such simple-hearted folk that they had shared their narrow quarters and scanty fare with the unknown waif their grandfather had found wandering alone, after dark, months before.

Amy, when we had leisure to ask questions and hear her experiences, declared they had treated her as they treated their own children. She could give no description of her kidnappers except that the woman had on a hat with roses in it and the man had a little yellow moustache. She could not tell how long they had kept her nor why they had left her to wander in the streets at night.

It needed no common language, far less any legal proof, to convince Amy's hosts that she belonged to us. I had a pocket full of Christmas money, new five and ten dollar gold pieces and bright silver quarters for the servants and children. I filled the old grandfather's hands and plainly overwhelmed him. They all jabbered at us, blessings, if I judged the tone right. I tried to tell the young woman we should see them again in a day or two and I gave her a card to make sure.

I told the cabman to stop the first taxicab he should see empty. In the hansom we hugged Amy alternately and hugged each other.

Once in the taxicab we were home in half an hour; more, much more than half an hour late. Helen whisked Amy in by the servants' door and flew upstairs with her by the back way. I faced a perturbed and anxious parlourful of interrogative relatives and in-laws.

'You'll know before many minutes,' I said, 'why we were both out and are in late. Helen will want to surprise you and I'll say nothing to spoil the effect.'

Nothing I could have said would have spoiled the effect because they would not have believed me. As it was Helen came in sooner than I could have thought possible, looking her best and accurately playing the formal hostess with a feeble attempt at a surprise in store.

The dinner was a great success, with much laughter and high spirits, everybody carried away by Helen's sallies and everybody amazed that she could be so gay.

'I cannot understand,' Paul's wife whispered to me, 'how she can ever get through the party. It would kill me in her place.'

'It won't kill her,' I said confidently. 'You may be sure of that.'

The children had arrived to the number of more than thirty and only the inevitably late Amstelhuysens had not come. Helen announced that she would not wait for them.

'The tree is lighted,' she said. 'We'll have the doors thrown open and go in.'

We were all gathered in the front parlour. The twins panted in at the last instant. The grown-ups were pulling motto-crackers and the children were throwing confetti. The doors opened, the tree filled all the back of the room. The candles blazed and twinkled. And in front of it, in a simple little white dress, with a fairy's wand in her hand, tipped with a silver star, clean, healthy-looking and full of spirits was Amy, the fairy of the hour.

ELLISON'S
CHRISTMAS
DINNER

by Dolf Wyllarde

Dolf Wyllarde (1871–1950) was a very popular
novelist during the first half of this century, but
is now (like many of her contemporaries) largely
forgotten. She wrote dozens of exciting stories
about Africa, Asia, and the Colonies. In her
introduction to *Tropical Tales* (1909), Dolf
Wyllarde assured her readers that 'Ellison's
Christmas Dinner' was based on an adventurer's
bona fide experience in Persia. 'I have only
altered names and developed supplementary
characters.'

(TO E. H. E.)

There was famine in North Persia. Cold and snow lay like a curse
upon the stricken land, and the long stretches of stony waste
mocked the cry for food with the bare earth that had yielded no
grain harvest. All the way from Teheran, Ellison had been sickened by
the suffering caused by the lack of food—men, women and children
dying by the roadside in their struggle to reach the northern capital,
where there was grain stored, and provisions might be bought. There
might be plenty to eat at Teheran, but the great drought had lasted for
two years and had made it almost impossible to get fodder for the beasts

as well as food for their owners, so the wretched Persians starved on the way before they could come in from outlying districts to the big cities.

Food was dear, of course, even at Teheran, but Ellison's English gold had bought it for him in the bazaars, and it had not occurred to him that things might become worse as he penetrated into the interior and that at smaller places even his money might not avail him to obtain what did not exist. He had drifted into Persia from the Caucasus, where, with an insatiable love of wandering, he had been exploring what was to him an unknown country. He was a stranger to Persia also, but had a half-formed plan of posting straight across it and going on to India as the mood took him. The famine was an incident of the journey; it had not struck him that it might prove an inconvenience as yet, and he was rich enough to pay his way. The Shah of those days was hardly more humane than his predecessors, and by a short-sighted policy had seized and stored what grain there was from the last poor harvest, intending to force up the price as food grew scarcer, and to drain his people for payment. But the drought that had stunted the grain had stunted the herbage—the horses and mules died by the roadsides, and the people died also before they could reach the selfish grain stores of the miserly cities.

Ellison had not been prepared for such sights and sounds as horrified him on his way from Teheran. In those days Englishmen travelled by caravan through the desert, and were not 'personally conducted', or even assisted, by Mr Cook. He had taken sufficient food to last him until he reached Koom, his next stopping place, but the sixty miles or so that lay between that place and the capital began to impress him with a sense of desolation, and he was glad that he had abandoned his first intention of travelling 'chupper' (post), and had provisioned himself to camp on the way as he felt inclined. He had been attracted to Koom partly on account of breaking his journey at a recognised stage, and partly to see the 'Woman's Mosque', the only one in the country. It being winter in the early '70s, few Europeans were likely to cross his path, and he looked to spend a lonely Christmas, but he was not quite prepared to fall short of Christmas cheer, and when he arrived in Koom—by chance on the twenty-fourth—he glanced with careless eyes at the usual aspect of the place. It was not exactly inspiriting—mud walls and undrained streets met him familiarly on all sides, and the people looked hardly less wretched than they had done on the way up. Part of the bazaar appeared to be closed, and the whine of children who had been deserted in the streets had a piteous effect. But still he did not realise the gravity of the situation until, having sent his servants to buy food, they returned to him with the information that none was to be had.

'The people are dying in the streets, sahib! They die, and none buries them. They gnaw their clothes, and kill each other for a few shahis [pence] wherewith to go and buy bread. Khok ber ser um! [Ashes on my head!] The curse of Allah is on this place. What will become of us?'

'And tomorrow is Christmas day!' said Ellison, with a grim sense of humour. 'I will make a good fight with the famine then, anyhow, for the sake of my traditions. For tonight, Abdul, I suppose we must go hungry.'

'But it is not only tonight, sahib!' remonstrated the Persian, shaking his head. 'It is all days in Koom! And how are we to buy food for the caravan in the desert? Teheran is sixty miles off.'

'Sag!' said Ellison disgustedly. This term of abuse—literally 'Dog'—he had already learned to use in dealing with his servants. 'If I can starve, you can fare likewise.' He left the man still grumbling, for the Persian demands bread at least as his right, and will eat almost any quantity, and strolled off to explore the town. The singular Mosque—the one door to heaven in all Persia for the Mohammedan woman—was not imposing save from a distance. Then, on nearing Koom, the golden dome dazzles out of the sunshine, even in winter, and welcomes the pilgrims who come at all times of the year; but Ellison found it but a poor distraction for an empty stomach, particularly as he might not enter. As he stood staring listlessly at the outside walls, a moonshi, or clerk, came out of the sacred building, and knowing that this class can usually speak English—of sorts—Ellison stopped him and asked him about the famine—was it really so bad in Koom as his servants reported? Was food not obtainable? The Persian shook his head much as Ellison's servants had done.

'If you could go into the mosques, sahib, you would find the people starving there, having come in from the villages round about, and taken refuge when too weak and ill to return! It is awful—and indeed the governors of the town seize what grain they can find for themselves and leave the poor to starve.'

'Then there is no food to be bought?' said Ellison blankly, wondering what he should do for his Christmas dinner.

The interpreter hesitated. 'There is one man—he asks much gold for what he gives, and he swears he has a flock of kids hidden in the hills where none may find them but himself. But he is, they say, luti [a scamp]—or worse! Mash'allah!' He made the sign of one who would avoid the evil eye. 'If his prices did not prevent the people buying, they would hesitate even in the famine.'

'By Jove! They can't feel hunger as I do! I will certainly hunt up this evil butcher. Where is his shop?'

'It is not far from here, sahib—in the bazaar that leads to the big bridge; but I pray that there be no curse attached to the eating of his meats, of which I have told you!' added the moonshi, with genuine fear. Ellison laughed. The man was evidently in holy horror of the only seller of meat in Koom, and he could not quite make out why. But, being without prejudice, and very hungry, he went on a search for the shop next day, regardless of the warning offered him.

A walk through the wretched, stricken city brought him to the place where he had been directed, and he easily discovered the shop, for it was the only one open amongst a row that had evidently been abandoned in despair. The salesman was not prepossessing in appearance, it must be owned. At Ellison's call a long, sinewy figure with a shaven head rose up from the dark recesses of the shop, where he had been sitting on his heels, and came quietly and swiftly to the door—so quietly and so swiftly that his motion was like that of a snake. In spite of its being winter he was dressed only in the blue shirt and zerejumah of the bazaar people, and in his kemmerbund was stuck a long sheathed knife. He stood in silence, looking at Ellison with curious eyes that never fairly met his own, and a peculiar smile lifting his lips. Though the famine was so apparent among the dwellers in Koom, this man at least was well nourished, which looked hopeful for Ellison's Christmas dinner. Nevertheless he felt an instinctive aversion to the silent snaky figure in the doorway, and made his wishes known in brief, terse sentences, not only because his Persian was limited (he had learned enough to enable him to travel without an interpreter constantly beside him), but because he did not feel inclined to waste words on the meat-seller.

'But certainly the sahib can have food,' said the man, with a sudden widening of the mirthless smile. 'He does right to come to me—I alone in all Koom can supply him. It is to my grief that I must ask gold—'

'I will pay you anything you like,' said Ellison shortly. 'Can you serve me now? The sooner the better.'

For a second the man seemed to hesitate, but he recovered himself almost at once. 'If the sahib will enter he shall be served!' he said smoothly. 'I will bring the kabobs at once!'

Ellison followed him into the little dark shop and sat down on his heels, Persian fashion, not without an instinctive movement to his own belt to feel that his pistols were there. The place was so dusky, and the kabob-seller and his long knife looked so wicked! He would have preferred eating his dinner in the road, where there was at least fresh air, to the stale odours and the confinement of the bazaar. If the surroundings were not appetising, however, the meat at least was beyond his wildest hopes. Never had he eaten such kabobs! They were tender and excellently cooked, and would have been so without his hunger to sauce them. Certainly the kids of the meat-seller's flock must be the finest fed and kept in Persia! Ellison ate his fill, nor grudged the gold that paid for his meal. He had eaten many Christmas dinners in England with less zest than he did the little mouthfuls of daintily flavoured meat from the sticks on which they are served. At length he rose, with the joyful feeling of a man who was at peace with Nature.

'You have served me excellently,' he said, in the geniality of his heart. 'You must have excellent kids!'

The salesman smiled in the old fashion, fingering the gold with which he had been paid with an uncanny fondness. 'Excellent, sahib!' he said smoothly. 'There is no doubt but that my flock is of the finest. The kids are young and tender. Is the sahib satisfied?'

'Very much so—and I thank you for one of the best dinners I ever ate!' said Ellison heartily, as he turned out of the shop.

'I hope I may have your custom again, sahib!'

'I will remember you if I am passing through Koom again, and come back for more kabobs!' said Ellison, laughing.

The meat-seller looked after him for a moment with an evil smile, clinking the gold in his hand.

Six months later two Englishmen met at Ispahan—the one on his way to Shiraz, the other just arrived from that place—and fraternised as Englishmen only do in a far land where national traits are forgotten. Keene, of the telegraph department, was going home on leave; Reynolds, who had just got his appointment to a small billet under the Indian Government, was going to take up station at Shiraz. Naturally enough the one man asked news of the other, as to whom he should find on the way up.

'I only came across one man since I left Shiraz, with whom I camped,' said Keene. 'That was a chap named Ellison—Harry Ellison. Ever met him?'

'Don't think so. What is he?'

'Nothing,' said Keene, laughing. 'Except an independent wanderer and vagabond! He has been hunting lions out at Muschir's Cap, and now he is after quail.'

'We might camp together. What's he like?'

'Oh, he's a very decent fellow. You can't mistake him if you fall in with him, though he looks just now as ragged as a tramp. He spends every evening mending his breeches with the tail of his flannel shirt! Says he's been wandering about Persia for six months, he got so fascinated with the country. And he can't get a European outfit!'

Ellison had, as a fact, found that his protracted stay in Persia had had its disadvantages. He had only brought clothes to last him a few weeks, and when he had lingered on for a few months—spent mostly in the saddle—his appearance threatened to become like Joseph's in the coat of many colours, from the constant patching of his moleskin breeches. But he was on his way home, having abandoned his half-formed plan of going on to India, and when Keene chanced upon him again at Deh Beed, which has the unenviable reputation of being the coldest place in Persia, he was glad to join forces and travel at least as far as Enzelli together. The caravanserai at Deh Beed was in ruins, and the two men made common cause and camped as best they might, sharing such comforts as they could obtain. Conversation turned naturally enough on the famine, which was now happily enough nothing but an ugly memory, and Ellison, in relating his experiences had a happy thought.

'I tell you what!' he said, as they sat over a fire of half-damp wood, and tried to forget the cold, 'we'll camp at Koom, and I'll introduce you to the best kabobs in Persia. Oh, they are good! They were cooked for me by the most villainous-looking wretch I have seen in the country: but they are worth all the journey to eat. I told him if I were in the neighbourhood again I would come back and taste his meats.'

Keene, being an old inhabitant in the country, knew how good a well-cooked dish of bazaar kabobs can be, and was perfectly willing to sample Ellison's vaunted dainty. Nor was his enthusiasm allowed to cool, for all the way to Koom, Harry Ellison referred hungrily to the Christmas dinner he had had there, when the tinned provisions palled, and the bread was bad from the last stage where they had bought it. There were always the kabobs at Koom to console them in fancy, and when they reached the town they only waited to see the horses rubbed down and given their corn at the chupperkhana (post house), which they had chosen in preference to the caravanserai, before they started in search of the noted shop.

The town looked no different to Ellison's eyes, save that the horrible sights of the dead and dying in the streets were there no longer, and when they reached the bazaar most of the shops had reopened. He led the way, his memory little strained to find the exact place owing to certain landmarks which had struck him—a certain quaint irregularity in the buildings that gave them a false air of perspective—when suddenly he stood stock still, his face a blank surprise. There were the two shops that had flanked the kabob-seller's—he remembered them well, though they had been empty at the time, and now one was a flourishing corn chandler's, the other a baker's—but between them, where the little dark place he remembered should have been—nothing! There was no shop at all there, nothing but a gap between the other shops, looking odd enough in the crowded bazaar, and more suggestive than if the shop had been merely closed, or altered to another trade. Ellison and Keene looked at each other, too puzzled even to laugh.

'There is more here than meets the eye,' said Keene quickly, and with some nameless suspicion. 'This shop has been razed—pulled down and utterly demolished. You are sure it is the same one, Ellison?'

'Certain. Poor devil! They said he had the evil eye—has their superstition run to violence? It's a thousand pities if those kabobs are gone beyond recall, though!'

He turned into the nearest shop left standing—the chandler's—and as the salesman rose up from his mat asked in Persian the meaning of the empty gap next door. The man cast a strange look at him, and made some sign equivalent to the European cross to avert bad luck.

'Sahib, the owner is dead!' he said, almost solemnly. 'He was a seller of meat—'

'I know he was,' Ellison interrupted. 'And very excellent meat, too!'

The corn chandler shuddered. 'The sahib was here in the famine?' he said anxiously. 'He did not eat of the accursed one's meats?'

'Yes, I did,' said Ellison bluntly, 'and I should be very glad to do so again. What's the matter, man? It wasn't poisoned—I felt no ill effects.'

'Sahib, it was human flesh!'

The pause which followed was like the silence before thunder—the calm that is no calm, because its breaking is inevitable. It was broken by both men looking at each other and going into sudden hysterical laughter.

'Great Scott! A cannibal—great Scott!' Keene gasped. 'Man alive! You couldn't—you'd know!'

'But I didn't!' Ellison almost shrieked. 'It was like chicken—I tell you I enjoyed 'em—I hoped for more. Oh, it *can't* be true!'

Both men had spoken in English, the Persian looking with a kind of solemn curiosity from one face to the other. There was nothing mirthful in their laughter, and yet he seemed to resent it as an unsuitable thing, almost indecent. It was Ellison who at last turned to him with nervous abruptness, and spoke in the vernacular.

'What do you mean? How could any seller of meat dare to play such a—a horrible trick on a stranger?'

But the corn chandler's gravity remained unmoved. 'Sahib, it is but too true. The sahib will himself remember that in the famine, when even gold could not buy food, this man had the kabobs for sale. He was feared and hated by his neighbours, who said that he had the evil eye, but for a long time we did not suspect the truth. Gradually, however—it was after the sahib left Koom—he grew too reckless a butcher—some little children were missed, and even a young girl. There was an outcry, and his house was searched. . . . There was a place below it, where he—he did it all, and the bones were there. . . . We burned his house down, and he died as they had died. That is all, sahib.'

The resignation of the Oriental made the quiet summary the more convincing, but, though he could not doubt, the idea was no more palatable to Ellison.

'How—beastly!' he said slowly. Then, as the fact realised itself in his mind, and would no more be controverted, he turned on his heel with scant ceremony, as though he shook the dust of the unhallowed spot off his feet. 'I'm going, Keene,' he said briefly, 'it seems I can't help myself.' Then with a touch of the brag that an Englishman depends upon to cover the least trace of defeat he added, looking steadily at his friend, 'Sorry I can't fulfil my promise of giving you the best dinner in Persia. Those kabobs were damned good, you know!'

The corn chandler made a quick protesting gesture.

'Aman Allah!' (God have mercy!) he said.

Time that softens all things has transformed Harry Ellison into the quietest member of a respectable club in St James's, content to find one corner sacred to himself, which is never intruded upon even by new-comers, and with the roving spirit almost unsuspected under his quiescent demeanour. But sometimes, when other men speak of their foreign experiences, he will rouse himself to tell younger travellers of the real adventures he had in the '70s, and with a twinkle in his eye will even own that he once ate a strange Christmas dinner in Persia, and invite the wildest guesses. No one has solved the problem as yet, and he has not divulged his secret, though it does not seem to him the horror that it did at the moment. He does not look like a cannibal—sometimes he even wonders at himself.

MARWOOD'S GHOST STORY

by Marjorie Bowen

Marjorie Bowen (1886–1952) had over 180 novels and collections to her credit, including a wide variety of mystery stories and 'twilight tales'. Her story 'The Prescription' appeared in *Ghosts for Christmas*, companion to this volume, and was presented on 'Woman's Hour', Radio 4, in 1989. Her less well known but equally powerful Christmas tale, 'Marwood's Ghost Story', appeared in the rare collection *Grace Latouche and the Warringtons* (1931), alongside the classic 'Kecksies', 'The Avenging of Ann Leete', and 'The Crown Derby Plate'.

H e went into the country to write a ghost story; he had written about most things but never about ghosts; he was a keen, practical, clever man and he could not admit that there was anything, in the writing way, that he could not do; since other people had achieved ghost stories, he meant to achieve one—a good ghost story.

He did not despise any of the usual effects, loneliness, snow, even Christmas Eve; he thought that if he went into the country for the winter and experienced all these sensations for himself he might be helped in the writing of his story.

Of course there were a great many trashy, flimsy, silly ghost stories written, but that did not prevent someone writing a really fine ghost story, a tale that would grip and chill and pester the imagination of the unfortunate reader.

Marwood had never been very successful as far as money goes, though the critics, those one or two or three or four that can really be called critics, always encouraged him; still he had sufficient means to be able to, sometimes, do what he liked; he was able now, for instance, to give up the winter to writing this ghost story; able, with the assistance of Janet, his wife, who came willingly into the country because the doctors, three very clever doctors, had said that Marwood was overworking, that he wanted quiet, a rest and change.

Doctors say that kind of thing very often, and sometimes rich, or lazy, or solitary folk are able to take advantage of the advice.

The cottage was very lonely, but not inconvenient; it was solid, compact, and could be made warm. Marwood paid so little rent for it that Janet felt she could be slightly lavish in comforts; Marwood had his big soft chair, his clear lamp, his roomy shelves, his thick curtains, his bright fires and his books.

The room soon began to overflow with books; Marwood began to collect ghost stories; he had never read a ghost story before, being a rational, sceptical man; his sharp, acrid studies of modern life had had as little to do with ghosts as with fairies.

'It is a queer thing,' said Janet, 'that you should want to write about ghosts—it is so silly, really, and so overdone.'

'I know; that's the interest, to see if you can put some new vigour into such old stuff—one ought to be able to do—it is just a question of applying your intelligence.'

Janet said:

'The best ghost stories have been written by those who believe in ghosts.'

Marwood didn't think so; he didn't really think that anyone believed in ghosts.

'Well,' argued Janet, 'I don't see how you can hope to scare anyone, if no one believes—'

'Oh,' said Marwood impatiently, 'the fools who read ghost stories—it's a special audience, of course.'

It was November and he had not begun to write; he just sat in his comfortable room and read the other fellows' failures.

He didn't think much of any of them, not even Defoe, or Poe, or Walter Scott.

'Stuff to frighten children,' he said. 'There must be a good ghost story somewhere, and I'm going to write it—''

Janet didn't care as long as he was quiet, resting; she was absorbed in making him comfortable; a plain woman who had never been enticed by pleasure, she did not miss the seductions of town, but sometimes she found the place rather lonely.

It was in a field, off a by-lane, and when the tradespeople (three times a week) and the postman, had 'called' there was no one else all day but perhaps a farm-hand trudging through the mud.

It had been a wet summer; when the Marwoods first came the trees were still green, a dank and sodden green, and for a month the low swollen clouds hung over the bistre-coloured uplands and the rain slashed, for many hours each day, into fields already like a sponge full of water. Then, in November, came the frost, and everything was dry and blackish against a sky the colour of iron.

Marwood continued to buy ghost stories; he searched old catalogues for anything remotely bearing on the subject; piles of books came from the library.

'I'm not trying to get ideas,' he explained to Janet. 'I'm just seeing what the other fellows have said, so I can leave all that alone and start fresh—it's amazing. The credulity, the childish nonsense!'

'You'll get swamped in all that rubbish,' replied Janet, who was a very practical woman. 'I should stop if I were you and begin to write—after all, we can't stay here for ever.'

'Of course not. I've got my plot, you know; it won't take me long to write it—I ought to have it ready soon after Christmas; that was part of my plan, you know, to spend Christmas here—'

'You won't know if it is Christmas or not here, no one comes near us, they think we are mad, or heathen.'

'Still it *will* be Christmas Eve and I shall get the atmosphere—'

'I don't see why ghosts should come out on Christmas Eve, never could; there's no logic in it—'

'Of course there isn't,' said Marwood, irritated. 'It is all an absurd invention. Haven't I told you that is what I want to do, take the stupid nonsense as it stands and make something out of it that's going to touch people up a bit?'

Janet thought that he was becoming rather bad-tempered and rude; she didn't believe much in his ghost story, she wished that he would get it over and done with and back to his usual work; with the cold the loneliness increased and Janet would have been quite glad to have returned to town.

When she ventured to make some remark of this effect, he returned a queer reply.

Janet said:

'If we stay away much longer you'll get out of touch with things.'

And Marwood answered:

'I'm just getting *into* touch with things!'

He looked vexed at her surprise and added sullenly:

'It depends what you mean by *things*.'

The first day of real snow Janet remarked that it might be a good occasion to commence the book.

Marwood said, yes, it was a good occasion, and he would go upstairs and write.

During their quiet meal that evening he seemed thoughtful, his lean, yellowish face was, Janet believed, paler than usual.

'Isn't it remarkable,' he asked suddenly, 'where they get it all from?'

'All what?' Janet was stupid at an emergency.

'All those things—ghosts, griffins, cockatrices, hobgoblins, vampires—if they never existed, how did people come to think of them?'

'Ignorance, of course.' Janet was alert now. 'They saw something that they didn't understand and they made up a tale—'

'But why? And how? *Where did they get the stuff for the tale?*'

'Imagination, obviously.'

'But what is imagination, Janet?'

Janet became impatient.

'I should think that you are reading too much of that trash.'

'I only want to know where they got it from,' he persisted obstinately. 'Some of those tales are so queer—'

'Inventions, fancies.'

'I know,' replied Marwood, exasperated, 'but where did they get them from?'

'Well, there's drink, and drugs.' Janet tried to humour him.

'That only starts it off—do you think the vision is in the glass? It's in your brain and the drink sets it free.'

'What's madness, then?' asked Janet finally. 'What's raving lunacy?'

Marwood sat up in some excitement.

'Now don't you ask me that—don't you ask me what madness is—'

'You needn't be personal over the stupid argument. I wish you'd finish your book so that we could get away from here—'

'You don't like the place?'

'I don't say that. But we've been here long enough. It's rather lonely.'

'Yes, it's rather lonely.'

They both glanced round the room, the one large low living room, as if to confirm this impression of loneliness.

'Fancy sitting up in bed at night and feeling the Devil pulling the mattress from under you, or hearing an empty box opening and shutting, or something with eight feet shuffling round the house—'

'Robert,' said Janet, 'you couldn't frighten a child with those things, nowadays.'

'Couldn't you? Couldn't you?'

'Of course not.'

'What would you say if I told you I saw a gigantic negress, very lean, with a huge red turban, prying round the house and staring in at my window?'

'I should say that it was a poor joke.'

'So it is,' responded Marwood grimly, 'a very poor joke.'

'Silly.'

'Silly,' agreed Marwood.

They sat in silence a little while.

It was real silence in the cottage, heavy palpable silence.

That night Marwood stayed up late, writing or reading, Janet did not know which; she heard him talking to himself—a bad habit that had lately increased upon him, a habit to be discouraged.

They awoke to snow so thick that the dawn could scarcely penetrate the heavy chilled clouds; the fields were pure against a dirty sky.

A few days off Christmas Eve now.

'I hope you got on all right last night,' said Janet.

'Splendidly.'

'Really begun the ghost story?'

'Really begun.'

'Well, I shall be glad when you've finished and we can get away.'

'That's the trouble,' said Marwood. 'It isn't so easy to get away, in fact it's extraordinarily difficult.'

'What do you mean, quite?'

'Oh, I can't keep explaining what I mean,' he replied testily.

She left him alone.

Queer how the snow added to the loneliness; they seemed absolutely cut off from humanity; if it hadn't been for that glimpse of the tradespeople and the postman Janet would have felt herself completely isolated; she wanted to go to the village, just to see people, but it was a long way and there was the snow, and her husband didn't seem to care to be left alone.

'Someone might come to the door and interrupt me—'

'Not likely.'

'You never know. The Vicar perhaps. And I really can't be interrupted.'

Janet stayed in.

That evening they sat alone round the fire; the snow had ceased, there was a wind and a frost; they had been to the door several times to look at the stars and to listen to the church bells, practising for Christmas Day, that could just be heard in the absolute stillness.

'Funny,' said Marwood, 'if something really came along—'

'What do you mean, Robert?'

'Ghosts, or devils—'

She laughed thinly: they evaded each other's look.

'Mind you,' Marwood added earnestly, 'if any were to come, I couldn't bear it; I've been thinking it over—and I really couldn't.'

Janet smiled at his joke.

'You aren't afraid?' she asked feebly.

'How can you be afraid of what you don't believe in? I never believed in them, did I?'

Still they didn't look at each other; Marwood lowered his voice and continued:

'What I am afraid of is *Fear*.'

'Afraid of being afraid?' she suggested.

'That's it—if you were afraid now, if you looked afraid—if I saw *Fear*—anywhere,' he answered confidentially.

'That is foolish,' said Janet stoutly. 'We are really shut up too much alone.'

Marwood looked sullen; he remarked that he had a bad headache; temper, translated Janet, who was beginning to be nettled herself—and it was lonely.

Lonely.

They locked and barred and bolted it all up, they put out all the lights but one candle, and went up to bed.

Janet could not get to sleep; she thought it was because the silence was oppressive.

But Marwood was asleep, and dreaming, she thought, by his mutterings and tossings.

Janet felt uneasy; what a lot of queer things her husband had said lately! He wasn't really a bit like his usual level-headed self; she would be glad when they got away from this place and all these ghost books.

Then Janet heard a faint noise.

Outside the house.

A shuffling, scrapping, peculiar sort of noise.

What had Marwood said about SOME thing with eight feet?

Janet struck a match and lit the candle by the bedside; in the spurt of yellow light she saw her husband's face staring up from the pillow.

'It's nothing,' she said quickly. 'Some stray dog.'

'Oh, you *do* hear it, then?'

'Of course—a stray dog, I say.'

Marwood sat up and they listened.

The noise seemed to encompass the house; it was as if they were being surrounded, beleaguered in the cottage.

'A dog,' said Marwood.

Then the shuffling was broken by a hoarse, quickly suppressed laugh.

Janet gripped her husband's shoulder; they stared at each other, shivering.

'If it IS,' whispered Marwood. 'I can't bear it.'

'Nonsense. It ISN'T.'

They peered forward across the murk of the room; the window space now showed faintly luminous, a square of reddish light; at the sight of this doubtless infernal illumination Janet winced.

'You're afraid,' gibbered Marwood. 'I can see that—you're afraid.'

'No—I'm going down to find out—'

He clung to her.

'No, you're not—'

A sudden clash, wail and howl tore the tension.

Marwood shrieked.

'I knew they couldn't have invented it all, I knew they'd got the stuff somewhere! It's true! It's true!'

'What's true?' mumbled Janet.

'Devils, ghosts—there outside—legions of 'em.'

The howl took form and substance; it became:

'Hark, the Herald Angels sing—'

With triangle and trombone accompaniment.

'The Waits,' sighed Janet, trembling.

Marwood never wrote his ghost story; he composed instead an essay on 'Fear,' but he could not care to have it published.

You see, he never believed they *were* the Waits.

THE MAN WHO
CAME BACK

by Margery Lawrence

Margery Lawrence (1889–1969) was a very
popular novelist (her *Madonna of Seven Moons*
was filmed successfully in 1944) and a long-time
researcher into spiritualism and psychic
phenomena. She regularly attended seances for
over forty years, and many of her novels and
short stories were based on first-hand
experiences with mediums. 'The Man Who
Came Back' appeared in her rare collection
The Floating Café (1936).

I t was a very merry house-party. The givers of it, Colonel and Lady
Garrison, were two pleasant, gregarious souls. Not peculiarly
interesting in themselves, but possessing that priceless gift, that, in
my opinion should be subsidized, when found, by the government of the
country to which the owner of it belongs—that gift that the Americans
crisply describe as 'mixing!'

The Garrisons, childless, well-to-do and middle-aged, gave, it was well
known, by far the most amusing parties in their particular coterie, and
fierce was the competition for invitations, especially to the annual
Christmas house-party, held in their country house, a rambling, old-
fashioned, but supremely comfortable old manor in a well-known
hunting county. The Colonel was a keen man to hounds, and despite his
increasing years and weight, still easily held his own with the younger
men, and several of his rivals in the hunting field were members of the

present party who, sitting round a blazing fire in the drawing-room after dinner, were eating chestnuts and cracking jokes, well pleased with themselves, their dinner and their hosts.

Ted Boulter, the M.F.H., and his pretty little wife, whose Dresden-china beauty belied her pluck across country. The two Symons, brother and sister. Londoners, dark, given to odd clothes and odder Bohemian jargon; altogether too 'arty and crafty' in the Colonel's private opinion. But indubitably young people to know, since they were rapidly becoming the only people who counted in the matter of smart house decoration. The Todhunters, travellers and explorers, Cecily Fleet, a county beauty, just embarking on a film career, and her two admirers, Len Ponsonby and Terry Walters; a couple of young nephews, all bounce and brawn, and two new acquaintances that Lady Garrison had picked up at the bridge club she frequented in town. Doctor and Mrs Playfair—charming people, thought the Colonel, as, with his glasses perched precariously on his forehead and his dinner-jacket rumpled as usual between his shoulders, he twiddled with the knobs on his beloved radio in a vain endeavour to get Rome or Milan. Charming people! Playfair himself was a brilliant young feller; one of the coming men in Harley Street, everybody said. And his wife was a dam' pretty woman! Small and slim and exquisitely dressed, with hair the colour of a new chestnut and golden hazel eyes.

The two were complete love-birds. At least, Playfair was obviously madly in love with his wife, never let her out of his sight unless he could help it; while she seemed sincerely fond of him—but between love and mere fondness lies a world of difference! Still, it seemed to be working all right, thought the Colonel to himself, as he struggled with the wireless. But neither Rome nor Milan responded, and, defeated, he turned to his guests.

'Something wrong with the blasted thing! Not that it matters. Anybody care for a game of billiards?' he demanded.

A chorus of assent came from the younger men, but Lady Garrison's motherly voice rose above them.

'Not a bit of it! I'm not going to let one of you out of here yet. I've got a surprise!'

'Not another ghost?' demanded Cecily Fleet, who had been at last year's gathering, and still retained vivid memories of the amazingly well-staged 'ghost' scare that Lady Garrison had got up for the amusement of her Christmas guests. Lady Garrison, plump and matronly in plum-coloured satin, shook her well-marcelled grey head.

'Nothing so ordinary!' She looked round the expectant circle with a smile of satisfaction. 'I've got another "stunt"—as you young people call it. I've got—what do you think? I've persuaded Madame Esperanza, the famous medium, to come and give us a sitting!'

There was a general chorus of acclaim.

'How splendid! How perfectly *marvellous!*'

The Boulters, who had a passion for bridge and considered any evening not spent at cards an evening wasted, smiled with tempered enthusiasm and said nothing. Cecily Fleet pressed her fingers, long and slender and tipped with shining scarlet nails, to her correspondingly scarlet lips and rolled scared blue eyes over them at the company in general.

'I shall be simply *terrified!*' she proclaimed, but from his post at one side of the fire Ned Playfair responded, smiling indulgently.

'No need to be in the least alarmed, Miss Fleet!' His rich, pleasant voice was comfortingly reassuring. 'It's only an amusing game, of course. I assure you there's nothing whatever in these so-called mediums. Nothing supernatural, that is.'

'What do you mean by "nothing whatever"?'

Lady Garrison's tone was faintly nettled. With a bend of his handsome head in her direction the young doctor deprecatingly replied.

'Please forgive me, Lady Garrison. But really, you see, as a doctor we know what this kind of thing is worth. And surely you, of all people, only regard a thing like this—this sitting, seance, whatever one likes to call it— as an amusing sort of game? You don't think there's really anything in it?'

There was a pause. Lady Garrison's plump face was faintly flushed, and her lips were pressed together. She was sharply irritated, in truth. Not that she herself was an ardent believer in spiritualism, in which, to be honest, she was merely a dabbler, half believing and half sceptical. But Playfair's undisguised contempt stung her at least momentary championship.

'I don't know.' She spoke defiantly. 'I'm not clever enough to argue the point, Doctor Playfair, and I freely admit that I, personally, haven't done enough of it to be able to speak with any authority. But if people like Marshall Hall and Oliver Lodge and—er, Conan Doyle, and so on— find something worth considering in it, it surely can't be dismissed so easily as that?'

There was an awkward pause. Cecily Fleet broke it, with a little gush of girlish earnestness.

'I'm sure the doctor didn't mean . . . er . . . that?' she said, skilfully skimming over what precisely she meant by 'that'. 'But I'm sure that the rest of us want to see Madame What's-her-name most frightfully! *I* do, for one.'

'We do!' chorused the Symons eagerly, and a general murmur of enthusiasm arose. It was obvious that the doctor's attitude of antagonism was not popular, and he was clever enough to see the wisdom of retreating at least a little way. He had no desire to quarrel with the Garrisons and their very well-to-do circle. He smiled disarmingly.

'I'm sure I apologise, Lady Garrison, if inadvertently I said anything you might have construed into a sneer or a slight on your "surprise".'

He smiled again at the old lady where she sat stiffly braced, upright in her favourite red satin Victorian chair, and against her will she thawed, smiling reluctantly back. Certainly Playfair knew how to handle women, reflected the Colonel, amused. Repute had it he had had plenty of experience with 'em! Even that his large practice was due to his extraordinary influence over—and charm for—women. But that was gossip in all probability. Mere jealousy directed against a rising man, and the Colonel, who was strictly fair-minded, scouted the idea almost as soon as it raised its head. Yet it would not be entirely banished . . . like a sardonic imp it sat there, in the remotest corner of his mind, listening and watching as the young doctor smoothed down the ruffled feelings of his hostess and re-established himself in her good graces.

'You know I didn't mean to be at all rude, Lady Garrison—far from it! I spoke on impulse, that's all—and I had no idea you took the thing so seriously. But since you do—why, then, I withdraw! Of course, I shall be only too pleased to join in anything you like to arrange.'

Lady Garrison arose, appeased.

'That's all right,' she said. 'I'll go and fetch Madame Esperanza. She's here already—resting and preparing in my room.'

Mrs Boulter gave a little squeak of delighted fear.

'Oh, is she here? Have you kept her hidden until this moment! Oh, Ted, how *thrilling!*'

'I only hope,' said Lady Garrison, 'that the sitting *will* be thrilling. But mind—I don't promise anything. She said herself that unless the conditions were favourable she couldn't guarantee anything at all.'

'The usual guff!' muttered Ned Playfair to his wife, as the Colonel, ever courteous, shuffled after his plump wife to open the door for her. Ida Playfair glanced up at him curiously, her hazel eyes starry under the shadow of her fringe of chestnut hair.

[99]

'Don't you like it, Ned? If you'd rather not sit, I'm sure we can get out of it. I'm a little bit scared, to be honest!'

He shook his head and glanced round the rest of the group, their eyes fixed expectantly on the door.

'I'm afraid not. I've rather foolishly put the old girl's back up by joking about it, and since I want to get 'em as patients, or at least, some of their friends—they've a hell of a lot of influence—I suppose we shall have to sit through it. But you've no reason to feel scared, Ida. It's all rot. Clever posing, with a spot of telepathy or hypnotism or guesswork thrown in as make-weight!'

He smiled down at her reassuringly, but her eyes were on the fire. Her expression was faintly dissatisfied.

'I don't know,' she began. 'If, as Lady Garrison says, all these brilliant men have come to the conclusion that there *is* something in it, surely it can't be *all* rubbish? And Tillie van Heyden told me . . .'

Impatiently he interrupted, his black brows drawn together in a dangerous-looking scowl.

'I don't care what Tillie van Heyden said. She's a silly twittering fool, anyway—just the type that likes to mess about with what it describes as "the occult". I tell you, it's fraud, and when it's not deliberate fraud it's a mixture of hysteria and self-delusion and hypnotism, and I don't know what all! If it didn't mean that I can't afford to offend the old folks— we've only just got to know 'em—I'd go upstairs to bed right away, and not waste time on their damn silly seance. But, however . . .'

He paused, for the door opened and Lady Garrison entered, followed by a strange woman. An insignificant little woman wearing a shabby black velvet dress ornamented with a conglomeration of cheap beads about the neck; she had greying hair, untidily bundled into a 'bun' at the back of her head, pince-nez, and a small, faded, indefinite face behind large horn-rimmed glasses. An almost audible hush of disappointment ran round the room, for nobody less like a professional sybil could possibly be imagined—but Lady Garrison, experienced hostess, instantly filled in the awkward moment with a flood of introductions.

'Madame Esperanza—Mrs Boulter, Miss Fleet, Mr and Mrs Todhunter . . .'

The little woman, warming her meagre hands at the fire, nodded and smiled vaguely at each fresh name until Lady Garrison ended her litany with:

'Dr and Mrs Playfair. And that's the lot!'

The medium, raising her eyes from the fire, surveyed the owners of the last two names—he still standing with one arm on the mantelpiece, watching the proceedings with a quizzical eye, she crouched on a black velvet pouffe at his feet, her white tulle frock billowing about her like a summer cloud. For a moment Madame Esperanza eyed the pretty woman at her feet, then spoke suddenly.

'Are you going to be at the sitting?' she asked.

Her voice was reedy, and she spoke with a faintly uneducated twang. Ida Playfair regarded her with a slight sense of distaste mingled with wonder and a rising sense of incredulity. Surely nothing that this common, shabby little woman could say could be really worth while! Probably as Ned declared, she was just a clever *poseuse*, some back-street pythoness who had somehow managed to impress dear old Thedosia Garrison—but quite obviously nobody to feel afraid of. She laughed breezily.

'Certainly I am! I'm not going to miss shaking hands with a spook!'

The medium looked down at her in silence. Behind, the room was in a cheerful uproar as chairs were hastily arranged in a circle, tables, cushions and whatnots pushed into corners, the door locked and a length of scarlet silk draped over the chandelier to dim its brightness to the requisite subdued glow; Lady Garrison, in her element, was bustling about directing operations, and for the moment the three beside the fire were alone, unnoticed, the shabby little woman with the intent eyes and the handsome young doctor and his wife. As if hypnotised by that strange, steady stare, for a moment Ida stared back without speaking— then Madame Esperanza spoke, suddenly and decidedly.

'I wouldn't, if I were you,' she said.

Ida's eyes flew wide with amazement, and her husband laughed drily.

'Why not?' he said curtly.

The medium looked at him, opened her mouth to speak, and changing her mind, looked back at the fire and went on warming her hands in silence.

But Ida Playfair's curiosity was aroused. Moreover, she felt faintly irritated that the woman's warning should coincide with a deep-seated sense of reluctance in her own heart. She did not want to take part in the sitting, in truth—but it was odd that Madame What's-her-name should have voiced, echoed, that feeling!

'Why don't you think I should go to the sitting?' she persisted.

The medium lifted her thin shoulders in an oddly foreign shrug. Perhaps, reflected the doctor sardonically, she actually deserved the name under which she worked. 'Esperanza!' It was a convincing name with which to tickle the groundlings, and she was quite a good actress, anyway. All this, of course, was according to type. She wouldn't be able to say *why* she had said that to Ida; would only hedge and hint. Yet . . .

'I can't tell you why I said that,' the medium said, almost brusquely, 'but sometimes before a sitting I get the feeling that for a certain person it would be better if they didn't join in. I don't know why—but it's always right.' She raised eyes, suddenly piercing behind their horn-rimmed glasses, to Playfair, standing leaning against the mantelpiece with his hands in his pockets, a barely-concealed smile of derision on his dark face. 'It applies to you, too, you know,' she said bluntly. 'I'd keep away from this sitting if I were you!'

Playfair's mouth fell open—then he laughed aloud and scornfully.

'My *dear* lady! What on earth have I to fear?'

Again that dark glance, and again the shrug.

'You know best. I don't know a thing about your life, of course. But if you've a secret in your life—if you've something to hide, or if you've done something—well, that you don't like to look back on—then if so, I'd find some excuse not to join in this circle.'

Ida Playfair's hand flew to clasp her husband's.

'Something to hide?' Her voice was sharp with affectionate resentment. 'What a perfectly idiotic idea! Darling . . .'

But for once an appeal by his adored wife passed Ned Playfair by. He did not hear, for he was staring at the woman with sudden attention. Staring fixedly—and for a moment it seemed as though his handsome brown face was a trifle white and strained. Then with a brusque laugh he seemed to dismiss the whole thing and turned away.

'Absurd! But I congratulate you,' he spoke coldly over his shoulder. 'I congratulate you on playing the part excellently, from the very first minute you came on the stage. Brilliant, really. You ought to go on the stage proper.'

The taunt was blatantly rude, but the medium did not seem to hear. She was staring down into the fire, apparently lost in thought—flushed with excitement, Lady Garrison bustled up, talking as usual at the top of her voice.

'Come on now—come along! It's all ready. That's right, isn't it, Madame?'

The medium turned, and surveying the room, nodded briefly.

'That's right—you have the door locked, so that servants can't come in and interrupt? Good. Then we'll start.'

Entering the circle she seated herself in the central chair, the huge leather 'grandfather' generally sacred to the Colonel, and glanced round the ring of eager faces that surrounded her. Taking off her glasses, she put them neatly away, like any maiden aunt, in a leather spectacle-case, and tucked them into the beaded bag that swung from her waist—and for a moment Ida Playfair blinked, surprised. For the eyes that the horn-rimmed glasses had hidden were dark and amazing, set in deep hollows that emphasised their darkness—piercing, oddly dominant eyes. Eyes that—suddenly—seemed to promise all sorts of possibilities . . . a faint sense of fear touched her once more like a passing wing, and she reached for her husband's hand and gave it a quick squeeze to give herself courage as she settled into her place. He glanced at her, surprised and touched—for as the Colonel had shrewdly surmised, their relations were definitely, as the old French song says, 'l'un qui baise, et l'autre qui tend la joue.' Despite his desperate love of her, it was still, with her, only a gentle turning of the cheek.

'There is one thing I must ask of you all, please.'

It was the medium speaking, and her voice already sounded oddly drowsy and slow. 'That is, that when I am once in trance you keep your places until I come out of trance.'

She blinked and paused, as though collecting thoughts already growing hazy.

'I—it may be very dangerous to me for anyone to leave their seat without permission from my control. If he gives it—all right, but not otherwise. I can't explain the—conditions—but I am sure you will accept my assurance that this rule is necessary.'

A subdued murmur of assent arose from the circle, and settling back into the chair with her head against the padded back, Madame Esperanza closed her eyes, and drawing a long breath, appeared to go to sleep. Playfair smiled faintly to himself as he watched her. Of course! The usual thing. Talk a lot of vague stuff about 'conditions' in order to *impose* conditions that made it utterly impossible for anybody to investigate the thing! The usual thing . . . except that it was odd that she had said . . . that; but here Dr Playfair, like the Colonel, hustled a certain thought deliberately and firmly into the background and settled down to watch events.

Everything was quiet. At first an excited giggle or two from one of the women broke out, a rustle of movement as somebody changed their position, a subdued whisper—but now, as though hypnotised, everyone sat very still, and dead silence lay like a deep unfathomable pool over the dimly-lit room. In the great chair the medium lay sunk in sleep, and the red light, falling almost directly upon her, etched curious lights and shadows on her shrunken little face. Watching, Ida Playfair shivered suddenly, thinking the face had changed, gained a curious dignity and power; the lines down each side of the mouth, the deep hollows about the eyes, looked as though carved in stone—the whole face looked, indeed, like the face of some old Crusader reclining 'mansize in marble' upon his tomb. Or the death-mask, stern, immovable, of some ancient king, long forgotten of mankind ... even as Ida Playfair stared and shivered, clutching her husband's hand, the medium shuddered violently, gave a smothered ejaculation in some unknown tongue, and then with an indescribable majesty sat upright in her chair. With eyes still shut she turned her head slowly from side to side, following the ring of faces as though she saw, indeed, through those fast-closed lids; and her face was sternly unfamiliar.

Mrs Boulter clutched her husband's arm.

'It's—it's not the same woman!' she whispered agitatedly. 'It's a man's face! Oh, Tony, I wish we hadn't started, I'm frightened. . . .'

A deep voice broke the silence, uttering a few unintelligible words. 'The usual bastard Hebrew or Egyptian,' muttered the doctor under his breath, but he dared not speak aloud. Although he was still utterly convinced that the whole thing was nothing but a clever fraud, against his will he was impressed. Impressed at least into silence . . . and that change in the face, that voice, heavy, masculine, rich, was certainly amazingly well done. Who'd have thought that shabby little Aunt Jane had it in her?

The voice was speaking again, but now in English.

'Peace be to this house!' The head bowed gravely in the direction of Lady Garrison, sitting upright, clutching the hands of her neighbours, her wholesome pink face flushed with excitement and nervousness. 'Peace!' The blind eyes went round the circle again as though seeking something, then paused. 'Peace and greetings to all, from the world of Spirit. I know what you would have—you would hold talk with those whom you call dead. With those who are on *this* side. And that is well— when you take care to whom you talk.'

There was a pause while the sitters, bewildered, looked at each other. Lady Garrison broke it at last.

'Er—how do you do?' The lame modern phrase sounded incredibly foolish. 'I—we are very glad to see you, and of course you are quite right about what we want to do. But we don't quite understand. . . .'

'I will explain!'

The deep voice paused, then continued.

'I am what you call the "control" of this instrument here on earth—and the name I use is Sekhet. On this side we do not like to allow these instruments—what you call mediums—to be used by anyone who chooses. We try to keep back those whom we do not think should speak to you; yet our powers are limited, and if the force is very strong—we must stand aside and permit it to speak. But—in this case I do not think it would be wise.'

'What *do* you mean?'

It was Ned Playfair's voice, brusque, unbelieving, that broke the puzzled silence that had followed on the control's speech. The figure bowed its head.

'I mean, that there is here, amongst other souls who wish to speak, one soul that I would try to keep from speaking. And for that reason I think it would be wise,' he bowed once more, with ineffable grace and courtesy, towards Lady Garrison, 'to what you call "break up" the meeting? Release your hands, thus shutting the current off, and I will bring the medium out of trance at once.'

A chorus of astonished and indignant voices answered him.

'Give it up—just when it's getting interesting? *What* an idea! But why?'

The chorus rolled round the circle while Ned Playfair sat back and smiled. Just as he had expected! The woman, seeing from the outset that he was not to be fooled like the others, had tried to frighten him—first through Ida, then directly away from the sitting; and now, finding he was not to be so frightened, she had recourse to this childish expedient! She was prepared to break up the circle, to lose her fee, and disappoint a group of eminently worth-while people sooner than risk discovery—now nothing in the world would persuade him to allow the circle to be broken, and he added his sharply-cut drawl to the chorus.

'Surely, Mr—er—Sekhet—you don't think you can frighten us in that way? I can assure you that we are prepared for any and everything that may happen! But we are *not* prepared to abandon the sitting.'

There was a momentary pause. The others looked gratefully at their champion, but Ida Playfair, suddenly white, half rose from her seat.

'I—I want to go!' she whispered. Her face was curiously strained, her great eyes ringed like a doe's. 'I don't know why—but I want to go.'

The deep voice answered from the centre of the circle.

'That is wise, little lady! You may go. But for you others—close the circle in as she leaves, friends, so that the current is broken as little as possible.'

[105]

Without a word the white-clad figure rose and fled, and as the door closed behind her the voice resumed.

'With regard to what you say, my son,' the blind eyes seemed to pierce right through the dark young doctor where he sat, 'if you insist—all have free will, and if it is the will of all to go on with this sitting, so be it! But— I still advise you against it.'

There was a faint pause. Lady Garrison, more impressed than she cared to admit, glanced uncertainly round the circle. The Boulters looked doubtful, the Todhunters puzzled, the Symons cynically amused, Cecily Fleet and her attendant swains definitely disappointed—a very little would have persuaded the good lady to take the mysterious Sekhet's advice and dissolve the circle altogether, but Ned Playfair's voice rose again, brusque, antagonistic.

'I suggest we are rather wasting time, Lady Garrison? I, for one, refuse to be alarmed by vague hints and warnings. We formed this circle for the definite purpose of seeing signs and wonders. And if Madame Esperanza feels that for some reasons' (the sneer was patent) 'she cannot tonight produce these signs and wonders, then let her say so plainly and candidly. But if she is *not* prepared to say so—why, then let her carry on!'

'And we'll take the consequences,' suggested Cecily Fleet with a giggle. 'If there are any?'

'And,' agreed Playfair suavely, 'we'll take the consequences. At least, if there are any consequences we shall all agree not to blame you, Mr Sekhet!'

The sternly upright figure in the centre of the circle bowed its head resignedly.

'So be it. You have, as I said, free will. And if you will insist, against my advice, upon opening this door tonight, then I will do my best to control the soul that already beats upon it, desiring to re-establish contact with the earth he has left. Be still, all! I go to prepare the way.'

There was a slight convulsion of the body, and the medium, drooped together, fell back into the chair. In the red light her face was again the face of a weary little middle-aged woman, lined and tired—Cecily Fleet, who was sitting on the other side of Ned Playfair, nudged him eagerly as she whispered.

'Look, isn't that odd! Her face looked just like a man when *That* was talking—and now it's herself again! Isn't that queer?'

But there was no time to answer, for the medium, muttering rapidly and unintelligibly to herself, was rising upright in her chair again. Her face was twisted and distressed, and the voice that came through her lips was hoarse, with a rattle now and then—like the voice of somebody striving, through the stress of furious excitement, to speak clearly and connectedly. A voice entirely and utterly different from the measured, level tones of Sekhet! Suddenly the hoarseness left it and it came clear, ringing, a strong masculine voice—and at the sound of it Ned Playfair bounded in his chair, his face suddenly chalk-white, his eyes blazing.

Yet the voice was not addressing him—it seemed to be arguing with someone unseen, so that it sounded for all the world like a human voice arguing with a telephone operator.

'Let me get through, will you—oh yes, I'll remember! I'll keep steady—at least, I'll do my best, but don't lecture me now, d'you hear? I've *got* to get through—I tell you I must, I know she's there!' Then, in a ringing shout that rang through the room like a clarion call: '*I want my wife, I say! I want my wife!*'

The call was so electric, so painful in its intensity, that a loud and startled gasp ran round the circle, Cecily Fleet, her flippancy vanished, gave a pitiful little cry that echoed Mrs Boulter's, and the hot tears pricked behind Lady Garrison's eyes, as in a strangled voice she stammered.

'Your wife? I'm afraid . . . who is it speaking?'

'Neil Ramsay!' came the answer instantly, sharp and clear, and Cecily Fleet, hearing a quick-drawn breath at her shoulder, turned and peered at the man beside her. Odd that Ned Playfair, who, of all people, had been at the start the hardest, the most defiantly sceptical, should be so shaken now! Even in the dusky red glow from the scarlet-draped lamp one could see how white he was.

'Did you know Neil Ramsay?' she whispered. But Playfair shook his head.

'No! No!' he muttered feverishly—and the entire circle started with amazement and alarm as the voice came again, this time in a furious shout.

'*Liar!* You to say you don't know me, Ned Playfair?'

With a huge effort the medium staggered from the chair and, standing planted firmly on her feet, faced the white-faced doctor. Half risen from his chair, Playfair stood shaking, endeavouring to steady himself with one hand upon his chair-back, but with the sweat of sheer terror running down his face, while within him two things fought fiercely for mastery. Cynicism—the bitter atheism that refused, even at this moment, to believe that he beheld anything other than a horribly brilliant *tour de force* of acting—and fear. That dreadful aching fear that turns a man's bones to water and his soul to a stone that sinks therein . . . madly he snatched at his vanishing self-control, and tried to laugh. But all that came was a cracked whisper, a ghastly echo of a laugh.

'Ha, ha! Of course I remember you now, old fellow. Neil Ramsay! But why . . .'

'You know why I come. You don't need to ask.'

The little figure in black was menacing now. Frail as a shadow, yet charged with a dreadful shattering power.

'*You* know why I come, Playfair. To find my wife. My wife—of whom you robbed me!'

A terrified shuddering ran round the circle, and Mrs Boulter slipped quietly to the ground in a faint—but held in the steel grip of sheer fascinated horror nobody could either move or speak. Playfair stood as though turned to stone, his eyes fixed on the grim little figure before him as the voice thundered on.

'Of whom you robbed me, Ned Playfair. *The wife for whom you murdered me!*'

With a spring like that of a coiled snake, on the last word she was on him, her lean fingers knotted in his throat. Shrieking, hysterical with fear, the women sprang up and scattered as the two fought, swaying and staggering wildly about in the centre of the circle, while the men, flinging chairs aside, seized the combatants and tried to force them apart—then suddenly in their arms the woman went limp and a great voice spoke, it seemed, from over their heads.

'Put her down—there, in the chair—and leave her to come round. I have removed the poor love-crazed soul who just possessed her—I warned you, I, Sekhet, but you would not be warned. Yet retribution is just . . . see to *him* now. Farewell!'

It ceased, and in silence the shaken group gathered about the prone form of the young doctor, lying just where he had fallen, among a welter of fallen chairs, scattered bags and scarves and fans, stark in the brilliance of the white light from which the shrouding red drapery had been removed. His face was set in a terrible expression of fear and rage, and there were red marks round his throat where the thin, vicious fingers had clutched—he lay deadly still, and with a sudden fear catching at his heart Colonel Garrison beckoned Todhunter over to his side. As becomes an explorer, the brown-faced man had a good working knowledge of medicine. Kneeling, in a dead and awful silence he opened the prostrate man's shirt, tested his heart and held a mirror to his lips, then looked up with a grave face. Cecily Fleet, reading the news in his eyes, burst into tears, and a general murmur of horror ran round the room as, soberly, Todhunter rose to his feet.

'Dead—of heart failure, as far as I can judge,' he said gravely. 'Those marks on the throat are nothing—only superficial. Although the spirit that moved her to attack him was a man—or so it seems—she was only a frail little woman, and it wasn't her attack that killed or even injured him. He died of shock. And if tonight's experience is as genuine as I believe it to be—no wonder!'

'But what is it all about—and who was Ramsay?' breathed the Colonel his healthy red face palpably pale with horror.

Todhunter hesitated for a moment.

'I don't like to say much,' he said. 'Especially as the man's dead now— and has paid for his sins. But—whoever spoke through the woman's mouth spoke what is thought, by many people, to be the sober truth. Ida Playfair was Ida Ramsay—the wife of Neil Ramsay—until a year or two ago, and they adored each other. Playfair met them and fell desperately in love with her. But she wouldn't look at him, so Playfair played a waiting game. Cultivated Ramsay, who was rather a simple soul; became his doctor as well as his bosom friend, and, one summer, about two years ago, they went on a fishing expedition together, and upon that expedition Ramsay was taken ill and died. Through—so Playfair said—eating tinned food that wasn't quite good. Playfair gave the certificate of death— natural causes—so that was O.K. for Playfair. And when he came back to London he made himself so indispensable to poor little Ida, who was completely lost and bewildered without Ramsay, that at last she married him. Though there were not lacking folks who said that Ramsay's convenient death, that left a charming and wealthy wife ready, as it were, to Playfair's hand, was rather too convenient to be convincing! That's the story. And—in view of what has happened tonight—it looks very much as though it were true.'

THE CHINESE
APPLE

by Joseph Shearing

Marjorie Bowen's second contribution to this
anthology first appeared, under her pseudonym
'Joseph Shearing', in the 1948 Christmas
Number of *The Illustrated London News*. As
'Joseph Shearing' she wrote many bestselling
novels of which the best known are *Moss Rose*
and *Blanche Fury* (filmed in 1947 and 1948
respectively).

Isabelle Crosland felt very depressed when the boat train drew into
the vast London station. The gas lamps set at intervals down the
platform did little more than reveal filth, fog and figures huddled in
wraps and shawls. It was a mistake to arrive on Christmas Eve, a matter
of missed trains, of indecision and reluctance about the entire journey.
The truth was she had not wanted to come to London at all. She had lived
in Italy too long to be comfortable in England. In Florence she had
friends, admirers; she had what is termed 'private means' and she was an
expert in music. She performed a little on the harpsichord and she wrote
a great deal about ancient musical instruments and ancient music. She
had been married and widowed some years before and was a childless
woman who had come to good terms with life. But with life in Florence,
not London. Mrs Crosland really rather resented the fact that she was
performing a duty. She liked things to be taken lightly, even with a touch
of malice, of heartlessness, and here she was in this gloomy, cold station,
having left the pleasant south behind, just because she ought to be there.

'How,' she thought, as she watched the porter sorting out her baggage, 'I dislike doing the right thing; it is never becoming, at least to me.'

A widowed sister she scarcely remembered had died: there was a child, quite alone. She, this Lucy Bayward, had written; so had her solicitors. Mrs Crosland was her only relation. Money was not needed, companionship was. At last it had been arranged, the child was coming up from Wiltshire, Mrs Crosland was to meet her in London and take her back to Florence.

It would really be, Isabelle Crosland reflected, a flat sort of Christmas. She wished that she could shift her responsibility, and, as the four-wheeled cab took her along the dingy streets, she wondered if it might not be possible for her to evade taking Lucy back to Italy.

London was oppressive. The gutters were full of dirty snow, overhead was a yellow fog.

'I was a fool,' thought Mrs Crosland, 'ever to have left Florence. The whole matter could have been settled by letter.'

She did not care for the meeting-place. It was the old house in Islington where she and her sister had been born and had passed their childhood. It was her own property and her tenant had lately left, so it was empty. Convenient, too, and suitable. Only Isabelle Crosland did not very much want to return to those sombre rooms. She had not liked her own childhood, nor her own youth. Martha had married, though a poor sort of man, and got away early. Isabelle had stayed on, too long, then married desperately, only saving herself by Italy and music. The south had saved her in another way, too. Her husband, who was a dull, retired half-pay officer, had died of malaria.

Now she was going back. On Christmas Eve, nothing would be much altered; she had always let the house furnished. Why had she not sold, long ago, those heavy pieces of Jamaica mahogany? Probably out of cowardice, because she did not wish to face up to writing, or hearing anything about them. There it was, just as she remembered it, Roscoe Square, with the church and graveyard in the centre, and the houses, each like one another as peas in a pod, with the decorous areas and railings and the semicircular fanlights over the doors with heavy knockers.

The street lamps were lit. It was really quite late at night. 'No wonder,' Mrs Crosland thought, 'that I am feeling exhausted.' The sight of the Square chilled her: it was as if she had been lured back there by some malign power. A group of people were gathered round the house in the corner, directly facing her own that was number twelve. 'Carols,' she thought, 'or a large party.' But there seemed to be no children and the crowd was very silent.

There were lights in her own house. She noticed that bright façade with relief. Alike in the parlour and in the bedrooms above, the gas flared. Lucy had arrived then. That part of the arrangements had gone off well. The lawyers must have sent the keys, as Isabelle Crosland had instructed them to do, and the girl had had the good sense to get up to London before the arrival of the boat train.

Yet Mrs Crosland felt unreasonably depressed. She would, after all, have liked a few hours by herself in the hateful house.

Her own keys were ready in her purse. She opened the front door and shuddered. It was as if she had become a child again and dreaded the strong voice of a parent.

There should have been a maid. Careful in everything that concerned her comfort, Mrs Crosland had written to a woman long since in her employment to be in attendance. The woman had replied, promising compliance. But now she cried: 'Mrs Jocelyn! Mrs Jocelyn!' in vain, through the gas-lit house.

The cabby would not leave his horse and his rugs, but her moment of hesitancy was soon filled. One of the mongrel idlers who, more frequently than formerly, lounged about the streets, came forward. Mrs Crosland's trunks and bags were placed in the hall, and she had paid her dues with the English money carefully acquired at Dover.

The cab drove away, soon lost in the fog. But the scrawny youth lingered. He pointed to the crowd the other side of the Square, a deeper patch amid the surrounding gloom.

'Something has happened there, Mum,' he whispered.

'Something horrible, you mean?' Mrs Crossland was annoyed she had said this, and added: 'No, of course not; it is a gathering for Christmas.' With this she closed her front door on the darkness and stood in the lamp-lit passage.

She went into the parlour, so well remembered, so justly hated.

The last tenant, selected prudently, had left everything in even too good a state of preservation. Save for some pale patches on the walls where pictures had been altered, everything was as it had been.

Glowering round, Mrs Crosland thought what a fool she had been to stay there so long.

A fire was burning and a dish of cakes and wine stood on the deep red mahogany table.

With a gesture of bravado, Mrs Crosland returned to the passage, trying to throw friendliness into her voice as she called out: 'Lucy, Lucy, my dear, it is I, your aunt Isabelle Crosland.'

She was vexed with herself that the words did not have a more genial sound. 'I am ruined,' she thought, 'for all family relationship.'

A tall girl appeared on the first landing.

'I have been waiting,' she said, 'quite a long time.'

In the same second Mrs Crosland was relieved that this was no insipid bore, and resentful of the other's self-contained demeanour.

'Well,' she said, turning it off with a smile. 'It doesn't look as if I need have hurried to your assistance.'

Lucy Bayward descended the stairs.

'Indeed, I assure you, I am extremely glad to see you,' she said gravely.

The two women seated themselves in the parlour. Mrs Crosland found Lucy looked older than her eighteen years and was also, in her dark, rather flashing way, beautiful. Was she what one might have expected Martha's girl to be? Well, why not?

'I was expecting Mrs Jocelyn, Lucy.'

'Oh, she was here; she got everything ready, as you see—then I sent her home because it is Christmas Eve.'

Mrs Crosland regretted this; she was used to ample service. 'We shall not be able to travel until after Christmas,' she complained.

'But we can be very comfortable here,' said Lucy, smiling.

'No,' replied Mrs Crosland, the words almost forced out of her. 'I don't think I can—be comfortable here—I think we had better go to an hotel.'

'But you arranged this meeting.'

'I was careless. You can have no idea—you have not travelled?'

'No.'

'Well, then, you can have no idea how different things seem in Florence, with the sun and one's friends about—'

'I hope we shall be friends.'

'Oh, I hope so. I did not mean that, only the Square and the house. You see, I spent my childhood here.'

Lucy slightly shrugged her shoulders. She poured herself out a glass of wine. What a false impression those school-girlish letters had given! Mrs Crosland was vexed, mostly at herself.

'You—since we have used the word—have friends of your own?' she asked.

Lucy bowed her dark head.

'Really,' added Mrs Crosland, 'I fussed too much. I need not have undertaken all that tiresome travelling at Christmas, too.'

'I am sorry that you did—on my account; but please believe that you are being of the greatest help to me.'

Mrs Crosland apologised at once.

'I am over-tired. I should not be talking like this. I, too, will have a glass of wine. We ought to get to know each other.'

They drank, considering one another carefully.

Lucy was a continuing surprise to Mrs Crosland. She was not even in mourning, but wore a rather ill-fitting stone-coloured satin, her sleek hair had recently been twisted into ringlets, and there was no doubt that she was slightly rouged.

'Do you want to come to Italy? Have you any plans for yourself?'

'Yes—and they include a trip abroad. Don't be afraid that I shall be a burden on you.'

'This independence could have been expressed by letter,' smiled Mrs Crosland. 'I have my own interests—that Martha's death interrupted—'

'Death always interrupts—some one or some thing, does it not?'

'Yes, and my way of putting it was harsh. I mean you do not seem a rustic miss, eager for sympathy.'

'It must be agreeable in Florence,' said Lucy. 'I dislike London very much.'

'But you have not been here more than a few hours—'

'Long enough to dislike it—'

'And your own home, also?'

'You did not like your own youth, either, did you?' asked Lucy, staring.

'No, no, I understand. Poor Martha would be dull, and it is long since your father died. I see, a narrow existence.'

'You might call it that. I was denied everything. I had not the liberty, the pocket-money given to the kitchenmaid.'

'It was true of me also,' said Mrs Crosland, shocked at her own admission.

'One is left alone, to struggle with dark things,' smiled Lucy. 'It is not a place that I dislike, but a condition—that of being young, vulnerable, defenceless.'

'As I was,' agreed Mrs Crosland. 'I got away and now I have music.'

'I shall have other things.' Lucy sipped her wine.

'Well, one must talk of it: you are not what I expected to find. You are younger than I was when I got away,' remarked Mrs Crosland.

'Still too old to endure what I endured.'

Mrs Crosland shivered. 'I never expected to hear this,' she declared. 'I thought you would be a rather flimsy little creature.'

'And I am not?'

'No, indeed, you seem to me quite determined.'

'Well, I shall take your small cases upstairs. Mrs Jocelyn will be here in the morning.'

'There's a good child.' Mrs Crosland tried to sound friendly. She felt that she ought to manage the situation better. It was one that she had ordained herself, and now it was getting out of hand.

'Be careful with the smallest case in red leather: it has some English gold in it, and a necklace of Roman pearls that I bought as a Christmas present for you—'

Mrs Crosland felt that the last part of this sentence fell flat. '. . .pearl beads, they are really very pretty.'

'So are these.' Lucy put her hand to her ill-fitting tucker and pulled out a string of pearls.

'The real thing,' said Mrs Crosland soberly. 'I did not know that Martha—'

Lucy unclasped the necklace and laid it on the table; the sight of this treasure loosened Mrs Crosland's constant habit of control. She thought of beauty, of sea-water, of tears, and of her own youth, spilled and wasted away, like water running into sand.

'I wish I had never come back to this house,' she said passionately.

Lucy went upstairs. Mrs Crosland heard her moving about overhead. How well she knew that room. The best bedroom, where her parents had slept, the huge wardrobe, the huge dressing-table, the line engravings, the solemn air of tedium, the hours that seemed to have no end. What had gone wrong with life anyway? Mrs Crosland asked herself this question fiercely, daunted, almost frightened by the house.

The fire was sinking down and with cold hands she piled on the logs.

How stupid to return. Even though it was such a reasonable thing to do. One must be careful of these reasonable things. She ought to have done the unreasonable, the reckless thing, forgotten this old house in Islington, and taken Lucy to some cheerful hotel.

The steps were advancing, retreating, overhead. Mrs Crosland recalled old stories of haunted houses. How footsteps would sound in an upper storey and then, on investigation, the room be found empty.

Supposing she were to go upstairs now and find the great bedroom forlorn and Lucy vanished! Instead, Lucy entered the parlour.

'I have had the warming-pan in the bed for over two hours, the fire burns briskly and your things are set out—'

Mrs Crosland was grateful in rather, she felt, an apathetic manner.

This journey had upset a painfully acquired serenity. She was really fatigued, the motion of the ship, the clatter of the train still made her senses swim.

'Thank you, Lucy, dear,' she said, in quite a humble way, then leaning her head in her hand and her elbow on the table, she began to weep.

Lucy regarded her quietly and drank another glass of wine.

'It is the house,' whimpered Mrs Crosland, 'coming back to it—and those pearls—I never had a necklace like that—'

She thought of her friends, of her so-called successful life, and of how little she had really had.

She envied this young woman who had escaped in time.

'Perhaps you had an accomplice?' she asked cunningly.

'Oh, yes, I could have done nothing without that.'

Mrs Crosland was interested, slightly confused by the wine and the fatigue. Probably, she thought, Lucy meant that she was engaged to some young man who had not been approved by Martha. But what did either of them mean by the word 'accomplice'?

'I suppose Charles Crosland helped me,' admitted his widow. 'He married me and we went to Italy. I should never have had the courage to do that alone. And by the time he died, I had found out about music, and how I understood it and could make money out of it—' 'Perhaps,' she thought to herself, 'Lucy will not want, after all, to come with me to Italy—what a relief if she marries someone. I don't really care if she has found a ruffian, for I don't like her—no, nor the duty, the strain and drag of it.'

She was sure that it was the house making her feel like that. Because in this house she had done what she ought to have done so often. Such wretched meals, such miserable silences, such violences of speech. Such suppression of all one liked or wanted. Lucy said:

'I see that you must have suffered, Mrs Crosland. I don't feel I can be less formal than that—we are strangers. I will tell you in the morning what my plans are—'

'I hardly came from Italy in the Christmas season to hear your plans,' replied Mrs Crosland with a petulance of which she was ashamed. 'I imagined you as quite dependent and needing my care.'

'I have told you that you are the greatest possible service to me,' Lucy assured her, at the same time taking up the pearls and hiding them in her bosom. 'I wear mourning when I go abroad, but in the house I feel it to be a farce,' she added.

'I never wore black for my parents,' explained Mrs Crosland. 'They died quite soon, one after the other; with nothing to torment, their existence became insupportable.'

Lucy sat with her profile towards the fire. She was thin, with slanting eyebrows and a hollow at the base of her throat.

'I wish you would have that dress altered to fit you,' remarked Mrs Crosland. 'You could never travel in it, either, a grey satin—'

'Oh, no, I have some furs and a warm pelisse of a dark rose colour.'

'Then certainly you were never kept down as I was—'

'Perhaps I helped myself, afterwards—is not that the sensible thing to do?'

'You mean you bought these clothes since Martha's death? I don't see how you had the time or the money.' And Mrs Crosland made a mental note to consult the lawyers as to just how Lucy's affairs stood.

'Perhaps you have greater means than I thought,' she remarked. 'I always thought Martha had very little.'

'I have not very much,' said Lucy. 'But I shall know how to spend it. And how to make more.'

Mrs Crosland rose. The massive pieces of furniture seemed closing in on her, as if they challenged her very right to exist.

Indeed, in this house she had no existence, she was merely the wraith of the child, of the girl who had suffered so much in this place, in this house, in this Square with the church and the graveyard in the centre, and from which she had escaped only just in time. Lucy also got to her feet.

'It is surprising,' she sighed, 'the amount of tedium there is in life. When I think of all the dull Christmases—'

'I also,' said Mrs Crosland, almost in terror. 'It was always so much worse when other people seemed to be rejoicing.' She glanced round her with apprehension.

'When I think of all the affectations of good will, of pleasure—'

'Don't think of it,' urged the younger woman. 'Go upstairs, where I have put everything in readiness for you.'

'I dread the bedroom.'

The iron bell clanged in the empty kitchen below.

'The waits,' added Mrs Crosland. 'I remember when we used to give them sixpence, nothing more. But I heard no singing.'

'There was no singing. I am afraid those people at the corner house have returned.'

Mrs Crosland remembered vaguely the crowd she had seen from the cab window, a blot of dark in the darkness. 'You mean someone has been here before?' she asked. 'What about?'

'There has been an accident, I think. Someone was hurt—'

'But what could that have to do with us?'

'Nothing, of course. But they said they might return—'

'Who is "they"?'

Mrs Crosland spoke confusedly and the bell rang again.

'Oh, do go, like a good child,' she added. She was rather glad of the distraction. She tried to think of the name of the people who had lived in the house on the opposite corner. Inglis—was not that it? And one of the family had been a nun, a very cheerful, smiling nun, or had she recalled it all wrongly?

She sat shivering over the fire, thinking of those past musty Christmas Days, when the beauty and magic of the season had seemed far away, as if behind a dense wall of small bricks. That had always been the worst of it, that somewhere, probably close at hand, people had really been enjoying themselves.

She heard Lucy talking with a man in the passage. The accomplice, perhaps? She was inclined to be jealous, hostile.

But the middle-aged and sober-looking person who followed Lucy into the parlour could not have any romantic complications.

He wore a pepper-and-salt-pattern suit and carried a bowler hat. He seemed quite sure of himself, yet not to expect any friendliness.

'I am sorry to disturb you again,' he said.

'I am sorry that you should,' agreed Mrs Crosland. 'But on the other hand, my memories of this house are by no means pleasant.'

'Name of Teale, Henry Teale,' said the stranger.

'Pray be seated,' said Mrs Crosland.

The stranger, this Mr Teale, took the edge of the seat, as if very diffident. Mrs Crosland was soon fascinated by what he had to say.

He was a policeman in private clothes. Mrs Crosland meditated on the word 'private'—'private life,' 'private means.' He had come about the Inglis affair, at the corner house.

'Oh, yes, I recall that was the name, but we never knew anyone—who are they now—the Inglis family?'

'I've already told Miss Bayward here—it was an old lady, for several years just an old lady living with a companion—'

'And found dead, you told me, Mr Teale,' remarked Lucy.

'Murdered, is what the surgeon says and what was suspected from the first.'

'I forgot that you said that, Mr Teale. At her age it does not seem to matter very much—you said she was over eighty years of age, did you not?' asked Lucy, pouring the detective a glass of wine.

'Very old, nearly ninety years of age, I understand, Miss Bayward. But murder is murder.'

Mrs Crosland felt this affair to be an added weariness. Murder in Roscoe Square on Christmas Eve. She felt that she ought to apologise to Lucy. 'I suppose that was what the crowd had gathered for,' she remarked.

'Yes, such news soon gets about, Ma'am. A nephew called to tea and found her—gone.'

Mr Teale went over, as if it were a duty, the circumstances of the crime. The house had been ransacked and suspicion had fallen on the companion, who had disappeared. Old Mrs Inglis had lived so much like a recluse that no one knew what she possessed. There had been a good deal of loose money in the house, the nephew, Mr Clinton, thought. A good deal of cash had been drawn every month from the Inglis bank account, and very little of it spent. The companion was a stranger to Islington. Veiled and modest, she had flitted about doing the meagre shopping for the old eccentric, only for the last few weeks.

The woman she had replaced had left in tears and temper some months ago. No one knew where this creature had come from— probably an orphanage; she must have been quite friendless and forlorn to have taken such a post.

'You told me all this,' protested Lucy.

'Yes, Miss, but I did say that I would have to see Mrs Crosland when she arrived—'

'Well, you are seeing her,' remarked that lady. 'And I cannot help you at all. One is even disinterested. I lived, Mr Teale, so cloistered a life when I was here, that I knew nothing of what was going on—even in the Square.'

'So I heard from Miss Bayward here, but I thought you might have seen someone; I'm not speaking of the past, but of the present—'

'Seen someone here—on Christmas Eve—?'

Mr Teale sighed, as if, indeed, he had been expecting too much. 'We've combed the neighbourhood, but can't find any trace of her—'

'Why should you? Of course, she has fled a long way off—'

'Difficult, with the railway stations and then the ports all watched.'

'You may search again through the cellars if you wish,' said Lucy. 'I am sure that my aunt won't object—'

Mrs Crosland put no difficulties in the way of the detective, but she felt the whole situation was grotesque.

'I hope she escapes,' Mrs Crosland, increasingly tired and confused by the wine she had drunk without eating, spoke without her own volition. 'Poor thing—shut up—caged—'

'It was a very brutal murder,' said Mr Teale indifferently.

'Was it? An over-draught of some sleeping potion, I suppose?'

'No, Ma'am, David and Goliath, the surgeon said. A rare kind of murder. A great round stone in a sling, as it might be a lady's scarf, and pretty easy to get in the dusk round the river ways.'

Mrs Crosland laughed. The picture of this miserable companion, at the end of a dismal day lurking round the dubious dockland streets to find a target for her skill with sling and stone, seemed absurd.

'I know what you are laughing at,' said Mr Teale without feeling. 'But she found her target—it was the shining skull of Mrs Inglis, nodding in her chair—'

'One might understand the temptation,' agreed Mrs Crosland. 'But I doubt the skill.'

'There is a lovely walled garden,' suggested the detective. 'And , as I said, these little by-way streets. Anyway, there was her head smashed in, neatly; no suffering, you understand.'

'Oh, very great suffering, for such a thing to be possible,' broke out Mrs Crosland. 'On the part of the murderess, I mean—'

'I think so, too,' said Lucy soberly.

'That is not for me to say,' remarked the detective. 'I am to find her if I can. There is a fog and all the confusion of Christmas Eve parties, and waits, and late services at all the churches.'

Mrs Crosland impulsively drew back the curtains. Yes, there was the church, lit up, exactly as she recalled it, light streaming from the windows over the graveyard, altar tombs and headstones, sliding into oblivion.

'Where would a woman like that go?' asked Lucy, glancing over Mrs Crosland's shoulder at the churchyard.

'That is what we have to find out,' said Mr Teale cautiously. 'I'll be on my way again, ladies, just cautioning you against any stranger who might come here, on some pretext. One never knows.'

'What was David's stone? A polished pebble? I have forgotten.' Mrs Crosland dropped the curtains over the view of the church and the dull fog twilight of evening in the gas-lit Square.

'The surgeon says it must have been a heavy stone, well aimed, and such is missing. Mr Clinton, the nephew, her only visitor and not in her confidence, remarked on such a weapon, always on each of his visits on the old lady's table.'

'How is that possible?' asked Mrs Crosland.

Mr Teale said that the object was known as the Chinese apple. It was of white jade, dented like the fruit, with a leaf attached, all carved in one and beautifully polished. The old lady was very fond of it, and it was a most suitable weapon.

'But this dreadful companion,' said Mrs Crosland, now perversely revolted by the crime, 'could not have had time to practise with this— suitable weapon—she had not been with Mrs Inglis long enough.'

'Ah,' smiled Mr Teale. 'We don't know where she was before, Ma'am. She might have had a deal of practice in some lonely place—birds, Ma'am, and rabbits. Watching in the woods, like boys do.'

Mrs Crosland did not like this picture of a woman lurking in coverts with a sling. She bade the detective 'Good-evening' and Lucy showed him to the door.

In the moment that she was alone, Mrs Crosland poured herself another glass of wine. When Lucy returned, she spoke impulsively.

'Oh, Lucy, that is what results when people are driven too far—they kill and escape with the spoils, greedily. I do wish this had not happened. What sort of woman do you suppose this may have been? Harsh, of course, and elderly—'

'Mr Teale, when he came before, said she might be in almost any disguise.'

'Almost any disguise,' repeated Mrs Crosland, thinking of the many disguises she had herself worn until she had found herself in the lovely blue of Italy, still disguised, but pleasantly enough. She hoped that this mask was not now about to be torn from her; the old house was very oppressive, it had been foolish to return. A relief, of course, that Lucy seemed to have her own plans. But the house was what really mattered: the returning here and finding everything the same, and the memories of that dreadful childhood.

Lucy had suffered also, it seemed. Odd that she did not like Lucy, did not feel any sympathy with her or her schemes.

At last she found her way upstairs and faced the too-familiar bedroom. Her own was at the back of the house; that is, it had been. She must not think like this: her own room was in the charming house of the villa in Fiesole, this place had nothing to do with her at all.

But it had, and the knowledge was like a lead cloak over her. Of course it had. She had returned to meet not Lucy, but her own childhood.

Old Mrs Inglis—how did she fit in?

Probably she had always been there, even when the woman who was now Isabelle Crosland had been a child. Always there, obscure, eccentric, wearing out a succession of companions until one of them brained her with the Chinese apple, the jade fruit, slung from a lady's scarf.

'Oh, dear,' murmured Mrs Crosland, 'what has that old, that very old woman got to do with me?'

Her cases were by her bedside. She was too tired to examine them. Lucy had been scrupulous in putting out her toilet articles. She began to undress. There was nothing to do but to rest; what was it to her that a murderess was being hunted round Islington—what had Mr Teale said? The stations, the docks . . . She was half-undressed and had pulled out her wrapper when the front-door bell rang.

Hastily covering herself up, she was out on the landing. At least this was an excuse not to get into the big, formal bed where her parents had died, even if this was only Mr Teale returned. Lucy was already in the hall, speaking to someone. The gas-light in the passage illuminated the girl in the stone-coloured satin and the man on the threshold to whom she spoke.

It was not Mr Teale.

Isabelle Crosland, half-way down the stairs, had a glance of a sharp face, vividly lit. A young man, with his collar turned up and a look of expectation in his brilliant eyes. He said something that Isabelle Crosland could not hear, and then Lucy closed the heavy front door.

Glancing up at her aunt, she said:

'Now we are shut in for the night.'

'Who was that?' asked Mrs Crosland, vexed that Lucy had discerned her presence.

'Only a neighbour; only a curiosity-monger.'

Lucy's tone was reassuring. She advised her aunt to go to bed.

'Really, it is getting very late. The church is dark again. All the people have gone home.'

'Which room have you, Lucy, dear?'

'That which you had, I suppose; the large room at the back of the house.'

'Oh, yes—that—'

'Well, do not concern youself—it has been rather a disagreeable evening, but it is over now.'

Lucy, dark and pale, stood in the doorway, hesitant for a second. Mrs Crosland decided, unreasonably, not to kiss her and bade her a quick good-night of a forced cheerfulness.

Alone, she pulled the chain of the gas-ring and was at once in darkness. Only wheels of light across the ceiling showed the passing of a lonely hansom cab.

Perhaps Mr Teale going home.

Mrs Inglis, too, would have gone home by now; the corner house opposite would be empty.

Isabelle Crosland could not bring herself to sleep on the bed after all. Wrapped in travelling rugs, snatched up in the dark, she huddled on the couch. Presently she slept, but with no agreeable dreams. Oppressive fancies lay heavily on her and several times she woke, crying out.

It was with a dismal sense of disappointment that she realised each time that she was not in Florence.

With the dawn she was downstairs. Christmas morning; how ridiculous!

No sign of Lucy, and the cold, dismal house was like a trap, a prison.

Almost crying with vexation, Mrs Crosland was forced to look into the room that once had been her own. The bed had not been slept in. On the white honeycomb coverlet was a package and a note.

This, a single sheet of paper, covered an opened letter. Mrs Crosland stared at this that was signed 'Lucy Bayward.' It was a childish sort of scrawl, the writer excused herself from reaching London until after the holidays.

The note was in a different hand:

I promised to let you know my plans. I am away down the river with my accomplice. Taking refuge in your empty house I found this note. The whole arrangement was entirely useful to me. I left the Roman pearls for Lucy, as I had those of my late employer, but I took the gold. No one will ever find us. I leave you a Christmas present.

Mrs Crosland's cold fingers undid the package. In the ghastly half-light she saw the Chinese apple.

DIARY OF A POLTERGEIST

by Ronald Duncan

Ronald Duncan (1914–82), English poet and
playwright, travelled widely, and lived for a time
with Gandhi in India. Later he was a founder of
the English Stage Company, Royal Court
Theatre, and wrote several libretti for Benjamin
Britten operas. Ezra Pound described Duncan as
'the lone wolf of English letters'. This story
originally appeared in *The Unlikely Ghosts*
(1967).

I t was my usual habit to leave my office in Berkeley Square at five-
fifteen precisely. But that particular evening it was well past six-thirty
before I walked to the lift. The reason for this lapse was that it was the
day before Christmas Eve. There had been a mild impromptu party: we
junior partners had indulged in no more than an couple of whiskies each;
our secretaries had had a bottle of sherry between them. But it had been
sufficient to relax us and give the illusion that there was something to
celebrate. Somebody had mysteriously produced a box of crackers; and,
before I left, paper hats had already appeared. I had sidled towards the
door unobtrusively, fearful that 'Auld Lang Syne' would be imposed at
any moment. I was feeling far from festive, having had an unusually bitter
quarrel with my wife that morning. In the circumstances, I didn't want to
be home late. If I were, I knew she would suspect that I had been to see
Janet. And since I was innocent I thought I might try to avoid being

punished for a pleasure I had not enjoyed. So I hurried towards the car park and then drove as quickly as I could through the Christmas traffic towards the A4.

The journey to Maidenhead usually took me an hour. But on the Slough by-pass I ran into mist rising from the river and had to slow down to a crawl. I found some music on the car radio. Then I began to trail behind an Esso petrol lorry, keeping twenty yards or so from its tail, content to let its driver penetrate the fog. I was careful not to get too near the lorry in case it should brake suddenly. There was ice on the road. But with it as a pilot, I was able to relax and listen to the music. But in counterpoint to it, I could hear the discord of the morning.

Like most serious quarrels, it had started by something infinitely trivial. One of our mutual friends had made the mistake of sending us a Christmas card which had been addressed only to me.

'I see your friends think you're no longer married,' she had said throwing the envelope into the marmalade, 'or maybe you've told them that I'm dead?'

I had stirred my coffee vigorously.

'Is that what you've told them, that I'm dead?'

'No,' I had said buttering my toast, 'anybody can see you are in your normal good health and full of your usual resentment.'

'And whose fault's that?'

That question had gone unanswered. It was one that didn't require a reply. I knew better than to speak when I was spoken to or to mistake a soliloquy for a conversation. But that morning my strategic silence had made her even more angry.

'The trouble with you,' she had screamed, 'is you are either faithless and unpleasant, or faithful and more unpleasant.'

'Yes.'

'Yes, what?'

'I will mend my manners and be as pleasant as you are.'

'Are you telling me you intend to start up with Janet again?'

'No, I haven't seen her for six months. . . .'

'. . . four.'

'And I don't know where she is.'

'You expect me to believe that?' she'd screamed, knowing it was true.

I was not unaware that I was being punished now because I had deprived her of the justification for punishing me.

'You expect me to believe that?' she'd repeated.

Now suddenly the Esso lorry came to a standstill. I slammed on the brakes: I reached for the handbrake too.

After this fright, I ceased going over the row of the morning and listened only to the music. I drove on unthinkingly as though with an automatic pilot. I did not stop until I got out of the car to open the gate at the end of the drive. As usual, cursing the hasp. Then I garaged the car and put the paraffin lamp under the bonnet, collected my brief-case from the back seat, and closed the garage door. Actions which I'd repeated so often I could perform them in my sleep. Then, as usual, I put my hand in my pocket five paces from the door to find my latch key so that I had it ready in my hand as I reached it.

I put my case on the hall table, hung my coat up then went into the sitting-room. The room was empty. I went to the foot of the stairs.

'Darling,' I called, 'come down and have a drink.' There was no answer. But I stood there, waiting. I felt no resentment in spite of the things my wife had said to me that morning. I am not an unkind man. Indeed, my kindness to my wife can be proved by the fact that I never believe a single word she or any woman says. And when I saw her coming down the stairs, I went up towards her, intending to embrace her, hoping that she felt as little resentment as I did. But to my surprise she walked past me coldly. I followed her into the sitting-room. She ignored my presence. This was ridiculous. I thought we'd had squabbles enough before, without making a war of it. But tonight there was no breaking the ice. She returned my smile with a stony stare. She didn't look particularly angry any more, just bored. After a few minutes of this awkwardness she stood up and switched on the television. With feigned interest we listened to the news. Then just as the next programme started, the front door bell rang. I made a move to go to open it, then saw my wife going to the door too. She still had not spoken to me.

'Don't bother,' I said, 'I'll see who's there.'

But she came on and shoved past me rudely as she drew back the latch.

A policeman stood there.

'Mrs Staniforth?' he asked.

'Yes,' my wife replied.

'May I have a word with you?'

'Come in,' she said.

I followed them back into the sitting-room and went to the sideboard to hand the man a drink.

'I'm afraid I have to give you some bad news,' he said awkwardly. 'Your husband has had a motor accident.'

'Is he hurt?' she said anxiously.

'I'm afraid he's dead.'

I almost dropped the bottle, then turned, to hear him say: 'It was about an hour ago. His car had skidded beneath the back of a stationary petrol lorry. He was killed instantly.'

'Nonsense,' I said, 'do I look dead?'

But neither of them listened and neither looked at me.

For the next ten minutes I had to stand there listening to the bobby mouthing platitudes of sympathy for my wife's grief which she did not feel. True, there were tears in her eyes. But she could always weep to order.

Then, eventually, she showed the man to the door, and came back to the room. She went straight to the mirror to repair her make-up.

I went up behind her. I saw to my horror that I had no reflection there. It was a personal loss. Feeling so sorry for myself I had some sympathy for her too. I bent to kiss the back of her neck. And as I did so my reflection appeared briefly as though it is that only love defines us. Seeing my features fleetingly in the glass beside her own, my wife cried out. But did not weep now there was no one there to see her tears.

My first reaction on realizing I was, though dead, still conscious, was one of irrepressible hilarity. This mood was heightened by seeing the mock grief about me which my sudden, if not sad, demise had caused. After drying her eyes and repairing her mascara, my wife had run upstairs and changed into mourning. She knew black suited her, especially in her underclothes. When she was suitably dressed, I had stood by her side doubled up with unheard giggles, as I had listened to her phoning round our relatives and friends to share her news and milk them of their sympathy. Not for me, of course: those who grieve, grieve only for themselves.

My next reaction was of sober exhilaration as I realized that death was something I need no longer fear. And I felt free, with all my senses and appetites still intact, yet without a tedious conscience to restrict them. I had no sense of responsibility except to myself. I valued my life, now I no longer had it. Though I was dead to others, I felt most alive in myself. The only thing I lacked was a sense of time. Perhaps this was necessary since I now had to bear the weight of all eternity? But within what had seemed to me only a few seconds since the bobby had left the house, I saw my solicitor, and my brother, Charles, enter the house. They were joined by my wife in my study. All were in mourning. They helped themselves generously to my whisky. Then my solicitor began to read my will. I enjoyed watching their mock approval at hearing of the small bequests I had made to others. With this succulent pleasure before me, I failed to notice anything untoward in the procedure. It was not until I heard my solicitor reading the final clause, in which my executors were empowered to defray my funeral expenses from my estate, that I realized I had omitted to attend that final ceremony.

'Unless my wife has any objections,' the man continued, 'I wish that my body should be cremated.'

I wondered if she had objected? I guessed not but instinctively glanced in the looking-glass above the desk to see if my hair was singed but there was no image there. The thought of the flames brought a cold shudder down my back. I resolved to find the urn which contained my ashes then sprinkle them facetiously on my head. For the dead feel no remorse for the sins they have committed, only for those temptations they needlessly overcame.

Busy as I had been with observing, if not attending, my last obsequies, I had failed to notice that there was no validity in any of the orthodox Christian threats concerning the after-life. Indeed, since I was still conscious, I refused to regard my life as past, though I could see, as country people euphemistically put it: I had passed beyond. But it was comforting not to see Saint Peter hanging around in the flesh as I was sure he'd prove a disappointment after El Greco's portrait of him.

I was in no doubt what I wanted to do next. My impulses in death were as definite as they had been in life. I now felt consumed with unusual malevolence. The sight of my pompous self-righteous brother Charles when my will was being read had focused these feelings against him. I had always resented him. When we were children, he, being two years older than I, got a bicycle before me: he was allowed to smoke and stay up for dinner while I was still treated as a brat. My hatred was as well rooted as it was natural. It had grown at the university where he had patronized me, and then flourished into full flower when, at my father's death, Charles had inherited the small estate in Somerset which I had loved and he had despised, and had then sold it without offering it first to me. With a private income and a flair for small talk, he had gone into politics, not out of any zeal for reform, but from self-conceit, choosing his party, not from conviction, but only with an eye as to which one was likely to obtain power and further his own fatuous advancement. While I, on the other hand, had had to go into business and had the humiliation even in my own obscure suburb of being known as Sir Charles Staniforth's younger brother. He had been knighted when he had become Minister of Education. It would have been more appropriate if they had made him a Dame. For in addition to his financial advantages, Charles was ambivalent, ambidextrous and homosexual: three valuable attributes in contemporary society. Yet, in spite of his predilection for his own sex, and his smug relationship with Geoffrey Mortimer, his private secretary, he had always managed to censure my heterosexual infidelities, safe in the assurance, I suppose, that from his way of life there could be no illegitimate issue. As for his boy friend and toady, Geoffrey, I hated him even more than I did Charles. This was because I know he really despised my brother and it made his fawning attentions to him all the more nauseating. My impulse was to pay them a visit as an invisible guest, especially as they were giving an important dinner party to which, alive or dead, I would never have been invited.

Charles's residence was in Tite Street. When I appeared, or to be accurate, arrived, the guests were just going into dinner. Amongst these I observed the Prime Minister and his lady; the leader of the House of Lords; a bishop, and various other leaders of the New Establishment. A more pompous parade of hypocrites, bores and prigs I had not seen. They had bestowed honours on each other and covered themselves in cant. As they seated themselves at the splendid Sheraton table resplendent with the family silver, of which I had only an odd pepper-pot, I longed for an Hieronymous Bosch to be there to paint the hideous features which lay behind their supercilious masks.

My brother had placed the Prime Minister at the head of the table and, as host, had taken the far end with Miss Maude Smith, the Minister of Transport, on his left and Lady Hartland on his right, with the Foreign Secretary on the other side of her. Lady Hartland had reached such eminent company, not by virtue of birth—she had suffered from the social disadvantage of not being a barmaid born, but sired by a backwood Earl, nor had she intelligence to recommend her; her only attributes were two aggressive protuberances in front and a couple of curvaceous buttocks behind. Carrying these features everywhere, she was welcomed wherever she went. Men with one eye on her milk ducts or her nates praised her as a conversationalist or wit, women were silenced by her vacuous effrontery. Knowing everybody and nothing at all she had become a TV personality. In the diplomatic language of the Foreign Secretary, she was 'a dish'.

As I surveyed the assembly sucking their soup, I realized that my intentions were no less than to reveal Geoffrey Mortimer's true nature to my brother, to unmask my brother to the world, to bring down the Government and reduce the dinner party to a shambles, if not a riot. But I wanted to have fun: I wasn't going to do it all at once. Indeed, I did nothing very alarming at the start, except to stand near the butler when he was serving the turtle soup to the Prime Minister's squaw and then gently steer the ladle into the lap of her dress. But unfortunately the man corrected its direction before it could reappear loaded with her breast.

But when the asparagus had been served I got busy: harmlessly touring the table and as each guest raised a piece to their mouth, I guided the buttered end either into their eye, their ear or down into their collar. After this course, they all looked a pretty messy lot. Neither dignity nor mascara is much improved with butter.

Next, while a cliché of sole was being served, I descended under the table to see what, if anything, was going on down there. Feeling particularly childish, no doubt engendered by the perspective, I amused myself by tying the episcopal boots together by their laces and then gently caressed Miss Maude Smith's calf with the point of my shoe till she was sufficiently encouraged to wrap her leg round Geoffrey Mortimer's. Then turning round I observed the Foreign Secretary lay a podgy left hand just above Lady Hartland's right knee. This didn't surprise her or me. But it gave me an idea when I saw my brother's right hand idle beneath the table. They were, of course, eating their sole with a fork alone. So firmly I placed my own right hand on Lady Hartland's other knee and then as it were observed which of these two crabs might crawl to shelter first. Presumably her ladyship must have been used to such attentions while she dined, for I could hear her chattering away above me quite unconcerned. This blasé attitude to our joint assault annoyed me. So I placed my other hand in between her thighs. For a minute she seemed only to respond to the contact; then presumably noticing that the men on either side of her were still using their only free hand to hold their fork, Lady Hartland concluded that the third hand came from the other side of the table. She struck out with her right just avoiding my spectacles and catching Geoffrey Mortimer, who sat opposite her, a mortal kick in the crutch, causing him and his chair to fall over backwards. Even so, I did not remove either of my hands, nor did the Foreign Secretary take his paw away from Lady Hartland's garter. With three hands upon her and only two arms within reach, she now emitted a horrible shriek.

'It's bad enough to be groped by the Cabinet,' she said standing up, 'but I'm damned if I can tolerate being raped by the Holy Ghost.'

'Dear, dear,' said the bishop and was then silenced when he noticed that I had removed his crucifix from the chain round his collar and replaced it by the more appropriate symbol of a corkscrew.

Hearing Lady Hartland's accusation against his colleagues, the Prime Minister playfully threw his bread roll at his Foreign Secreatry, unfortunately missing him and catching Miss Smith so firmly in her open mouth that when she removed the roll her dentures still adhered to it. Now this example from 10 Downing Street occasioned the subsequent Battle of the Rolls in which bread bounced from pate to pate or was forcibly stuffed by the ladies down one another's corsage. This brawl incited the servants who, not to be outdone by the guests, went round the table squirting syphons of soda on to bare backs or napes of necks.

It was then that my brother revealed himself as both a man of action and a resourceful host: bellowing above the din, he announced that he intended to give a recital of Chopin. Being of a sadistic nature, he always enjoyed inflicting this upon his guests. They, now without any ammunition left to express their reaction to their host's threat, rose to their feet and followed us both from the room.

Immediately the quieted company was seated and when coffee had been served without incident Charles strode with feigned bashfulness to the concert grand. As usual, Geoffrey stood at his side to turn the pages and with subtle gestures of patronizing approval indicate that he himself had taught Charles everything he knew. While he played the Polonaise I did nothing more than cause Geoffrey to turn two pages together. But my brother knew the piece so well he was not thrown except for tempi and a mounting irritation against his protégé. After this piece, he began on one of the Études. I allowed him to get into the run of the piece, then brought the lid of the piano down on to his hands when Geoffrey's fingers had happily strayed near enough to it for him to be blamed.

'You clumsy bugger,' Charles shrieked, dancing with the pain from his wrists.

'You old queen,' Geoffrey countered. 'It serves you right. Now you won't be able to carry on with Lady Hartland any more.'

This witty exchange also ended in a brawl in which somehow Lady Hartland's necklace was broken. When she bent to pick the pearls up I approached her from behind and dexterously reached for the hem of her skirt which I slit up to her buttocks, then with one hand I pulled her black panties down and with the other stuck a head of celery in between her legs just as my brother came to her assistance, and consequently stood there blamed for the whole, blushing like Lady Hartland's pretty bottom which I had playfully slapped. Complete chaos now ensued. But I got bored with my evening as a poltergeist and promised myself not to repeat it. It was far too easy making those who were ridiculous appear as absurd as I knew them to be.

After leaving the shambles of Tite Street, I next found myself in my bank, Cox & King's, at the bottom of Pall Mall. I suppose I wandered in there with the vague intention of taking advantage of my condition and absconding with a few thousand pounds. I sat on the counter for some time watching clients coming in to exchange one paltry piece of paper, and stuffing other bits of the same material into their wallet. And when one of the cashiers had a slab of new fivers before him I teased the poor fellow by taking half of them, intending to slip them into my pocket. There must have been £500 or more. But they were bulky and, realizing suddenly that I had no need of valid currency, I stood up on the counter and scattered the fivers like confetti over the astounded clients. But I didn't feel generous: I felt an all-consuming sense of indifference. In this mood, I walked up Bond Street. How often had I done that before stopping at one shop or another to admire a scarf, a picture or a piece of furniture which I could never afford, and then hurrying on empty-handed? But this time I went straight to Asprey's: they had been displaying a gold and platinum cigarette case there which I had lusted after for months. I took it out of its case, admired its casing and delicate workmanship, and was about to put it into my pocket when I realized something: I had not smoked a single cigarette since my demise. The shock of this nearly killed me. I had always been a compulsive smoker. I had not even wanted a cigarette. And now I remembered something: my wife had always said that she would never believe I was dead unless a lighted cigarette was placed in my mouth and I failed to draw it. I now found myself replacing the case. To me it had become a bauble. I hurried from the shop and crossed the road, and went towards the Burlington Arcade where there was a little shop whose hand-painted silk ties had always arrested me. But now I found I had passed this shop unaware of its window. My mind must have been on less substantial things. Irritated by this apparent lapse into abstract thought, I retraced my steps deliberately and stared blankly down at these tawdry bits of cloth which, only a month ago, had attracted me so much. Suddenly a sense of panic seized me. I had found I had lost my desire to smoke; could it be that I was now losing interest in all material things too? I felt indignant at the thought. But glancing at the other objects in the shops in the Arcade convinced me this was true. Even jade, which I always admired, now interested me less than lumps of unfashioned clay. This realization did not give me a sense of liberation but of resentment. It is one thing to achieve spirituality by abnegation, fasting and other self-imposed disciplines, quite another to find this condition forced upon one, especially without any religious belief as a compensatory illusion. Having lost one vice had I also been deprived of my others? What of my natural appetites? I now recalled that I had not eaten since, but I could answer that for I had no more sense of time than Cleopatra's Needle. I now ran to put this to the test. My direction was easily chosen. It had been my habit to treat myself occasionally to my favourite dish of crab meat at Rayner's Bar at the top of the Haymarket. I ran down Piccadilly towards this place: fear, not hunger, pursuing me. As usual, George stood behind the bar opening oysters. They were Imperial Whitstables. Normally I would have eaten two dozen at least. Now plate after plate passed over the counter before me and no greed arose. At this failure I felt saddened beyond words, and outraged too, like a Las Vegas croupier who wakes up from a trance to find he has involuntarily become a Yogi. Astounded, I reached over the bar and helped myself to a great dollop of crab meat, and then taking some brown bread and butter, I retired to a corner. It was a test, a question of life or death to me. I heaped the fork with the brown crab meat and slowly lifted it to my mouth: not only did the saliva fail to meet it, my mouth refused to open. And sitting there I began to weep noiselessly. At least my tears still flowed. Then I realized there was one appetite which surely had not forsaken me. I stopped weeping and smiled to myself as I got up and strode vigorously out of the pub, taking the first car I found at a parking meter. I drove straight to Janet's mews cottage in Gloucester Place, causing some alarm to drivers in the traffic who were unused to seeing a Lagonda propel itself or weave so dexterously round Piccadilly. I did not find my condition extraordinary. After all, I had long been of the opinion that many of my friends were dead and didn't know it.

Such is habit, that even now as I parked the car, I found myself making up excuses to give to my wife. Catching myself at this again pleased me: at least my invention had not left me. Feeling comparatively cheerful again, I let myself in with my latch-key.

Janet was nowhere to be seen downstairs. I called up. There was no response. But I knew she was in: her handbag was hung over the back of a chair. I guessed where she would be: upstairs taking a bath. Janet was a compulsive bather. And I recalled that the geyser was so noisy she would not have heard me. I opened the bathroom door: there she was with her giant sponge lying on her pretty belly. It had been months since I had seen that navel. I found myself flooded with affection for her and glanced at the mirror now confident that my reflection would be there— but the glass was covered in steam.

Janet now got out of the bath and sat on its edge, her legs outstretched before her. As she reached for a towel I let her take me into her arms. I kissed those lips I had so often kissed and my tongue imitated what I performed below. Was this what they meant by rigor mortis? I always knew sex would be my last sense to go. I had thought that Janet had responded to my passion. But later, as I lay within her arms, I realized that she was not even aware of my presence. She perceived that she was sexually excited but doubtless explained this to herself as being due to some erotic fantasy which had passed through her fertile mind. How often, I wondered, had I ploughed such a futile furrow before?

Janet was never a girl to hesitate to put inclination into effect.

'Henry,' she called coquettishly, 'come and dry my back.'

A young man walked obediently into the bathroom wearing my dressing-gown. I now suffered the humiliation of seeing my mistress lifted out of my own arms and carried manfully into the bedroom. I had been nothing but an aphrodisiac for another.

With the agony of a voiceless Rigoletto deprived of his strangled cry, I stood there and watched them make love before my eyes. And I wept again, not for my loss of love, but my loss of pain. The beast with two backs filled me with no revulsion, just indifference.

Then, as if I had not suffered enough from my lack of suffering, something occurred which makes even the dead die again. Standing there watching my beloved in her playful transports I saw her visibly age before my eyes. The apples of her breasts drained of their pretty pout. Next, the thighs sagged, her waist thickened and the neck wrinkled. At first I dared not look at her face. When I did, I saw the double chin, the tight lips of age pursed with wrinkles lying over her toothless gums. And her hair? Oh, pity the dead, who without a sense of time, stand and stare and see on an instant what the living are spared, blinded as they are by the gradualness, the mercy of years.

At this moment of compassion for her, my features must have taken on definition again. Janet, opening her eyes, saw me. She always said she wanted me to be the last thing she saw before she died.

When I left her cottage, I do not know where I walked or for how long. My last recollection was standing on some cliff edge looking down at the interminable breaking waves. With all the earth and all that's on it accessible to me, I felt nothing but consummate indifference to it. That is what death is. And why so few ghosts appear: we are too bored with you all to be bothered to haunt you.

So, I walked into the mist and finally let the yawn of space envelop me.

THE
LEAF-SWEEPER

by Muriel Spark

Several of Muriel Spark's earliest books
(including *Tribute to Wordsworth, Letters of J.H.
Newman,* and *My Best Mary: Letters of Mary
Shelley*) were co-edited with Derek Stanford,
another contributor to this anthology (see 'The
Illuminated Office'). 'The Leaf-Sweeper' was
one of Muriel Spark's earliest works of fiction,
and originally appeared in the Christmas issue of
the *London Mystery Magazine* (1956), shortly
before the publication of *The Comforters*—first
in a long line of highly acclaimed novels (*The
Prime of Miss Jean Brodie, The Girls of Slender
Means, The Abbess of Crewe, The Driver's Seat,*
etc.).

Behind the town hall there is a wooded parkland which, towards the end of November, begins to draw a thin blue cloud right into itself; and as a rule the park floats in this haze until mid-February. I pass every day, and see Johnnie Geddes in the heart of this mist, sweeping up the leaves. Now and again he stops, and jerking his long head erect, looks indignantly at the pile of leaves, as if it ought not to be there; then he sweeps on. This business of leaf-sweeping he learnt during the years he spent in the asylum; it was the job they always gave him to do; and when he was discharged the town council gave him the leaves to sweep. But the indignant movement of the head comes naturally to him, for this has been one of his habits since he was the most promising and buoyant and vociferous graduate of his year. He looks much older than he is, for it is not quite twenty years ago that Johnnie founded the Society for the Abolition of Christmas.

Johnnie was living with his aunt then. I was at school, and in the Christmas holidays Miss Geddes gave me her nephew's pamphlet, *How to Grow Rich at Christmas*. It sounded very likely, but it turned out that you grow rich at Christmas by doing away with Christmas, and so pondered Johnnie's pamphlet no further.

But it was only his first attempt. He had, within the next three years, founded his society of Abolitionists. His new book, *Abolish Christmas or We Die*, was in great demand at the public library, and my turn for it came at last. Johnnie was really convincing, this time, and most people were completely won over until after they had closed the book. I got an old copy for sixpence the other day, and despite the lapse of time it still proves conclusively that Christmas is a national crime. Johnnie demonstrates that every human unit in the kingdom faces inevitable starvation within a period inversely proportional to that in which one in every six industrial-productivity units, if you see what he means, stops producing toys to fill the stockings of the educational-intake units. He cites appalling statistics to show that 1.024 per cent of the time squandered each Christmas in reckless shopping and thoughtless churchgoing brings the nation closer to its doom by five years. A few readers protested, but Johnnie was able to demolish their muddled arguments, and meanwhile the Society for the Abolition of Christmas increased. But Johnnie was troubled. Not only did Christmas rage throughout the kingdom as usual that year, but he had private information that many of the Society's members had broken the Oath of Abstention.

He decided, then, to strike at the very roots of Christmas. Johnnie gave up his job on the Drainage Supply Board; he gave up all his prospects, and, financed by a few supporters, retreated for two years to study the roots of Christmas. Then, all jubilant, Johnnie produced his next and last book, in which he established, either that Christmas was an invention of the Early Fathers to propitiate the pagans, or it was invented by the pagans to placate the Early Fathers, I forget which. Against the advice of his friends, Johnnie entitled it *Christmas and Christianity*. It sold eighteen copies. Johnnie never really recovered from this; and it happened, about that time, that the girl he was engaged to, an ardent Abolitionist, sent him a pullover she had knitted, for Christmas; he sent it back, enclosing a copy of the Society's rules, and she sent back the ring. But in any case, during Johnnie's absence, the Society had been undermined by a moderate faction. These moderates finally became more moderate, and the whole thing broke up.

Soon after this, I left the district, and it was some years before I saw Johnnie again. One Sunday afternoon in summer, I was idling among the crowds who were gathered to hear the speakers at Hyde Park. One little crowd surrounded a man who bore a banner marked 'Crusade against Christmas'; his voice was frightening; it carried an unusually long way. This was Johnnie. A man in the crowd told me Johnnie was there every Sunday, very violent about Christmas, and that he would soon be taken up for insulting language. As I saw in the papers, he was soon taken up for insulting language. And a few months later I heard that poor Johnnie was in a mental home, because he had Christmas on the brain and couldn't stop shouting about it.

After that I forgot all about him until three years ago, in December, I went to live near the town where Johnnie had spent his youth. On the afternoon of Christmas Eve I was walking with a friend, noticing what had changed in my absence, and what hadn't. We passed a long, large house, once famous for its armoury, and I saw that the iron gates were wide open.

'They used to be kept shut,' I said.

'That's an asylum now,' said my friend; 'They let the mild cases work in the grounds, and leave the gates open to give them a feeling of freedom.'

'But,' said my friend, 'they lock everything inside. Door after door. The lift as well; they keep it locked.'

While my friend was chattering, I stood in the gateway and looked in. Just beyond the gate was a great bare elm tree. There I saw a man in brown corduroys, sweeping up the leaves. Poor soul, he was shouting about Christmas.

'That's Johnnie Geddes,' I said. 'Has he been here all these years?'

'Yes,' said my friend as we walked on. 'I believe he gets worse at this time of year.'

'Does his aunt see him?'

'Yes. And she sees nobody else.'

We were, in fact, approaching the house where Miss Geddes lived. I suggested we call on her. I had known her well.

'No fear,' said my friend.

I decided to go in, all the same, and my friend walked on to the town.

Miss Geddes had changed, more than the landscape. She had been a solemn, calm woman, and now she moved about quickly, and gave short agitated smiles. She took me to her sitting-room, and as she opened the door she called to someone inside.

'Johnnie, see who's come to see us!'

A man, dressed in a dark suit, was standing on a chair, fixing holly behind a picture. He jumped down.

'Happy Christmas,' he said. 'A Happy and a Merry Christmas indeed. I do hope,' he said, 'you're going to stay for tea, as we've got a delightful Christmas cake, and at this season of goodwill I would be cheered indeed if you could see how charmingly it's decorated; it has "Happy Christmas" in red icing, and then there's a robin and . . .'

'Johnnie,' said Miss Geddes, 'you're forgetting the carols.'

'The carols,' he said. He lifted a gramophone record from a pile and put it on. It was *The Holly and the Ivy.*

'It's *The Holly and the Ivy,*' said Miss Geddes. 'Can't we have something else? We had that all morning.'

'It is sublime,' he said, beaming from his chair, and holding up his hand for silence.

While Miss Geddes went to fetch the tea, and he sat absorbed in his carol, I watched him. He was so like Johnnie, that if I hadn't seen poor Johnnie a few moments before, sweeping up the asylum leaves, I would have thought he really was Johnnie. Miss Geddes returned with the tray, and while he rose to put on another record, he said something that startled me.

'I saw you in the crowd that Sunday when I was speaking at Hyde Park.'

'What a memory you have!' said Miss Geddes.

'It must be ten years ago,' he said.

'My nephew has altered his opinion of Christmas,' she explained. 'He always comes home for Christmas now, and don't we have a jolly time, Johnnie?'

'Rather!' he said. 'Oh, let me cut the cake.'

He was very excited about the cake. With a flourish he dug a large knife into the side. The knife slipped, and I saw it run deep into his finger. Miss Geddes did not move. He wrenched his cut finger away, and went on slicing the cake.

'Isn't it bleeding?' I said.

He held up his hand. I could see the deep cut, but there was no blood. Deliberately, and perhaps desperately, I turned to Miss Geddes.

'That house up the road,' I said, 'I see it's a mental home now. I passed it this afternoon.'

'Johnnie,' said Miss Geddes, as one who knows the game is up, 'go and fetch the mince-pies.'

He went, whistling a carol.

'You passed the asylum,' said Miss Geddes wearily.

'Yes,' I said.

'And you saw Johnnie sweeping up the leaves.'

'Yes.'

We could still hear the whistling of the carol.

'Who is *he?*' I said.

'That's Johnnie's ghost,' she said. 'He comes home every Christmas.'

'But,' she said, 'I don't like him. I can't bear him any longer, and I'm going away tomorrow. I don't want Johnnie's ghost, I want Johnnie in flesh and blood.'

I shuddered, thinking of the cut finger that could not bleed. And I left, before Johnnie's ghost returned with the mince-pies.

Next day, as I had arranged to join a family who lived in the town, I started walking over about noon. Because of the light mist, I didn't see at first who it was approaching. It was a man, waving his arm to me. It turned out to be Johnnie's ghost.

'Happy Christmas. What do you think,' said Johnnie's ghost, 'my aunt has gone to London. Fancy, on Christmas Day, and I thought she was at church, and here I am without anyone to spend a jolly Christmas with and, of course, I forgive her, as it's the season of goodwill, but I'm glad to see you, because now I can come with you, wherever it is you're going and we can all have a Happy . . .'

'Go away,' I said, and walked on.

It sounds hard. But perhaps you don't know how repulsive and loathsome is the ghost of a living man. The ghosts of the dead may be all right, but the ghost of mad Johnnie gave me the creeps.

'Clear off,' I said.

He continued walking beside me. 'As it's the time of goodwill, I make allowances for your tone,' he said. 'But I'm coming.'

We had reached the asylum gates, and there, in the grounds, I saw Johnnie sweeping the leaves. I suppose it was his way of going on strike, working on Christmas Day. He was making a noise about Christmas.

On a sudden impulse I said to Johnnie's ghost, 'You want company?'

'Certainly,' he replied. 'It's the season of . . .'

'Then you shall have it,' I said.

I stood in the gateway. 'Oh, Johnnie,' I called.

He looked up.

'I've brought your ghost to see you, Johnnie.'

'Well, well,' said Johnnie, advancing to meet his ghost, 'Just imagine it!'

'Happy Christmas,' said Johnnie's ghost.

'Oh, really?' said Johnnie.

I left them to it. And when I looked back, wondering if they would come to blows, I saw that Johnnie's ghost was sweeping the leaves as well. They seemed to be arguing at the same time. But it was still misty, and really, I can't say whether, when I looked a second time, there were two men or one man sweeping the leaves.

Johnnie began to improve in the New Year. At least, he stopped shouting about Christmas, and then he never mentioned it at all; in a few months, when he had almost stopped saying anything, they discharged him.

The town council gave him the leaves of the park to sweep. He seldom speaks, and recognizes nobody. I see him every day at the late end of the year, working within the mist. Sometimes, if there is a sudden gust, he jerks his head up to watch a few leaves falling behind him, as if amazed that they are undeniably there, although, by rights, the falling of leaves should be stopped.

THE
ILLUMINATED
OFFICE

by Derek Stanford

Derek Stanford (b. 1918) is a distinguished
critic, editor and poet, and author of studies on
Muriel Spark, Dylan Thomas, Christopher Fry
and John Betjeman. He has also published
several anthologies and articles on the 1890s.
Among his other writings are *Movements in
English Poetry, 1900–1958* (1959) and *Inside the
Forties: Literary Memoirs, 1937–1957* (1977).

They started—the strange happenings in Old Square—the night
that Maurice Daimler moved in for his short stay in a friend's flat
which had been vacated for Christmas.

Old Square was more than two-thirds empty. The barristers and
solicitors had mostly closed their chambers and offices, while the
residents of that sober zone had—all but a handful—decamped for
holidays in country cottages, houses, hotels, or on the Continent.

The square, with its bewigged magpie counsels, wore a decidedly
sombre look; bleak, even. It was Christmas Eve, with the Christmas
spirit—holly, mistletoe, tinsel and the trimmings—present, if at all,
behind heavy oak doors in just the few flats of those tenants remaining.
There was one exception: a lighted Christmas tree which stood in New
Square, outside the Library, just inside the gates. Strangely, this single
festive touch, in lonely splendour, only served to emphasize the general

bleakness. Perhaps also one should not forget a berried evergreen wreath fastened to a large brass knocker, displaying itself in New Square, but then—as Maurice's friend had told him, he regarded New Square, with its more open prospect, the stone dryad by the fountain on the lawn, as the light side of Lincoln's Inn. Old Square, he had asserted, was its more shadowy Victorian aspect.

At first Maurice was inclined to believe that the initial occurrence was a dream or a trick played by his eyesight, used to the brazen glare of roads at night and not the glimmery silver-fish glow of gas, less baleful but also less pervasive and extensive as to visibility.

The morning after, he'd been inclined to dismiss it, since Christmas Day dawned so preternaturally bright that it seemed impossible to think of fog drifting about the buildings at four a.m. But the fact remained, he *had* seen it there—the swirling swathing fog—or dreamt he'd seen it. Anyway, there were more things, better things, to think about: the script of the play he was directing, and which he'd brought with him, to bring to a finish in this quiet seclusion.

It was not only the momentum of composition which had driven him to celebrate Yuletide in so hermetic a fashion. He was licking his wounds from a love that had gone wrong—a relationship he'd hoped would be long-term, for life. Deirdre had been the one to draw out—out and away with some better man presumably. His plans had been laid for Christmas with her; when she pulled out, he did not feel like enduring the pity of kind-hearted friends who vied with each other to help him fill the vacuum.

Hearing that Frank's flat would be unoccupied for a week, he applied for the office of unpaid caretaker. Frank was glad to have him there: a precaution against all those burglars playing Father Christmas.

Christmas lunch he would get from an Indian restaurant. Their curry would help to keep out the cold, even if it couldn't remove the chill within. Apart from that, he'd two large bags of groceries and greengroceries: a tin or two of Campbell's soup, Heinz baked beans, a few apples and satsumas—with, of course, a spot of booze—would adequately serve his stomach in its present uninterested state.

It was, then, in the small hours of the morning that Maurice had got up for a pee. His wristwatch on the mantelpiece told him it was four o'clock. Four a.m. on Christmas Day; and a vestigial sense of wonder, remaining from childhood, caused him to cross the room and part the curtains for a quick look at the square. What he expected to greet his glance, it would be hard to say. A moment's vision of things motionless—a kind of still-life vision of peace?

What his eyes encountered was something quite different—something which communicated to his brain a far other feeling than that suggested by the silent holy night of the German carol. The visibility was troubled, obscure; and there was a sense of unrest, the gas-light patchy, part-haloed by mist which rose in after-midnight billows between the two gas-lamps and the tree in the square, and between the tree and the buildings opposite—all of their chambers and offices closed, with perhaps one aged bachelor resident staying put, flat-bound, till relatives arrived, with presents, to cook the lunch.

Maurice found it hard to say why these misty modulations disturbed him. Was it because he could not really trust himself to say whether what he saw was a matter of external visibility or whether it was an optical disturbance, something momentarily troubling the nerves of sight? He was reminded of a film version of Shakespeare's *Richard III*, when the King—on the morning of Bosworth Field—had stepped from his tent and seen, by dawn, mist shapes moving across the meadows, taking on the face and figure of those he had assassinated or killed. He recognised no analogy in those movements of mist in the Square, but did not like the feeling of the scene before him. In the morning, five hours later, with church-bells ringing and the sun, a confident sphere, shining in the wintry blue sky, Maurice was inclined to query whether what he thought he saw had substance.

After a two-hour stint on his script—the end drawing tantalizingly nearer—he put down the purple pen he favoured for 'significant' composition, and decided to go for lunch: the idea of a curry for Christmas, in a Pakistani restaurant, tickled him. It was a plan to hold misery at bay. He did not wish to be reminded, by the sight of roast turkey and all the trimmings, of Deirdre's sudden defection when she had been scheduled to play the part of the fairy on the top of the Christmas tree.

Distraction and concentration—these were his two anodynes. His manuscript offered him concentration (focusing something vital, seemingly untouched by late disaster), and a walk down Red Lion Street, across Gray's Inn Road, and then on to the end of Lamb's Conduit Street, in search of poppadums . . . what better ruse to distract himself than this unseasonal prandial exercise? In the afternoon, he might return, after brandy-laced coffee, to sleep. Whisky in his tea at four; fiddle with correction of his script till six. A simple supper of soup and beans on toast. Then the telly, with a bottle of advocaat beside him. Work, food and alcohol—and no human faces, no friendly voices, expressing sympathy, asking questions. Maurice had got it all worked out, but the programme was subject to interference.

The after-lunch coffee had been truly well laced; and on his return to Old Square, Maurice had opted for an early tea. He toasted a slice of unspeakable white bread, spreading it first with cinnamon paste—a jar of which, belonging to Frank, he found in the kitchen dresser. Tea, with no sugar but plenty of whisky, soon had him pacifically soporific. It was then, as he almost reeled into the kitchen for a rag to wipe up tea he had poured, with an unsteady hand, not into the mug but on to the little folding table in the front room, that he noticed something which seemed odd—un-Christmas-like in the extreme—and, surely, he was a judge of that, right enough.

The kitchen window overlooked an office on a lower floor, just across the way from Frank's flat, and separated from it by a little passageway which led into the Inn garden. What surprised Maurice, in his state of semi-stupor, was that the lights were on in the office; and, there, with his back to him, sat a man in black pinstripe, writing he supposed at a table.

Working on Christmas Day—wasn't this carrying the protestant work ethic to extremes? He bet the man was not such a stickler for morning communion—even with Inigo Jones' lovely little chapel, next door to the Old Hall, not five hundred yards away. That was the trouble with the protestant work ethic: it couldn't spare the time for church service first.

Such were Maurice's profound reflections before he drew on a warm camel-haired dressing-gown, and falling on the small truckle bed in the tiny guest bedroom, fell into a deplorably drunken sleep.

When he woke two hours later, his tongue like a piece of parched leather, his first thought was: a drink of water. He staggered into the narrow kitchen and ran himself a couple of icy glassfuls. The window was above the old-fashioned stone sink; across the way was the office with its lights still on. And the man Maurice had seen, before his drunken sleep overtook him, was still there, with his back to him, as if he had never moved for one instant.

But even as Maurice stared with surprise at this gross example of industry, the lighted window began to dim and the figure of the man to become indistinct. It was as if an india-rubber was being passed over a drawing, pencilled in by light, on the space opposite. Maurice, still confused by the drink, could not make out what was happening—though, whatever it was, he did not like it. Then he realised that it was mist; and he supposed that it gathered from the lawns and flower-beds of the Inn gardens less than fifty yards away. It reminded him, however, of the troubled swathing forms he had seen in the night from the front room windows. Quickly, the mist performed its work of obfuscation.

The utter dispiritedness of his grief—his loss of Deirdre—now came back upon him. 'Deirdre of the Sorrows'—she had been that to him! It was as if the mist had subdued and overcome all that temporary provisional warmth which curry and alcohol had lent him. Like a conquest of red by white corpuscles, emotionally speaking. What moved pallidly outside the window seemed to draw out, and drain away, such Dutch courage as Maurice had succeeded in preserving, leaving him, as it were, a mere man of mist.

He pulled down the kitchen blind over the sink, and returned into the front room to put on the television. Even a shadow can watch the flickering screen.

After a while, Maurice—slumped in an armchair—became aware of a muffling silence in between the blatant clatter and chatter of two programmes. Only a few seconds between the perpetual trumpeting and spieling; but in that space, it made itself felt as a pressing silence, an impingement of soundless air upon the walls and windows of the flat. He remembered, now, he had heard no church-bells ring, and surely the little Inn chapel where John Donne had preached from the pulpit as chaplain to the Honourable Society ... surely that small sanctuary would be holding a Christmas Evening service for those few residents and old faithfuls from outside? He did not think he had slept through the few admonitory strokes of its bell—a sober and chastening invitation.

By rights, there should be a service now. Nothing easier than to check since the lighted windows of the chapel should be clearly visible from the flat. He crossed the room and, drawing back the curtains, looked down from the height of three stories up, expecting to see those little lozenges of stained glass glowing gold and blue-gold in the night. To his utter amazement—quickly changing to dismay, and from this transforming itself to fear—he could see no lights, since no chapel was visible. Neither, for that matter, was anything else. The tree in the centre of the Square, the buildings opposite, the lamp-post at the entrance to the flats and the gas-lamp bracketed to the wall on the corner of Old and New Square—

all of them had been removed by the eraser of mist; but mist so thick that it blotted out the very existence of the external world: no sky, no ground, no sense of things between—just space without any bounding dimensions.

So dense was the mist—or was it an illusion, resulting from the high-lighted candelabra throwing its glow against the impenetrable wall outside?—seeming to be tinged with the faintest bilious tint as of fog. The window was jammed, so Maurice went to unchain the heavy solid door of the flat which opened on to the landing and descending stairway. Yes, by God, he was right: there was just the slightest sulphur-and-saltpetre smell as if someone had been letting off fireworks! No doubt about it: despite the Clean Air Act of the Fifties, this mist had the essence of a traditional pea-souper.

Just then, the weatherman came up on the box, the forecaster speaking of 'a bright sunny Christmas Day and a cold but clear night over London and the South-East . . . the sort of night to see the stars if you feel like venturing out.'

Well, there were no stars over Lincoln's Inn, and Maurice wondered what other parts of London were enjoying this murk prevailing in West Central. On the off-chance, he rang a friend in Wimbledon:

'Happy Christmas, and all the trimmings, Doug. How're things with you, weather-wise in Wimbledon?'

'Perfect, perfect; but bloody cold now! Just been out to see the Star of Bethlehem . . . that's my religious observance for the day. I daresay it's really Venus; but Bethlehem sounds right at Christmas. How are things with you and where are you for Christ's sake?'

'Over at Holborn, caretaking for a friend. We're in a real pea-souper here. I can't see a yard in front of me.'

There was a pause. 'It can't be, Maurice. We haven't had one of those for thirty years! You all right, Morrie? Not been drinking, by any chance?'

'Only a few brandies to keep out the cold.'

'Ah, well; that's it. Smoke gets in your eyes, and fog gets in your throat—in your case, inside your head.'

Pity veiled as humour—he saw through that ploy; all his friends knew about Deirdre's defection.

'Don't hit the bottle too hard, old boy.'

'What I drink wouldn't fill a hot-water-bottle! Blessings on you and Sara. Bye-bye.'

He returned to the telly but couldn't settle to it. West Central had long been a smokeless zone; and what held good for Wimbledon ought certainly to apply here. There was only the river up which fog might drift; but surely it couldn't all come from there.

Fog everywhere. Fog up the river . . . *Fog on the Essex marshes, fog on the Kentish heights.* Wherever did these lines come from, as if some tape-recorder in his brain suddenly turned itself on and off? One of the world's masterpieces read and, alas, forgotten.

After fidgeting with the television and changing channels listlessly, Maurice reached for the phone again. This time it was a Highgate chum he contacted.

'Hi, Len! How's Highgate, this Christmas? We've got a genuine Victorian fog in Holborn.'

'Good to hear from you, Maurice. Wondered where you'd got to. A fog, you say. You must be joking. Been a marvellous day. A grand night. Stars all over the sky. Some as large as fifty-p pieces. Can't believe you've got a fog. Sure you're not kidding?'

'Listen, Len. I can't see the houses opposite!'

'You're not joking, are you, Maurice? Don't believe they make those heavies any more.'

'I'm serious, Len.'

'Oh, well, of course, you're a lot lower down in W.C. Highgate's halfway up Mont Blanc and about as cold! Look after yourself! Things are a bit rowdy here . . .' The sounds of stereo, the stomping of feet and singing voices momentarily made it hard to hear Len's words. 'And, as I say, look after yourself. You're a *rara avis*, Maurice. Ring me in the New Year.'

A half-pitying, half-indifferent note of concern. A strange horse, our Maurice. That was how 'our Maurice' interpreted Len's words. So back to gazing, without much recognition, at the tireless screen—a *perpetuum mobile* of inanities—until, with more brandy, he became drowsy, falling asleep while the programme chuntered on.

He woke, with the channel he had chosen quite blank. Either there was no all-night programme or the set had broken down. Perhaps it was the intense cold which had affected reception. With a splitting headache inserting itself as soon as he rose from the chair, he did not care either way and pulled out the plug.

Another visit to the kitchen for a glass of water to cool his hot parched throat. Better, but the headache persisted. A kind of fearful curiosity led him to pull up the blind some six inches. Wonder of wonders: the fog was gone; but, in the office across the way, the lights were still on, and the black-coated figure presented his back to him as he sat, seemingly motionless, at his desk as before.

Then the light bulb fused in the kitchen. Surreptitiously lowering the blind, Maurice made his way—benumbed by these phenomena—to the little guest bedroom where, semi-dressed, he tumbled into bed.

His first thought, on waking in the morning, was to check on the illuminated office—since that was how he thought of it.

Gingerly, as if he was afraid of attracting attention, he lowered his head and raised the blind a few inches. Yes, there it was; its window a vertical oblong lit with strip-lighting. Many of the offices in the Inn had lights on most of the day in winter, but *not* on Christmas or Boxing Day. And, there too, unbelievably, were the same black-suited back and shoulders of that man sitting over his desk. Ten a.m. when most Christmas wassailers were just getting up or lingering over a slow coffee-laden breakfast: what sort of a workaholic was this one?

Had he sat there all night with his head on the desk (Maurice had journalistic colleagues, some of whom could sleep on their hands in their office between consignments)? At that moment, someone entered the office carrying what looked like pink-ribboned briefs. It was a woman and Maurice noticed straightaway that her dress and hair-style were Victorian. As she approached the man at the table, he turned towards her so that his face appeared in profile to Maurice—a countenance somehow known to him—but from where? The man smiled, but his smile was a mixture of love and desperation: a look of pleading and rejection. The young woman shook her curls and flounced out. The young man, too—something of a dandy—was, by his hair-style, not of this century. It all seemed incredible—and terribly wrong. He could sense the resonance, the vibration of deep sadness. Being rejected gave one insight into others.

Maurice had noted that Frank possessed an instant-developer flash-bulb camera. He had seen it on a shelf of a blue bookcase; and decided he would photograph this round-the-clock all-night sitter. He slipped back into the front room and, as he picked up the camera, noted that the tree outside the window was already disappearing in the returning mist. He hurried back into the kitchen, raised the blind a little higher and pressed the camera-switch.

Swirls of mist were appearing now, drifting in from the lawns and nearly bare beds of the Inn gardens. Maurice thought he might just have been in time to catch the lit window and sitting figure detected in his viewfinder; but when the film was ejected and dried, there was nothing in the photo. Just an overall greyness which may well have been the wall of the office opposite and an odd space which, conceivably, could have been the window-frame. Frank's was a colour camera, but nothing of the glowing gold window was evident; nothing of a black-suited figure contained within that golden oblong.

In those few moments needed for the film to be ejected and dry itself, the mist had made good its hold on all outside the kitchen window. The external scene was now as grey and characterless as the photograph. Had Maurice been just a second or so too late in snapping the scene, or was he himself seeing something which the camera did not register? The slender possibility of this latter was too disturbing to be properly considered.

Yet, despite his reluctance, events forced this consideration upon him. The fog (too dense for even the heaviest mist) continued unabated during the morning. Just as the image of the newscaster appeared on the television at one o'clock, a greyness, like billowing oceans of mist, swept across the screen and extinguished it. For a few seconds, the voice could be heard, then the channel went off the air. Maurice tried the other wavelengths, but the set had gone entirely dead. Was it, he wondered, the transmitter and were all areas affected?

After his enquiries about the fog yesterday, he didn't feel like ringing either of those two friends. He would have to choose someone between Wimbledon and Highgate. What about Bryan in High Street, Ken? Far enough from both of these and quite a distance from Holborn.

He knew Bryan's number without resorting to his pocket-book; but, reaching for the phone, he found the line dead. Neither was the operator to be obtained. He was besieged; cut off by the fog, since he somehow associated the TV-breakdown and the number out of order with that eerie surrounding element, immersing him inside the flat with all lines of communication to the outside world severed.

The idea of being walled in—walled up, was how he almost felt it—produced so gripping a claustrophobia that he felt he must run the gauntlet of the fog and see if he could get beyond the gates of the Inn. To a greater degree than all other Inns of Court, Lincoln's Inn is contained behind its walls, like a small mediaeval town or Oxford college. Maurice, in a mood of panic and desperation, shut the front door behind him and, without locking it, descended the cold spacious spiral of stairs. He was out into the open air of Old Square within moments. His footsteps rang out along the stone-paved landing as he hurried past each closed chamber, empty of their residents or workstaff. The sound emphasized his isolation.

Down below, the suffocating mist blanked all things out and hedged him in immediately. Yes; he must turn right, and then right again. Had he not known his way, he would be lost. As it was, he kept close to the black railings in front of the neighbouring buildings in the Square, turned round the corner, feeling his way past the white stone war memorial and the open entrance to the gardens, until he was touching the walls of the Buttery, below the Library and the New Hall. And where was that Christmas tree with its tinsel and electric baubles? Not a hint of coloured lights in the murk.

Whether or not there was a porter at the gates—a green-uniformed sentry in his snug little lodge—Maurice was unable to say, being on the outside of the roadway. Then, to his amazement and joy, once past the confines of the Inn, he perceived a loosening in the noose of the mists— an experience of something, which had been almost palpably throttling, abating its pressure. Across the road, just in front of the entrance to Lincoln's Inn Fields, he discerned, though dimly, an image of the drinking-fountain—one of those all-too-few remaining elaborate ornaments of Victorian or Edwardian easement for man and horse. The fog seemed now a swirling mist rather than swathes of thick opaque air; and as he passed into the Fields, with their all-but-leafless sycamores and planes, the mist appeared to fall away every yard he put between him and the gateway to the Inn. Just as the fog had descended like the lights turned down at the end of a play, now it was as if a theatre-curtain had slowly risen to reveal a lighted stage with all its props and figures clearly defined. Three or four of these latter occupied the little paved piazza in front of the Fields' outdoor cage. With the utmost relief Maurice noted that not one of them wore Victorian costume. He had left the nineteenth century behind him.

These lawful truants from business on Boxing Day were joined by Maurice, who thought how much better both he and they were occupied than that workaholic in the illuminated office. Here, the air was bracingly keen but not chill enough to be unendurable. One could drink a cup of coffee without becoming too aware of the cold's penetration. Up above, a frail blue sky boasted a twelve o'clock sun which had not yet commenced its wintry descent. From where he sat, between the trees, he had no prospect of the Inn. Here, at any rate, there was no suggestion of the fog which for two days had enshrouded him. What sort of a misty vapour was it which could locate itself so exactly within an area of a square quarter mile; and would it, he wondered, be there when he returned? He felt the time of his reprieve was up, having proved to himself that he could make good his escape.

Well, a humble lunch of asparagus soup and camembert awaited him. It was time he returned if he was to put in an afternoon's proof-reading.

Rising from the table, he ambled back; and, entering the Inn, its Christmas tree resplendent in the late morning sunshine, heard the cheery voice of the porter at the gateway greeting him.

'Good morning, sir. Staying at Mr Dunmore's flat, ain't you? Security; forgive me enquiring.'

'Yes, that's right,' responded Maurice. 'Caretaking for him over Christmas, so to speak. Hope you had a good one yourself.'

'Thank you, sir. Quiet, but pleasant. Put my feet up for a few hours.'

Maurice had already observed that the Inn now seemed completely free of fog. It had vanished within forty minutes as if it had never laid siege to these venerable courts and square.

He climbed the stairs, finding the front door closed but unlocked as he had left it. He entered, and made straight for the kitchen to see what was happening at the illuminated office. There, too, a change was evident. No lit-up windows. No figure at the table. Only empty space expressive of after office hours. Stage Two of these haunted happenings seemed over.

After lunch, Maurice sat back in an armchair and picked up a book lying on a side table which he had not remembered noticing before: an old tatty copy of a Collins Clear-Type pocket edition. He opened it without seeing the title, but noting the inscription on the fly-leaf:

Christmas 1926
To Dulcie
With Best Love
and Wishes
from Phyllis

Odd, since Phyllis had been the name of Deirdre's mother, no longer living.

He flicked the book open, and on page 31 found in italics a letter from Kenge and Carboy addressed from Old Square, Lincoln's Inn to Miss Esther Summerson referring to Our client Mr Jarndyce. Turning to Chapter One was like the recollection of a poem, first read in schooldays, once loved and then forgotten.

London. Michaelmas Term lately over, and the Lord Chancellor sitting in Lincoln's Inn Hall. Implacable November weather ... Smoke lowering down from chimney pots, making a soft, black drizzle, with flakes of soot in it as big as full-grown snow-flakes—gone into mourning, one might imagine, for the death of the sun . . . Fog everywhere, fog up the river where it flows among green and meadows; down the river where it rolls defiled among the ties of shipping, and the waterside pollution of a great (and dirty) city. Fog on the Essex marshes, fog on the Kentish heights.

Extraordinary! And now the source of those phrases which had come to mind earlier—mysteriously yet aptly—was revealed: the opening paragraph of Charles Dickens' *Bleak House*—however could he have forgotten it? The fog must have blurred his memory.

He went into the little kitchen, and raised the blind a few inches. Yes, all was back to normal: no vertical oblong of lit-up window—only the innocuous space with the still-life appurtenances of office furniture; and no black-coated figure seated at the table, writing, napping or day-dreaming; whatever he had been thought to be doing.

Maurice thought now he would see him no more; and recognised who it had been when the figure had turned sideways, showing his profile at the entry of the young woman carrying ribboned briefs. It was the author Dickens himself, before his literary career was under way and when he had made, initially, a start in the world of law as a solicitor's clerk, followed by a period as legal and parliamentary stenographer.

Maurice guessed, too, who the young woman was: a handsome flirtatious daughter of family with money and pretensions. While welcoming Dickens—a good-looking witty dandy—at their social soirées, they had every conceivable objection to regarding him as prospective son-in-law. So what, on the young lady's part, remained only a drawing-room relationship (emotionally she regarded 'dear Charles' as 'a boy') was on his side a desperate love affair, with its social and emotional wounds of rejection. It was one of those experiences which go to inform and deepen the artist; one of those turn-offs which set the seeds of art.

At three that afternoon the phone came to life. Automatically, he reached for it. Unbelievably, it was Deirdre; repentant, tearful, pleading. She was, unstoppably, in full spate, her language heightened by her headlong feelings. Her Christmas moonlighting with Hugh Insbrough had clearly come unstuck. She related events in the speech of melo-drama—a drama in which Maurice silently shared.

'Dearest, how could I have done it? There must have been a fog in my brain. Hugh's life-style . . . all that glitter . . . bowled me over. That ghastly affluence turned my mind. I've always loved you. I think you know it. But you know how afraid I was of the breadline. Being on the breadline with an unpaid genius. You never seemed to get a chance to direct.

'Hugh caught me when I was feeling extra low. Extra low and more afraid than usual. It's a horrid time, Christmas . . . always counting one's pennies.

'I certainly mistook the man for his means. Sort of munificent, I thought him. It's only his gold that has any glitter. Underneath it all, he's dull. With a bit of a mean streak, too.

'I hoped all that glitter would distance me. I was trying to bury you underneath it. What a ridiculous ploy to play on us both! I hurt you and covered myself with contempt. I can't bear to see myself in a mirror.

'All along, it was you I loved; but, as I said, I'd a fog in my mind. My love was a street-lamp extinguished by it.

'Will you just let me see you, Maurice, sweetheart? You will? Bless you; loved one!

'Shall we meet in the Fields? Yes, I know where you are. Who told me? Well, I had a Christmas card from Phyllis Raeburn—she was my mother's dearest friend. She said I was to call her. N.B. Ring me. Important. So I rang her. First she spoke of mother. Then of you. Very affectionately. You've never met her? Well, she seemed to know about you. How? Well, I didn't ask. Everything was like something in a dream.

'Anyway, she said she knew where I'd find you. Yes, I think she knew the chap whose flat you're staying in. Frank MacBryde she said he was. Said I should get to you pronto. She sounded very emphatic about it. Thank God I rang her! Thank God she knew!

'And I *can* see you, sweetheart? OK then, the kiosk at four. It'll be closed, I know; but we can go somewhere. Back to Old Square? What a beautiful idea. Love you, dearest, see you.'

Yes, it *was* like something in a dream. A dream-disc playing marvellous music, after all that ghost music on the ride! Could Deirdre really be returning to him, as suddenly, unexpectedly, as she'd departed?

As in a daze, he picked up the Dickens—that dog-eared copy of *Bleak House*. Had it been there on the table all the while, unnoticed by him; or had someone smuggled it in? Yes, he *had* left the door on the latch.

But, who could it have been:

Phyllis? . . . Dulcie?

THE CASE OF THE SEVEN SANTAS

by H.R.F. Keating

H.R.F. Keating (b. 1926) has written nearly
thirty highly acclaimed mystery novels since
1959, over half of them featuring Inspector
Ghote of the Bombay CID. He has also edited
the invaluable *Whodunit? A Guide to Crime,
Suspense and Spy Fiction* (1982) and *The Bedside
Companion to Crime* (1989).

Mrs Craggs, *former cleaning lady, secure in her retirement to the
remote village of Princefinger, lying somewhere between the
Dartmoor cragginess of Princeton and the mild Buckinghamshire
comforts of Princes Risborough, wondered silently why she had ever agreed to a
visit from her co-worker of old, Mrs Milhorne.*

'Yaiss,' *Mrs Milhorne was saying with elegant reflectiveness,* 'I do love the
countryside. So peaceful and what you might call 'armon- hhharmonious.'

She looked round.

'Why,' *she went on,* 'I don't suppose as 'ow—as hhhow you'd find anywhere
in all England peacefuller than your Princefinger. Though, mind, I like a touch
of class meself. That little bit of, you know, excitement.'

'Good thing you wasn't here last Christmas then,' *Mrs Craggs replied.* 'Dare
say you'd of found it a mite too exciting.'

'Oh, I don't think so. I'd of enjoyed a real country Christmas. All the jollity.'

'Yeh, well, it was a real country Christmas all right up at the Manor. Old
Mr Ebenezer, 'e really liked that sort o' thing. The 'ole Charles Dickens bit.

'Olly, carols, plum pudding, Santa Claus, Yule log, presents round the tree. Pity 'e 'ad to go an' get murdered right in the middle of it.'

Mrs Milhorne choked.

'O' course,' Mrs Craggs resumed when her friend had been patted on the back and was able to manage another sip of tea, 'asked for it, old Eb did. No getting past that. I mean, when you're a rich bachelor living all on your ownio 'cept for a valet 'oose 'alf daft any'ow, to go bringing down fer Christmas seven different people as you've told are coming in fer something under the will an' then to threaten to cut some of 'em out of it . . . Signing your death stiffticicate, that is.'

'So it was one of them as done—as was doing it?' Mrs Milhorne breathed, pale eyes glowing.

'Well, there they was, each one of 'em due fer a cool 'undred thousand, an' there was 'e saying some of 'em might not 'ave the right Christmas spirit . . .'

'So one of them—one of those seven did—No, I'm wrong. There was eight. There was that valet.'

'You're counting 'im in then? That's more than what the police did. Soon as they 'eard old Tiny Tom—that's what I called 'im on account of 'im being so tall—as soon as they 'eard 'e was provided for with a nice little annuity started years before, they ruled 'im right out.'

'So it was just the seven then? Just the seven.'

It was Mrs Craggs who discovered the body. When she came plodding into the big, stone-flagged kitchen at the Manor on Christmas morning, stamping off her boots the snow that had fallen overnight, she was greeted by old Mr Ebenezer's ancient valet, Tiny Tom, in even more of a dither than usual.

'Oh, Mrs Craggs, Mrs Craggs,' he moaned in his dungeon-deep voice the moment he saw her. 'I can't find him. I can't find him. Not in his bed when I took him his morning tea. Not in his bathroom. Not in his bed when I went back to look again. It hadn't been slept in, Mrs Craggs. That's what I can't understand. It hadn't even been slept in.'

'Then perhaps 'e never got into it,' Mrs Craggs replied with a sharp sniff.

'Never went to bed? You mean, he—he never went to bed?'

'Yes, you daft lummox. Fell asleep in 'is chair down in what 'e calls the 'all, most likely. Decked with boughs 'o 'olly indeed.'

'He could have, Mrs Craggs. He could have. They passed the steaming bowl of punch about enough last night, the smoking bishop as Mr Ebenezer said in his very own words.'

'I'll give 'im bishop,' Mrs Craggs replied, setting off, tramp, tramp, tramp, towards the manor's lofty hall, with Tiny Tom trailing along behind her like an outsize question-mark.

But bishop Mrs Craggs was unable to give old Mr Ebenezer. He was in his chair all right, but there was a neat little bullet hole in the middle of his forehead.

There was more to the scene of the crime, too. Mr Ebenezer's corpse was buried up to the chest in Christmas crackers. Bright red and vibrant green with here and there a little glued-on picture of a robin or a reindeer, they were piled up by the hundred round his tall carved armchair. And, more, stuck on the knob at the chair's top there was a sheet of paper. It bore in neat printed letters the simple words 'Old Scratch has got his own at last.'

'Well, don't just stand there with your mouth 'anging open like a blooming codfish,' Mrs Craggs said to Tiny Tom. 'Phone for the police. There's been murder done, you know.'

But, of course, in the end it was Mrs Craggs who got herself put straight on to Inspector Hummbugg. She woke him from his bed, at the end of which dangled the stocking his faithful spouse, Martha Hummbugg née Wilkins, had filled the night before with fifty-two tins of his favourite tobacco, one for each week of the year.

'Yes,' Mrs Craggs pounded into his scarcely woken ear. 'Murdered. That's what I said. Murdered. An' plenty o' clues fer you, too. So you'd better get 'ere just as fast as you can. An' bring yer fingerprint set. I think you're going to need it. Princefinger Manor. Princefinger Manor. Now, 'ave you got that, or 'aven't you?'

'I shall arrive in due course,' said Inspector Hummbugg, and the sigh he gave as he comtemplated the crammed stocking at the foot of the marital bed floated like a gale down the telephone line.

But eventually Mrs Craggs showed his bulky form, and that of the pale young sergeant who came with him, into the hall where Mr Ebenezer in his tall chair, a bullet hole in his head, sat surrounded by the high-piled Christmas crackers beneath the sheet of paper bearing the words 'Old Scratch has got his own at last.'

It was this that seemed to puzzle Inspector Hummbugg most.

'Old Scratch?' he said. 'Now who on earth can Old Scratch be? Find out that, and, mark my words, sergeant, we'll have our murderer under our thumb.'

For a long moment he comtemplated that thumb, a formidable piece of pig-pink flesh.

'Scrooge, sir,' said the pale sergeant.

Inspector Hummbugg's little porcine eyes darted him a look of quick suspicion.

'It's Dickens, sir,' the sergeant said, with haste. 'His story, A *Christmas Carol*. Sir, it's about a man called Scrooge, and—'

'I'll thank you not to teach your grandfather to suck eggs, sergeant. I know who Scrooge is, if you please.'

'Yes, sir. But—' He was a courageous young man, this pallid sergeant. 'Sir, in that story by Charles—In it, sir, when the Spirit of Times Yet to Come is showing old Scrooge the future they hear a City merchant saying just those words, sir.'

'Just what words, sergeant? What are you blathering on about now?'

But that pale sergeant was a very courageous young man.

'Just "Old Scratch has got his own at last", sir. They're in the book, A *Christmas Carol*. Look, there's a copy in that bookcase over there. I'll show you.'

He advanced towards a tailor-made bookcase containing each and every one of the works of Charles Dickens, old Mr Ebenezer's favourite author, as he had been of his parents before him. Hence Mr Ebenezer's addiction to old Christmas and all its traditions, right down to steaming bowls of bishop.

'Stop,' said Mrs Craggs.

'Stop?'

'Don't you touch that book, sonny.'

Inspector Hammbugg bristled. He might treat his sergeant as if he were a schoolboy, but he did not at all care for anyone else doing so.

'I'll thank you,' he said to Mrs Craggs, 'not to come between me and a piece of vital evidence.'

'Vital it may be,' Mrs Craggs retorted. 'But it won't be 'alf so vital if the sergeant o' yours puts 'is fingerprints all over the ones what's probably there already. Can't you see that Christmas Carol book's the one that's sticking a bit out from the row? Like as not, the person what wrote that silly note on the chair went to that book to find the words for it. So you'd better get out your fingerprint set. If you remembered to bring it.'

'Sergeant,' said Inspector Hummbugg. 'Prints apparatus. In the car. Get it, lad. Get it.'

But just as the sergeant returned Mrs Craggs addressed Inspector Hummbugg once more.

'O'course,' she said, 'them fingerprints won't lead you to the one what done it, not necessarily. I mean, what about the clue o' the thousand crackers?'

'The thousand—'

Hummbugg, and his sergeant, turned to look at the great heap of crackers almost burying Mr Ebenezer's dead body.

'One thousand,' said the inspector. 'How do you know there's a thousand there?'

'I don't, though I dare say I'm not far out. But what I do know is that only yesterday afternoon one o' the seven folk old Ebenezer invited 'ere, an' threatened to cut out o' his will, said to 'im, "I 'ope I see you buried under your damn Christmas crackers".'

'Sergeant,' said Inspector Hummbugg. 'Notebook.'

Mrs Craggs waited till the sergeant's pencil was poised.

'Young woman by the name o' Yettercumb,' she said.

The sergeant coughed.

'Would you be so kind as to spell that?'

'For heaven's sake, man,' Hummbugg exploded. 'Didn't they even teach you spelling at school?'

'Yeh,' said Mrs Craggs. 'I'd better spell it. Funny old name.'

Letter by letter she spelt it out.

'That is funny all right,' the sergeant commented.

'I'll give you funny,' Hummbugg snapped. 'Just put down what you're told, and keep your mouth shut.'

'An' you know why it's funny, that name,' Mrs Craggs went on, just as if Hummbugg's huge pink bulk was not there at all.

'Will you kindly get on with it, woman,' Hummbugg boomed.

'I am. If you'd listen. That name, Yettercumb, remind you of anything, sonny? You've read that old Christmas Carol story, didn't yer say? Just like I was brought up on it.'

Slowly light dawned on the sergeant's pale face.

'Yettercumb,' he said. 'Yet to come. The Spirit of Times Yet to Come.'

'You got it. That's why old Ebenezer 'ere even knew 'er, the silly young chit. Collected 'em up, 'e did. Names in that story. We ain't only got young Fifi Yettercumb. We got Mr Parst, what speculates in what they calls Stock Exchange futures whatever they may be, an' we got Mr Pressent, what's a theatrical angel, which I takes ter be a real-life devil. Times Past an' Times Present. An' more. We got Marylee Jacob, actress an' no better nor what she ought ter be.'

'Marylee Jacob?'

The sergeant's pallid face wore a frown. And then cleared.

[159]

'Jacob Marley,' he exclaimed. 'Old Scrooge's dead partner, Jacob Marley, just turned around.'

'All right then,' Mrs Craggs went on. ''Ow about Mrs Feswick, failed authoress so I 'eard 'er called?'

'Easy. Wife of Jolly old Mr Fezziwig, Scrooge's employer when he was an apprentice.'

'You're doing all right, son. So let me tell you that old Mr Ebenezer acksherly 'appened to 'ave a nephew name o' Fred. Readymade, as you might say.'

'Yes, yes, Scrooge's nephew was called Fred. At least I think he was. Any others?'

'Just the one. Try the Hon. Robert Crayshett-Clark.'

The frown on the sergeant's face deepened and deepened.

Then with a snort that would have done credit to a prize porker Inspector Hummbugg broke in. 'Bob,' he said. 'Bob Cratchit. I remember seeing it all on the stage when I was a kid. Bob Cratchit, clerk. But where's his son, Tiny Tim, then? He was the one I really liked. "God bless us every one".'

Hastily he wiped away a pair of tears that had oozed one from each of his piggy little eyes.

'What about Tiny Tim?'

'You'll 'ave to make do with Tiny Tom, the valet,' Mrs Craggs replied. 'Only other living soul in the 'ouse last night when that snow was a-falling. He's a regular muttonhead, but that's the best we got.'

But a ferocious gleam had suddenly come into Inspector Hummbugg's little eyes.

'Sergeant,' he said, 'get that fellow in here. Always suspect the butler. First rule of investigation. And I reckon a valet's as good as a butler any day.'

'O' course,' Mrs Craggs told Mrs Milhorne, 'when that Hummbugg 'eard as 'ow Tiny Tom, God bless us every one, 'ad 'ad that annuity of 'is fer years already 'e put 'im out of account straightaway.'

'Yaiss,' said Mrs Milhorne. 'Yaiss, 'e— hhhe'd hhhave to, wouldn't 'e?

'Not but what old Tom didn't do 'im a bit o' good.'

'I saw him though, I saw him,' Tiny Tom said as Inspector Hummbugg waved him exasperatedly away.

'Saw who, man? For heaven's sake, speak up if you've got anything to say.'

[160]

'Saw the one what done it, Inspector.'

'Saw him? Saw him? Then why the heck didn't you say so?'

'Couldn't, Inspector.'

'I'll give you couldn't. It's an offence, you know. Withholding evidence. Now, who did you see?'

'Santa Claus, Inspector.'

'Santa—'

But Mrs Craggs stepped in and deflected the mighty porcine wrath.

'I get it,' she said. 'It's this. The whole blooming lot of 'em came down 'ere with Santa outfits, saw 'em meself doing out the rooms. Wanting ter please the old devil, I suppose. An' what Tiny Tom 'ere's saying is the one what crep' down an' shot 'im wore that outfit to do it.'

'Then we'll have each manjack of them in and—'

'Oh, no, Inspector,' Mrs Craggs interrupted again. 'It ain't manjack. It's womanjack as well. Behind one o' them bit white beards it could 'ave been a woman just as well as a man. An' I tell you something else. They're all of a height. Each an' every one of 'em. Noticed it yesterday. So there'd be no telling one from another, dressed up like that.'

'Bother,' said Inspector Hummbugg.

But his pendulous pig-cheeks did not stay droopily despondent for long.

'Ha,' he exclaimed scarcely five minutes after the door had eventually closed behind Tiny Tom. 'Something was said about a threat. I haven't forgotten. Someone in this house threatened to bury the late Mr Ebenezer under one thousand of his Christmas crackers, and I want to know who.'

'Yettercumb,' Mrs Craggs answered. 'I was telling yer.'

'Sergeant. Why isn't Miss Yettercumb here? You're never going to solve cases, me lad, if you don't follow up a clue pretty sharpish. I'll tell you that for nothing.'

'No, sir. Yes, sir.'

And in no time at all little blonde Fifi Yettercumb was confronting the inspector in Mr Ebenezer's next-door study. On the broad desk the ancient typewriter had been thrust aside in favour of a generous sample of the Christmas crackers together with the sheet of paper from the top of the chair. Once again the sergeant's pencil was poised.

Inspector Hummbugg pounced.

'So,' he said, glaring ferociously at the black leather-clad curvaceous little creature in front of him, 'You buried Mr Ebenezer's body under a pile of his Christmas crackers after all, did you? Afraid he'd cut you out of your hundred thousand pounds soon as Christmas was over, eh?'

'No, Inspector, no. No, I never.'

'No use denying it, my girl. Saying "No, I never" won't get you out of trouble. Not here, and not in court.'

'But it's the truth, most like.'

It was Mrs Craggs, stepping out from the dark shadows of the oak-panelled room where she had been careful to hide to get a ringside view.

'What do you mean it's the truth?' Inspector Hummbugg thundered.

'Look,' said Mrs Craggs. 'If you was going to murder a bloke what was going to cut you out of 'is will, would you go an' do to 'is corp just what everyone 'ad 'eard you threaten to do? I didn't think it was very likely all along, an' when I 'eard the young lady deny it I was sure.'

'But—But—But why were those crackers there if she didn't put them there as per her threat?'

'Simple,' said Mrs Craggs. 'It was because the real murderer wanted to put the blame on 'er. Make 'is or 'er share o' the dibbins all the bigger, wouldn't it, if this young lady was found guilty?'

'Yes,' Fifi Yettercumb put in with palpitating haste. 'It musta been one of the others, trying to put the blame on a girl. I mean, have you thought about that mysterious typewritten note there, Inspector? That's words out of that Christmas Carol thing, ain't it? And joo know somethink?'

Inspector Hummbugg blew down his nose till the crackers on the desk began to tumble to the ground below.

'I dare say I know more than you think, my girl,' he said.

'Well then, what joo know?'

For a moment, for a good many moments, Inspector Hummbugg did not speak. Then at last he looked at Fifi again.

'Suppose you tell me,' he said.'

'Well, last night when we were all sitting round that Yule log thingy, and the nails in it going off every few seconds like ever so many pistol shots, old Eb asked us if we'd all read that Christmas Carol book. And only one of us said right out they had. I mean, who could get through all that?'

'Right then,' said Hummbugg. 'Who was this person?'

'That Mrs Feswick,' Fifi replied promptly. 'Her and her sarky remarks.'

So it was just a few minutes later that Inspector Hummbugg had in front of him at the late Mr Ebenezer's desk Mrs Bonny Feswick, fiftyish, bouncy, tweeds-clad.

'Jolly good, Inspector,' she said. 'Thought you'd want to see me. Interviewing all round, what? Well, here I am. Always ready to do my duty. Spread a little happiness, don't you know.'

Hummbugg's huge pink face assumed an expression of immense cunning.

'Glad to hear that, madam,' he said. 'And I think you can indeed help us. We're interested in this note found on the chair above Mr Ebenezer's body.'

Mrs Feswick looked at the sheet.

'It's a quotation from A *Christmas Carol*,' she said, rather slowly. 'What someone says about Scrooge after he's dead. In the future, you know. Bit awful, what?'

'Mrs Feswick,' Hummbugg said with a sudden ferocious glance. 'What would you answer if I told you that of all the people in this house you are the only one to know that story through and through?'

'I—I—'

'And what would you say if I added that I strongly suspect this note was typed on this very machine in here?'

And Mrs Feswick gave a huge smile.

'I'd tell you to look at the note a little more closely, Inspector,' she replied. 'I think you'll find that it wasn't produced on a typewriter at all. I think you'll find it was produced on a word-processor.'

At this the sergeant peered forward and examined the sheet that hitherto Inspector Hummbugg had kept as his personal possession.

'Yes, sir,' he said. He was a very, very young sergeant. 'That's quite right, sir. You can easily tell that sort of word-processor print. Dot matrix.'

'Dot—Dot—I'll dot you one in a moment, my lad.'

But the inspector did turn to Mrs Feswick.

'Thank you, madam,' he said. 'That will be all.'

'Oh,' said Mrs Feswick. 'But aren't you going to ask me if I know whether anybody in this house has a word-processor?'

'I was about to put that question to you when you elected to depart.'

'Well then, let me tell you in confidence, Inspector, that Miss Marylee Jacob has a word-processor in her room, wrapped up in sheets of paper with snowmen on them. She intends to give it for Christmas to Bob Crayshett-Clark, the sweet boy. As if that would do any good . . .'

And out she flounced.

'I think,' said Hummbugg, 'it'd be no bad thing to have a word with Miss Jacob, Marylee.'

It was Mrs Craggs who was despatched to find this new witness, not to say suspect.

And once again Hummbugg, that man of cunning incarnate, adopted shock tactics.

'Tried out your nice little present for Mr Crayshett-Clark, did you?' he asked without preliminary.

But Marylee Jacob, brassy as a brass door knocker—and, thought the sergeant, who young as he was had a good vulgar streak hidden away inside him, with a pretty good pair of knockers on her, too—showed not the least sign of guilt or dismay at the shot-out question.

'Oh, no, Inspector,' she said. 'I mean, I wouldn't know how to work something like that. No, all I did was to creep into Bob's room late last night, all dressed up as Santa Claus if you can imagine, and leave my little present for him to find this morning. It did look as if the paper round it had been disturbed, though. Perhaps that was what made you think I'd tried it out.'

She gave the inspector a sweet, sweet smile. If hammered brass can smile sweetly.

'Nevertheless,' he said, ignoring the smile, 'a certain note found not a foot away from the corpse was written on a word-processor. You can tell by the print, you know. What we call dot mattress.'

'Matrix, sir,' said the sergeant, who despite his notions about knockers was a very innocent young sergeant.

'Well, Inspector,' Marylee answered. 'All I can suggest is that somebody very naughty tapped out that note on the word-processor before I gave it to sweety-pie Bob.'

'And why would they do that?'

'Oh, Inspector, haven't you worked that out yet? If whoever murdered that awful old man can pin it on someone else it means all the bigger share of what he's left, doesn't it?'

'I am quite capable of working out whatever I have to work out for myself, madam,' Hummbugg answered, giving no credit at all to Mrs Craggs who had pointed this out to him in the first place. 'But that leaves the question of who, in fact, did murder Mr Ebenezer.'

'And haven't you worked that out either, Inspector? I mean, you've surely only got to find the weapon, and there'll be some nice, nice fingerprints on it for you. It'll be easy as falling off a Yule log, and I'm sure you can manage that.'

Exit Miss Marylee Jacob.

'Sergeant,' roared Hummbugg. 'Find the weapon.'

It took the sergeant, who despite his youth and innocence was a very active young man, just seven and a half minutes to find the gun that had put that bullet so neatly into Mr Ebenezer's forehead. It was down at the back of the tub in which stood Mr Ebenezer's enormous Christmas tree. Carefully taking it out, the sergeant blew powder on to it from his insufflator and revealed even to the naked eye splendidly clear fingerprints. Expertly he photographed them, and then, zooming off like a demented ice-skater, he secured in no time the prints of each of the seven suspects.

And it was clear beyond doubt that the ones on the gun belonged to none other than Mr Ebenezer's nephew Fred.

'I shall make the arrest at the very spot where the deed took place,' Inspector Hummbugg announced, leading the way, swaying and swinging, back into the holly decorated hall.

Nephew Fred was brought before him, sleepy-eyed and yawning.

'Don't know how it is,' he said easily, 'But I just dropped off. Always doing it, you know, having a bit of a zizz. And it's not as if I don't go off at night. I do. From ten o'clock on I'm out to the wide. Always have been. Dare say I always will be.'

Solemnly Inspector Hummbugg interrupted these self-revelations.

'Mr Frederick Ebenezer,' he began.

But before he could pronounce another word Mrs Craggs, who had been taking a good look at the gun with those clear, clear prints on it, called out.

''Ere, wait a sec.'

Deflated as if by a suddenly injected pin, Inspector Hummbugg wheeled round.

'What—'

'You 'ave another dekko at these 'ere finger marks,' Mrs Craggs said. 'I've taken 'old of enough brush 'andles in me time to know where your fingers come on 'em, and I tell yer this: nobody never 'eld this 'ere gun in a way they could of shot anybody with it, not never.'

Inspector Hummbugg peered. Nephew Fred peered. The pale sergeant peered.

It was this last who had the temerity to speak.

'She's quite right, sir, now you come to look.'

'Yes, yes,' said Nephew Fred. 'I promise you I never touched that gun. But I'll tell you what did happen to me. I was fast asleep last night, dreaming of something. Forget what. And then—this has hardly ever happened to me before—I woke up. I woke up and had the distinct impression somebody had been holding my hand.'

He gave a violent blush.

'Thought it might have been Bonny Feswick,' he said. 'Afraid she's rather keen on me. Or it might have been Marylee. Afraid she's a bit keen on me, too.'

'What you're telling me,' Inspector Hummbugg said, 'is that somebody came into your room last night while you were sound asleep and put your fingerprints on the weapon here.'

'Yes, yes, old boy, that is what I was telling you. Got it in one.'

He gave a tremendous yawn.

'Well,' he said, 'I suppose as those fingerprints have been sort of disposed of I may as well take the gun. Belongs to me now, you know. Uncle Ebenezer always said I'd get the house and everything in it. Only trouble was he was never too sure about leaving me enough actual cash to keep the old place going. Said I was too lazy. Can't think why.'

With another prodigious yawn he picked up the gun and wandered out.

'But then,' said Mrs Craggs, 'a funny thing 'appened.'

'No? What?' said Mrs Milhorne, eyes popping.

'Sleepy-clogs came back in again in just a brace o' shakes an' asked old Hummbugg did 'e know something about that gun.'

Inspector Hummbugg knew nothing about the gun. To judge from his massive silence.

So his sergeant evidently felt it up to him to save the honour of the country police.

'We know you were making off with the weapon in a somewhat suspicious manner, Mr Frederick Ebenezer,' he said, drawing himself up to his full formal height.

'Oh, no, old boy. It's just this. You see, there aren't any more bullets in it, and Uncle always kept it fully loaded. Happen to know that.'

'And so?' the redoubtable Hummbugg came trundling in.

'Well, and so, Inspector, find the bullets taken out of the gun, and I'd say you'd found your murderer.'

Fred yawned again.

'Sergeant, search the house.'

It took the sergeant, who in spite of his pallor, was a robustly active youth, only two and a half hours to search the house. But at last he came back to the study with in his hand five fat revolver bullets.

'Well,' Hummbugg grunted, 'where d'you find 'em? Took you long enough.'

'In the bedroom assigned to the Hon. Robert Crayshett-Clark,' the sergeant replied. 'Hidden.'

'Then why haven't you brought Bob Cratchit back down with you, lad? He'll have made his escape by now.'

'He's just outside, sir.'

'Then why isn't he standing here in front of me? Jump to it, lad, jump to it.'

The sergeant jumped. Bob Crayshett-Clark, man-about-town, debonair, not quite wearing an eyeglass, was standing in front of Inspector Hummbugg.

'God bless us every one,' Hummbugg said, sadly shaking his great pink head. 'I'm disappointed in you, Crayshett, father of a boy as good in every way as Tiny—'

'Father?' Bob Crayshett-Clark exclaimed. 'I assure you, Inspector, I have never even contemplated matrimony. Much less . . . Well, much less.'

'That is as may be, sir,' said Hummbugg, loudly blowing his snout to remove the two tears that had crept from his eyes at the thought, however mistaken, of Tiny Tim. 'But there's still the matter of certain bullets concealed in your room.'

Bob Crayshett-Clark flicked a minute scrap of lint from his beautifully tailored suit.

'Come, Inspector,' he said, 'I'm not such an idiot as to hide bullets from a gun I'd just shot someone with in my own room.'

'That's what I calls common sense,' Mrs Craggs put in from the shadows.

'Well, then—' Hummbugg began.

But the Hon. Bob at once answered the question the inspector would eventually have got round to asking.

'Last night,' he said, 'a person dressed as Santa Claus entered my room thinking I was asleep. I cannot name a name, but I feel it my duty to mention that that fellow Parst, hardly one's idea of a gentleman, had been going about all morning searching for his spectacles. Should you by chance have seen a pair at the scene of the crime, I think I can leave you to draw your own conclusions.'

He withdrew.

[167]

Mrs Craggs, still watching from the shadows, drew her conclusions. The pale sergeant drew his conclusions. They waited. At length Inspector Hummbugg arrived at his conclusions.

'Sergeant,' he said thoughtfully, 'have you observed anything in the hall in the nature of a pair of spectacles?'

'Yes, sir. I have just been looking. There's a pair caught up in the Christmas tree. And, sir, I have asked Mr Parst to step in.'

Mr Parst, blinking so distractedly that his future as a speculator in futures seemed particularly in doubt, forestalled the question working its way up Inspector Hummbugg's capacious gullet.

'You're a policeman,' he said. 'Ought to be good at finding things. You noticed my glasses anywhere? Can't see a damn thing without them.'

'Yes, sir,' Hummbugg said portentously. 'A pair of spectacles has been found caught in the Christmas tree not five yards from the body of the late lamented Mr Ebenezer.'

'Ah, good. Well done. Credit to the force. Let me have them, will you?'

'It will be my duty,' Hummbugg pronounced, yet more portentously, 'to retain them as evidence in any criminal trial that may or may not take place.'

'Ah,' said Mr Parst, 'so you've got someone in your sights, eh? Good work. Spotted something clenched in the corpse's fist, I dare say. Fine piece of detection.'

Another question was perhaps moving slowly up Inspector Hummbugg's gullet. But before it had reached the air Mr Parst had gone.

The sergeant coughed. A pale cough, but enough to draw attention.

'Shall I take a close look at the corpse, sir?' he asked. 'At his fists, or something?'

'No, lad, you will not. If a close search is in order, it'd better be done by an expert.'

The three of them returned to Mr Ebenezer's body, still half-buried in bright Christmas crackers. Ponderously Inspector Hummbugg peered at both the fists, which were every bit as clenched as Mr Parst had indicated.

'Nothing,' he said at last. 'Trying his tricks, mark my words. Sergeant, have you ever seen a man arrested for murder? Well, if you haven't, you're just about to see that happening to a certain Mr Parst.'

'Only one moment,' said Mrs Craggs. 'If you'd spent as much o' your life a-looking fer little bits o' dirt as what I 'ave, you'd of seen what's just peeking out between them third an' fourth fingers there.'

Inspector Hummbugg returned to the corpse. His sergeant peered over his massive shoulder.

'Why, yes, sir,' he said. 'A tiny bit of green material. And, sir, when I was taking fingerprints I saw that Mr Pressent—he's the one who's a theatrical angel, sir, backs shows and that—though dressed in a green country suit, with green socks and even a green handkerchief in the pocket was wearing a pink bow-tie.'

'An' when 'e arrived 'ere,' added Mrs Craggs, ''e was wearing a green 'un. You can draw a conclusion from that, if you like.'

'Sergeant,' said Inspector Hummbugg, 'didn't I tell you five minutes ago to bring Mr Pressent down here?'

'No, sir, you—Yes, sir. Yes, Inspector, you did.' The sergeant was learning, perhaps.

Soon Mr Pressent, green as the holly decorating the hall, was brought in.

'Charles Pressent,' Hummbugg began without preliminary, 'I am arresting—'

''Ere,' said Mrs Craggs, 'shouldn't you be asking 'im, afore you go saying who you was a-going to arrest, why 'e put all them crackers round the corpse?'

'And why,' said Hummbugg, before he had time to think, 'did you put all them—that is, all those crackers round the corpse?'

Green-clad Mr Pressent went green to the gills.

'Ask 'im if it weren't to make it look like Fifi Yettercumb done the murder,' said Mrs Craggs.

'Was it to make it look as if Fifi Yett—Was it to create the appearance of Miss Yettercumb—er—doing the murder?'

Mr Pressent turned from green to blushful red.

'Look, Inspector,' he said, 'I happened to be coming down here last night to—to see if Ebenezer, whom we had left half-asleep in his chair, was all right, and—'

'Or p'raps,' said Mrs Craggs, 'you was creeping down dressed up as a Santa to see if it was a good time to put the poor old devil out of 'is Christmas misery.'

'Inspector, never mind why I was coming down. The fact of the matter is I found Ebenezer dead, and I thought that the police might, well, might suspect me myself.'

'Which,' said Mrs Craggs, 'seeing as 'ow it was probably your intention to murder the poor old feller anyhow was pretty much on the cards.'

'Be that as it may, Inspector. The thing is I—er—thought it better your attention should be directed elsewhere, and recalling that awful little Fifi's threat earlier in the evening I decided to put all Ebenezer's crackers where she had said she would like to see them. Why, it is quite probable she did in fact kill him.'

At which the door burst open and that awful little Fifi flung herself in.

'You rotten swine,' she said, 'what for joo pick on me? I may've thought old Eb was a bloody bore, yacking on about Christmas and that. But I wouldn't ever have murdered him, not however much I could do with a hundred thousand quid.'

'Well, I don't know what to say,' Inspector Hummbugg murmured.

'But I do,' said Mrs Craggs. 'I got this to say to you, Miss Fifi. If you think it's so bad o' Mr Present 'ere to try to plant the job on you, why did you go an' write that note on old Ebenezer's typewriter an' put it on the chair to make it look as if it was Mrs Feswick what done it?'

Now it was the turn of Fifi Yettercumb to look ashamed, though she hardly managed as deep a blush as Mr Present.

'Oh,' she said, 'might as well own up. What I did was look through and through that book till I found some good words, and then I picked them out on old Eb's typewriter. I thought that'd teach that snobby bitch to say I didn't even know how to read.'

'But, wait a moment,' the sergeant broke in, his pale face alight with intellectual triumph. 'That note wasn't typed. It was written on a word-processor. Dot matrix.'

'O' course it was,' Mrs Craggs said. 'An' who do you think by? That Mrs Feswick, o' course.'

At once the door opened, and Bonny Feswick stood there. 'Well,' she said, 'when I came down to the hall here, dressed up as Santa Claus I don't mind admitting, and found someone had already done the deed and tried to make it look as if it was me, I wasn't going to take it lying down.'

'Do you mean to say, madam,' the young sergeant jumped in with youthful outrage, 'that you went up to Miss Marylee Jacob's room and used her word-processor?'

'Look,' Bonny Feswick replied cheerfully, 'I wasn't going to let her cut me out with that dishy young man if I could help it, was I?'

And then to the surprise of everyone—except perhaps Mrs Craggs—the door burst open again and Marylee Jacob came storming in.

'You bitch,' she said to Bonny Feswick. 'Why, if—'

She got no further.

Mrs Craggs had a word to say.

'Just a minute. Suppose you tells us who it was what crep' into young Fred's room, knowing the way he slep' an' slep', an' put 'is fingers round the gun. After you 'ad come down 'ere, all in your Santas too I dare say, an' found old Ebenezer dead with a clue pointing to you?'

Marylee was made of too much brass ever to blush. But she did look a little put out.

'All right,' she said, 'But I didn't like the way Fred kept hinting I had a thing about him. As if I would. When he'd fall asleep before I'd even . . .'

'Sergeant,' said Inspector Hummbugg, going a pinker shade of pink, 'suppose you go and fetch Mr Frederick. I dare say you'll find him dozing off somewhere. Ho, ho, ho.'

'In an armchair next-door, sir,' the sergeant said, half a minute later, leading in a yawning, stretching Fred.

And this time Hummbugg turned directly to Mrs Craggs.

'Well?'

'Now let's 'ave the truth,' Mrs Craggs said to Fred. 'When the inspector 'ere accused you o' the murder just now you thought you'd better be on the safe side an' make it look like someone else done it, didn't yer? So you went off an' put them bullets in Bob Crayshett-Clark's room. That gun was never as empty as what you made out, was it?'

'Got it in one,' Fred said, with a rueful shake of his head. 'Not very decent to try and pin it on old Bob. But I couldn't think of anything else.'

And the door burst open. Once again.

It was the Hon. Robert Crayshett-Clark.

'Well, damn it all,' he said, 'I do think you might have hit on somebody else. I mean, a fellow doesn't like to be accused of murder, even if he hasn't done it.'

'Then why,' said Mrs Craggs, stepping smartly forward, 'did you go an' pinch poor old Mr Parst's spectacles from 'is room an' leave them a-dangling on that there tree?'

'How do you know that!'

'Well, stands to reason Mr Parst couldn't never 'ave shot old Ebenezer, not without 'is glasses, 'im being blind as a bat when 'e ain't got 'em on. So someone must 'ave tried to plant the job on 'im. An' you was as likely as any, seeing there ain't 'ardly no one else left.'

The Hon. Bob looked round the room.

'There's Mr Pressent,' he said. 'He is, ha, ha, present.'

Now Inspector Hummbugg, almost all the suspects eliminated, moved into resolute action.

'So, Mr Pressent,' he said, 'suppose you account for the dead man having in his clenched fist a tiny piece of green material, which I happened have to observed. Taking into account you are no longer wearing your green bow-tie.'

Mr Pressent went pink as the tie beneath his chin.

But Mrs Craggs came at once to his rescue.

'That green tie, which I 'appened to point out to yer, Inspector, bein' clutched in the dead man's 'and, can't mean our friend 'ere murdered 'im. Old Ebenezer was shot, you know, 'e couldn't 'ardly 'ave wrenched off the tie o' the man what shot 'im, could 'e?'

'No,' said the young sergeant, careless at last of all promotion. 'Of course he couldn't have. So how did that tie get there?'

Mrs Craggs went over to the door and jerked it open. Mr Parst, speculator, was standing there, ear pressed to a panel attempting to see the future without having to speculate.

'Well?' said Mrs Craggs.

'Oh, well, dash it. Might as well admit it. When I found my specs had been taken from my bedside table I wondered if they'd been made away with for a purpose. So I came down here, and could just make out that poor old Ebenezer was dead. Not moving, you see. So I groped my way up to the first room I came to—I suppose it was Pressent's—grabbed an article of clothing and managed to stuff it into the body's fist. Did I get it all in?'

'You did, you swine,' remarked Mr Pressent.

And now from somewhere inside Inspector Hummbugg there came a curious, querulous rumbling.

'Well,' he said at last, 'if none of them murdered Mr Ebenezer, who for heaven's sake did?'

'Why,' said Mrs Craggs, 'simple enough. Tiny Tom's the one. 'Im an' 'is talk o' seeing a Santa creeping in. Nothing to 'ave stopped 'im being the killer 'imself. An' as to motive, provided for 'e may 'ave been but 'ow well was 'e provided for? Not with a hundred thousand quid. You can bet yer boots on that. So when 'e 'ears all this lot was getting that much each, what should 'e do but shoot the mean old Scrooge what gave 'im such a pittance.'

'And hhhad he done it, that Tom?' Mrs Milhorne asked, blinking.

'I told yer, didn't I?'

'Yaiss. Yaiss, but what I can't understand is I never saw nothing about hhhim in the paper. On trial and that.'

'Nah. Well, you wouldn't 'ave done, would yer? Not with old Hummbugg needing almost till New Year's Eve to catch on. Tiny Tom just 'opped on the nearest reindeer, I reckon, 'an skedaddled. 'Cos 'e ain't never been seen since.'

MAGE OF THE
MONKEYS

by Sydney J. Bounds

Sydney J. Bounds (b. 1920) has been a prolific
writer of science fiction, and westerns (under
the pseudonyms 'Wes Saunders' and 'James
Marshal'), during the past forty years, and
contributed several tales to the Fontana *Horror*
and *Ghost* series of anthologies.

It was going to be a hard winter. Outside, in the Gray's Inn Road,
carriage wheels had churned the snow to frozen mud and icicles hung
like stalactites. Inside, my office filled with smoke from a coal fire
that didn't want to burn, and I felt a persistent draught from the window
at my back.

I wore my thick coat and wondered if there was any point in staying.
It seemed unlikely that a client would turn out in this weather. I had just
made up my mind to leave early when footsteps echoed on the stairs.

The door opened, a man came in from outdoors and my eyes opened
wide.

My prospective client was a beefy man with reddish hair; his face was
flushed and he had a moustache like the bristles of a scrubbing brush. He
wore a shirt with short sleeves, wide open at the neck, thin cotton
trousers and he was sweating.

Tears ran down his face and he swore as he tore off his shirt, dropped
his trousers and collapsed in the chair on the other side of my desk.

[174]

I controlled my dismay. Either he was drunk, or mad, but I felt confident I could handle him if I had to.

He was panting as he blurted out, 'Can you lift a curse? I'll pay you. I'll pay anything. I can't stand much more of this.'

'Do you mean a spell?' I asked.

'I suppose so—I don't know. That's your department, isn't it? I'm jinxed. I keep dropping things because they're too hot to hold. I keep drinking and sweat till I stink. I've tried cold baths. Nothing helps for long—'

He broke off, and leapt out of the chair. Smoke curled up from the seat.

'Hell! I've lost my girl—she broke our engagement because I had to strip off. I can't sleep properly. I could lose my job—I work at the zoo and the uniform's thick and heavy. I've sent a message to say I'm off sick.'

I frowned. This sounded like a thermocular spell, where the molecules of a body are speeded up. It was a spell discouraged by the Magician's Guild as dangerous; obviously, it could lead to spontaneous combustion. It wasn't banned because it had a use in special circumstances.

'Your name and address?' I asked quickly.

'Haley. "Ginger", my mates call me. Thirty-three Gloucester Road, St Pancras.'

I put a communications spell on my crystal ball to call the Guild's registrar. She was snappy as a turtle and came back scowling.

'I do wish people wouldn't waste my time. There's nothing listed under that name at that address.'

The crystal clouded and I frowned again. All spells on human beings have to be registered. I didn't like what this indicated, but I was bound to help.

I got out a release form and handed Haley a pen. 'Just sign here and—'

He fumbled the pen like an English cricketer and threw it from him. 'My hand!'

I sighed. It wasn't strictly legal, but I felt sorry for him, so I ran an interference spell first. Immediately he began to calm down.

'This is only temporary,' I warned. 'I'm superimposing on the original spell, so the worst effects cancel out. This will give me time to locate the mage—and his client—and see what I can do to persuade them to lift the spell.'

'You're taking my case then, Master Weaver?'

I nodded. 'As soon as you sign, I can get started.'

Haley hesitated, and I thought he might try to bluster his way out of the situation but finally, reluctantly, he picked up my pen and signed. I wondered what he was trying to cover up.

I got the name of his girlfriend and her address while he was putting his clothes on. Then he left in a hurry.

I opened a file and jotted down some notes, intrigued by the case. Who would have cast such a spell? It was a particularly nasty thing to do, and I wondered about the reason for it.

It couldn't be a Guild member because the spell hadn't been registered. And a black magician wouldn't risk death for such a minor spell. A wild talent? Possible, but the case didn't have that sort of feel to it.

I put on my fur hat and went downstairs. A few snowflakes were falling and the sky was dark. The magic carpet operators had quit, and I couldn't blame them. I struggled up the Gray's Inn Road and signalled a carriage.

'Barnsbury Road, Islington.'

It wasn't warm inside the carriage, but at least I was out of the wind. The horses plodded, passing shoppers with Christmas trees and turkeys, and I felt every icy rut we jolted over.

Barnsbury Road was long and dreary, filled with houses depressingly alike and grey with soot. Number fifty-seven was no different. I paid off my cab and knocked on the door.

A buxom woman in an apron answered.

'Julie Beeson?' I asked.

The woman turned and shouted, 'Julie! Another bloke for you.'

'Really, Mrs Soames!'

The girl hurrying along the passage was plain with brown hair, a pointed nose and a sniffle. Her voice was common, but she dressed up, cosmetics overdone and her scent overpowering.

'I don't know you,' she said.

I flashed my card, the one that glowed and magically vanished.

'Ooh, a private mage! You'd better come in.'

I followed her along the passage to a small room filled with knick-knacks. It was warm compared to outside, and smelt musty.

'I've only just got in,' she said. 'The shop shut early due to the weather.'

I perched on a padded chair and offered a cigarette. She refused, and I lit one myself.

'It's about Ginger Haley. I understand you've broken your engagement.'

Julie sniffed. 'That's true. It was his own fault, the way he behaved. No young lady can be expected to—'

I raised a hand. 'I'm not criticising. It appears that Mr Haley is under a spell, and he's asked me to remove it.'

'Mr Haley's a rough sort of man,' she said coldly. 'I like a man who is a man, but he could be cruel at times. Anyway, I prefer Ted.'

She was easy to read. She intended to move up the social scale, and Ted was the next rung on her ladder. I couldn't see her paying a mage to lay a spell on her ex-fiancé. As far as she was concerned, Haley's behaviour was just an excuse to make the break.

'Fair enough,' I said mildly, and asked for Ted's surname and address. Her new boyfriend certainly had a motive for getting rid of Haley.

Apparently he had a studio in York Road, only a few streets away. I stubbed out my cigarette, wished Julie Merry Christmas and decided to walk. The sky was darker as snow clouds thickened and it looked as if we'd have a white Christmas.

The studio was a converted warehouse and Ted Dench a big man wearing cords and a sweater. He carried a hammer, and a powdering of dust covered the hairs on the back of his hands.

There was a stove, but it didn't throw out much heat in that barn of a place.

'I can't take on another commission at the moment,' Dench said abruptly. 'As you see, I'm busy.'

He was working at a large block of stone, shaping it with hammer and chisel to carve—? I wasn't sure, but I was curious.

'It's not about your work,' I said. 'I've called about Julie and Mr Haley.'

'Is he bothering her?'

'No, no.' I introduced myself. 'Someone's paid a mage to make life hot for him.'

'Well, it wasn't me,' Dench said, and went back to chipping at his stone. 'I don't need to hire any mage. I've heard about Haley from Julie and, if he doesn't leave her alone, I'll deal with him my way.'

He raised his hammer threateningly. Obviously the sculptor was no mage. Artists rarely are, I've noticed.

'Hear me? I'll flatten 'im.'

'I hear you,' I said, and gestured at the half-finished statue. 'What is it?'

'What is it?' He glowered at me. 'Should be obvious enough. It's a statue of Julie.'

[177]

'Oh,' I said, and left with the feeling that Julie Beeson would be moving on again when she saw it.

I walked to the hire station at the corner and, while I waited for a cab, warmed myself at the brazier and bought a baked potato and hot chestnuts. Then I went home and put an extra blanket on the bed, realising I was no nearer the who and why of Ginger Haley's tormentor.

The next day was Christmas Eve. I struggled out of bed, made a hot drink and looked out of the window. Snow was still falling, so I took a carriage to Regent's Park. Outside the zoo, street vendors were selling holly and mistletoe and toy reindeer.

The only animals on view were the polar bears and sea-lions. I went straight to the office and asked to see the Head Keeper.

I waited in reception while they sent a messenger. He was not in a festive mood when he arrived.

'Some people don't realise that looking after animals is work,' he grumbled.

I showed my card and told him I needed information about Haley.

The Head Keeper, after introducing himself as Mr Michelmore, looked sharply at me.

'You know him? When's he coming back? I'm not happy when a keeper goes sick—especially at this time of year. You can tell him from me he'll lose his job if he isn't careful.'

'I'll tell him. What sort of man is he?'

'All right, I suppose. It's a problem getting good keepers. Haley does his job, though he's a bit rough with the animals at times. I have to keep an eye on him.'

'Is anyone after his job?'

'Not that I know of. I'd be glad to have someone apply.'

'Will you let me know if anyone does?'

Michelmore nodded curtly, as if he considered that an unlikely event. But it could be a possible motive, I thought, if somebody was after Haley's job.

'Which animals does he look after?'

'The monkeys.'

I went outside and trudged through the snow, following signs pointing to the monkey house. There were few people about and not many inside, even though it was heated. The smell nearly made me choke.

The monkeys were bigger than I'd imagined, with grey fur, black faces and long tails. They chattered incessantly as they swung from branches or poked a paw between the bars as someone offered a handful of nuts. I studied the few visitors, but only one caught my interest.

He was huge, coffee-coloured and balding. He wore a heavy top-coat and was big enough to make Ted Dench look ordinary. What attracted my attention was the way he talked to the monkeys and the way they seemed to listen, as if what he said made sense. I moved closer but couldn't understand a word; he spoke a language I didn't recognise.

He bowed to the monkeys and glided towards the door, moving with a kind of dignified grace. I'd never seen a big man move like that and it startled me.

I noticed that a keeper had been watching him too, and engaged the man in conversation.

'Funny bloke, that Indian,' the keeper confided. 'He comes here every day and chats away to the langurs. Bonkers, if you ask me.'

I asked about Haley.

'Ginger? He's lazy, I reckon—we'll see 'im back in the New Year. Me, I'm an elephant man and I'll be glad to get back to 'em. Maybe Michelmore'll get someone else—cruel, Ginger can be, with animals.'

I left, stopped at a café for a kidney pie and hired a cab to take me back to the office. On the way, I spotted a poster:

Grand Christmas Eve Performance
INDIAN DANCE TROUPE
Exclusive to the Tivoli

The face on the poster was that of the man I'd seen in the monkey house and it gave his name: *Ramada*.

I called to the driver and changed my destination to the *Tivoli*, where I booked a seat for that evening's performance. Just out of curiosity, really.

The audience was sparse so I had a clear view of the stage from the stalls. I'm not much of a dancing man, but these Indians got me excited. I'd never imagined dancing could be so thrilling and Ramada, the leader of the troupe, was something special. The way he weaved among the other dancers, leaping high in the air and spinning like a top as if he were made of india-rubber made me wonder if he had any bones at all in his body.

But it was the climax of the show that made me catch my breath.

When the curtain swept back after the interval I saw, on stage, a golden statue of a monkey. Now the dancers moved solemnly, their brightly coloured robes forming a kaleidoscope as they bowed and swayed before the statue. When they ended up on their knees, I realised they were worshipping a monkey god.

My scalp prickled. If Ramada truly worshipped a monkey god and it wasn't just a stage show . . .

I could hardly wait for the performance to end so I could go backstage and confront him.

I found him sitting alone before the mirror on his dressing table, calm and breathing easily after his exertions. I hoped I was doing the right thing in coming alone; close up, he looked as if he could break me in two without raising a sweat.

I told him who I was and that I represented the Guild.

'It's about the zoo keeper, Haley—'

Ramada frowned. 'White trash, red hair, right?'

'Did you pay a mage to put a spell on him?'

He smiled benignly.

'Did you think I need to, Master Weaver? In my country, too, we have witch doctors who can work a hex. This man Haley insulted the monkey god, Hanuman. Monkeys, you must understand, are sacred animals. Your Guild was not involved. I worked the hex myself.

'I caught him jabbing a monkey with an iron point on a stick. Such behaviour could not be tolerated. I was disgusted, and punished him myself.'

'That's fair enough,' I said mildly. 'I don't approve of cruelty to animals either, but he's been punished enough. He's lost his girl and reached the end of his tether. He may lose his job, too. I suggest you can now remove your spell.'

Ramada shook his head. 'I disagree, Master Weaver.'

'If he dies, you'll be held responsible.' I was stretching a point; I could run interference indefinitely and, anyway, I couldn't prove a thing.

The Indian said nothing, so I pressed him harder.

'I imagine your tour is doing well? And you've practised magic without a licence, which is illegal in this country. The Guild won't like that, and could have you deported.'

White teeth flashed in a brown face. 'Blackmail?'

'I prefer to put it another way. In England, we call this time of year the season of goodwill.'

Ramada looked at me steadily.

'Very well. But goodwill should work both ways, don't you think?'

So I got the hex lifted from Ginger Haley and collected my fee. I don't know what he's doing now, and don't want to, but he's no longer working at Regent's Park.

I agreed readily to Ramada's condition, and a quiet word with the Head Keeper ensured that he didn't get his old job back.

NOSTALGIA

by Maggie Ross

Maggie Ross studied art and qualified as a
teacher before taking up a career as a writer. Her
first novel, *The Gasteropod*, won the James Tait
Black Memorial Prize for the best novel of 1968.
During the past twenty years she has written
several plays and short stories, and was a regular
contributor to the *Ghost Book* series edited by
Rosemary Timperley.

The memory plays tricks. I think I remember it all so clearly but the two festivals keep merging into one, leaving me perplexed. Could the weather have been so identical—both Christmases icy cold with the frost sparkling on the turned earth? When daylight faded I twice remember the stars flickering huge and blue in the blackness of the evening sky. I remember the snow, I remember my feelings. On both occasions I was filled with a strange elation compounded of unfulfilled desires and my release from them. What I had wanted was taken away from me. When he'd gone it was a whole year and another festival later before I realised my good fortune. I try not to think of him.

All I'd wanted was to be near him. I had no feelings of guilt that he was married to someone else and that she was supposed to be my friend. After the Christmas that James disappeared I stayed close to Emily as a friend would, comforting her as best I could with phrases she clearly didn't need, spoken as Mother would say, with a forked tongue.

It seems now such a stupid waste of twelve months repining someone's disappearance when he'd clearly wanted it and clearly willed it with all his being. I should have spent my time looking for a more tangible man worthy of my spirit, not consoling his widow (if widow is the right word) in the small hope of being close by at his reappearance. For it was Emily who was convinced that James hadn't gone for good, her certainty so believable that if I didn't at least once a month make the trip to their house, to hang about however unhopefully, I was unsettled.

It was no surprise that she asked me to spend the following Christmas with her, for visitors were few since James had gone. People watched Emily from a distance, comparing notes, putting her through their own private guilt tests. And there was plenty for them to chew on. Over the year of James's disappearance her eccentricities had proliferated, so that when she proposed celebrating this Christmas in exactly the same manner as the previous year, exactly as if James hadn't gone at all, I took it as another sign that she was losing touch with reality. The same guests were to be invited, the same decorations hung, the same food eaten, the same games played. She said he would like it.

As far as I was concerned she'd let me down. I told her. For one whole year hadn't all my conversations been about breaking with the past, facing the future with a new attitude, preparing for a new existence alone? She'd seemed to agree, if one discounted the number of times in a day she felt obliged to mention James. From that I couldn't veer her: how right he was; how erudite; how commanding. And each time I heard his name a tiny part of me willed him to come back and fulfil her promise. But I was genuinely trying to point her towards a future in which she would stand like me on her two feet; like me enjoying single life; a good job with promotion. It was tiresome to hear her quoting James's praise of the good old days; irritating that she was forever harking back to the times when everyone—women most of all—knew their place in their small and cosy world. If my arguments overstressed the advantages of living now, they only served to convince me that Victorian times were not as marvellous as she kept claiming. I'd said the same to James, but his persuasion was altogether more alluring. He could paint me pictures of a past age that made the heart positively ache. 'There's a lot to be said for not knowing about the ills of the world, Marie. You should not be part of this dreadful nuclear planet,' he'd say. 'Think of being pollution free, media free and care free! Imagine living as a woman should—provided for and cared for somewhere where nothing changes.'

Surely, I said to Emily, she could now see how insidious was his attitude. He had stopped her working outside the home. Didn't her new single status mean the freedom to make a total break with the past?

Unable to do so totally myself, I charged her to forget James. If he returned, as she said he would, he should find her changed, not repining him and preparing in his memory an old-fashioned Christmas party.

And what if the family refused to come? With a small show of venom she replied that I had a very singular idea of singularity considering how attached to him I'd been. Besides, she said, James wanted it and that was that.

Mother declined Emily's invitation but she was the only one. She said it had been more than she could bear last year to see her so-called liberated daughter making a fool of herself over a married man. Be blowed if she was going to come again this year to watch her being hypocritical with his wife. Besides, why should she spend another Christmas Day of unutterable boredom dressed up like Mrs Cratchit playing charades? No electric light, no TV, her dog cowed and herself treated like a second class citizen. Positively barbaric. None of it would bring back a man who was probably either sunning himself in Bermuda, or lying in a shallow grave somewhere. I told her of Emily's idea that reconstructing the scene of James's disappearance might bring him back, but she merely sniffed and said 'poor Emily' in that special tone of hers. Unspoken was my feeling that if James had gone off on a whim, he was just as likely to fulfil Emily's prophecy by returning on the anniversary of his escape.

The others accepted—Bella and Edgar, Susan, Grandfather Poslate and cousin Denys. Uncle Ronald rang to say that Deborah wanted to know if it was going to be one of those Agatha Christie reconstruction-of-the-crime type of do's. Since there had been no crime as such it was difficult to grasp her meaning. Emily wanted us, I patiently told him, merely to come dressed in last year's costumes and enjoy ourselves. Ronald said they had decided to accept in a spirit of Christmas charity.

I got there early exactly as I had the previous year. It was approaching dusk. This time it was Emily who was in the back garden cutting the Brussels sprouts. All year she'd been busy in the garden, returning it to what it had been before the police dug it up. Her hands were purpled by the frost. In the long dress with the shawl round her shoulders she resembled some working woman in an old painting, even to the strange transparency of her cheeks. James's face had looked the same when I'd sought him out in the garden cutting sprouts last year. He'd smiled at me with a curiously triumphant smile which I knew was signalling 'Can't keep away from me, can you?' On the spot I'd made a small pledge to be more resistant.

'He'll come tonight,' Emily said, 'at eleven.' I thought her eyes looked slightly wild. Lately she had been distant with me and a little wary. A DC 10 making for Heathrow flew low over us, leaving in its wake a great stillness. A single star had appeared over the housetops.

'Will it snow?' I said. 'It did last year.' I remember it, the big flakes dropping and melting on my hot eyelids as I stood outside, staring unbelieving through the lit windows.

We went into the kitchen. I looked round me in amazement at the changes, trying to remember how many weeks it was since I'd last been there. The place was worthy of a museum.

'Everything is prepared but the gravy,' Emily said. 'It must be put to seethe. There will be apple sauce. And horseradish.'

Elderly iron pots were simmering on the cast-iron stove which, against all my advice, she had had installed some months previously. She picked up a cloth and lifted a saucepan lid. I heard her mutter, 'My, but the wood took a time to draw this morning.' On an ornate dresser was arranged a collection of ancient dishes and pans I'd never seen before. What, I asked, could have possessed her to replace the new steel sink with such an inadequate shabby stone one surmounted by a single elderly brass tap? She didn't reply. I'd noticed lately her withdrawal, the way she'd taken to ignoring questions and talking to herself.

'"Damask for the table makes it fair and suitable",' she said. She had lately acquired the habit of muttering to herself in doggerel: 'Sweet oil, emery, and turpentine assist the grate to make it shine'. 'If in me you put your trust, we shall never turn to dust.' Sometimes she sang snatches of old songs to herself. It did no good to remind her that thirty year olds did not as a rule go about the house in long skirts humming to themselves, or talking in riddles about preparations for departure.

'The chiffonier cleaned well,' she said. 'Ox gall was a good idea. Never would I have thought of it myself. And nothing exceeds the value of candle snuff. It brought up the pier glass quite wonderfully.'

She bent to the stove again. I saw how carefully her hair had been smoothed; how at ease she was in her constricting dress. '"Make your house fair as you are able, I rim the hearth and set the table."' She turned and smiled at me. 'Marie, I would be greatly obliged if you would see that the fires in the grates are drawing properly. I must busy myself a little while in here. So much to do. He's needed more than ever tonight, is he not?' I didn't like her brilliant smile.

There was a delicious smell of roasting goose in the house, commingling with such scents of polish and lavender and smoke a pang of

[185]

nostalgia momentarily pained me. And I thought there lingered another fainter perfume which wrinkled the nose and irked the memory. It followed me as I went from room to room, remarking the transformations with increasing amazement. All previous signs of modernity had been removed, even down to the banishment of gas fires in favour of open ones. In the fireplaces fenders and fire irons gleamed, coal scuttles were full. I poked at the coals with the toe of my buttoned boot wondering what had possessed her to turn her home into such a complete Victorian replica. How had she managed it? Then it occurred to me that for some months I hadn't set foot in many of these rooms, whose doors had been shut to me. Now they were framed, like the pictures, in green holly and ivy swathes. Great bunches of mistletoe hung from each ceiling.

I entered the dining room and stared about me. The table was already laid; two oil lamps with their engraved glass putti; last year's familiar china centre-piece; all the best cutlery. She'd remembered everything from last year, down to the cut-glass finger bowls, celery vases and cruets. I knew that madeira and port filled the shining decanters. On each fragile china plate she'd placed a favour exactly as before. Without looking at mine I knew it would be a MIZPAH silver heart with a ribbon knot. Now cosy it all was. How claustrophobic.

In a corner of the parlour the tree stood, its candles as yet unlit, its reflectors, tinsel and coloured baubles shimmering and twitching at my step. It stood beside the pianoforte that James used to play. By the fire the buttoned footstool was ready for Grandfather Poslate. Two strange metal stags at bay stood guard beside the lamps on the mantelpiece. There were only two Christmas cards. Both held James's signature. The room was more crowded than when I'd last seen it. Every surface had its scattering of ornaments and photographs, every chair its worked antimacassar and moquette cushion, every mirror its fringing. By comparison my shoulders looked exceedingly bare. I put a concealing hand to my throat for I could see in reflection James's photograph on the wall behind me. He was staring at me with his special knowing look, his pale face framed by the stiff white collar erect round his ears, the hair curling over it. I hadn't noticed before how tense he seemed and how his hands were clenched on the ludicrous rustic cork fence. It was hard to take my eyes from the twin sight of myself mirrored, so vulnerable in the antique costume, and the dominating man behind me. The skin of my neck began to creep, as if his fingers were lightly brushing away my make-up. And I was overcome by a momentary nostalgia for the time when a woman needed a man to lean on. As I left the room it could have been me that sighed.

Susan came first, complaining about the frost and the coldness of the bedroom where I took her to leave her reticule and cloak. She pulled a face at the bed with its old fashioned sheets and blankets, the hand-worked quilt, the warming pan on the wall. I felt constrained by nothing more than the sight of James's nightshirt lying neatly folded beside Emily's long, white nightdress.

'At least she still sleeps in here,' Susan said.

'Why not? Her conscience is clear.'

'He's never been found. They trawled the reservoir, you know.' She peered into the dim lead mirror on the chest of drawers, pinching her cheeks to bring some colour. I thought how essentially modern she was despite her clothes. She had none of my doubts and yearnings. 'He went out without his Ulster, or that ludicrous Gladstone bag. In the snow, remember? Nobody goes out at eleven p.m. in the snow in a velvet suit. But she can't have done him in later, can she? She was besotted with him.'

I remember the snow. I remember the ormolu clock had chimed hollow under its glass dome. We were sitting in a clutch in the parlour, waiting. We waited for a long while, watching Emily from the corners of our eyes to see what she would do next. She'd sat ramrod straight, her crinoline billowing out as if she would take flight upward. For some time she stared ahead as if in a trance, then the corners of her lips turned up in what passed for a smile. But her eyes were watery and cold. Mother was the one brave enough to ask what had happened to James. 'Gone,' Emily replied.

Gone just like that in mid-charade, leaving us all marooned in our foolish fancy dress wondering what to do next. 'He's gone without me,' she kept saying like a woman bereft. 'He's gone.' Only later did she admit to me privately that he'd begged her to go with him and she'd been too afraid. She wasn't ready then. Go where with him? But she wouldn't tell me. 'Go where?' I'd asked. 'Somewhere very safe,' she'd said. Her quivering white fingers had fluttered in the air. On each visit I had tried to extract from her the truth of his disappearance. But as the year progressed and Emily became more vague, less willing to take me into any confidence however small, I gave up and decided that she truly didn't know where her husband had gone that Christmas night. All I knew was that she wore no widow's weeds.

'He was in the house, Susan,' I said. 'I'm sure of it. I heard a door bang. She left him in the kitchen.'

'I don't know why you keep saying that when the front door was open.' Susan was always irritated by my defence of Emily, whose meek exterior she considered hid something more sinister. She shuddered. 'Cold, isn't it? Beastly things coal fires.' She removed a lace handkerchief from between her breasts and fanned herself. A strange gesture for one so patently modern. 'I don't know why everyone these days makes such a fuss about Victorian times. Look at it in here. Smoky. Draughty. Ghastly wallpaper. A wash-stand with a jug and basin for heaven's sake! Something disgusting in the cupboard underneath, I bet! Knick-knacks everywhere.'

'I like it,' I said. But all she replied was, 'Watch out she doesn't influence you. She's getting more and more peculiar. The other day I saw her talking to herself outside the library.'

'That's where James worked.'

She stared distastefully about her. 'Nothing but old books and knick-knacks. "A positive dust-trap", as Mother would say.'

'You needn't have come. You could have stayed with her and the dog!'

'And miss the fun! It was quite exciting here last Christmas,' she said. 'But I don't suppose it will be any good without James.' The arch look she cast in the direction of his photograph on the dressing table had me almost persuaded that she too had been attracted to him. I felt an urge to pick it up and look at his face more closely. He was staring at me with the same knowing expression as in the parlour portrait. Hastily I set him down, my thumb leaving a damp print on the velvet frame.

As we went downstairs Susan said, 'Funny smell in there. What does it remind me of . . .?'

The others arrived in pairs, carrying their umbrellas; it was going to be a replica of last year's weather. They stamped their feet and talked loudly, embarrassed to be in the house they hadn't set foot in since the previous Christmas. Emily was totally at ease and I admired her. She took muffs and mufflers, bonnets and top hats, apologising for her absent spouse who, she said, would be arriving later. She complimented each of them on their costume. Ronald complained that hiring charges had gone up since last year. Bella and Edgar were unnecessarily polite as if she were a stranger and not a niece. How they eyed the room as they stood over the fire sipping their negus, noting the changes with avid eyes.

I was cool with Bella, long suspecting her of having informed the police of my tête-à-tête with James in the pantry. She must have seen how I followed him there. Had she seen how I'd kissed him passionately, full on the lips? He nearly collapsed with the force of me. I can feel his moustaches still. She seemed not in the least put out by my coldness, whispering in my ear that she sincerely hoped we weren't going to have a seance, or one of those Ouija board experiments to try and bring James back from wherever he'd gone. Denys remarked how decorative the house had become since ... then he faltered. Edgar said he'd never beheld such a plethora of ornament and books. The house was taking on quite a vintage look. Ronald, wearing the Mr Pickwick suit that was too small for him, with the watch chain stretched tight across his belly, said that if the food was as good as last year he wouldn't be complaining. Last year after a surfeit of alcohol he'd disgraced himself by trampling the lawn before the police could stop him, shouting 'James, you bastard, where are you?' into the snowy night. I thanked heaven that temperance wasn't part of Emily's philosophy, for it was my determination to dim my faculties as soon as possible with drink. The others, I noted later, seemed to have taken the same vow.

Just like last year we ate formally in the dining room, using the old blue and white china and the best silver. A vacant chair was left for James. As before Ronald carved and Emily dished the vegetables; Grandfather set fire to the pudding. At the start everyone was subdued, casting odd glances at James's chair, and at Emily as if checking whether she might not break down in the face of such a heavy reminder of her loss. But she sat there like royalty in her garish tartan dress with the flounced sleeves, seeming not to notice how much liquor her guests were downing throughout the meal.

Gradually our spirits rose to last year's heights and we tucked into the goose and trimmings and pulled our crackers and put on our paper hats as if nothing unusual were happening. If now and then Emily turned to the empty chair with a wistful gaze, she seemed generally to be enjoying herself. For one usually so self-effacing she was behaving quite assertively, even managing to be charming. There was no doubt that by the end of the meal the tide had turned in her favour and everyone, including Uncle Edgar, was willing to give her the benefit of any doubt. The goose came and went. The pudding like a white cannon ball sizzled in a flurry of blue flames. Presents were opened just like last year: there were warm mittens for Grandfather and Edgar, for Denys a puzzle map of the Empire, for Ronald a writing box with sealing wax; for Bella and Deborah and me French plums and cinnamon sticks just like last time. Susan who had never been known to hold a needle, pulled a face at the replica of the silver thimble she'd been given last year. An embossed album—Emily's gift to James—was reverently laid on his empty place.

The oil lamps were lit and the curtains drawn. Fire flames danced on the shadowy ceiling. The decanters went round and round.

When darkness had long since fallen, I felt a kind of tension creep in among us. I began to watch Emily. There was a certain excitability discernible in her demeanour. She had gulped down two glasses of port and was fluttering her arms and pushing at her bracelets, much as she did on the night James went. But then her looks were all anxiety as if she really had had some premonition that he was about to go.

And Mother afterwards was convinced that James had walked out on Emily, although she was given to frequent changes of mind. Good riddance too, she'd said. Right that minute he was probably sunning himself on a Caribbean island with Constance Chisling. Why her? Mother said she'd seen them hobnobbing in the library last June twelvemonth; the implication being that James couldn't resist anyone in skirts. She didn't understand that his wonderful erudition drew women to him like a magnet. Not for him the everyday banalities of common conversation; he could hold one enthralled on any subject however esoteric.

Emily never appreciated his intellect. All she ever said was that James's fragile psyche needed careful nurturing lest it be pushed beyond the bounds of reason. She certainly took for granted that we should all defer to him. Once she confided to me how long it took to polish his boots. Denys's opinion was that he was touched, although he admitted that James knew more about things than the average person. James, he said, could take you on an historical tour of the past as if he lived there. Dates, details, nothing escaped him. He'd select a period and chew it right down to the bone. Denys it was who claimed he'd seen James riding a penny farthing along Back Lane. Mother had said that conversation with James was like running the marathon, except that with him you didn't know where you'd wind up. Eccentrics, she said, had never been to her taste, but that is probably because she is one herself. 'Can't see what you all saw in him,' she said to me. 'He was a terrible philanderer. Although I suppose anyone married to that mouse would have a wandering eye.' I told her it was character that mattered and she huffed at me. 'But I think I know what he saw in her,' she said. 'Take a good look at her one day.'

Mother was right, the resemblance became clearer every time I looked at Emily. That evening it was remarkable. She had the aquiline nose and bulbous eyes of Queen Victoria in her younger years; the sloping shoulders, the same slight but regal stature. The hair looped over her ears accentuated the likeness, and I felt as if, over the past year, that likeness had increased. I could also see in her face how fear and eagerness combined; how she tried to disguise her desire to get the dinner over and done with as quickly as possible. Her eyes went constantly to the clock. Grandfather Poslate, garrulous throughout the meal, was not to be rushed; he startled us all by suddenly wondering aloud what had become of James.

It was still in all our minds. Where had James gone? The police weren't at all satisfied with any of our explanations. How can one man disappear in a house full of people on a Christmas night? they'd asked. Didn't anyone see the going of him? Emily had said she did, but they discounted her, accepting that the distraught wife might answer a little strangely in the face of such an occurrence. And she had said some wild things. Once she'd said that James had just faded away; another that he was in a better place; she'd said that from time to time he came and gave her advice. Grandfather was of the opinion that Emily ought to have him back, as if, Ronald exclaimed, the fellow were wandering about outside waiting to be let in. All I could do was be grateful Mother wasn't there to egg Grandfather on, or put in unhelpful words about what I'd been up to that Christmas night. Not to mention Pugh her dog who, last year, had behaved so strangely.

At last our glasses were empty. There was nothing left on the tablecloth but opened walnut shells, one or two withered grapes, the cratered Stilton and the holly from atop the pudding: the remnants of a feast the equal we said to that Emily had prepared for us on the last occasion.

'Now it is time,' she said firmly.

Obediently we followed her into the parlour. Only I heard Grandfather complain that at least the fellow could open his present instead of leaving it lying there. Emily settled him with his drink and his stool by the fire. Little spots of colour had appeared on her cheeks. In the grate sharp flames flew upward. I saw Susan approach it and shudder. She raised one hand and brushed her shoulder as if brushing something away. Although the parlour was warm I too felt chilled. The trinkets on the Christmas tree had set up a rattling. Was there a draught coming from the windows? I went to release the heavy curtains from their cords. Outside the garden gleamed under a sky in which bright clouds were beginning to hide the stars. The scene was too familiar. It would have been preferable to shut it out but Emily stopped my hand. 'We must have them open,' she said. 'Remember? He wants it this way.'

She had forgotten nothing. Every minute of that previous Christmas

[191]

she seemed to have memorised. The candles were lit on the Christmas tree. She chivvied us into sitting in the same places; into eating roasted chestnuts whether we wanted them or not. We burned our fingers all over again picking raisins from the snapdragon, and ate her mince pies even though we were replete. I swear she instigated the same conversations and tried to elicit the same replies. We played only one uneasy game of Blind Man's Buff because no-one would admit to having knocked Ronald over. At exactly the same time of nine thirty-five Grandfather was nudged into wakefulness to hear Deborah's rendition of 'Cold was the Yule-tide fair' on the pianoforte. At the end the piano lid came down inexplicably on her fingers. 'Pay no heed,' Emily said. 'Time is short.' There was an increasing urgency in her behaviour that made us all nervous.

'She must be mad about charades,' Deborah whispered.

The clock chimed ten. 'We shall each perform our own charade in the same order as last year,' Emily announced. 'Susan first. Denys. Deborah and Edgar, then Uncle Ronald. Then myself. And James after me.' We exchanged glances. 'Last year circumstances ordained that Aunt Bella and you, cousin Marie, did not participate. But you must still play your parts. We can only pray that the absence of Aunt Mona and Pugh does not affect the outcome.'

Why such a feeling of apprehension came over me as I listened to her curious speech I do not know. I felt unable to breathe, as if the stays of my bodice had inexplicably tightened. The tiny house with its overloading of ornament was entrapping me. There was no escape until we, her cast of actors, had played out the drama to her satisfaction. She paid no heed to Susan's remonstrations at having to act the same word as last year. She set the chairs in order and told her with something like command in her voice, to go outside, wait as long as she did last time, then enter and begin.

Susan did as she was told, flouncing through the performance of AFFECTION with a slightly sullen air. I thanked heaven Mother wasn't there to comment on the stupidity of it all. Denys, whose memory frequently failed him, needed Emily's prompting before he could sort out his performance of DOMINATE exactly as the last time. Ronald managed to act out THEATRE well enough; dividing it as last year into THE and ATE HER. We argued the mispronunciation of his word almost as if we hadn't done it before. And Emily was beginning to look pleased. She had stopped begging us to slow down. She had even ceased reminding us not to reach James's turn until a quarter to the hour. Edgar fumbled through SEDUCE with bad grace, while Grandfather woke occasionally to sip his brandy and ask if it was all over yet.

'Now it is my turn to go,' Emily said. Ronald reminded her that last year at that very time James opened several bottles of claret. She was very excited. The hectic colour of her cheeks had spread right down to her lace tucker. The candlelight couldn't disguise her tense expression. 'Yes, we must behave exactly as we did last year,' she said. Dutifully we charged our glasses and drank.

At the door there was a moment's hesitation as Emily looked back at us. Her skin was pale and gleaming with sweat. Her lips parted; she seemed about to say something else. Then she silently gathered up her skirts and left the room.

I remember exactly what happened last year. James got up and followed Emily, saying she would doubtless need his help in making up a suitable charade, for she always relied on him in everything. His look in my direction told a different story. In his eyes I thought I saw an invitation.

Grabbing Pugh by the collar I pulled the dog to the door saying we both needed fresh air. Only Mother realised that my goal was James.

Pugh escaped from my grasp in the hall. There was no sign of James or Emily. The front door was open. Pugh ran through it and disappeared into the darkness of the garden. I ran out after him. The night had changed and it was very cold. White clouds were hiding the stars. It had begun to snow. The light from the windows lay on the lawn in yellow squares. Huge snowflakes were speckling the air.

I saw the family sitting in the parlour: Grandfather nodding by the fire; the back of Edgar's head; Ronald holding out the claret bottle to Mother; Susan saying something to Deborah, her face beautiful in the candlelight. I went round to the back of the house in search of Pugh. He was lifting a steaming leg at the sundial, lit by the lamplight from the kitchen window.

Despite the falling snowflakes I could clearly see the scene inside the kitchen. Emily was standing stiffly confronting James's wagging finger. Her head was moving from side to side. I couldn't see her face but I knew she was afraid. In his velvet suit, dark as the darkest shadow, he towered above her. The white finger threatened. The red curls shook with the vehemence of his words. My heart jumped as he moved towards her. She stood where she was. His expression changed and he began to stroke her hair. Some kind of pleading was taking place. Their hands met, their fingers were entwining, twisting together, separating. I was witness to something I didn't understand.

The dog was at my feet, and in bending to grab him I lost sight of the couple in the kitchen. When I looked again the room was utterly empty.

Once more I made a circuit of the house, dragging Pugh with me. Through the open curtains of the parlour I saw my relatives, now all sitting unnaturally still like waxworks. Emily was seated in their midst, upright and unrelaxed. All eyes were fixed on her. Later they told me she had come back into the room in some kind of strange trance. She wouldn't speak to them.

It was with difficulty I managed to get Pugh indoors again. An unusual silence seemed to have descended. There was no festive noise from the parlour. No sounds at all but the dog's claws on the boards as I dragged him resisting past the foot of the stairs. He looked up with real terror in his eyes. A great howl escaped him. Nervously I called out, 'Who's there?' But it was only James upstairs, looking at me from the landing. He came down slowly, ignoring Pugh who, on being released, slid whimpering on his belly into the shadows. I followed James into the kitchen, my only excuse being the amount of alcohol I had consumed, and the consuming passion that burned in me. I didn't want to remember Mother's words that I practised a one-sided form of liberation if the other woman always got the blunt end of the deal.

As I closed the kitchen door his arms came out to me. His hands clasped my waist and pulled me to him. I could feel his beautiful red whiskers on my face and smell the pungent patchouli. Round and round I turned him in my excitement. He put his lips to my ears and murmured something tense and excited that was lost as I sought his lips. I thought I heard 'I implore you!' and 'Come!'—a wonderfully open invitation. I kissed him so hard he reeled backward. His lips were cold on mine, but I thought they burned. I thought he said, 'Come with me. Come,' and it crossed my foolish modern mind that it would take precious minutes to remove the cumbersome crinoline, the stays, the petticoats.

Then it was that Aunt Bella came in and spoilt everything. I remember exactly what happened last year.

'We must behave exactly as we did last year,' Emily said before she gathered up her skirts and left the room. The others sent me after her, saying that it would do no harm to humour her by pretending to go in search of the absent dog.

The front door was open as before. As before I went outside. A few large snowflakes had begun to fall. I could feel them melting on my hot skin. White clouds were hiding the stars. I walked round to the parlour side of the house and saw the family sitting almost exactly as they had sat last year. Had it not been for Mother's and Pugh's absence I might have thought time had stood still: Grandfather Poslate nodding by the fire. Susan talking to Deborah and smoothing her side plaits in the mirror. Ronald holding the claret out to Edgar, Aunt Bella's mouth moving in animated conversation with Denys. Reluctantly I made my way to the back of the house as if in search of the dog. The yellow light from the kitchen window fell across the frosty lawn; shadows flickered over it and over my face as I reluctantly peered in.

I saw Emily standing in the kitchen beside the scrubbed table. Her body looked stiff and unnaturally slanted. It looked as if she were either leaning backward against a wind, or resisting some unseen force that was pulling her. I saw how her hands were stretched in front of her, the palms flattened by something I couldn't see. Her head was moving from side to side in negation, but even from outside in the garden where I watched I could tell how weak she was. Her head was shaking no, and no, and no again as she was inched inexorably towards whatever or whoever was coercing her. Unseen hands were tugging at her wrists. They had her by the sleeves, the shoulders. They were pulling her with incredible strength, and this time she could not refuse.

This time there was no dog to distract me. My eyes never left that scene. All my apprehensions had exploded into one terrible sense of urgency. I rapped on the window until my knuckles hurt in an effort to make her hear. But my eyes—or was it the window?—were clouding over. I shouted 'Don't go!' but she didn't really want to stay. She was already fading. With each shout she was disappearing from my sight. I heard myself calling 'Emily! Emily!' then both their names over and over. Then despite my heavy skirts I ran like a sprinter round the house and through the front door, bursting into the kitchen crying 'No! No!' just as Emily must have done before she gave in to his persuasions.

For she had gone. There was nobody in the kitchen. I gathered breath beside the glowing stove, with nothing but the steady hiss of steam from the big black kettle and distant laughter from the parlour to keep me company. It was no use going in search of her. I knew she couldn't be found. I knew James had called her and she'd gone to him.

Aunt Bella found me standing there. Wasn't it she who had discovered James and me together in the kitchen last year?

'What's all the hullaballoo?' she said. 'Where's Emily?' She hoisted up her crinoline and perched on the corner of the table. 'Funny smell in here. What is it? Patchouli? No wonder they call it grave dirt!' She wrinkled her nose in disgust. 'A lot of nonsense this charade thing. But I suppose we'd better get on with it.'

She seemed the worse for drink. 'Now,' she said, 'What next? Oh yes! I remember last year when I came in here to look for you, I found you talking to yourself.'

'You're wrong,' I said. 'Last Christmas James was in here with me.'

She shook her head.

But I distinctly remember last year. Bella came into the kitchen. James smiled as I sprang away from him. She asked who was I talking to? She said there was something wrong with the dog in the hall. She'd asked if James had thought of a word yet?

And James had replied, 'SUPERNATURAL' in an amused tone of voice. But Bella just waited, a questioning look on her face as if he'd said nothing at all. I should have known why. At the time I only thought she was hard of hearing.

'SUPERNATURAL,' I repeated for him.

She told me off. I shouldn't have given the word away, she said. Now James would have to think of another word, and I would have to go and tell him so. It wasn't clear to me then what she was saying.

She hadn't looked at James as he brushed past her. She didn't seem to see him go into the hall. I thought I heard the dog whine. I heard the bedroom door bang. I remember her asking what the devil was the matter with me. And who had been maltreating that dog? Couldn't I do something about the noise? I remember her pushing me out of the kitchen, telling me I must find James because they didn't want to wait all night; calling instructions after me again as if I were deaf or crazy.

'You do talk nonsense, Marie dear,' Aunt Bella said. 'Of course James wasn't in here last Christmas. Don't you think I'd have noticed? Where's Emily? We're waiting for her to tell us what we do next.'

She said later that my answer had been to push past her and make for the foot of the stairs shouting at the top of my lungs, 'Emily! Don't go with him. Don't go!'

I remember. I remember going upstairs, where they found me in the empty bedroom staring at my dim reflection in Emily's mahogany mirror. They said my dress was round my ankles, the petticoats piled like meringue on top. I was unlacing my bodice with feverish fingers. Had they not stopped me I would have stripped to my skin. I was babbling about putting away the past; about escaping from that house with its cloying atmosphere as far as fast as we all could run.

Months later I was still imploring them to listen to me. I told them he'd come for any one of us next. But they wouldn't listen. They said the house had a right to its history. How could I talk of destroying it? It must remain as it was until its owners came back. They talked about us all getting together there again this year to wait for them; of starting what they hoped would become a Christmas tradition. But I stopped my ears and refused to hear and made myself a promise never to go back.

THE RELUCTANT MURDERER

by Roger F. Dunkley

Roger Francis Dunkley (b. 1943) is a
schoolteacher with many excellent short stories
to his credit, most combining mystery and
horror with memorable black humour.

Midge, the gentle giant, picked up the carving knife, its steel blade glittering in the Christmas candlelight, and waited for his brother to return.

His fingers tightened round the handle.

He listened to Anthony's light, easy laugh from the hallway. 'Another of his women on the phone,' he thought. Couldn't his young brother give the professional charm a rest even on Christmas Day?

His knuckles whitened.

In front of him on the neatly laid table the turkey, which he'd spent all morning preparing, basting and garnishing, glowed crisp and golden, dispensing its tantalising odours around the cramped and shabbily furnished room. He'd attempted to garnish the room too—with bunches of holly from the landlady and streamers of tinsel left over from the act—but the effect was unconvincing. Nothing could transform theatrical digs into home—not even the magic of The Great Antonio and Midge—especially at Christmas.

'Tony!' he called. 'Happy Christmas,' he muttered grimly.

He twisted the knife-blade, scattering icy spangles round the room like the flashing of the scimitars they used on stage.

Another laugh, smoothly polished, from the hallway.

Midge stared into the lights dancing on the knife, feeling them begin to splash and flicker inside his brain. He gave an involuntary shudder. His breathing deepened, laboured. He tried to speak. 'Tony . . .' It was like calling from the abyss, reaching across the stars . . . Foreboding filled his mind, black shadows thickening in his head. He reached for words, struggled for gestures, but impossible forces weighted his arm. Danger. There was danger! Why could he not speak of it? . . .

'For heaven's sake, Midge! The knife. Give me the knife! . . .'

With a hollow rush darkness swallowed the lights and Midge found Anthony, his eyes wide and terrified, cringing beneath him.

'That's right, Midge. Give me the knife . . .'

Midge felt bewildered. Meekly he allowed himself to be settled back in his chair.

Tony took the knife, took charge—the capable one, as always.

'I'll carve,' he said. 'You take it easy. Are you feeling better now? . . . Look, Midge, you've got to tell the doctor about these blackouts. Next time we're home. Get some tablets. Hell, you could have killed me just then—you know that?'

Midge shook his head. 'Never,' he said.

'You don't know your own strength.'

'Kill my dearest kid brother?' said Midge.

'Your *only* kid brother!' Anthony poured two generous sherries and pushed one across the table. 'This really is a splendid turkey.'

Midge watched him pick up the knife. Memory sparked in his head. He struggled to capture it, hold it.

'That was Mrs Logan-Pearce,' said Anthony, savouring the juicy slivers of turkey as they peeled off his knife. 'On the phone. She was confirming the New Year's Eve booking, bubbling with champagne and Christmas spirit—full of call-me-Janice and why don't we make magic, perform a trick or two together sometime . . . Women!'

Midge stared at him, deftly wielding the knife. With a sudden glint of candle light the memory focused.

'Pass your plate, Midge.'

'No!'

Anthony's brow furrowed. 'Midge?'

'No,' he repeated. 'We mustn't do it. The New Year's Eve show. Let's say no. Cancel.'

Anthony sighed. 'She was only kidding,' he began. 'Flirting. Like all the others. It's nothing serious . . .'

Midge reached across and grasped his brother's wrist. 'I've got this feeling,' he said. 'I don't understand it.' He gestured helplessly, at the shining knives, the crimson tears amidst the holly thorns. 'I . . . I smell blood,' he said simply.

Anthony looked with concern into his big brother's eyes. 'You'll be talking about vibrations next,' he said, 'and opening at the end of the pier with your crystal ball! Look, we're in the magic not the mumbo-jumbo business. The only fortune we can tell is the one we make—and that'll be even smaller if we go around cancelling engagements. Right?'

Midge shook his head and released his grip.

'The dinner's getting cold,' said Anthony. He picked up his glass. 'Here's to us. A happy Christmas!'

'God rest ye merry gentlemen; let nothing you dismay . . .' sang the radio from the ornate mahogany sideboard.

'And a happy new year,' said Midge, shifting unhappily in his seat.

But on the whole Midge loved his younger brother and, despite these occasional bleak and bewildering moments of resentment, he had no real desire to murder him. When, therefore, the new year arrived and their hostess approached, he drained another quick whisky and dutifully bared his teeth in a fulsome smile.

'Goodwill to all men,' she said, earrings tinkling. 'And especially to the Great Antonio.' She produced a much-abused sprig of mistletoe and, stopping slightly, pressed a lingering New Year's kiss on Anthony's handsome cheek. She giggled lightly. 'Oh, and one for the magician's assistant.' She reached up to Midge, who towered awkwardly above them both, and delivered an appropriate peck. Midge's smile faltered; his hackles rose. It had always been the same. As a kid he'd always been The Other One, tall and ungainly. Likewise in the early days of the act during the tedium of bazaars and vicars, the panic of pigeons, squashed eggs and tangled bunting: 'Boys and girls, I want a big hand for Uncle Tony, the Kiddies' Friend, and . . . sorry, who? . . . Ah, yes . . . And Midge!' It would be the same tonight: 'Presenting the Great Antonio . . . And Midge.' Overgrown and overlooked, thought Midge; he had gone through life in parenthesis. He had gone through life like a ghost.

But, of course, he'd never seriously wanted to murder his brother.

'Look!' The lady had turned back to Anthony. 'Can I be just *un poco* presumptuous? I want a man. A stranger. The darkest, best-looking one

I can lay hands, so to speak, on!' The Great Antonio smiled. His chest enlarged. Midge looked down at them both, and winced. 'When the act's over and you've done, as they say, your thing,' she persisted, 'would you pander to the ethnic whims of our Scottish contingent'—she waved a jewelled hand towards an outbreak of loud laughter and kilts—'if they're still conscious by then, and bring in the New Year for us? You know, "first foot" it over the doorstep after midnight bearing good luck, coal and so forth . . .'

The Great Antonio reached out a small, immaculately groomed hand and pressed her fingers to his lips. 'Yours to command,' he said, and bowed.

The earrings flashed. 'Delicious,' she said: 'Isn't your brother just too—mm, delicious!'

Midge growled. 'Much too delicious,' he muttered. 'One of these days I shan't be responsible . . .' He helped himself to another whisky, and realised that a large lady, sprigs of tired heather straggling from her tartan head-band, was conferring with the hostess and pointing at him. He swigged defiantly.

'Wait a moment!' The hostess fluttered eye-lashes heavy with apology and mascara. 'A technical hitch! I'm reliably informed—by our Celtic friend here—that first foot has to be the *tallest* man available. So sorry.' Anthony shrugged with nonchalant charm. 'Your brother'll do. He'll have to.' She turned to Midge, on tip-toe. '*Would* you? So kind . . .' And without waiting for a response, she stepped forward, stilling the guests with an elegantly uplifted palm.

'Cabaret time, everybody!' she announced. The party-goers ceased glittering expensively at one another and turned expectantly to the small stage. Lights dimmed promisingly.

'A warm welcome, ladies and gentlemen, for the Great Antonio and—' she hesitated, remembered '—and Midge.'

Midge glanced at Anthony. Of course he loved his brother—really. Anthony grinned and squeezed his arm. Grimly Midge rearranged his features into professional jollity and, with a splash of cymbals, the show began.

Baubles came and went in predictable puffs of multicoloured smoke; pigeons fluttered on cue, more or less; blinking rabbits and miracles occurred with routine panache. Not until they were well launched upon the mystifying marvels of the hypnotic mind-reading routine did drama interrupt the polished suavity of the performance.

It was standard procedure: Midge, after a few histrionic passes and incantations from his brother, had sunk into the usual deep-breathing trance, which he could now contrive quite convincingly, and had suffered the transparent, black-velvet 'blindfold' to be wrapped with extravagant care about his eyes; Anthony was moving purposefully among the audience, the star of the show, asking the customary coded questions.

'My left hand. What do I hold in it?' demanded the Great Antonio of his supine assistant on the stage.

Midge stirred. He pressed white fingers against his damp forehead. 'Take your time.'

'It's a wrist-watch,' he said heavily. 'A lady's . . .' But his voice was slurred and thick. His chest heaved and his breathing deepened.

Anthony grew uneasy. He'd warned Midge earlier about drinking before an act.

'The spirit's been meddling with spirits it doesn't understand,' chuckled a drink-heavy voice behind him.

'Cheers!' called a red-cheeked youth anxious to impress the blonde at his table, and raised his glass. 'Tell us the future then, great spirit. Will there be a New Year at midnight, eh?' The girl tittered, pouted him a kiss across the table, then lapsed into silence with an abrupt and startled whimper.

'The future!' The voice was deep and thrilling. It came from Midge, but it resonated strangely in the room.

The Great Antonio stifled his alarm and admiration. This was a new Midge, a Midge with initiative, a consummate actor. He took his brother's lead. 'Look into the seeds of time,' he said. 'Tell us about the future.'

Midge raised an imperious arm. The audience leaned forward.

'A man,' he intoned hollowly, 'will die tonight.' He gestured impressively. 'It is determined. When the bells ring.' The audience followed his pointing finger. 'I will murder that man!'

The guests stared at the Great Antonio, suddenly pale before the finger's unequivocal sentence.

The Great Antonio stared at his brother.

Midnight approached.

With order restored, guests raised glasses and voices, assured each other this was a New Year's Eve to remember, and waited for the cabaret to resume. Behind the scenes, voices were lower and more intense.

'I wasn't pretending!' Midge shivered again recalling his involuntary trance. 'It must happen,' he repeated bitterly. 'If the future's fixed, there's nothing we can do to alter it.'

'The show,' insisted the Great Antonio, with more urgency than originality, 'must go on.' He helped himself to a couple more indigestion tablets.

'But the prophecy, Tone. . . Believe me: that wasn't *me* speaking . . . The future . . .'

Brother Anthony, the erstwhile Kiddies' Friend, snorted. 'There'll be no future,' he said, 'if we don't finish the show.' He glanced at his watch. 'No future for us. We both die.' He looked sadly back down the long, struggling years. All that effort and experiment; all those despairing rehearsals; all those Women's Institutes from Peebles to Pangbourne . . .

Midge watched his brother, the inspiration of their act, the brains, the personality behind their success. 'He has more to lose than me,' he thought. 'How *could* I murder him?'

Their hostess reappeared. 'Well? . . .'

Midge shrugged helplessly. 'The question is,' he murmured, 'how to alter an unalterable fate?' Suddenly his brow uncreased. 'There *is* one way, only one *sure* way . . .'

Anthony looked at him puzzled. 'I don't know what you mean.'

'The show? . . .' asked the lady.

Midge nodded slow approval.

'. . . Goes on!' pronounced the Great Antonio.

'Delicious!' She turned to Midge. 'And you won't forget to knock thrice and cross the threshold exactly on time, will you? We're so looking forward to your surprise midnight appearance!'

Midge nodded absently, his face haunted by dark ghosts of doubt and determination.

The earrings sparkled.

Light spangled the black and silver cabinet. Saccharine music subsided beneath the low, tense susurration of the cymbals. The audience watched Midge move towards the box, turn to embrace his brother, then allow himself to be elaborately chained and padlocked and, finally, immured within the garish, upright coffin.

The two men's eyes met. Midge raised his left eyebrow—the standard signal. All was well.

With a typically suave, theatrical flourish, the Great Antonio slammed shut the coffin doors. More rattling of padlocks and cymbals. He wheeled forth a sheaf of silver scimitars.

Apprehension tautened in the audience. The blonde gripped the young man's arm. 'Why doesn't he kill the big one . . . while he's helpless? . . . That'd foil the spirits,' she whispered.

'Shush,' said the youth, forgetting himself. 'Darling!' he added. 'It's a trick. All part of the act. Nobody's going to murder anyone.'

And they watched the Great Antonio lift up the first glittering sword, introduce it to a central vent in the cabinet, pause for the drums to roll to a crescendo, and—with much plausible if rather melodramatic exertion—plunge it home.

It was muffled, but perfectly distinct. Everyone in the room heard it: the cry, half agony, half triumph, escaped from the depths of the box.

Everyone in the room shuddered when, with a fumbling of chains and padlocks, the bleeding body of Midge, the magician's assistant, was released and displayed beneath the glare of the spotlights.

And everyone knew that the Great Antonio's grief was as genuine as his bewilderment.

People despatched other people with contrary instructions for doctors, ambulances, police, and even, in one over-zealous instance, the fire-brigade. Confusion seized all the company—save one: Anthony cradled Midge's head in his arms, and saw it all with complete clarity.

'He didn't bother to slip the master catch. He killed himself deliberately. To foil a ridiculous prophecy. To save me. To give me a future . . .'

He lowered his head, choking at the futility, the finality, the absurdity of such a death.

'It was all back to front anyway, Midge,' he groaned. 'Perhaps it's my fault: perhaps *I've* been killing *you* all our lives.'

Distantly he became aware of a clock clicking, whirring and launching into the chimes of midnight. Across the city the first bells began to clamour and rejoice.

'Ring out the old, ring in the new,' murmured the hostess to no one in particular. No one in particular listened. She shook her head. The earrings glistened like tears. 'The poor man's luck is out. We shan't have our first foot now.'

She looked up. Silence had fallen across the room like a sudden black shadow.

Three hammer blows, strangely resonant, sounded in the hallway. Murmurs of unease and excitement thrilled through the company. They clustered together. They stood on tip-toe, on other toes, to see the door.

Hollow footsteps approached.

Anthony lifted his head. His eyes moistened with terror; his pulse drummed along his veins. He beheld the blood-gashed figure of his brother, pale but punctual, forming slowly in the doorway.

Midge gazed over the company, the tall, triumphant stranger holding spectral New Year's gifts in his upraised hand, and spoke:

'You see,' he said. 'We did it. We changed the future, Tone, and thwarted misfortune. It was the only way. *Dead men can't kill.* We altered the unalterable!'

The Great Antonio, however, saw accusation not rejoicing in the pointing hand. And he was never able to register Midge's words.

His body slumped against his brother's on the stage.

'Weak heart,' said the doctor. 'Simple shock. That—sight—in the doorway killed him outright!'

CYANIDE FOR CHRISTMAS

by John S. Glasby

John Stephen Glasby (b. 1928), distinguished
chemist and astronomer, joined the Imperial
Chemical Industries (Nobel) Division in 1952,
where he carried out research on detonation and
rocket research. He was elected a Fellow of the
Royal Astronomical Society in 1960; among his
books are *The Dwarf Novae* (1970) and *The
Variable Star Observer's Handbook* (1971). He
has written over 500 stories in various genres,
notably crime and horror, including two in the
companion volume *Chillers for Christmas*.

I t was the week before Christmas when Charles Tremayne met the
gypsy.

He was making the rounds of his estate, as was his usual custom,
when he turned the corner in the narrow path leading through the wood
and there she was, standing directly in front of him as if daring him to
proceed any further. His first emotion on seeing her was one of anger,
then fear. Ever since childhood he had been obsessively afraid of gypsies.
There was something about them which made his flesh creep and filled
him with a deep-seated disquiet.

She was an old woman, thin as a stick, and the heavy woollen shawl
across her shoulders hung on her bony frame like a shroud. Small, bird-
like eyes stared intently at him and the mere sight of her made him grip

his walking stick more tightly. He felt his arm muscles tighten of their own accord.

Somehow, he found his voice. 'What are you doing here?' he demanded harshly. 'Don't you know this is private property? You're trespassing on my land.'

'Why are you so afraid?' The old crone's voice was like the dry rustle of wind through rime-coated branches.

Tremayne stiffened. In spite of her bent, diminutive build, there was something oddly menacing about the old woman which struck a responsive chord deep within his subconscious.

'Get off my land.' He forced the words out through tightly clenched teeth. 'If I see you hanging around here again, I'll have you arrested.'

The gypsy raised her right arm. A skinny claw protruded from below the voluminous folds of her garment, the long forefinger pointed directly at him. 'Don't worry, I'm going. But first you'll hear the warning I'm going to give you. Whether you heed it or not is up to you.'

Tremayne had the sudden conviction he had heard all of this before, a long time ago. The memory came swiftly. It must have been just after his sixth—or was it his seventh?—birthday. An old gypsy had come to the door selling pegs and other bric-a-brac. A warning had been delivered then, he remembered; a warning to his mother not to go out that day.

To the mind of a child such solemn and frightening words had held a terrible seriousness. But his mother had merely laughed at his fears and told him such things were superstitious nonsense. She had gone out that afternoon, leaving him with his aunt—and she had never come back. It was two days later that his father had told him she had been struck by a car and killed instantly.

Recalling the incident, he experienced a sharp chill of fear but his anger remained uppermost in his mind.

'I'm not interested in any of your foolish warnings,' he retorted sharply. He raised the walking stick in his clenched fist. 'Now be off.'

The old gypsy shook her head and held her ground. 'Like it or not you're going to hear what I've got to say, Charles Tremayne. I see death. Not by your own hand but by another's and before this Christmas Day dawns. And those who seek to find your murderer will fail.'

'Nonsense!' There was now undisguised scorn in Tremayne's tone.

'Is it? Are you so sure? Perhaps you've heard a similar warning before, long ago. One which also went unheeded.'

'How could you know—?' Tremayne choked the words off.

'You blind fool! I know and foresee many things.' The thin, reedy voice ended in a dry chuckle that sent a shiver along Tremayne's spine. 'Heed my words well and perhaps the course of fate may be changed. Sometimes we have it in our power to alter the path of destiny. If you should live to see Christmas Day there will still be many years ahead for you. But—'

'But what?' he demanded roughly. For the moment his initial anger and the stick in his hand were forgotten.

'But should you see the light, you will die.'

Even as she uttered the final words, the gypsy was shuffling past him and moving rapidly along the path through the trees.

Tremayne was aware that his arms and legs felt oddly numb and it was several seconds before he could turn. The stooped figure had vanished among the trees and although he forced himself into a shambling run, there was no sign of her when he reached the edge of the wood and stared across the empty fields.

Somehow, he got back to the house and poured himself a stiff brandy, gulping the raw liquor down quickly. Part of his mind was still perfectly clear. Had it really happened? The logical explanation, of course, was that he had suffered some kind of hallucination, that he had simply imagined it all. He had been feeling off colour all week and, looking at everything objectively, there seemed no possible way that old woman could have disappeared in such a short space of time.

But there was no point in taking chances. He had made a lot of enemies in his lifetime, not least among his family. There had been that violent quarrel with his son, Philip, a couple of months ago when he had threatened to cut him out of his will. And Philip's wife, Margaret, was an avaricious little bitch who would go to any lengths to ensure that Philip inherited his share of the family millions. Then there was his daughter Anne and her second husband Mark. He didn't doubt that they, too, were impatiently waiting for him to die. And they would all be there for the Christmas festivities giving any one of them an ample opportunity to commit murder.

He poured himself a second drink but sipped this one slowly. Already, his mind was engaged in formulating plans. Forewarned was forearmed and whether his recent experience was an hallucination or not he intended to take it seriously and see to it that he lived to enjoy this Christmas and many more.

Apart from himself, and the servants, the big house was empty for the next five days. It was Christmas Eve when the family arrived. First Anne and Mark and then, just as it was growing dark, Philip and Margaret drove up. Everything had been made ready for their coming and, by this time, Charles had made up his mind exactly how he intended to spend that evening.

Deep beneath the house was a vault where he stored most of his art treasures and other prized possessions which he had collected over the years. Many of them had been obtained through illegal channels, old masters which had disappeared from art galleries all over the world and which he had bought at a fraction of their true worth.

It was here that he intended to spend most of the night, protected by thick concrete walls with no windows and only the one thick steel door to which he had the only key.

The previous day he had gone over everything down there with Luigi, the electrician from the village, ensuring that all was in perfect working order. He had known Luigi as a prisoner of war and over the years they had become firm friends. Now he was confident that, no matter how hard they tried, no matter what diabolical plan any of the family may have made, no one could reach him there.

Throughout the evening, he tried to appear his usual self although he knew that the family, particularly Philip, gave him odd glances when he refused to eat or drink anything, pleading an upset stomach.

He forced himself to listen to, and join in, the conversation around the table. Philip went out of his way to ingratiate himself in the hope that their quarrel had been forgotten. Anne chattered incessantly about how difficult it was to live in London with everything so damned expensive and Mark being continually passed over for promotion.

After dinner, they had all insisted on paying a visit to the vault. Over the years, this had become a tradition, when he allowed them to select some item of jewellery as a present for Christmas. He, himself, had long since renounced the true spirit of Christmas, ever since Mary had died. But he had seen to it that the usual decorations and the Christmas tree had been put up in readiness.

As the time passed, he could not hide from himself that he was scared and it was an emotion utterly foreign to his nature. If he could only get through the night without anything happening, he would be all right.

He awaited ten o'clock, when everyone retired, with a growing sense of trepidation. During the evening he had unobtrusively scrutinized them all closely, watching their facial expressions, marking every word they said, wondering which one of them harboured thoughts of murder.

Now there were only two hours left.

He knew that if one of them was contemplating murdering him it would have to be some fiendishly clever scheme, one which would so closely simulate death from natural causes or an accident, that the doctor and police would be completely fooled. The old gypsy had said that his murderer would never be found. But she had also said that it was possible to alter the course of fate—and that was what he intended to do.

He felt drained physically but all of his senses were sharp and alert as he made his way down in the small lift, along the short underground passage to where the door of the vault stood at the end. Inserting the key, he unlocked the wheel and spun it slowly, withdrawing the thick steel bolts and thrusting the door open. The overhead lights, set close to the ceiling, came on brightly as he flicked down the switch. Closing the door, he locked it securely, letting out his breath in a single exhalation.

Now he was absolutely safe. He checked his watch. Ten-fifteen. He would stay here until two or three in the morning and then go to bed. If there was any truth in the gypsy's words, he would have beaten fate and there would be nothing to fear.

In the harsh actinic glare of the overhead lights, every detail of the chamber stood out with blinding clarity. The stacks of old masters along one wall; the large safe which contained a fortune in diamonds and precious stones. All he had amassed over the years and really cared for was here.

He spent more than an hour poring over them with a loving care. Then he sat down at the desk in the middle of the room and made himself comfortable.

At precisely 11.58, Charles Tremayne died. Death came so swiftly that he was not aware of it.

Detective-Inspector Challon mounted the imposing flight of stone steps with a growing sense of irritation. Why did people have to go and get themselves murdered at the most unpropitious times? Christmas Day wasn't exactly the best time to be called out on a case. Particularly one which was really outside his area of operation. Still, as a lifelong bachelor it was probably less annoying for him than for Sergeant Eddison.

He paused at the top and surveyed the surrounding countryside while he waited for Eddison to join him.

Milthorpe Manor was a large, rambling building almost an hour's drive from London. It had obviously been extensively renovated several times since it had been originally built. In summer, the scene would undoubtedly be picturesque and relaxing. Now, with the bare, white-covered hills and the boughs of the stately elms bowed down with snow, the place held a desolate look under the leaden sky.

'Do we know anything about this Charles Tremayne, Sergeant?' he asked. 'The name sounds familiar.'

'Not much, sir.' Eddison stamped his cold feet in the snow. 'A self-made millionaire. Suspected of receiving stolen paintings two or three years ago but he was never charged.'

Challon gave a brief nod. He recalled the case. Tremayne had amassed a fortune by some dubious deals with a group of international financiers. There had been the collapse of a major finance house in Rome, he remembered, but Tremayne had had inside information and had pulled out before the crash and associated scandal.

'So he probably made a lot of enemies,' he said, speaking his thoughts out aloud.

'Very likely, sir.' There was a note of puzzlement in the Sergeant's voice. 'What I don't understand is why we were called in. Couldn't the local force have handled it?'

'Maybe there's some mystery here that's got them stumped. Anyway we'll soon find out.' He rang the bell.

The door was opened a couple of minutes later by a young, uniformed constable. He eyed them suspiciously.

'Detective-Inspector Challon,' Challon said. 'And this is Sergeant Eddison.'

'Oh, sorry, sir.' The constable stepped hastily to one side to allow them to enter. 'I thought you might be reporters. We've had a couple here already but the Inspector isn't giving out any information to the press.'

'Quite right,' Challon said.

'Would you like to see the family?'

'Later,' Challon said, stamping the snow from his shoes. 'Where's the body?'

'If you'll follow me, sir, I'll take you down.'

Challon threw Eddison an enigmatic glance, then fell into step beside the constable. 'Down?' he asked.

'That's right, sir. Mister Tremayne was locked in the vault when he died. We had to burn through the door.'

Challon restrained his growing curiosity with an effort. Over the years he had developed a strange kind of sixth sense when it came to murder cases. He could invariably tell when they were going to be reasonably straight-forward or when they held some baffling aspect which made them notoriously difficult to solve. Right now, he sensed this one had all the hallmarks of one of the latter.

The instant he saw the door of the vault, Challon knew he had seen one almost exactly like it. That had been at the scene of a major bank robbery in the East End. On that occasion, too, there had been the characteristic black marks where the crooks had burned through the thick bolts with an oxyacetylene torch.

He eased himself warily through the narrow opening. There were three men in the brightly lit chamber. Two were standing beside the desk in the middle of the room. The third lay slumped across it. One arm hung limply by his side, the other lay across the base of the heavy, ornate desk-lamp which had evidently been knocked over in his death-throes.

There was a very faint smell in the air which Challon didn't recognize for a moment. Then it came to him. Bitter almonds!

The taller of the two men introduced himself. 'Inspector Wilmington.' He turned to his companion. 'This is Doctor Graham.'

Challon shook hands, then turned his attention to the body. 'Has anything been touched?'

Wilmington shook his head decisively. 'Nothing. I thought it best to leave everything just as we found it until you arrived.'

'And there's obviously no doubt as to the cause of death. Hydrocyanic acid.'

Graham gave a terse nod. 'My opinion is that it must have been self-administered.'

'Suicide?' Challon looked surprised. 'Then why were we called in?'

Wilmington coughed nervously. He suddenly looked uneasy and unsure of himself.

'Perhaps I should explain what happened a couple of days ago.'

'If you think it has any bearing on the case, I'd certainly like to hear it.'

'Tremayne came to see me two days ago. He claimed that someone was out to murder him and asked if I could give him police protection until Christmas. Naturally, I asked him if he had any concrete evidence to support such a statement. He was extremely reticent at first and I got the impression he was a very frightened man. Something was scaring him.'

'Go on.'

'Well, he spun me a yarn about meeting a gypsy in the wood yonder a few days earlier. Seems she warned him he was to be murdered before Christmas Day. If he lived to see today, he'd be perfectly safe.'

'Did you believe his story?' Challon asked pointedly.

'About meeting the gypsy—yes. There've been several around these parts lately.' Wilmington paused. 'But I didn't attach any importance to this so-called warning.'

'Quite right, too,' muttered the doctor.

Challon rubbed a hand across his chin. 'Yet he came down here where he obviously considered himself to be quite secure from any murder attempt. That doesn't strike me as the act of a man intending to commit suicide.'

He leaned across the desk. 'Nor does this.' He pulled something from beneath the dead man's arm and held it up to the light.

'His pocket watch.' Wilmington said.

'Exactly. He must have put it on the desk in front of him, watching the time closely until he figured it was past midnight when he'd be safe.'

Eddison walked over from the far wall where he had been making a complete circuit of the chamber. 'So how was it done, sir? Cyanide acts fast. There are no windows and those walls are solid concrete and several feet underground. There's only that one door and if it was locked from the inside—'

Challon knew what the Sergeant was getting at. There was no way the murderer could have got into the vault. Even if he had come down with Tremayne, which seemed highly improbable in view of the latter's intention to remain completely isolated until he reckoned the danger was past, he could never have got out. Unless—

'Have you checked how many keys there are to that door?' he asked the Inspector.

'That was one of the first questions I asked when I questioned the family. Tremayne had this place specially built. There's only the one key and he never let it out of his possession. It was in his pocket when we found him.'

'You were here when those doors were burned through?'

'Yes. There seems absolutely no doubt he came down alone some time after ten o'clock and he locked the door from the inside.'

'And do we have any idea when he died?'

'Some time between eleven-thirty and midnight,' Graham said. 'That's as close as I can put it at this moment.'

Challon experienced a sense of utter bewilderment. He could see now why Wilmington had called him in. If it hadn't been suicide, he could see no possible way Tremayne could have been murdered. As a last resort, he retraced his steps and examined the door just in case there was some tiny aperture through which cyanide could have been introduced into the room.

There wasn't a keyhole or the minutest crack. The key clearly unlocked some internal mechanism in the door which allowed the massive bolts to be withdrawn by turning the wheel on either side.

Wilmington spoke from beside the desk. 'I can guess what you're thinking. But once that door is closed this room is virtually hermetically sealed. Nothing can get in—or out.'

'What you're suggesting is that unless Tremayne killed himself, we're faced with an impossible murder.'

'That's exactly what I'm saying.'

'Perhaps you're right.' Challon walked back to where the body lay sprawled across the desk.

'Goddammit, man! I know I'm right.'

Challon's reason told him that the Inspector had to be correct in his deduction. But reason alone could not combat the odd instinct he had that this was murder—and a diabolically clever murder at that. Everything that Tremayne had done cried out that he had taken the old gypsy's warning to heart and ensured that no one could get near him until after midnight.

Yet how had it been done? He felt certain that the vital clue was there, staring him in the face if only he could recognize it. He was equally sure that Tremayne had not unwittingly brought the cyanide with him when he had come down to the vault and locked the door securely behind him.

No; it must have been already there, waiting to do its deadly work. And that was the bit of the jigsaw which didn't fit into place. Because Tremayne had obviously been in the vault for well over an hour before he had died and, since cyanide acted within seconds someone—or something— must have been present to have administered the poison.

He realized he was thinking in circles. With an effort, he forced his thoughts to fly off at a tangent. There was an elusive little thought at the back of his mind but it refused to be dragged out into the open.

'You still think it was murder, Inspector?' Graham asked.

'To be quite honest, I'm not sure of anything at this stage. From what you've told me, all of Tremayne's actions of the past week, and especially last night, were not those of a man contemplating suicide. Yet all of the facts as we see them here show that it's impossible for him to have been murdered.'

It was at that moment that the fleeting notion in his mind crystallized into something more definite. At first, he was inclined to reject it utterly. But it persisted and the more he considered it, the more certain he was that he knew how Tremayne had been murdered. Yet there still remained the problems of proving it and—more importantly, forcing the killer to reveal himself.

His glance shifted towards Eddison. 'Sergeant, I want you to get hold of the family and bring them all down here. I'd like to question them at the scene of the crime. In the meantime, I want a word with the butler alone.'

When Challon returned to the vault twenty minutes later, he found all of the family gathered there. The two women were standing together well away from the desk, their eyes averted from the corpse.

He waited until Wilmington had identified them for him, then walked across to the desk.

'I've no doubt you're all wondering why I asked you to come here instead of asking questions in the drawing room,' he said. 'However, if you'll indulge me for just a little while I'm sure everything will be made clear.'

'I certainly hope so.' Philip spoke with ill-concealed irritation. 'Personally, I can't see why you were brought in at all. Doctor Graham has said that my father died of cyanide poisoning. And since no one can get either in or out of this place once that door is locked, he must have killed himself.'

'So you don't believe in the warning the gypsy gave him?'

Philip's thin lips curled in a sneer. 'Certainly not. A gypsy's warning, indeed. Jenkins told us all about that when we arrived. I'd have thought the police would have something better to do than listen to such nonsense.'

'Evidently your father did.'

'Then he was a bigger fool than I took him for.'

'On the contrary, I think that, in the circumstances, he did everything he could to prove her wrong. Unfortunately, the murderer had conceived an extremely clever way of killing him—one which he couldn't possibly have foreseen.'

'You think you know how he was killed?' Margaret asked.

'Yes. And I intend to show you exactly how it was done.' Challon turned to Eddison. 'Would you ask the electrician, his name's Calecchi I think, to come in for a moment.'

Eddison returned with the electrician; a diminutive, dark-complexioned man of indeterminate age although probably on the wrong side of sixty, Challon judged.

'I understand you came down here two days ago with Mister

Tremayne and checked that everything was in perfect working order,' Challon said.

'That is correct, Inspector.'

'Did Mister Tremayne give any reason for this?'

'He told me he had a feeling that something was going to happen to him.'

'An accident?'

'Not at all. I would say he was convinced that one of his family intended to murder him. He said this was the only place where he would be safe.'

'I see.' Challon nodded. Turning slightly, he allowed his gaze to pass over the two men and their wives. 'And according to the butler all four of you came here last night. I understand you spent at least half an hour in this room with the deceased.'

'Are you accusing one of us of murdering him?' Mark demanded harshly.

Challon gave a grim smile. 'I'm saying that all four of you had both the motive and the opportunity.'

'You're just fishing in the dark, Inspector,' Philip said belligerently. 'You're simply trying to pin this on us because you're completely baffled.'

'I can assure you I'm deadly serious.' Challon picked up the heavy lamp and replaced it carefully on the desk near the body. Sliding his hand beneath the wide shade, he clicked the switch.

Nothing happened.

'The bulb was smashed when he knocked the lamp over as he died,' Graham said. He indicated the shards of broken glass close to the dead man's outstretched hand.

Challon motioned to the electrician. 'See if you can remove the broken end from the socket. Be careful you don't cut yourself. And you'd better switch it off first at the mains, it's still live.'

'You're not suggesting that Tremayne was electrocuted, sir?' Eddison asked.

'Nothing quite as simple as that, Sergeant. Whoever did this wanted it to look like suicide. It would have been easy for us to prove that the lamp had been tampered with. It was definitely the cyanide that killed him.'

'While he was completely alone in a locked and sealed vault?' Wilmington shook his head in bewilderment.

'Once we get a little more light on the desk I think you'll see what I'm getting at.' Challon fished inside the capacious pocket of his overcoat. He brought out a light bulb. 'I took the liberty of taking this from the hall. Would you put it in for me, Mister Calecchi?'

The electrician took the bulb, checked it, then took a step backward.

'Damn you, Inspector!' He spat the words through clenched teeth. Then, with a savage lunge, he started for the door.

'Grab him, Sergeant!' Challon called.

A moment later, the electrician was held firmly in Eddison's grasp. His face was twisted into a mask of defiance.

'How on earth did you—?' Wilmington began in a bewildered tone. He stepped forward and took the bulb from Calecchi's hand, holding it up to the light. 'There's something inside it.'

'Just a little ordinary tap water,' Challon said. 'But the one he fitted into the lamp two days ago contained a very different mixture. At a guess I'd say it was ether and hydrocyanic acid. The instant Tremayne switched on the lamp the ether ignited and the bulb exploded. Tremayne got a lethal dose of hydrocyanic acid in the face. He must have died within seconds, falling across the desk. Our friend here was banking on him knocking over the lamp so that he completely destroyed all evidence of his murder.'

'But how did you cotton on to this, sir?' Eddison asked.

'I suppose it was a case of following the advice of Sherlock Holmes, Sergeant. Once you've eliminated the improbable, look for the impossible. When I'd convinced myself this was murder and not suicide, it was obvious the cyanide had to be down here in some kind of container which would be readily broken, be close enough to Tremayne to prove lethal and yet leave no obvious trace once his body had been discovered. Only the bulb in the lamp satisfied all three criteria. It had to be that which contained the cyanide.'

He turned to Wilmington. 'You can take him away now,' he said. 'I don't think you'll have any difficulty convicting him for murder.'

Once they were in the car heading back to London, Eddison said, 'What made you suspect Calecchi, sir? If there had to be a murderer my bet would have been on Philip Tremayne.'

Challon gave a wry grin. 'I must confess I had considered him as a likely suspect. Then I recalled the conversation we had on the steps when we arrived. There was a man named Calecchi who was one of the directors of that finance house in Rome which collapsed shortly after Tremayne pulled all of his money out. It seemed too much of a coincidence to me.'

Eddison remained silent for several moments, concentrating on the road ahead where it wound endlessly between tall hedges.

Finally, he said, 'You know, sir, a case like this makes me wonder.'

'About what, Sergeant?'

'About these old superstitions. That old gypsy Tremayne met. Everything she told him came true.'

'Not quite, Sergeant.' Challon gave a smile of pure contentment. 'She was wrong when she said his murderer would never be found.'

THE CLOAK OF
deSOUVRE

by Elizabeth Fancett

Elizabeth Fancett has been one of England's
most prominent and talented writers of ghost,
horror and mystery fiction during the past
twenty years, and has contributed to many
anthologies in addition to Capital Radio's
Moments of Terror series.

'The entire Christmas supplement!' gasped Jason. 'For a conjuror!'

'He's more than that,' growled the Editor. 'Here, listen to this—from a leading national daily: "In the great deSeever the art of stage magic has reached its highest peak. He is a worthy successor to—no, even greater than—the renowned deSouvre who died so tragically in 1920."'

'Who cares?' yawned Jason.

'"Using only his cloak,"' continued the Editor, '"he places it over a volunteer from the audience, who rises from the ground and remains in the air until lowered at the Magician's command."'

'So what?' sneered Jason. 'He uses paid stooges. I don't suppose anyone managed to interview the so-called volunteers? Hey, that's an idea!'

'I don't want to know how it's done,' said the Editor, 'I just want you to get an interview with him. This is a rush job and I don't know if we can make it, but I want to go to press the day after tomorrow. That gives you two days to come up with something. I've already had pictures taken of his performances but I want to know more about the man himself. Christmas Eve is his last appearance in our town and he may not come our way again. Concentrate on his family background, get him to talk about his private life. And I want facts, Jason—not an exposé of how he does his acts!'

'If that's what you want,' shrugged Jason. 'But to me he's just another conjuror.'

Scowling and impatient, Jason sat among the crowded matinée audience. He was further irritated by the almost reverent hush that fell when the magician finally appeared. DeSeever came on stage with nothing, an immaculate masked figure in his impressive red-lined black cloak, about whose slender person scarce a brace of birds could be concealed let alone the numerous coloured doves with which he ended his spectacular performance.

The magician stood in the centre of a darkened stage, a single spotlight framing him. He reached out into the dark air and the doves came fluttering into his hands, then went winging over the heads of the now wildly cheering audience. Not once did deSeever go near the back curtain or make any move towards the wings. He stood isolated and motionless except for the movements of his arms and hands as they plucked the birds from the air about him.

Before the end of the act, Jason slipped backstage. He had expected to see someone—or even the stage hands—sending the doves to deSeever. Instead, they had their work cut out catching the birds as they flew in from the stage.

He studied the magician, his hands outstretched into the darkness and the birds still coming into them. Jason picked up one of the doves perched on a piece of scenery, stroked its crimson plumage. Dyed of course, but in splendid condition. No cruelty angle here.

He went in search of the stage manager.

'I understand,' said Jason loftily, 'that deSeever always visits beforehand at every theatre where he plays. Comes to arrange a few things, eh?' he winked.

'We went over the lighting arrangements,' said the manager firmly, 'and the music—and that's all.'

'He brought no apparatus with him?'

'Did you see any?' challenged the manager.

'No,' admitted Jason. 'But that's black light out there. Anything— anyone—could be with him even now.'

'True,' admitted the manager. 'But I assure you he's alone, as the audience will see when the lights go on again.'

'Oh sure,' grunted Jason, '*after* his assistant comes off stage!'

'You can wait here and see,' grinned the manager. 'But you're on the wrong track, son. DeSeever comes with nothing and leaves with nothing—not even the doves. At every theatre where he performs the doves are afterwards given to the local zoo or some reputable aviarist. I don't know how he does any of his acts and I don't want to. He's a great magician, so let's leave it at that.'

But Jason had no intention of leaving it at that. He waited on until the curtain closed on deSeever to thunderous applause. The magician came off stage alone. Jason waylaid him.

'I'm Jason, the local paper's chief reporter,' said Jason. 'We're devoting a special Christmas supplement to you.'

'I am honoured,' smiled deSeever. 'Please—' he motioned Jason to accompany him. In the dressing room, he removed his cloak but retained the mask.

His age? wondered Jason. Impossible to tell with that mask. He wondered if he could persuade him to remove it.

'Certainly,' said deSeever. He removed the mask, to reveal a fine, strong face and dark, compelling eyes.

'I'll be honest with you,' said Jason bluntly. 'I'm not interested in magic. And I don't want the usual type of interview, though it will be difficult to find a new angle on the conjuring profession—although the dove act *is* spectacular,' he added grudgingly. 'But as far as I'm concerned conjurors have little appeal. However, perhaps between the two of us we can cook up some fresh approach.'

'No doubt,' said deSeever gravely. His eyes held Jason's for so long that Jason shifted uncomfortably.

'Perhaps it would interest you to know,' said deSeever, 'that there are other even more spectacular acts I haven't as yet performed on stage. Let us go to my home, we can talk much better there.'

'Your home?' asked Jason, surprised. 'Here in Abbotsville? I didn't know that.'

'Few people do,' smiled deSeever. 'I return here secretly from time to time—to rest, to improve my acts, and to think up new ones.'

Despite himself, Jason felt excited. This was more like it! At the magician's house anything could happen, and by now he was determined on an exposé. He could always sell his story to some other paper that wasn't averse to ruining a man's career.

'We will have to take a cab,' said deSeever. 'I do not drive.'

DeSeever stopped the cab at the point on the main road some distance away from the town centre.

'From here we walk,' said deSeever.

Grumbling inwardly, Jason walked.

The magician's house was an old, strange looking building enclosed entirely by trees, off a quiet lane and in a part of town Jason had never seen before.

'Built to my own specifications,' said deSeever proudly.

No doubt! thought Jason grimly. A house of secrets fit for a magician, and before this day was over he hoped to discover some of those secrets!

'A drink?' asked deSeever.

'Whisky,' said Jason. He relaxed in the warmth and elegance of the room, switched on his tape recorder and placed it beside him.

DeSeever touched a wall panelling, which swung open to reveal a small bar. He brought a whisky bottle and two glasses to the table beside Jason. He filled two glasses with whisky and handed one to Jason, then he raised his own in greeting.

'To magic!' he said, then, smiling, put down his glass. 'But I forgot— you don't believe in magic, do you.'

Jason said nothing. He sipped his whisky, then drank deeply. Best stuff he'd ever tasted—or could afford! He put down his empty glass. DeSeever filled it up again. Jason began to glow.

'How did you get started in this rack—er—business?' he asked.

'It goes back a long time,' answered deSeever.

For the moment, Jason had the impression that he was about to say something else. He was studying Jason, his dark eyes absorbing every feature.

'Why do you always wear a mask?' challenged Jason.

'Why not?' countered deSeever. 'Enhances the mystery, don't you think?'

'Some say you're the son of deSouvre,' said Jason.

'Some say that, do they?'

'*Was* your father a conjuror?'

'No,' answered deSeever. 'And the correct word is magician.'

'I don't believe in magic,' said Jason belligerently.

'So you said,' said deSeever. 'Magic is my life, my life is magic. I have never been able to contemplate not being what I am, I have never been able to contemplate not *being*.'

'Seems a strange profession to me,' grunted Jason, 'and an even stranger way of wanting to be entertained. Where's the fun in trickery?'

'Trickery?'

'Sleight of hand . . . fixed apparatus . . .'

'I use no apparatus,' said deSeever. 'You must have seen that for yourself—except the cloak, perhaps, which, you will recall, was examined before and afterwards by the volunteer.'

'Who could have been a stooge,' said Jason. He poured himself another whisky.

'But was not,' said deSeever. 'The volunteer was as surprised as the audience.'

Jason began to glow with something else beside the drink. Was the magician implying that he could do *real* magic? He patted his recorder, listened anxiously for its slight humming as reassurance it was still running. One never knew with magicians. DeSeever was in his own specially designed house where dear knows what gimmickry was installed. He didn't much like the smile of the magician and he looked—well—different somehow. He looked slightly older, less supple in his movements, and there was a touch of grey about his hair.

'Are you saying,' asked Jason somewhat slurredly, 'that you can do *real* magic?'

'Would you believe me if I said yes?'

'Probably not but—well—what sort of magic?'

'For instance, I can make anything materialise in any place I choose.'

'But how about anything in any place *I* choose?' sneered Jason.

'I am at your command,' smiled the magician.

'Alright, materialise me a—a real live lion!'

'Where would you like your lion?'

'In the corner by the bar,' said Jason, his eyes challenging deSeever's. When Jason looked at the corner, a lion was there.

The lion opened its mouth. So did Jason—in a great gasp of fear and disbelief. The lion moved, so did Jason. He was out of his chair and heading for the door.

'You can't leave yet,' called deSeever. 'The show has only just begun.'

Jason looked back at the corner, but saw no lion. He came back shakily. He groped for his chair, sat down, reached for the whisky bottle, decided against it.

'It was a h—hologram, that's what it was—and that's not magic!' This time, Jason, did pour himself a drink. He looked at it suspiciously.

'It isn't drugged,' said deSeever, smiling.

'There's no such thing as real magic, there isn't,' said Jason. He took a deep draught of whisky. The room seemed to be much larger now, and the door farther away. He looked again at the door. It had gone entirely now.

'You wish to see something else?' asked deSeever.

'Just the door,' said Jason, alarmed now. He had an odd sense of spinning yet he was still sitting upright in the chair, and the door had definitely gone. 'The door!' he demanded. 'What have you done with it? Put it back, I want to go home.'

'You may leave any time you wish,' said deSeever.

'Then why can't I see the door?'

'Get up and walk towards it.'

Jason rose unsteadily. He remembered just in time to pick up his recorder then walked towards where the door was supposed to be. Almost immediately the door was back in place again. He opened it and shot through. The front door opened automatically at his approach. He sped through the grounds, uncertain of his direction, and only hit the lane by chance. Once he reached the main road he stopped, leant heavily against a telephone booth. Must have been all that whisky he'd been plied with, and deSeever had taken cunning advantage of it!

The crisp early evening air gradually cleared his brain. Phew! What an interview! And he hadn't finished with deSeever yet! Meanwhile, how to get home? There was no bus stop in sight and little chance of a cruising taxi way out at this end of town. And that was another thing—just what part of town *was* this?

He decided to ring for a taxi, but the one number he could remember was far from helpful. How did he expect to be picked up, said an irate voice, from some God-forsaken part of town when he could give no instructions as to how to get there? There was nothing for it but to walk and hope he was walking in the right direction.

It took him a long time and he lost his way twice but eventually Jason arrived home. He flopped down thankfully into the nearest chair and took out his tape recorder. The tape, to say the least, was a disappointment.

'I might have known it!' shouted Jason with fury. He'd played the tape twice over but each time it came out blank. Nothing of his interview with deSeever had been recorded. Somehow the magician must have blocked it! He decided to keep out of the editorial way until he could decide what to do.

Press day came and he was summoned to the editorial sanctum.

'Where the hell have you been?' growled the Editor. 'We were supposed to go to press this morning. Didn't you see the man?'

'Oh yes, I saw him,' said Jason.

'Well then, what did you get?'

'A peach of a story!' said Jason. 'But I haven't got it all yet. It's too good for a rush job, but I'll soon have enough for a special supplement that'll make your hair curl!'

'I won't have any hair left to curl', snapped the Editor, 'if you don't come straight with me! Now, what have you got so far?'

Jason told him.

'So what *have* you got?' asked the Editor. 'A blank tape which you *say* the magician blocked, an unlikely tale of holograms and dear knows what other figments of your imagination. Admit it—you forgot to switch on the recorder. Anyway, it doesn't matter now. I'm cancelling the supplement. The pictures we took of his performances just didn't come out—and don't try to tell me that it was deSeever doing real magic and all that nonsense!'

'But don't you see—it must have been!' said Jason excitedly. 'Or rather what he *claims* to be real magic. The pictures . . . my tape . . . and I *did* see a lion.'

'I've warned you before about drinking on the job,' said the Editor.

'I wasn't—well—he offered me one or two—'

'And after that you saw the lion,' scowled the Editor. 'It seems as if I'm surrounded by incompetents. But I can reduce that to one less—you!'

'But I'm on to something big, I know it!' protested Jason. 'If I can expose him—'

'You're on to the unemployment queue,' growled the Editor, 'unless you forget this whole business. Just do the things you usually do until we close shop on Christmas Eve. And don't expect me to wish you a merry Christmas, because it appears you've been having a very merry one already!'

But Jason had no intention of forgetting the whole business. The national dailies now seemed a very inviting proposition. He took in the next two nights of deSeever's performances, wondering if the magician would include his hologram act, but there was nothing new or different to what he'd seen before.

On Christmas Eve Jason decided to return to the house while the magician was conveniently at the theatre. A thick fog had descended on the town, so he took a powerful torch and a slow-crawling cab driven by a protesting cabbie along the main Abbotsville road in search of the phone booth. The taxi driver didn't take too kindly to Jason's repeated instructions to 'crawl just a little bit farther'.

'Who do you know lives in a phone box then?' asked the driver sarcastically.

'I'm not sure where my friend's house is,' said Jason, 'but it's somewhere behind the main road and near to a phone booth.'

The driver stopped and Jason got out at his impolite request. He grudgingly paid the treble fare originally agreed upon and groped his way through the thick shroud. His torch was useless in the impenetrable gloom and he found the phone booth by barging into it, but he was too relieved to feel any pain. He trod the next few yards very cautiously until he felt the rough track of the lane leading to deSeever's house. So far, so good. A few yards more, and the gravel drive way scrunched beneath his feet. Reaching the house was simply a matter of walking straight ahead.

He put out his hands, feeling through the dark murky air until at last he touched the wooden surrounds of the front door. If his calculations were correct, the end right window belonged to the room he'd been in with deSeever. The magician appeared to have no housekeeper and he could quite easily have overlooked locking one of the windows. He groped his way along the wall until he touched a window ledge. To his relief, the window opened when he exerted pressure on it. He climbed in.

His torchlight broke the darkness of the room. The furniture was shrouded, the pictures gone from the walls, the curtains removed. The sweep of his torch brought a further shock. By the empty fireplace stood the figure of a woman. He was in the wrong house!

'M—madam,' he stumbled, 'I'm so sorry . . . the fog, you know . . .'

His voice fell on dusty silence and echoed hollowly through the shrouded room. The woman did not even turn to him. His torchlight was full upon her face. In her eyes—no expression. Was this a housekeeper after all? And why the covered furniture, the missing pictures, the unlived-in-for-ages look of the room? Perhaps deSeever was closing house? But how to explain the woman? Another illusion—like the lion? She could even be a robot.

She was moving now. He followed her with his torch. She reached the closed door but she kept on moving, until she disappeared from Jason's sight.

Well, thought Jason grimly, it wasn't the whisky this time! Cold stone sober, he'd seen a woman walk through a closed door! Had deSeever been expecting him to come back some time? For this *must* be the magician's house. All this must be more of his carefully planned trickery.

But he needed more evidence if he was to make a true exposé of the man who claimed he could do real magic. There must be something around the house that he could use.

He lit his way to the door, which opened easily to his touch. The passage was dark, empty, silent. He thought he saw something move, a swish of greyness in the gloom, like a small cloud, turning a dim corner ahead of him. He sped to the corner. A light blazed from somewhere, spilling out into the dark of another passage. He crept to the source of light, looked in upon it.

A bright, large beautiful room, a high chandeliered ceiling, a leaping fire in an enormous grate, a glittering Christmas tree—a room of warmth, colour, life. Was deSeever expecting guests? A farewell party perhaps?

Jason entered the room. He spotted a photograph on the huge mantelpiece, a picture of an exceedingly beautiful woman, a very handsome man. The man—was that deSeever, that dark hair, the strong face, those compelling eyes? DeSeever and his wife?

He opened a bureau, seeking a diary, papers, letters . . . He found a leather book, gold lettering on its cover—Press Cuttings. He opened it eagerly, ran a practised eye over the clippings.

'*The brilliant magician, Michael deSouvre, continues to amaze and mystify millions . . .*'

He glanced swiftly through the glowing accounts.

'*DeSouvre could become one of the greatest magicians of all time.*' . . . '*DeSouvre electrifies audiences with his superb magic, his wondrous wizardry . . .*'

Jason flicked through page after page of similar notices. What, he wondered, was the book of another magician's press cuttings doing in deSeever's house? Or perhaps they were *about* deSeever and at some time he had changed his name from deSouvre?

He searched vainly for a date. He came to the last entry.

END OF A LEGEND.

'*Today deSouvre died. On Christmas Eve, death came to this brilliant artist—dramatically, suddenly, terribly—before a horrified audience while attempting to perform the most spectacular and daring act of his career—escape from a burning coffin. A technical fault? An error of judgement? No one will ever know. He died with his secrets, as he would have wished. The theatre was immediately closed and the manager himself broke the tragic news to deSouvre's wife.*

'*Said the manager: I will never forget that beautiful gracious room in* deSouvre's house, alive with colour, warmth, light, the lovely Mrs deSouvre happily decorating the Christmas tree, waiting for him—and her face, her cry of anguish, when I told her that he would not be coming home.'

Jason stopped reading, aware of a sudden uncanny silence. Not even the fire crackled in the hearth, not a clock ticked. He glanced nervously about him before he continued reading.

'There may never be the like of deSouvre again. In him, the art of stage magic reached its highest peak. He once said of himself: "Magic is my life, my life is magic. I have never been able to contemplate not being what I am, I have never been able to contemplate not BEING."'

Again, Jason paused. DeSeever had said those same words to him. Apparently he had not only copied deSouvre's words but probably even his acts! I wonder, thought Jason grimly, if he'd ever copy the coffin act? Perhaps that's why he keeps the cutting—to remind him never to do it! But why was he living in deSouvre's house? For this must be deSouvre's place. Could he be his son?

He finished reading the notice of deSouvre's death.

'But deSouvre is no more. Death came too soon, too terribly. And there is none about whose shoulders his famous cloak may fall. He leaves no son to succeed him.'

But someone has succeeded him! thought Jason. He looked at the cutting again. It had been badly pasted in and a piece at the top had been caught and folded over. He smoothed out the crease, read the date—December 24th, 1920.

Seventy years ago! What kind of trickery was deSeever capable of? thought Jason angrily. The shrouded room, the strange woman, and now these cuttings—all put here especially for his sake no doubt. He sensed someone behind him, turned swiftly. A woman was coming through the doorway, the same woman he had seen in the other room. Instinctively he drew back as she advanced. There was something so unreal about her, matching the uncanny silence of the room. She made no sound at all. Not even her gown rustled as she moved towards the Christmas tree.

He watched her as she rearranged the baubles, adjusted the lights, redraped the tinsel. And still no sound from her actions. Suddenly she turned, looked towards the open doorway. For a moment she stood there, watching, smiling as if someone were advancing towards her. Then he saw her face change from serene beauty to incredulous horror. Her mouth opened as if in a silent scream. Then she wept, quietly, but he could see the tears upon her cheeks.

[228]

A phrase from one of the cuttings leapt into his mind. 'Her cry of anguish when I told her that he would not be coming home.'

'No!' shouted Jason fiercely. But even his own voice was lost to him and no sound broke the deathly hush around him. He turned away, tried to will himself towards the door, but he could not move. Then the silence of the room broke into many gentle sounds—the crackle of the flames from the fire, the rustle of the baubles on the Christmas tree, a faint tinkling of the chandelier. And somewhere a clock began to tick.

Jason grabbed his torch from the bureau where he'd left it and ran out into the dark passage. Unsure of his bearings, he switched on the torch to find the hallway. As he turned into it, a dark shape seemed to hang in the air before him. Fearfully he shone the light upon it, realised it was a cloak hanging on a peg—deSeever's cloak? Yes, it must be—or one of them. That was an idea! If he took it away, inspected it closely . . . he didn't know what he hoped to find but it might reveal something. Not only that, he could do with its warmth. He felt so extraordinarily cold.

He took the cloak off its peg, slung it over his arm and hurried out of the front door.

The fog had lifted slightly but the cold was intense. He placed the cloak about his shoulders and began to make his way out of the grounds. He clasped the cloak at his neck and drew it tightly around him. He cried out, unprepared for the force of memories that came flooding into his brain, experiences he had known and yet not known, strange yet familiar sensations crowding in upon his confused mind. Almost mechanically, he kept on walking until his feet sounded hollow on the hard surface of the dark and lonely road.

No traffic passed him. He walked about a mile in the continued emptiness, in quietness, darkness and cold. He tried to think, to remember, but his thoughts were strange and unfamiliar, and yet in some unknown way they *were* familiar—memories of things done, of people known, of places he'd been to, and sometimes he remembered being conscious of a bright light surrounding him and of darkness beyond the light, and there had been clapping and cheering within the darkness and there were birds . . . yes, doves . . . about him and . . .

He broke into a run, as if to speed away from the memories that haunted him and touched in teasing fantasy upon his troubled mind. Lights ahead of him now, piercing the mist, a city's lights, spelling shelter, comfort, sanity. He ran on, stopped only when he was well into a lighted street. He stood still, trying to get his bearings. This was his town—he felt it—but what was it called? And most important of all—where did he live?

He moved on slowly, searching for familiar signs. One sign stirred his memory: *To the Theatre*. Some instinct took him into the semi-darkness of the stage door entrance. The door keeper, engrossed in a book, did not even look up as Jason glided silently past him. From somewhere he could hear music. It seemed familiar, yet unfamiliar. The double impression, so often recurring, added to his confusion. Several stage hands emerged from behind some scenery. Jason stepped back quickly into the shadows. The men were carrying some wooden apparatus on to the stage. He watched as they began to assemble it, and it looked, thought Jason, like a coffin.

He frowned uneasily. The grim word had a special meaning in his mind, something he'd read recently . . . He made his way to the dressing rooms. A name on one of the doors caught his eye—deSeever. Where had he seen that name before? It was hot in here. He tried to remove the cloak but it would not unclasp. He flung it away from his shoulders. That was better, he could think a little clearer now. DeSeever—or should that be deSouvre? He opened the door and went in.

'Just in time,' said deSeever. 'My act is due in five minutes. And good—you have brought my cloak.'

'*Your* cloak?' said Jason. 'But why am I wearing it?'

'If you were not,' answered the magician, 'you would not have come here to the theatre tonight.'

'But how did I come by it?'

'Do you not remember? You went back to my house.'

'Went *back*?'

'Three days ago, after the matinée—I took you there.'

Jason shook his head.

DeSeever came towards him, removed the cloak from Jason's shoulders and laid it over a chair. Almost immediately Jason's mind cleared.

'You tricked me!' he said, his old belligerence returning. 'You knew I'd go back! The house was rigged with all sorts of gimmicks. You planned all those silly illusions, didn't you!'

'What did you see?' asked deSeever gravely.

'What you *intended* me to see—the shrouded room, the woman—and why are you living in deSouvre's house? I saw the cuttings. Or were they part of the whole set-up?'

'The cuttings were real,' said deSeever.

'And the woman?' demanded Jason.

'She was my wife,' answered deSeever sadly.

'Your wife?' gasped Jason. 'I didn't know you were married.'

'And you a reporter!' said deSeever, gently mocking.

'So why didn't I see her the other afternoon?'

'You didn't stay long enough,' the magician reminded him. Jason flushed, remembering his sudden desire to be gone when the lion appeared and he'd thought the door had vanished.

'But even if you had stayed,' continued deSeever, 'I doubt if you would have seen her then. You saw her tonight because it is Christmas Eve.'

'But why didn't she see *me*? Is she blind . . . deaf?'

'To *you*—yes. She is dead.'

'D—dead?' spluttered Jason.

'For nearly seventy years now. She died soon after me.'

Jason groped for a chair and sat down heavily. He had to drag his voice from the depths of his dried throat. 'S—soon after *you*?' he croaked. 'But—but it was a magician called deSouvre who died seventy years ago!'

'Death is limited in its power, Jason. Only the flesh perishes. The personality, the inner spirit, goes on forever. DeSouvre died on stage, but I did not intend to perish with him.'

'Then—then what you are saying,' said Jason hoarsely, 'is that *you* are deSouvre, and that you're a ghost too?'

'How else,' smiled deSeever, 'would you explain my seemingly impossible acts and illusions? No *living* magician could do the things I have done—not without assistance, and not without all the techniques of stage magic. When I lived—in the body, that is—I too had to rely on what is commonly known as apparatus. I performed great illusions, but they were contrived—trickery no doubt you would call it. Today I am even greater than when I was deSouvre, who perished in a failed illusion through his own fault and mortal weakness. But the magician in me refused to die. I wanted to go on to even greater things. I couldn't stop, I *wouldn't* stop—'

'Come off it!' interrupted Jason rudely. 'First I see a woman you pretend is your wife's ghost, then you claim that you're deSouvre a ghost in fact. Who do you think you're fooling? You may be living in deSouvre's house, but that's where it ends!'

'Tonight is where it ends, Jason,' said deSeever. 'I am growing tired, weaker in substance, my hold is lessening upon this world. So tonight I retire—as it were.'

'Oh yes? Then perhaps it's time to do the burning coffin act,' grinned Jason. 'Why have you never done that before?'

'Because,' explained deSeever, 'for that I must use some apparatus. I have built my reputation on using no props, having no assistant, except the occasional member of the audience, who themselves were as mystified as all the rest.'

'Hypnosis—that's what it was,' snorted Jason. 'Must've been!'

'What will it take to convince you?' sighed deSeever. 'But you are right about my last performance. It will be the coffin act, for which I will need some assistance. That is where *you* can help me, Jason.'

'Me! Not on your life! Besides, if you're a ghost you can perform wonders without any help at all. You do it on your own, deSeever! Why do you want to do it, anyway? So you can go out in a blaze of glory? Supposing,' he added slyly, 'you just go out, like deSouvre did?'

'Not quite like deSouvre, Jason. For instance, I did not wear the cloak.'

'You think the cloak will save you? It has magic properties I suppose,' sneered Jason. 'I think I'll have to stay and see this!'

'Yes, you will stay,' said the magician gravely. 'And tonight the cloak will be worn.'

His dark compelling eyes fixed on Jason's own, deSeever picked up the cloak and came towards him. Before Jason could move away the magician put the cloak around his shoulders.

'What are you doing?' demanded Jason. But he couldn't think so clearly now and once again strange yet familiar sensations began to fill his mind.

'Yes,' said deSeever, 'you have a right to know. From the moment you wore my cloak until I removed it, your mind was muddled, your brain confused. You had vague memories of other days, other places, other skills, and yet with it all you were still Jason. But you were also partly me, my mind beginning to mingle with yours—as now, Jason, as now.'

'No!' cried Jason, but weakly. 'You can't play your fool tricks on *me*! I'm going home!'

'You can't go home—not any more. It is *I* who am going home. I don't want you to *help* me, Jason—I want you to *be* me. You see, I have this strange fear that if I re-enact my death tonight I will be banished to some strange place where my wife cannot find me. So I must leave this world quietly, peacefully, to rejoin my wife who waits so patiently for me.'

DeSeever picked up the mask and placed it on Jason's face, turned him round to look in the long mirror.

'See,' he said, 'the same height, the same build, and the mask will take care of the rest. As for make-up—well, we won't bother with that tonight.'

Jason stared at his image in the mirror. He tried hard to think, fighting still to retain his own identity. He was Jason, he told himself, his mind screamed that, but he was also deSeever, with the mind and skills of deSeever—and his fate! Why? What power had the magician to do this to him? While he wore the cloak—only while he wore the cloak? He tried frantically to tear it from him but the cloth would not yield.

DeSeever came close to him and fastened the cloak around his neck.

'As long as you wear the cloak, Jason, you will know what to do. Perform it well, no matter what the outcome, for this is my last appearance. After tonight, both deSeever and deSouvre will be no more.'

He smiled wryly. 'What a pity, Jason, that you will never be able to use the greatest story that you will ever know!'

The magician's reflection vanished from the mirror. Jason stood there alone. The distant sounds of Christmas songs floated in through the half-open doorway. He was calmer now, confident. As the sound of the last carol faded away, he sensed the expectant hush upon the audience.

A knock on the door startled him momentarily, though half of him had been expecting it.

'Last call, Mr DeSeever!' came a voice. 'Last call!'

He could hear the orchestra striking up the famous introductory music. He knew that all was ready, the apparatus in position on stage. His performance was about to begin. Automatically, he straightened up, adjusted his mask with a practised, professional hand, smoothed down his hair, re-arranged his cloak about him. He walked to the door, Jason and yet not Jason, deSeever and yet not deSeever.

His audience was waiting.

Time to go on stage.

Time to go.

THE SOLDIER

by Roger Johnson

Roger Johnson (b. 1947), author of 'The Night
Before Christmas' in last year's companion
volume *Chillers for Christmas*, here contributes
an atmospheric tale set in the unfamiliar back
streets of the City of London.
This story was particularly inspired by the
writings of Arthur Machen.

'A Christmas ghost story,' I prompted.

Julia Kirkby's eyes widened. 'Did I say that?' she murmured. 'Perhaps I was exaggerating a little.'

'Oh, I do hope not,' said George Cobbett in a dangerously polite tone that warned of dyspeptic ill-temper. Its import wasn't lost on Julia.

'Well, at least it took place towards Christmas, and if there was an end to the story then that came on the day itself.' She flashed us a brief, slightly nervous smile and added, 'Mystery there to start with. And more to come. As to ghosts . . . I think you'd better make up your own minds about that.'

'Straightforward advice,' said George. 'Here's some for you. There's a good fire going, your glass is full, and you're among friends—so begin at the beginning and stop when you think you've reached the end.'

'Very well,' said Julia, 'though I must tell you that it isn't actually my story. If it were, perhaps I'd be able to understand it more clearly.' She took a sip from her gin and tonic and continued: 'As far as I was concerned, it began with some research I was doing for an article on the

City of London and its peculiar institutions—the livery companies, the Lord Mayor's Show, the Trial of the Pyx—that sort of thing.

'Well, I came across a letter in an issue of *The Athenaeum* from some time in the 1890. The writer simply asked for any information about The Worshipful Company of Militia—'said to be the oldest volunteer corps in the British Army, and drawn entirely from men of the City'. The name was quite new to me. You may not think that's surprising, but my father was something of a military historian, and I do actually know something about the subject. I looked through the following half-dozen issues of the magazine, but there was nothing further. Perhaps someone had got in touch directly with the inquirer. There was no way of telling. It did seem a little odd, though, that he'd been unable to satisfy his curiosity by simply asking at the War Office. I wondered idly if the whole thing was a mistake. Maybe the body in question was actually the Honourable Artillery Company. Still, I had work of my own to do.

'The article eventually appeared a few months later in a magazine called *Your England*, which is distributed only in North America, aimed at expatriates and potential tourists. By the time it came out, I'd written several other pieces and had quite forgotten about the Worshipful Company of Militia. I'd certainly forgotten making a brief reference to it in my article, so that when a package arrived for me from British Columbia, the Worshipful Company was not the first thing I thought of.

'That was the reason for it, though. Inside the package—it had been forwarded by the publishers of *Your England*—was a small batch of typed A4 sheets and a covering letter. My correspondent—his name was Davies, which is of no importance whatsoever—had been interested by my reference to this mysterious body because it was something he'd known of, by name, for several years. And he too had run up against a blank wall in trying to find out more. He actually had got as far as writing to the War Office and the National Army Museum, but the replies had been courteous and totally unhelpful. He could add nothing concrete to the little I already knew except what I should read in the enclosed pages. Yours sincerely, etc., etc.

'The typed sheets were a transcript from a notebook kept in about 1880 by a boy who was some sort of relation to my correspondent's grandmother—uncle, cousin—something like that. Though more obviously important and valuable things had been discarded over the years, this notebook had somehow been preserved. There wasn't much to tell about its owner. His name was Richard Henry Wenlock, and he was nearly sixteen years old when he wrote this brief journal. Physically, he was stocky and well-proportioned, but mentally—well, I don't know. Not actually backward, in any usual sense, but distinctly strange. He was the youngest child by several years, which wasn't uncommon, I suppose, in those days of large families. At least one sister had died in early childhood, and there was a brother killed at Balaclava. Perhaps it was the brother's career that set the lad to the notion of becoming a soldier himself, or perhaps it was just the experience of being brought up in a garrison town. I can imagine the clash there'd be between that military ambition on the one hand and the over-protectiveness of an ageing mother for her last and youngest darling.'

Julia paused and looked meaningfully at the glass in front of her. George hastily emptied his own glass of beer and handed it to me. Plainly this was my round. When I returned from the bar, I found that Julia had taken out of her briefcase a neat loose-leaf folder. She thumbed quickly through the pages before turning back to the beginning.

'This is young Wenlock's story,' she said. 'I can grasp the significance of some of it, but . . . Well, let's see what you make of it.' And she began to read.

I really did not think that I should be happy when I came here. They told me that it was not just London, but the City of London. Of course I knew that London is a city. It is the greatest city in the world. But that was not what they meant. The City of London is a very small place, they said, like a village, and very special. It does not seem to me much like a village, but I have learned that it really is special.

It was strange at first, not being able to go out into the countryside, and not seeing soldiers everywhere, as I used to in Colchester. I loved to visit the Garrison at Colchester. It was even exciting to go into the chapel there, because it was a soldiers' church and had regimental flags and battle trophies. I made up my mind quite early on that I wanted to be a soldier, but somehow things did not seem to go right. My Father had served in the army, and he used to tell me wonderful stories of wars and campaigns, but Mother never liked to hear them and she never wanted me to be a soldier. When Father died, she tried to stop me going again to the barracks, but it was not hard to go without her knowing. But then Mother died too, of what the Doctor said was her weak heart, and I was sent here to the City of London to live with my Aunt. I have been here now for nearly three months. Soon it will be the twenty-fifth of December, God's birthday, and then I shall take my first steps towards being a real soldier.

It did not take me long to find that where we live in Spicers Lane is not very far from the castle which is called the Tower of London. I think it is rather strange that the Tower of London is really in Stepney and not in London at all, but there are many strange and special things still to learn about this City. Still, there are soldiers at the castle, and just occasionally I am allowed to see them. They are mostly rather old men and wear funny old-fashioned clothes. I have read also that soldiers come to the great Bank of England, which is quite near, but they only come in the evening to stand guard, and I have not seen them yet.

I am going to be a very special kind of soldier, and that is only right, for I am a special person. I know that, for Mr Pater told me so. I must write down all that has happened so far, so that it is clear in my mind. It is most important for a soldier to have a clear mind; Father told me that. Some things, though, are secret things and must not be written down, and if the wrong people were to find out about them I should not be allowed to become a soldier.

So I must not tell where the church is, except that it is only a short distance from Spicers Lane and it is in a little square churchyard which you get to by going underneath a building and along an alleyway.

There is a metal gate with a bull's head on it, and Mr Pater told me that the gate is usually locked, but I have never found it locked.

Many of the churches in the City have strange names. I have found this out while walking around the streets, with my Aunt or on my own. There are Saint Katherine Cree and Saint Lawrence Jewry and Saint Andrew-by-the-Wardrobe. So I was not surprised when I saw the board just outside the iron gate with the name upon it, Saint Denis Mitre. But I was surprised and excited to learn that it was a soldiers' church, the first I had seen since I left Colchester. I knew, because under the name on the board was written, The Church of the Worshipful Company of Militia. Militia means soldiers, so this church was a soldiers' church.

It was a Sunday afternoon, and the City was very quiet, like death, it was as if there had never been anyone alive there at all. Even the public houses were shut, and there were no shops open at all. If I had chosen to walk towards the Tower of London, then there would have been many shops open and busy street markets, because so many people who live just outside the City of London are Jewish and do not keep Sunday as a day of rest as most of us do. But in the City, all was still. I like to be here on a Sunday, because then I can feel that I have the whole special place to myself, and even the Lord Mayor is not more important than I am. It is even more peaceful than on Saturday afternoons, when so many of the people who work here go home for luncheon and do not come back until Monday morning. The stillness on Saturday afternoons is one of the reasons why the City of London is so very special.

My Aunt had been taken ill with a headache while we were at church, but it is not that church that I shall tell of. It was only our parish church, called Saint Michael Cornhill, which is very old and gloomy and rather dull. After luncheon, Aunt said that she would lie down for a while, and as Cook and Ann, who is our maid, said that they were very busy, I asked if I might walk about the streets for a while. I said that I had not lived in London long, and it was important that I should know where famous places were, like the Guildhall and Saint Paul's Cathedral. That is what I said, but really I wanted to get out of the house and away from Aunt and Cook and Ann, because I could not make them see how very important and special to me it was that I should become a soldier. When I mentioned it to them they would laugh, but in a secret kind of way that they hoped I would not understand, but I did.

The sky that Sunday was grey and watery, and the sun looked like a dull sixpence, casting uncertain, fleeting shadows. It was the sort of day that suits well the greyness of this City, which was now mine. I am of a clever and inquiring mind, and I already knew where the Cathedral was, and the Guildhall in its secret square, back from the empty road. However, I resolved to follow the streets where my nose led me, now this way and now that, so that I might know my new home fully. In this way I discovered many special and important buildings and places, such as the Royal Exchange and the Mansion House, which is where the Lord Mayor lives, and the Founders' Hall and Leadenhall Market, and it seemed to me that I ought soon to return to Spicers Lane and my Aunt's house. But my nose led me to turn to the left off one of the main roads and into a narrow lane where tall grey buildings seemed to reach up to the grey sky, almost shutting out the light.

As I walked along this lane, I noticed, for I am very observant, that there were a number of older and generally smaller buildings among the big grey ones. One of these, which looked very old indeed, had a narrow passage or alley underneath it, leading away from the lane. I should have passed this by, thinking it a private way, if it had not been for the sign. It was just inside the passage, screwed to the wall with bolts that had rusted over very many years, and there was an arrow painted upon it which pointed away from the street. Underneath the arrow were the words, To The Ch—. But that is all it said, because the rest had faded entirely.

The passage was rather dark beyond, and it still looked to me like a private and secret place, but if I had not been meant to go in, then there would not have been a sign with an arrow. So I went along the dark and narrow alley and found at the end of it a gate made of strips of black iron, shaped into strange shapes and with a metal bull's head in the centre of it. Beyond the gate I could see a small square, whose grass looked colourless and unhealthy. There were tombs of blackened stone and patches of bare earth, but the grass was neatly shorn. Someone tended this little churchyard. Looking to the far side of it, I saw the church itself.

At first, and for a moment, I was disappointed, because I had seen several churches that afternoon, and even the dullest of them were more handsome than this one, which seemed rightly to hide away from the streets where people go. But then I saw the notice board which told me that this was a very special church. It stood just within the gate, and it was cracked and faded, but I could clearly read the words, The Church of Saint Denis Mitre, and underneath, The Church of the Worshipful Company of Militia. So then I knew that it was right that I should go on, because this was a soldiers' church.

I pushed open the iron gate and walked across the grass to the big wooden door of the church, where I lifted the heavy latch and pushed, but the door was locked. I was about to go away, disappointed, when I noticed the knocker on the door. It was made of iron, black like the gate, and shaped like a bull's head. Almost without thinking, I raised the knocker and rapped smartly upon the door. The sound was very loud, like a martial drum. I expected it to rouse angry people in the buildings that surrounded the little churchyard, but nobody appeared at any of the blank windows, and I remembered that it was Sunday. Probably these houses and offices were all deserted. Almost before the sound of that loud rap had died away, the big door was opened, and in front of me stood a tall man who wore a dark robe and had a curious kind of cap upon his head. As he saw me, he smiled. This was my first meeting with the priest.

He said, My dear son, I have been waiting eagerly for you. I thank God that He has led you to us this day.

This was strange, because I had not known myself that I should even find this hidden church, so how could the priest know that I would come?

But he was speaking again, and he said, Come in. It is good to have another soldier to swell our ranks.

I started to explain that I was not really a soldier, but that I hoped to become one, and he said, In God's good time you shall. We must give thanks to God and to the Mother of God that you have arrived. This is a special church indeed, and you are a special Son among the Sons of God.

He said that he was the Priest of this Church of Denis Mitre, and that he was known as Pater. Because of the cap that he wore, I was so bold as to ask if he was a Roman priest, and at that he only smiled in a singular way and did not reply. But I thought that he was a Roman, because of the smell of incense that was all around the church. It was not very strong, but it was like the incense that they use in the big churches in Flanders, where my Mother had taken me when I was quite a small boy. I found this rather exciting, but I was not sure that my Aunt would like the thought of me visiting a Roman church.

It was a soldiers' church, though, and I had been welcomed as a soldier. That was very special and important.

I asked if the church was very old. Was it as old as Saint Michael Cornhill, which was our parish church? And Mr Pater said that it was very much older, older than all the churches that were used in the City of London, even Saint Paul's Cathedral. And it had always been a church of soldiers.

He said that he would show me something of the upper part of the church, and tell me a little about the soldiers who worshipped there. Alas, he said, there are very few of them now, but once they were numerous. They were the strongest and bravest of all the soldiers of the empire, and they worshipped God from all its wide dominions. Those who are left still remember in thier bones the great deeds that were done, and even now those few are proud to be of the Worshipful Company of Militia.

I said that I had never heard of this Company of Militia, and Mr Pater told me that it was very old, like the church. It is the oldest company in England, he said, and for a long time now it has met only here in the City of London. Ah, my son, he said, this City of ours is a very special place. It is more strange and special than you can imagine, and you are a privileged young man to know something of its secrets.

He took me to the altar and made me swear that I would say nothing to my Aunt or to anyone else of what he told me and what he showed me, and his eyes were dark and terrible as he said it. When I asked why, he said that a soldier must be a fit person to have secrets entrusted to him, and that if I could not keep the secrets of the church then I was unfitted to be a soldier. Besides, he was an officer of very high rank, and I must learn to obey his orders. So then of course I swore as he demanded, by God and His great sacrifice, by which the world was saved.

Then he lifted up the embroidered cloth and showed me the altar itself. It was made of a single great block of stone, and on it were carved the signs of the stars and the words, Lord of Ages, only the words were in Latin, and I could not read them. This, he said, is the altar of our Lord, even as the other is. Now come and see what a proud tradition we soldiers have.

The stone walls and even the strong, low pillars, with their rounded arches, seemed to be covered with plates and tablets of stone, recording the lives and deaths of soldiers who had worshipped at this church. All the names were of men. There were no women's memorials there at all. Many of these monuments were framed with stone wreaths, and above them was written the word, Deo. Mr Pater explained to me that this too was Latin and meant simply, To God. The names on some of the stones were quite ordinary, but many of them were strange names. They are among the secret things, and I must not write them down. Mr Pater was able to tell me something about these soldiers, how they had fought bravely for their country and for their God, and how they had died uncomplaining when they were called. It was remarkable that he could tell me a little about all the men whose names were there, no matter how long ago they had lived. This one, he said, was a true lion, and this one a faithful Persian. I may not mention the name, but it did not seem Persian to me.

Before I left that afternoon, Mr Pater asked me to kneel with him in front of the altar and say a prayer of thanks to God for sending me to the Church of Saint Denis Mitre. The battle continues, he said, and we must have soldiers. Life and Death, Light and Darkness await the outcome.

When may I come again? I asked.

When you will, he said.

And will you be here?

When you come I shall be here, he said.

That was my first visit to the Church of Saint Denis Mitre and my first meeting with Mr Pater.

When I got back to my Aunt's house in Spicers Lane I found that I had hardly been missed. I was able to tell of the streets I had walked along and the buildings I had seen, but I said nothing about the church and the Worshipful Company of Militia.

In the evening, while Aunt read to me from the Bible, I thought of the stories that Mr Pater had told me. Stories of great battles, of brave soldiers and mighty deeds, of victories won and enemies defeated. The stories that Aunt was telling me were not exciting, but those that Mr Pater had told me thrilled my martial blood even as I remembered them. I called to my mind the great wars in which the Sons of God had fought, the mighty clash at Maranga and the battle of Chalons, when the plains were rich with the red blood of brave men. I remembered these secret and terrible things, and I said no word to anyone.

It was not always easy for me to leave the house alone and to go about the City. On the next Sunday I was kept indoors because my Aunt fancied that I did not look well, and that the winter chill would be unhealthy for me. Twice at the weekends Aunt told me to stay with her because special company was coming to tea. The people who came were not special at all, though perhaps Aunt truly thought they were. They were an old woman, who was about Aunt's own age, and her son and daughter. I had hoped that the son might be a soldier who could tell me exciting stories of wars and battles, but he was only a lawyer and very smartly dressed and dull. Aunt told me to be very agreeable to the young woman, and I did as well as I could, though I could not think why. She was pretty enough, but not interesting. I wanted more than anything to visit the hidden church and to learn more about the soldiers.

Once, on a weekday afternoon which I think was a Wednesday, I was sent on an errand to Aunt's bank, and I thought that on the way I might go by way of the church. The day was covered in a greasy yellow fog, so that I could not see many paces in front of me, and I had to take care not to jostle people or to step into the road. There were boys here and there with torches in their hands, to guide gentlemen along their way, and after I had called at the bank I followed one of these boys because it seemed to me that he would lead me in the right direction. As he passed the corner of a counting house I saw clearly in the light from his torch the sign with the name of the lane which led to the secret narrow passage and the church, but when I walked along the lane all was so dark and uncertain that I could not find the old building with the entrance to the passage. When I got back to Spicers Lane I tried hard to hide my disappointment, but my Aunt noticed that something was wrong. Happily, she thought that I must have taken a chill, and she made Ann light the fire in my room and give me a hot drink and see that I went to bed early. I did not mind this in the end, because in my sleep I dreamed of being a soldier and fighting in the most glorious battles.

I was at last able to visit the church again, and it was a Sunday afternoon just as before. Three weeks had passed since my first visit, but

Mr Pater was there as he had said, and he welcomed me like an officer welcoming a faithful soldier. I felt very proud and very humble at the same time. With him was an old man who must have been over fifty years of age. I may not tell his name, but Mr Pater said that he was a brave and faithful member of the Worshipful Company of Militia. He had risen high in the ranks and was soon to be promoted again, to the rank of Courier.

I said that I had not heard of an officer being called a Courier, even though I knew of Colonels and Generals, but he explained that it is a rank that is very special to the Worshipful Militia.

I asked the old man when and where he was to receive his new rank, and at that he pointed to the rounded west end of the church and said, I am to be buried at the great Festival on the twenty-fifth of December, when we celebrate the birth of God and His coming into the world.

I did not like to hear that, because he was a fine old man, and I did not want to think of him dying, but the two of them laughed kindly and told me that no harm would come of it. He will pass through death to a new life, said Mr Pater, and on that joyful day he will be reborn. God will take care of him. You have much to learn, my son, but if you are willing to be taught you too shall share in our feast and be recruited with the rank of Raven. God has shed the Eternal Blood for you. Can you refuse Him your service?

So then I knew that this good man had accepted me as a fit person to be a real soldier. It was the most important thing that had happened to me, and I resolved that I should be brave and strong and worthy of my brother, who died in battle far away. How proud he would be! You will be a true Servitor of the Lord, said the old man, and I felt very much honoured.

Mr Pater left me in the care of this good old soldier, and he told me many more things about the great and honourable military company that I am soon to join. Some of them are secret things and may only be spoken of among those who know. They made my head swim with the wonder and the glory of it all. At last Mr Pater came back and told me that it was time for me to go. They will miss you at home if you stay longer, he said, but you shall come once more before the great day.

That was my second visit to the soldiers' church, and it was near the end of November.

The third time I went to the church was on a Saturday afternoon, just two weeks ago. Of course there were more people about in the streets, and the public houses and some of the shops were open, but all the City seemed very quiet when I thought of how it had been only that morning. The sky was all over clouds of a greyish blue, and towards the west a great uncertain patch so dark that it was almost black. The air itself felt heavy with excitement, as if it had been charged with electricity. But I did not need excitement from the air, for this was my third visit to the secret church, and my last before the great festival, when God is born, and the year turns.

The priest and the old soldier were there again to greet me and to conduct me into the church. We knelt in front of the altar to offer our eternal service to the God of Battles, and the flames that burned in little pottery bowls shook a little, even as my heart shook, with the majesty and glory.

Mr Pater said, Now, my son, you have seen what may be seen of this church above the ground. Today you shall see beneath, where lie the heart and bowels.

They led me behind the altar to where an archway was covered by a hanging curtain. In the archway was a wooden door, which Mr Pater unlocked. Then, with two candles to light us, we proceeded down a narrow and winding stone stair to the church beneath the church.

It was the same shape as the church above and no smaller. The walls were of a plain white, and on the floor was a design in stone to remind us always of God and His sacrifice. Beside the door that we had entered through stood a statue of a most beautiful Lady, whose face was proud and commanding, and whose eyes looked steadily upon the altar. She is the Holy Virgin, Who is to be revered. The smell of incense and wine was strong.

Mr Pater said, Here is the real church, of which that above is but a shadow. See the benches and the tables, where the Communion Feast is taken! See the high altar, where the Holy Mysteries are celebrated! My son, this shall be your glory when you join us.

He told me and showed me much more, of the roaring of beasts and the croaking of birds, of the liquid sweetness of the honey wherein the Lions bathe, of the spiced sacramental wine. This much I may write down, but the rest is secret. I knew and gloried that I was to be admitted to the ranks of an ancient and blessed company.

When the time came for me to leave, Mr Pater said to me, You are God's gift to our cause, for we are few in number now and grow old. Our faithful friend here is the youngest of our company. I myself am older than you think, old beyond your reckoning. Your youth and vigour are sorely needed in the great fight.

How shall I arrange to leave the house and come here on the day of the Festival? I asked.

Never worry, he said. I shall arrange that. Pay no heed to those who celebrate other gods upon the twenty-fifth of December, but set your heart and mind upon the one true God. They have kept us under foot for so long! But we are soldiers, you and I, and we will prevail. If by chance you cannot come to us on the great day, then we shall come to you. Be assured!

And so I left the Church of Saint Denis Mitre and the Worshipful Company of Militia, but soon I shall return, for soon it will be the twenty-fifth, the day of the Festival of God's birth, and I shall hear in my ears the terrible pain in the bellowing of the dying bull.

'Yes,' said George, 'it's certainly a strange story. Powerful strange. What became of the boy?'

Julia took a thoughtful sip from her gin and tonic. 'There,' she said, 'we have to rely on third-hand evidence. My Canadian correspondent found some while ago a letter, written to his grandmother from a cousin. In it she tells what she had heard from someone else in the family—oh, dear! this is getting very complicated. What it comes down to is a very brief report on the death of a younger cousin, who isn't named, but is certainly the Wenlock boy.

'You'll remember how amused he was at his aunt's notion that he'd taken a chill? Well, apparently he really had, though he ignored it. He was such a withdrawn, secretive lad that he managed to to keep the worst of it from the rest of the household until a few days before Christmas, when it became clear that he was seriously ill. His mother had a weak heart, and it looks as if the complaint was hereditary. At all events, he was confined to his bed, and the doctor was called in. Pneumonia. That was the diagnosis, and the boy wasn't to be left alone. The pneumonia aggravated the heart condition, and he died shortly after ten o'clock on Christmas morning. Not a very merry Christmas in that house, I fancy. He ate little and spoke little, though he seemed, they thought, to be waiting for something important to happen. When he died, he was smiling.

'There. Now you know just about as much as I do. What do you make of it?'

I started to say, 'One or two things seem pretty plain—', but I was interrupted by George's voice. He spoke in an almost dreamy tone, quite as if no one else had said anything.

'Some years ago,' he said, 'your old friend Michael Harrison wrote a book* setting out the theory that much of Roman London can still be traced in the names of the present city. Street names and so forth. He went into considerable sound detail. One point I particularly remember is the notion that a few of the City churches, too, have names which indicate Roman origins. Dionis Backchurch and Magnus Martyr, for instance, at the very least suggest *Dionysus Bacchus* and the *Magna Mater*.'

'Now that,' said Julia, 'is something that hadn't occurred to me. And you think . . .?'

He waved a hand, deprecatingly. 'Well, the City certainly is a curious place—very secret and special, as young Wenlock put it. And I suppose that a hidden cult would tend towards corruption, mental or spiritual. My knowledge of the later Empire is limited, and I wouldn't dare offer it as proof, but—well—to me, at any rate, the name Denis Mitre strongly suggests *Deus Mithras*.'

'I think you've got it,' I said. '"Mithras, also a soldier . . ." *Pater* was the highest grade, if I remember rightly. And wasn't Cybele—the *Magna Mater*—also known as the Mother of God?'

The old man nodded in approving silence. Then he turned his sharp eyes to Julia. 'Young lady,' he said, 'you haven't told us everything, have you? I appreciate that you weren't able to find out any more about the ancient militia company, but what of the church, heh?'

She laughed. 'You're right, of course, Yes, I've been doing some research there, and I can tell you that St Denis Mitre was one of those churches that escaped the Great Fire. The parish was small and neither rich nor populous, so in about 1710 there were proposals made to demolish the church. Instead it was extensively renovated. Some of it has been attributed to Hawksmoor, but the few surviving pictures of the building don't show anything that looks like his work.

'The church certainly existed, though it was eventually pulled down. It had stood empty for something over twenty years, having been closed on the authority of the Archbishop of Canterbury on account of "certain un-Christian practices".'

She hesitated for a moment, looking to each of us in turn. 'Now,' she said at last, 'here's the shock. That journal was written in about 1880. The Church of St Denis Mitre was destroyed in December of the year 1855. Make of it what you will.'

'Bullseye!' I said. 'George, you've got your Christmas ghost story after all. How about another drink?'

---

* *The London That Was Rome* by Michael Harrison (Allen & Unwin, 1971)

THE CASE OF THE FIERY MESSENGERS

by Ron Weighell

Ron Weighell (b. 1950) has written several
short stories and articles, and a forthcoming
novella (*The White Road*), reflecting his interest
in the writings of M.R. James, Arthur Machen,
De Quincey, and the western magical tradition.

I t was late in the December of 1895 that Mr Sherlock Holmes became
engaged upon a most singular and disturbing case. Indeed, I can think
of no other that displayed the full range of his prodigious talents, or
offered quite so chilling a denouement. Furthermore, it brought us into
contact with two quite remarkable—if very different—individuals.

I see from my notebooks that the affair began one bitterly cold
afternoon but three days before Christmas, when all London lay under
a freezing fog that reduced the view from our Baker Street window to a
sea of wreathing vapours. Only the occasional figure, looming like a
muffled phantom under the gas lamps, and the clatter of hooves on black
ice, hinted at a world outside.

Holmes had been locked in his room all morning and had taken no
lunch. I was glad enough to stay by the roaring fire with a volume of
military memoirs, for the season had not been kind to my old wound.

At a little after two o'clock, Holmes emerged, cast down upon the
table a pair of old brown boots, and began filling a pipe from the Persian

slipper. Judging from his choice of the cherry wood that he was in a disputatious mood, I asked innocently if the boots signified that he had added the trade of cobbler to his many accomplishments. A faint smile played upon his thin lips, but he refused the bait.

'You are doubtless aware, Watson, that there may be tongues in trees, books in the running brooks and sermons in stones. To this exalted list we may now add a source of information unguessed even by the Bard: autobiography in boots. There is matter there for another monograph, I fancy. In any event, I may have saved a poor wretch's life today. The near miscarriage of justice was Lestrade's doing, I fear. He brought these boots round yesterday afternoon and asked if I might look them over. According to his account, they were last seen on the feet of a clerk named Mottram, who went missing a week ago, and whose body was recovered from the Thames yesterday, minus the boots. They were found wrapped in a week-old newspaper in the wardrobe of one of Mottram's drinking friends, a man named Rodgers, who cannot account for his whereabouts at the time of Mottram's disappearance. As a result, Rodgers now languishes in goal, and Lestrade anticipates criminal charges within twenty-four hours.'

'It seems a damning enough piece of evidence, Holmes. Did Lestrade say how Rodgers explained his possession of the boots?'

'He claims they are not Mottram's, and that he obtained them in a parcel of clothes given in part-payment for a gambling debt. Lestrade hopes that I can furnish evidence linking the boots to Mottram. Naturally, I asked Lestrade for a description of the victim, and was told that he was a large, fat man with heavy nicotine stains on the fingers of his right hand. Lestrade seemed particularly proud of his powers of observation. Personally, I do not see how anyone but a blind man could have observed less! However, it has proved sufficient to discomfit our friend the Inspector. I am now satisfied that the owner of these boots was a lightly built, left-handed pipe smoker, who favoured a dark shag tobacco. He had calloused hands, and worked outdoors—probably as a gardener—for a strict employer.'

'Oh come now, Holmes,' I said. 'You can't possibly tell all that from a fellow's boots!'

'On the contrary, Watson, it is all quite obvious. Let us cast our eyes over the offending articles and see what they tell us. A supple, much-used boot of the serviceable working kind, but not the style I would associate with a City clerk. The uppers well worn, but the soles—which are original—hardly worn down at all. Light on his feet, then.'

'I concede as much. But why a gardener?'

'Traces of soil and compost on the sole, not picked up in an office!'

'Calloused hands?'

'The faint line worn across the sole of the *left* boot, running parallel to the face of the heel: surely caused by repeatedly pushing a spade down into the earth. There is nothing quite like regular spadework for raising callouses on the hands.'

'Could not such a mark be caused by some other means—such as a stirrup?'

'An interesting suggestion, Watson, but there is no corresponding mark on the right sole.'

'Very well then. How can you tell he was a pipe smoker?'

'The circular burn marks on the inside of the right heel, and traces of ash in the seam. He has often tapped out a pipe there. I could hardly fail to identify the ash as dark shag tobacco—it is by chance a variety I have used myself. And incidentally, since it is natural, merely for balance, to raise the foot *opposite* the hand that holds the pipe when tapping out, there is further evidence for a left-handed man.'

I made one last attempt. 'The strict employer, then. Surely that is a guess?'

'Come, come, Watson; do you deduce nothing from the fact that there are not merely ashes, but burn marks, upon the heel? Our man has often knocked out his pipe while it is still burning. Would he repeatedly waste the best part of his smoke unless often interrupted by someone who does not approve of smoking in his presence?'

'Bravo, Holmes, that is masterful.'

'It is quite straightforward if you—'

The sound of the doorbell came faintly from below.

'Ah, that will be a client, on a matter of some urgency, I think.'

'Can you tell *that* from the boots?' I asked. Holmes chuckled amiably.

'No, Watson, I think we have exhausted that particular oracle. I merely observe that this is not the weather for social calls. There are steps upon the stair. Let us be ready.'

Mrs Hudson knocked and entered.

'Mr Holmes, there's a Mr George J. Barker to see you. He says it is a matter of some urgency.'

Holmes cocked a triumphant eyebrow at me and gestured with his pipe. 'Show him in, Mrs Hudson, show him in.'

Our visitor was a well-built, bespectacled man of perhaps thirty years. A certain pallor and softness in his fine features suggested that his was an inherited, rather than a cultivated physique. His suit was well cut, but in some disarray, and his hair was uncombed.

'Come in, Mr George J. Barker,' said Holmes. 'I see you have been walking around for some considerable time.'

Barker replied in a rich east country accent.

'Now how did you know that, Mr Holmes?'

'Your clothes did not become so thoroughly fog-bedewed during a short step from a hansom to our door.'

'You are right enough there, sir. I *have* been walking back and forth. I have come all the way from Suffolk to talk with you—and now that I am here—why, I scarcely know how to begin.'

'Is that so? Then let me make your task a little easier. That you came hurriedly and in some distress is apparent from the fact that you did not shave this morning and have omitted to comb your hair. But I do not think you have come *quite* so far. Perhaps you might save time by telling us what has occurred in Cambridge?'

Barker's reaction was comical. He gaped and sat down heavily in a chair.

'How could you know that?' he asked in a cultivated voice that betrayed no hint of an accent. Holmes laughed.

'I wish I could say it was by miraculous powers of deduction, but there is a return ticket to Cambridge sticking out of your waistcoat pocket.'

'Very well, Mr Holmes. I apologise for my little charade. I confess that I thought to test the powers so vividly chronicled by Dr Watson. Let me be honest with you. My name is not Barker, but James.'

'Doctor Montague Rhodes James?'

'This is too much! Is there nothing you do not know about me?'

'Oh come, Doctor, you are too modest. I see before me a scholarly-looking gentleman of around thirty whose name is James, and who comes hot-foot from Cambridge. Even so stumbling an amateur of Palaeography as myself could hardly fail to make the connection. You have been known to me since that very subtle piece of deductive reasoning on a manuscript fragment at Bury was published in the *Academy* some years ago. And your recent attainment of a Doctorate at the age of 33 has not gone unnoticed.'

Our guest bowed.

'Very kind of you, Mr Holmes. May I say that I have read your monograph on the dating of documents. It is exemplary—quite exemplary.'

'Come,' cried Holmes. 'I observe you are a pipe smoker. Try some of this tobacco if you will, and while you smoke, tell us in as much detail as you can what misfortune has brought you here.'

Doctor James produced a shiny new pipe and began to fill it from the proffered slipper.

'Misfortune indeed, gentlemen. Theft and assault and the threat of extreme public embarrassment at the least. But let me begin at the beginning. Aside from my college duties, I spend a good deal of time, as you know, examining manuscripts and compiling catalogues. I have recently undertaken work on certain Greek and Latin texts in the Library of Trinity College. Trinity also possesses a number of manuscripts pertaining to Doctor John Dee—'

Holmes raised a hand.

'One moment, please. Watson, my commonplace book, if you would be so kind. Dee, ah yes—born 1527, studied at St John's College—graduated MA—under reader in Greek—founding fellow of Trinity—lectured on Euclid—profound Mathematician, great book collector, inventor of navigational instruments, Astrologer Royal, confidante of—and probably spy for—Queen Elizabeth! A fascinating individual!'

'Indeed, Mr Holmes. Dee has always been of intense interest to me. I have had it in mind for some while to give my attention to this material when time permitted, and perhaps publish the results. That time is not yet, unfortunately, but once in a while I do devote an hour or so of my leisure to that end, and recently I was looking over Dee's own list of his books. In my experience it is not uncommon to find fragments of valuable writings appended to quite unrelated matter, so you can be sure that I am very close in my examination of manuscripts. One day quite recently I made an intriguing discovery. A page of Dee's list, which I had thought to be of somewhat thicker paper than the rest, proved to be two sheets gummed back to back. Of course I would not have dreamt of inflicting any damage upon them, but they succumbed with surprising ease to a little gentle coercion, and between them I found a third sheet of very thin paper closely written over in Dee's hand.'

Here Dr James showed signs of embarrassment. Holmes leant forward in his chair.

'Go on, Dr James, go on.'

'There are, of course, strict rules governing the loan of valuable manuscripts, but there is a certain degree of flexibility where trusted members of the University staff are concerned.'

'And you were permitted to take this very interesting page away with you. I will resist the temptation to anticipate you further. Pray continue.'

'Well, over the following days I devoted what time I could to the concealed sheet. It proved to be even more cryptic than my first brief perusal had led me to expect. I have my notes here—first there was a biblical quotation, from the second book of Chronicles, concerning the building of Solomon's temple. It begins "But who is able to build Him an house?" and ends "for the house which I am about to build shall be wonderful great". There follows what I take to be an invocation of spirits called Fiery Messengers: probably Angels, with whom Dee was always trying to get in contact. I quote:

If ye would learne the secret of th Fiery Messengers, first cast yr circle linking th High Priest to the release of Spirittes. Then fashon an arc by which ye shall be encrowned and bewailed, therebye enfolding ye moste high within th vesica piscis. Thus, arise again as one blindfold and mocked, on ye arms of ye crosse. Look then to th circle whose centre is everywhere found, its circumference nowhere.

Then there are a number of geometrical diagrams reminiscent of Vitruvian architectural designs, and an oblong divided vertically into three equal strips, the left and right of which are further divided by horizontal lines.'

'And what did you make of all this?' asked Holmes.

'At first, very little, but I have developed a tentative theory. That subdivided oblong reminds me of a mnemonic diagram in one of Robert Fludd's works, in a section entitled *Ars Memoria*: I should perhaps explain that the Art of Memory is an elaborate system dating from Greek times, in which symbolic images were visualized within an imagined building as aids to the memorizing of vast amounts of information. Vitruvian architecture became a popular setting for these 'memory images'. Now, Dee was a near contemporary of Giordano Bruno, who developed the Art along magical lines. Given the reference to 'building' a house, the later use of that oblong by Fludd, and the Vitruvian drawings, I think the hidden sheet may be the surviving fragment of Dee's notes for a method of memorising magical invocations. In any case, I thought it worthy of an article for publication, and made the notes I have here. In fact, I was just completing them last night when I received a message to the effect that Dr Verrall of Trinity wished to see me urgently. Evidently he was entertaining a guest named Kelly, with whom he was discussing a matter which I alone could settle. I assumed it to be some question of Apocryphal writings, or the dating of a manuscript. It was highly inconvenient, but it is a matter of principle that I make myself available to my friends at all times. Besides, I felt a walk in the cold night air would do me no harm, so I set off for Trinity. Dr Verrall was very pleased to see me, but denied any knowledge of the message, or of anyone named Kelly! We concluded that I had been the victim of a silly practical joke. Then I remembered something that should have occurred to me sooner. Kelly was the name of John Dee's associate!'

Holmes smiled grimly.

'A touch, that. Definitely a touch.'

'I fairly raced back to my rooms, but when I got there I found the door open, the manuscript gone, and Muir, the porter, sprawled semi-conscious on the floor with a nasty bruise on his temple. It seemed that he had noticed the door open, entered and had been struck a blow from behind.'

'What is Muir's age?' asked Holmes. Dr James seemed puzzled by the irrelevance of the question, but replied, 'Over sixty, I should say.'

'And his size?'

'Small, rather frail, but very courageous. He was on his feet in no time, expressing disappointment that he had been given no chance to defend himself.'

'Now Doctor, please answer with extreme care. Was anything else taken?'

'Well, that is the odd thing, Mr Holmes. I keep a quire of paper on my desk; early that evening I had noticed there were only six sheets left, and made a mental note to replenish the supply before retiring. After the incident, I noticed that only four sheets remained. Seemingly the thief had stolen two sheets of completely blank paper!'

Holmes clapped his hands. 'Better and better! I'm sorry, Dr James. I was speaking from my own point of view.'

Our client seemed a little out of countenance.

'I know this must seem very trivial to you, Mr Holmes—hardly a matter of life and death—'

'Not at all, Doctor. I fear Watson's flair for the melodramatic sometimes gives a false impression. I deal with many cases from which the element of crime is totally absent. The only criteria for acceptance are that the case should be unusual and offer a real challenge to the deductive faculty. Yours fulfils these requirements in plenty. It has some very interesting features; the blank paper, for instance, is of the utmost significance.'

'I confess it seems to me quite inexplicable.'

'On the contrary, it is crystal clear, and suggests there is more to the case than meets the eye.'

'Then you will give it some thought?'

'Leave your notes with me. There is a question of some errant footwear to be sorted out—we cannot leave poor Mr Rodgers to Lestrade's tender mercies—and a little research will be necessary, so it may be a while before I can visit the scene of these curious events. Watson, are you prepared to undertake a short trip to Cambridge?'

'Of course, Holmes.'

'Then be so good as to pack for a stay of three nights, and accompany Dr James back to King's. Learn what you can without making yourself conspicuous. Above all, lock the remaining blank leaves away without disturbing them. I will join you at the first opportunity. And take heart, Doctor. We may yet bring this matter to an early conclusion.'

Within the hour Dr James and I had completed the cab journey to King's Cross and were on a train racketing through the frozen countryside. Of the journey to Cambridge I need say little. James seemed in better spirits after Holmes's words of encouragement, talking animatedly about the published accounts of our cases. I was surprised to learn that he was himself a writer of mysteries, though of the fictional, supernatural variety.

It was already dark, but the sky was clear, with the smell of snow on the wind, when we reached journey's end. Little time was lost in taking a cab to King's College and making our way to Dr James's rooms.

Here was the dwelling place of a prodigious scholar. Books were ranged two deep around the walls and stood in piles, interleaved with notes at points of reference. On the cluttered desk lay the few remaining sheets of blank paper, which we carefully locked in a drawer, as Holmes had requested.

'I thought', said James, 'that we might have our evening meal here. Even at this season there are sufficient residents in Hall to ask awkward questions, and enough avid readers of *The Strand* magazine to make Dr Watson from London as instantly recognisable as Dr James from Cambridge was to Mr Holmes! Had you thought of a false identity?'

We talked the matter over as we ate, and decided that I was to be Mr Crossley, representing David Nutt with plans to publish a little book by Dr James on the subject of John Dee. This, we felt, would justify any questions I might ask concerning the Trinity papers.

Dr James was occupied with some College business early the next day, so it was late in the morning before we began our investigations at the Porters' Lodge.

Fortunately we found Mr Muir on duty. Dr James's description of him as small and frail proved accurate, but he was not wanting heart. Despite a livid bruise on his right temple, he stood to attention, pigeon chest stuck out, and told us what he would have done to the intruder had they met on equal terms!

'Did you get a look at him?' I asked.

'Not at all, sir—first I knew was when 'e struck me.'

'Who left the message for me?' asked James.

'That I couldn't say, Doctor. It was found by Mr Clifford, and passed on to me in the course of events, so to speak.'

'Well, go carefully, Mr Muir. That is a very nasty bruise. Well, Dr Watson, that gets us no further. Let us see what our next port of call brings.'

We walked to Trinity library under driving clouds white with snow— it seemed not at all unlikely that there would be a blizzard before long— and entered the library through the north cloister.

My first glimpse of that wonderful interior left an indelible impression of magnificence. The immense proportions of its arcades, dully illuminated by winter light through many high windows; the rows of statuary depicting past luminaries; the great oaken bookshelves that lined, and broke out from the walls, forming bays of bookish solitude; all combined to create a place perfectly adapted to the noble pursuit of learning.

As we approached the desk, a thin, dapper individual of pallid aspect came forward and wished Dr James 'good day'.

'Good morning, Mr Biggs,' said James; 'I wonder if you could help us? Mr Crossley here has a professional interest in those Dee lists, and would like to know whether anyone else has studied them in the last few months.'

'Funny you should ask that, Dr James. If you'd come to me before this morning I'd have said only one other—an undergraduate—Trinity man, I have the name here somewhere—yes—Crowley, Edward Crowley. Spent some time with the Dee material over the last few months. Very keen, he seems. Then, just today—not long ago—a white-haired old gentleman with those long side whiskers—what d'ye call 'em—Piccadilly Weepers—he took them for about half an hour or so. Eldred, the name was. He seemed to know Crowley by name. I thought the old gentleman might be his tutor, though I can't say I recognised him.'

'Thank you, Mr Biggs. Most helpful. Shall we go, Mr Crossley?'

As we departed, James gripped my arm. 'Well, Dr Watson, what do you make of that? A definite clue, I think. You see, I happen to know that Dr Verrall is young Crowley's tutor. Verrall has spoken of him. It seems he came here after some trouble at Oxford. He is by all accounts a gifted student, with a real flair for Latin and Greek, but something of a *Decadent* and a poet *manqué*: you know, adopts the fashionable Diabolism of Baudelaire, and dresses very foppishly. He told Verrall that God and the Devil had fought for his Soul and that he could not decide which had won! Remember that Verrall was mentioned in the message that decoyed me from my rooms! Could it be—?'

I nodded. 'That Crowley and this other fellow Eldred are behind the theft? It is a distinct possibility. One may have delivered the note while the other waited to slip into your rooms.'

'My thought exactly, Dr Watson. Would Mr Holmes object if we visited young Crowley's rooms?'

'He told us to learn all we could.'

'Then let us go at once!'

It took but little time to locate the young undergraduate's rooms. At our knock a voice called 'enter' and we stepped into another world.

The contrast with Dr James's spartan quarters was very instructive. Books covered the walls and filled several revolving walnut bookcases, but this was more than a scholar's workshop. Everywhere the eye fell upon tomes of obvious rarity and tremendous value. I had never seen so many sumptuous bindings; vellum, morocco, and calf, all glittering with heavy gold blocking and intricate decoration. Here was the collection of a bibliophile with the wealth to indulge his passion to the full. I noted, too, a well-worn ice-axe and a bag of fishing rods. Staunton chess pieces stood about a board. The heady aroma of incense mingled with the smell of books.

The young man who rose to greet us was even more remarkable. My readers will know that I had confronted powerful men before that date, and would do so after, but never have I felt so strongly a sense of immediate danger. From the comments of James I had expected the silken shirt and floppy tie, the hands full of rings heavy with semi-precious stones. I could not have anticipated the brooding, hypnotic eyes, determined jaw and immensely powerful frame. He was, I now think, only a little over average height, but his erect, almost arrogant, carriage and the bulk of his upper torso created the impression of exceptional stature.

Dr James introduced us, and explained about the supposed book on John Dee. 'When Mr Crossley here heard that someone else had been studying the material at Trinity, he feared that another book was in production. I have explained that undergraduates have better things to do with their time, but he insisted we talk to you.'

Young Edward Crowley laughed.

'You need have no fear, sir. I am not writing a book—not of *that* kind anyway, though I *am* the greatest poet since Shelley. No, the Dee manuscripts of Trinity do not interest me in themselves. Oh, I did hope they might reflect his occult researches, so misunderstood by that clod Casaubon, but as they do not, I have hardly glanced through them.'

'Yet,' I interrupted, 'you have requested them on several occasions.'

Crowley gave me an odd look.

'Yes, but not to study their contents. I see you are puzzled, gentlemen. Let me explain. I have recently discovered that I possess quite remarkable psychic powers. You are probably not aware that we leave subtle impressions upon every object we touch. To hold such an object is to read its history. By holding manuscripts once written by Dr Dee, I seek to identify myself psychically with him.'

This seemed to me absolute madness, but young Crowley appeared to be completely sincere.

'Though I can tell you little of the actual manuscripts,' he went on, 'I *can* tell you what Dee was wearing when he wrote them, describe the aspect of his library at Mortlake, what thoughts were passing through his mind on certain days when he referred to them.' He assumed a dramatic pose and added impressively, 'I have even seen Queen Elizabeth when she visited him.'

I was now convinced that we were in the presence of a raving lunatic, but Dr James remained quite calm.

'That is most interesting, but hardly relevant to the matter in hand. One other thing—there was a gentleman at Trinity library today, a man with long side whiskers—'

'Mr Eldred? How strange that you should mention him!'

James shrugged. 'He gave the impression that he knew you well.'

'That was a little premature, as we did not meet until an hour ago! In fact, he left not long before you came. We played a game of chess. I am the best chess player in Britain, but he gave me quite an interesting contest. It took some little effort on my part to defeat him. In fact he spoke of the Dee manuscripts while we played!'

Crowley's eyes narrowed, and his lips hardened into a cruel line. 'You know, I begin to find this a little strange. One could be forgiven for thinking there is more to your visit than meets the eye.'

Clearly Crowley was beginning to see through our little pretence. I rose and fastened my coat.

'Well, we have wasted enough of your time, young man. I am satisfied that David Nutt will not be in competition with any rival publisher on this occasion. My mind has been set at rest. Shall we go, Dr James?'

Crowley gave me a penetrating look, then smiled. 'I am glad I could help. Tell me Mr—Crossley did you say?—would you be interested in a volume of poetry? I am, as I told you, the best poet since Shelley.'

'Unfortunately Mr Crossley does not deal with poetry,' said James smoothly. 'Another department.'

'That', said Edward Crowley in a distinctly menacing tone, 'is most unfortunate for him.'

Outside I breathed the clear air with some relief.

'Well!' exclaimed James, 'What did you make of that?'

'I didn't believe a word of it.' I replied. 'Psychic powers indeed! He's hiding something, I'm sure.'

'I thought so too. He owns a copy of Trithemius, as well as Bacon's *de Augmentis Scientiarum* and Selenius's *Cryptographia*. Young Mr Crowley is obviously interested in the decipherment of secret documents!'

We walked back to King's in a state of high excitement, weighing the possibility of actually solving the case without Holmes. However, a shock awaited us at Dr James's rooms.

For as we approached, it became evident that the door, which had been locked when we left, was now standing open. Creeping forward quietly, we peered in.

There, bending over the desk, was a hunched figure with long side whiskers. Adjusting the grip on my stick, I stepped into the room and said, 'Would you mind telling us what you are doing here?'

The old man turned slowly and leered at us with a rheumy insolence. The effect was unnerving.

'I might ask you the same question,' he piped. 'Dr John H. Watson.'

I hefted my stick.

'How do you know my name? Out with it, man! You will not leave this room until you have told us everything!'

'Then', said the old man, straightening up and pulling off his whiskers, 'I had better reveal myself, before you break my head!'

'Holmes!' I cried.

'I'm afraid so, Watson. You can strike one suspect from your list. I apologise for the deception, gentlemen. It was not intentional, but my business in London was concluded sooner than I expected, and it occurred to me that I might undertake at least some of my investigation incognito. I must confess I have enjoyed being Mr Eldred!'

He began to remove his wig and makeup.

'You have been with us every step of the way,' said the crestfallen James. 'Ahead of us, in fact.'

'I got Crowley's name from Biggs. A singular fellow, our Mr Crowley, who will one day make his mark upon the World. Whether it will be for good or ill I cannot say. In any case, I intend to add another "C" to the index. To play chess with someone is always revealing. I held a rearguard action against him for almost thirty minutes, but it was like crossing swords with a fencing master. A powerful mind!'

'An unhinged mind,' I corrected. 'Do you know, Holmes, he thinks he has met Queen Elizabeth!'

Dr James quickly recounted the gist of our conversation. Holmes seemed uninterested.

'These are matters quite outside my brief. There are enough mysteries to exercise my mind in the natural world, without confusing the issue with spooks.'

'Talking of mysteries,' said James, 'are you any nearer to a conclusion?'

Holmes seemed surprised by the question.

'I had arrived at a conclusion before I left Baker Street, Doctor. However, I have found the confirmation I needed. The manuscript is quite safe, and should be in your hands by Christmas Eve.'

'You have no idea how relieved I am to hear that, Mr Holmes. But how could you have solved this so soon?'

'You handed me a pretty problem, I'll admit, but it offered obvious possibilities. The first clue was the blank paper.'

'So you said, but what could that tell you?'

'That this was not merely the theft of a manuscript. Do you have the remaining pages? Good, let us examine them.'

Taking up a pencil, Holmes gently shaded over the topmost sheet. The imprint of words began to show through. Holmes read them aloud.

'Building a house—Vitruvian—five-panel square mnemonic?—Fiery Messengers—As I thought. Whoever stole the manuscript took the time to copy your notes.'

'But why not just take the notes themselves?'

'A good question. Because he did not wish you to *know* that they were of interest to him. Clearly you had stumbled upon some clue of which you yourself were unaware.'

'Clue? Clue to what?'

'That brings us to another point which interested me: the nature of your original discovery. You commented that the gummed pages yielded with surprising ease. I wondered why that should be, when they had held for centuries. There seemed to me one likely answer. That yours was not the initial discovery. My brief examination of the material this morning confirmed the hypothesis. There were two other pages with faint signs of having been gummed back to back. So someone had already found one hidden sheet, and stolen it. On the same, or a subsequent occasion, he began to open the other pair of gummed pages, but was interrupted, and pushed the joint back together. Then you came along, discovered the second sheet, informed the staff and arranged to borrow it. Using that very apposite Kelly hoax, the thief retrieved the other half of his puzzle, coolly picking your brains as he did so!'

'But why go to so much trouble over a few lines of ritualistic nonsense? The value of those pages is surely academic rather than financial. And even academic rivalry rarely descends to the level of physical assault and robbery!'

'You are forgetting young Crowley,' I said. 'Surely he has taken them in order to perform this ritual of the Fiery Messengers. He admitted his initial interest in the Dee material was occult.'

'That is true, Watson, but consider another possibility. You, Dr James, told us with admirable succinctness of your Art of Memory hypothesis; it certainly fitted the facts, but it is possible to be too erudite, to see complexity where it does not exist. Think of that Biblical quotation about building a house, coupled with Vitruvian architectural designs. Dee was a Cambridge man through and through. Can you not think of a building not far from here, completed in Dee's own lifetime, which represents the epitome of Vitruvian architectural principles?'

Dr James threw up his hands.

'Good heavens! King's College Chapel!'

'Quite so,' said Holmes drily. 'And in the light of that, does not this cryptic "ritual" with its circles, arcs and crosses, rather suggest a way of locating something hidden in the Chapel? It would not be the first time such a document has lent itself to such a solution, eh, Watson?'

'The Musgrave Ritual!' I exclaimed. 'I had quite forgotten!'

'If this case has taught me anything,' rejoined Holmes, 'it is that a consulting detective ought to know everything and remember everything! Well, Dr James, are we to solve this puzzle?'

'There is nothing I would like more, Mr Holmes, but the thief is now in possession of all the clues. He had the advantage of that other page.'

'Yet we are three, Doctor, and we have your great ecclesiological knowledge at our disposal. Now, I suppose you can lay your hands upon a ground plan of the Chapel? Good; and as the creator of this mystery was an authority on Euclid, it is perhaps fitting that we will also require rule, compasses and ink for a little geometry. The time has come for a guided tour of King's College Chapel.'

Luckily for us, the Chapel proved to be deserted, though we knew well enough that there might be an interruption at any moment.

Despite myself, I was so moved by the great and solemn interior, with its intricate vaultings and blazing expanses of coloured glass, that I could not help but look around me in wonder.

'It is beautiful, Doctor,' I whispered. 'Such workmanship—and the stained glass! Is it original?'

Dr James did not answer. He was gazing upwards as if he too was seeing the windows for the first time.

'What a fool!' he cried. I felt a little hurt, for I had not thought my question so deserving of ridicule, but it seemed I had misinterpreted his words.

'What an absolute fool I am!' he went on. 'Mr Holmes, Dr Watson, I have been blind! You were right, I was too clever for my own good. When the context is understood, it is all absurdly simple! Where are those notes—here—d'you see? the oblong with the central panel surrounded by four smaller! It is the layout of each of these windows! And in the centre panel of each is a figure sometimes called a Messenger!'

'A *messenger* in *fiery* colours,' observed Holmes. 'Well done, Doctor. I was sure your knowledge would prove invaluable. The windows mark the positions on our ground plan, then, but which?'

Dr James looked about him. 'Let me see—I think the east end. Yes— now "first east yr circle linkying th High Priest to th release of Spirrittes—" Yes, the second to last window on the North side depicts Christ before the High Priest. And that of the South shows Christ releasing the spirits!'

Holmes rubbed his hands and chuckled. 'A circle on the ground plan that touches those two windows. Go on. Doctor, go on.'

'Where are we? Yes—"Then fashion an arc by which ye shall be encrowned and bewailed." The last window on the North side has Christ crowned, and on the last South window, Christ mourned by the women. Absurdly simple, why didn't I think of it? Have you got that, Mr Holmes?'

'Yes—the arc thus formed cuts through the circle, forming an eclipse around the altar.'

' "Thereby enfolding ye most high"—*altus*, meaning high, an altar!—"Within the vesica piscis". Now, "Blindfold and mocked on ye arms of ye crosse". The third to last windows on each side show Christ blindfolded and Christ mocked. A cross, then, with the arms touching those two points. May I see?'

He peered over Holmes's shoulder.

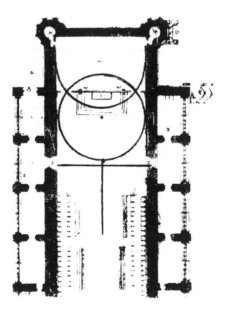

'The Hieroglyphic Monad!' he exclaimed. 'It is Dee's own symbol.' Holmes nodded. 'But our puzzle is not quite complete. Have you forgotten the reference to a circle whose centre is everywhere?'

'Wait, you are right. The symbol usually has a dot at the centre of the circle.'

'Then let us add one: and as it is described as "everywhere" we can take it that its position—before the steps leading up to the altar—is all important. It is surely to the flagstone at that spot that we must look.'

'Do we dig it up?' I asked.

'There is no need, Watson. Our man will do that for us, *and* return the stolen pages, if we only wait for him.'

At that moment, the sound of movement sent us swiftly into a side chapel, from which James peeked out.

'It is an undergraduate named Wimbush. An excellent young man, but somewhat talkative. If he sees us here, I fear it will be all over the University by nightfall.'

'Then', whispered Holmes, 'we may turn the situation to our advantage. Stay out of sight—and hold my coat.'

Rolling up his sleeves, Holmes ruffled his hair and tied his handkerchief about his neck. By the time Wimbush drew near, the consulting detective had disappeared, and in his place stood a rather truculent workman.

'Can I help you, sir?' I heard Wimbush ask in a frankly suspicious tone.

''Elp us?' rejoined Holmes. 'If yer've got a cold chisel or a lump 'ammer about yer.'

'I thought', persisted the youth, 'that the renovations were in abeyance at present.'

'Did yer! So did we till the word came to get back 'ere. We'll be workin' on the *floor* right up ter Christmas Eve.'

'Who gave you the order to resume work?' Wimbush asked. It was an awkward moment, but Dr James saved the day by shouting from the shadows in an accent every bit as convincing as that of Holmes, 'Are you gunner stand there jawin' all day?'

'Keep yer 'air on,' Holmes called back. 'There's a young genelman 'ere wants ter 'elp us wi' the liftin'.'

'I'm sorry, gentlemen,' said Wimbush in quavering tones, 'but I am really rather busy—good day to you.'

Holmes chuckled as he pulled on his jacket. 'Well done, Dr James.'

'Well done both of you,' I said, 'but would it not have been better just to hide?'

'No, Dr Watson,' replied James. 'I think Mr Holmes wants our talkative young friend to spread the word that workmen are examining the floor of the Chapel.'

'You anticipate me in every particular, Doctor. The thief will not risk any accidental discoveries by workmen. This should force his hand. If we are lucky, tonight might well see the moment of confrontation.'

Holmes's plan was to mount a vigil in the Chapel. To this end we prepared, arming ourselves with dark lanterns, rugs and walking sticks for weapons. Dr James was given a stout oak cudgel, Holmes had his cane weighted with lead, and I elected to settle any differences of opinion with the aid of a Penang Lawyer.

There followed, let me confess it, a tedious time for me. Holmes and Dr James became engrossed in a discussion of the ways in which the principles of detection might be applied to the dating of documents. So the time passed profitably enough for them, but little of what was said proved intelligible to me, or, I suspect, to the general reader. I did take the opportunity to write up my notes in detail, then dozed by the fire. The next thing I remember was Holmes standing over me in the firelight saying, 'Come, Watson—it is time.'

The walk to the Chapel cleared my head. It was bitterly cold, and the hoar frost crunched beneath our boots like a light fall of snow. There was a curious stillness in the air that suggested the impending blizzard could not be long delayed. Dr James produced a key and unlocked the heavy door to the Chapel.

It was Holmes's plan that we should conceal ourselves among the side chapels that lined the building. Holmes settled in the shadows on the north side, James and I in separate places to the south, so that we could converge from three sides upon our prey. With the dark lanterns shuttered, we sat in complete darkness, gazing out at the slightly lighter area of the Chapel.

I do not remember the hours that followed with any pleasure. The chill of the building soon penetrated to my old wound, causing a nagging ache that I did not dare to ease by movement. The nature of the forthcoming confrontation began to play on my mind. Holmes would see it merely as the culmination of an investigation, and James seemed too excited by the adventure to think ahead, but I recalled the menacing figure of young Crowley, and remembered the ice-axe on his wall. It seemed to me the likeliest implement to choose if one sought to combine the functions of leverage and defence. The final confrontation might prove distinctly unpleasant.

Just when I was beginning to think that our wait had been in vain, I became aware of a disturbance of the air, betokening movement somewhere. The sound of a door closing echoed faintly through the darkness, and the light of a partly unshaded lantern approached through the ante-chapel. As it came closer, I could discern a heavily muffled figure with sheets of paper clutched in its gloved hand. I could see no weapon of any kind. Crouching over to see the papers by the half-light of its lantern, the figure began to move back and forth across the floor of the Chapel.

There was a certain grim humour in witnessing that slow decipherment of the clues. More than once features of the Chapel quite unconnected with the solution were examined, and steps retraced. But inexorably the lines were drawn, and at length the figure stood on the spot before the steps to the altar. Only then was a prise-bar produced from his coat, and the lifting of the slab begun. Then the stone was turned aside and something taken from the hole.

'Now!' roared Holmes, and shone his lantern full upon the scene. Struggling from my place of concealment, I glimpsed our quarry already in flight, with Holmes in pursuit. My lantern cover had jammed, but that of Dr James shone out to reveal a second man standing on the edge of the surrounding shadows. He was tall, white-bearded and grim, but too old and frail to pose much of a problem for a healthy young man. I therefore decided that Holmes had greater need of my help. Calling out 'Detain him, Doctor,' I set off in pursuit.

That long, cold vigil had so aggravated my wound that I had little expectation of overtaking Holmes, but my efforts to keep pace found unexpected assistance outside the Chapel.

The night was a swirling mass of white flakes, and the ground underfoot had become very slippery. Such conditions are a great leveller. The two men in front of me were hardly capable of a better pace than I. None the less, it proved an epic chase. Our quarry led us out onto the stretch of land called the Backs, a very pleasant walk, no doubt, on summer evenings, but on such a bitter night of snow, with the ground rutted and slippery under ice, a treacherous place.

Just as my strength was giving out, and I felt I should have to leave Holmes to continue the chase alone, I came upon him crouched over a fallen figure.

'Holmes,' I gasped, 'you caught him.'

'No, Watson,' he replied grimly. 'He fell before I reached him.'

With that, he turned over the muffled form, to reveal the distorted face of Biggs. Forcing open the clenched hand, Holmes retrieved some small object. I laid my hand upon the fallen man's neck.

'He's dead, Holmes. What was it—a seizure brought on by the chase?'

'Probably—and yet, Watson, I would swear that some dark shape rose up and dropped upon his back just before he fell.'

'A trick of shadow,' I observed. Holmes did not reply. 'In any case, I hope Dr James has been able to detain the other man . . .'

Holmes rose up with a cry.

'The other man? I saw no other man! Come, Watson!'

'But what of Biggs?'

'We can do nothing for him now—come!'

Returning to the Chapel with all possible haste, we found Dr James standing alone, his left hand raised to his brow, as though dazed. The thought that the old man had produced some weapon and attacked him suggested itself to me. However, he was not injured, but the figure I had glimpsed had gone. Clearly I had expected too much of the amiable scholar. Holmes was keen to salvage what we could from the débâcle.

'Did you by any chance recognize him, Doctor?'

'Yes—yes, I'm afraid I did.'

'Then tell us his name. Come on man, out with it.'

'I cannot—I will say only that he was a distinguished fellow of the University—I can tell you no more.'

'Dr James,' I cried, 'I am surprised and disappointed! I had thought you a man of honour, yet you cover up for this man. It is misplaced loyalty!'

'Watson is right,' added Holmes. 'You cannot be partial in this matter.'

'You mistake me, gentlemen. I am not defending him. He is far beyond your reach. It was Dr John Dee.' Seeing our disbelieving expressions, James added quietly, 'I have seen his likeness often enough in the Ashmolean at Oxford. It would seem, gentlemen, that the originator of this mystery returned to witness its solution!'

'We cannot stand here all night,' said Holmes abruptly. 'Pick up your missing pages; we will replace the slab.'

As if by agreement, not another word was spoken about James's remarkable claim until half an hour later, when we were warming our chilled limbs by the fire.

'I cannot help feeling guilty about leaving Biggs out on the Backs,' James said suddenly.

'If you wish this whole matter to remain secret, there is nothing else to be done,' replied Holmes.

'I was so sure it was Crowley!' I said. Holmes shook his head.

'I have warned you before not to be too precipitate in your conclusions, Watson. Young Mr Crowley is strong and fit enough to be a mountaineer, and if I do not misjudge his character, is possessed of a violent temper when crossed. If *he* had been cornered by Muir, I think the resulting injury might have given us a murder case! No, the culprit was barely strong enough to knock down a frail old man. From the first I was looking for a comparatively weak individual, although', he added ruefully, 'his stamina over the flat mile surprised me.'

'I wonder', interjected James, 'if that was because he was fleeing from more than you and Dr Watson? I have been reading the first of the hidden pages:

"In nomini Jesu Christi. Amen. Unus est Deus, et unum est opum nostrum." (There is one God, and there is one work of ours.) *"Tabula locorum rerum et thesaurorum absconditorum."* (A table of the locations, the objects and the hidden treasure)—then a section that is indecipherable. Then, *"Quam hic, familiarissimorum consensu, aliquando ad nostratium commoditatem et auxilium abscondere et sepelire decrevi: qua quidem intellecta facile passunt ad lucem abscondita effere."* (Which I ordered here to be hidden and buried, with the consent of those closest to me, for the benefit and advantage of those of us returning at some future time: which having been interpreted, they may easily bring what was hidden to light.)

'It was, I believe, customary to leave some demonic guard over treasure. That is why I wonder if it *was* just a shadow that fell on Biggs. The text ends with the words *"Depositum Custodi"* (Keep that which is committed to thee).'

To my surprise, Holmes said nothing but stared into the fire.

'But I almost forgot in the excitement, Mr Holmes,' added James. 'What *was* this treasure?'

Holmes drew from his pocket a curiously shaped phial of turbid liquid.

'The fruit of a lifetime's studies, vain or otherwise. The Elixir of Life.'

'Then surely,' I cried, 'this has all been an enormous folly!'

'An hour ago I would have agreed with you,' said James. 'But after looking into the face of a man dead for almost three hundred years, I am no longer sure.'

'In any case,' said Holmes, 'it is the strangest conclusion to an investigation that I can remember. In fact, there can be no question of a fee. The interest of this case has been payment enough. But if you wish me to name a price, I will take this phial.'

'Of course, Mr Holmes. It is of no use to me. I prefer to leave the hour of my demise in the hands of the good God who made me. But surely you do not intend . . .'

'No, Doctor, I merely wish to extract a sample for chemical tests.'

'And if you find a composition unknown to science?'

'Then—then the temptation will constitute an interesting test of character. By the way, Doctor, when the time comes to publish that list of Dee's books—'

'No detail of this episode shall ever appear in print, Mr Holmes, unless it be as fiction. When the time comes, I will exercise editorial discretion.'

It was the day of Christmas Eve, on which Dr James was to attend the carol service in the Chapel. After a much-needed breakfast, we packed our things. Later in the morning James was called away, and returned to tell us that Biggs had been found, but that the carol service would go ahead as planned.

Since the blizzard had curtailed train services, we were forced to wait until late in the afternoon, when at last we set off, stopping on the way to say our goodbyes at the Chapel. The snow was still falling in heavy flakes, but they came slow and straight out of a still sky. As we drew near the Chapel, Dr James approached in his surplice, looking every inch the scholar dignitary.

'Gentlemen,' he called. 'I'm so glad I had the chance to give you these. Seasonal gifts—tokens of my gratitude. For you, Mr Holmes, a copy of one of my latest catalogues, *The Manuscripts of Jesus College*, which I have inscribed. I think it is rather nicely "got up", don't you? And for you, Dr Watson, nothing so grand, I'm afraid. Just the Christmas issue of the *Pall Mall* magazine, but I've written some words of thanks on the cover. It contains one of my little efforts at fiction entitled "Lost Hearts". A poor thing, but not, I promise you, *quite* as sentimental as it sounds! And now I really must go. Are you sure you cannot come in for the service? Later there will be dinner in Hall, and I generally have a few friends over for talk and drinks. I usually tell the latest of my tales.'

'Alas,' said Sherlock Holmes, 'we cannot. Even at this season there is work to be done. In the great City, Evil never sleeps.'

We shook hands and James made his way into the Chapel. We stood a while, looking into that great space, now starred with a hundred points of flame. Columns of figures filed in from various points of the Chapel, a faint hum sounded and the soft voices of the boys struck up 'Once in Royal David's City'. The whole scene seemed the very embodiment of Christmas.

Holmes touched my shoulder. 'Are you ready, Watson?'

As I stood there, a sudden desire took me to go in and listen to that beautiful music, to enjoy a hearty dinner, then accompany Dr James to his rooms, there to exchange tales over drinks by the fire. In short, to keep Christmas in the good old-fashioned way. It was an unworthy thought. Turning up my collar against the snow, I straightened my back and said, 'Yes, Holmes, I'm ready.'

Many years have passed since that day, but on the shelves at Baker Street there still stands a now brittle copy of the *Pall Mall* magazine, and a well-thumbed volume, reminders of a singular adventure, and of two—or should I say three?—very remarkable men.

THE CODEX

by David G. Rowlands

David G. Rowlands (b. 1941), one of England's
best modern writers in the classic ghost story
tradition (who contributed 'Gebal and Ammon
and Amalek' to *Ghosts for Christmas*, and 'On
Wings of Song' to *Chillers for Christmas*), here
makes his welcome third appearance in the
series. Several friends and colleagues of M.R.
James are featured in 'The Codex', some under
disguised names. Henry Elford Luxmoore was
his tutor at Eton and remained a good friend,
assuming a paternal role, for half a century
(from 1876 to 1926).

'A capital view of Luxmoore has come out in the photograph of the function in
his garden.'

M.R. James, letter to Gwendolen McBryde, 14th June 1933.

Being the product of a grammar school education in an industrial
township, Mr Batchel—sometime Chaplain of a famous Cambridge College, Vicar of Stoneground and presently Librarian
emeritus at the Minster Church—had never quite understood the
fixation of public schoolboys with their early years in venerable
establishments; their preoccupation with tradition and their close
relationships, extending well into middle age, with their former House-
masters or Tutors.

These thoughts had arisen in their generality from a specific example,
of course. Mr Batchel was thinking of a friend of many years standing,

once Provost of the Cambridge College where he had been Chaplain and who had returned to be Provost at the public school that had predestined his donnish career.

He was in fact on his way to visit that friend for Christmas at the same school; mindful as they both were of many previous years at Cambridge and always aware, as the years rolled by, that each present meeting might be their last. Not that they viewed it in any morbid light or that the years had in any way dulled the sparkle and cutting edge of their repartee.

Mr Batchel was aware, though, from their correspondence, that his friend's former Tutor who had lived in retirement within the precincts, had died a few years previously and that the personal loss had been immense.

It was the last weekend of the Michaelmas term and the teeming throngs of boys and Scholars at the College with their exuberance and noise, and the imminence of departure for Christmas made Mr Batchel smile in rapport with the mood of festivity, as he made his way carefully across the cobbles of School Yard, beneath the arch of Lupton's Tower, round to the left into the Cloisters and so to the Provost's Lodge.

A bitter wind was whipping round the covered walk and Mr Batchel reflected that he had changed the freezing cold of his fenside Minster, for the chill of this venerable Thames Valley pile.

He came at last to the nail-studded door bearing a forbidding brass plate 'The Provost' and, wheezing slightly as a token of his threescore and ten years, knocked on the oak with his stick. An elderly lady opened the door, framed in a welcoming glow of warmth and light from the passage behind her. Mr Batchel removed his hat.

'Good afternoon, Mrs Keating. Bitter-cold weather.'

'Good afternoon, Mr Batchel; come in, sir, and get warm, do.'

He was shown along a dimmish corridor of rush mat flooring and lined with pictures, into a panelled room where a welcome warmth was given out by a large, open-hearth, log fire: little of the smoke seemed to be going out of the flue high above. He coughed, his eyes streaming.

'R.B., my dear chap!' His friend, the Provost, rose from his chair, not without a certain caution, and limped across, hand outstretched. They banged each other lustily on the shoulder blades and lapsed briefly into the brickfields jargon of Mr Batchel's former parish.

'Whaffor are yer come, then, moulder?'

'Better ter greet yer, pug boy.' They laughed and sat down beside the fire, returning to normal accents.

'I thought we'd have dinner in College Hall tonight. You've got your usual room by the way. Ramsay and Lombard are looking in after dinner. Which reminds me . . .' The Provost shuffled to a side table heaped with books and papers, handing a slim brown volume to his guest.

'It's a few years old now, but I haven't remembered to give it you before. It's the story I told to Ramsay and Lombard's scouts at Worbarrow camp. One of the hundred and fifty copies printed.'

'Ah, yes, indeed. Thank you, M! It was included in that handsome "Collected" volume you sent me a year or so ago. I was amused by your statement about belief in ghosts: that you were prepared to consider evidence; you old sceptic!'

The Provost started slightly and smiled. 'Well, what else could the Provost say? But I may have something to say to you later on that score!'

Mr Batchel coughed. 'I had no notion you'd written so many ghost stories.'

'Nor I. It came as a bit of a shock to have them all put together like that. So many of our Cambridge Christmasses and other occasions, eh? Now, thanks to Millar's radio set we can listen to the Cambridge service on Christmas Eve, but it isn't the same any more. The Lessons and Carols: a bit overdone. Too rich a diet for one sitting.'

Mr Batchel nodded and the two lapsed into reverie, as old men will; each remembering past years and events.

Mrs Keating's entry with teapot and cups stirred them into conversation, once more, and they talked briskly about the Codex Sinaiticus which the Provost was embroiled in purchasing for the British Museum, about the novels of Dorothy L. Sayers and attempted to finish *The Times* crossword, unsuccessfully; before making their way up the spiral wooden stair to robe for chapel and the last choral evensong of the Half-year.

While putting on his surplice and hood, Mr Batchel looked out of the bedroom window. It was already dusk and he could barely see across the Siam garden to the fields beyond. Something round and white moved briefly in the foliage below and he grinned, thinking of what his friend had written in a story concerning the playing fields after dark! Then the booming of the chapel bell dispelled that notion as effectively as it was supposed to exorcise evil spirits!

Evensong in the chapel was very pleasing. Even the faded wall paintings (an enthusiasm of the Provost's that Mr Batchel could not share) did not cast their usual gloom, and the choristers put real spirit into the settings and anthem; possibly in the knowledge that this was their last stint of the year and that there was only the exuberance of the

Lower Master's party to come before the holidays. The Provost hobbled out of his stall to read the first lesson; Mr Batchel read the second. As for the concluding hymn: 'O, Little Town of Bethlehem', Mr Batchel did not think it had ever been better sung.

He was in pleasantly mellow mood therefore as he followed his old friend down the private stair from the rooms above to College Hall, and took his place at the top table. One of the few buildings to have proceeded according to King Henry's plan and dating from the mid-fifteenth century, the open fireplaces filled the room with the pungent reek of wood smoke and had not been improved by the more recent alterations. Mr Batchel avoided looking at the hideous west window, happily not very visible against the dark outside, and enjoyed instead the panelling and portraits: among which he could discern a new canvas of the Provost's former Tutor, Luxmoore.

They were joined at dinner by the new Headmaster, Dr Elliott, the Vice-Provost, Lombard and Ramsay, just returned from Magdalen, all friends known to Mr Batchel and conversation flowed easily despite the rising crescendo of exuberance from the Collegers' tables, and even from the Sixth Form just below High Table.

Just before nine, there was a stir among the tables and a few older boys of the Auxiliary Choir joined the choristers (who had been spirited thither from the Lower Master's party) in the dark Gallery over the East door and softly sang 'In dulce jubilo' (this being a known favourite of the Provost). Once again Mr Batchel was strongly reminded of the Cambridge years. The attendants had turned out the main lights and when they were raised again and the choristers packed off home with a mince pie apiece, the smallest of the Collegers was impelled toward High Table clasping a book.

The Provost's eyes twinkled as the lad stumbled over his request for one of the ghost stories to be read to the Scholars. He rose heavily from the table, taking the book, and limped over to the Oriel window where stood the old desk, from which in former times improving passages of Scripture had been read.

Save for the lectern glow, the lights were turned down, and the Provost read the story 'Canon Alberic's Scrapbook' in his dry, unemotional tones to a spellbound silence.

During the reading Mr Batchel allowed his eyes to wander up to the gallery and all but started. Looking over the rail was the craggy, hawk-like face and bushy eyebrows of the late Mr Henry Luxmoore. Then, of

[273]

a sudden, the face was withdrawn. He nudged Lombard, looked at the new portrait, and whispered.

'I'll swear I saw Luxmoore up in the Gallery.'

Mr Lombard nodded, repacking his pipe. 'You're not the first; but Monty doesn't want to believe it,' he confided, sotto voce.

After dinner, a handful of those from High Table adjourned to the Provost's apartments, sitting round the fire in the panelled room where the valuable portraits of former scholars, Oppidans and dignitaries looked down on the convivial flow of conversation, and the splash of soda water in tumblers of spirit. Topics were mostly bookish and ran from comments on Mr Batchel's own *Story of the Minster Church* via the Provost's current *Excluded Books of the New Testament*, to S.M. Ellis's recently published *Wilkie Collins, Le Fanu and Others*, at which juncture Ramsay quoted from some rather sprightly letters of Collins to a young niece, that had surfaced a few weeks earlier, to the discomfort of relatives. Finally they managed between them to complete *The Times* crossword before leaving for their various apartments and billets.

The Provost saw his friends out, then returned to the fireside and stirred the embers to life, placing on another log.

'A night-cap, R.B.? I've got a little story for you.'

Mr Batchel nodded, repacked his pipe and settled back in his chair. His host brought his glass and from a drawer in his desk took out a framed photograph.

'Tell me what you see there,' he said, rather in the manner of Williams of 'The Mezzotint'.

Mr Batchel looked at the print.

'Why,' he said, 'it's a garden party surely? And on a festive day. There's you and Alington and Ramsay—oh, lots of donnish folk on a platform with bunting: *very* vulgar, M! Facing a sort of pavilion or summer house . . . why, it must have been your . . .'

He was interrupted by the Provost, speaking briskly.

'In the foreground, man! With his back to the camera?'

'Well,' said Mr Batchel slowly, 'it looks like your old Tutor, Luxmoore—though mind you, it's a good few years since I last saw the old chap. When was this taken, then?'

'June this year,' said his friend quietly.

'Phew,' said Mr Batchel and meant it; for as the reader will have gathered, Luxmoore had been dead for more than six years. He looked very closely at the picture, screwing up his eyes to use a hand-lens from his waistcoat pocket. 'No doubt about it, I'd say: Luxmoore, unquestionably. What's the story?'

'I wish I knew! All I can tell you is that this year after many protracted negotiations with his executors, and even more wrangles with the Fellows, I managed to secure for the College the garden Luxmoore created across the stream there, on Tangier island. We had a summer house erected on the site and it was all formally opened this June. Kissack's the Photographers came along to take some pictures of the occasion.

'It must have been about a week later, when Mundy from Kissack's was banging at the door downstairs in great excitement. I was en route to a Bursary meeting, but he thrust a photographic print into my hand.

"Mr Provost! Mr Provost! Just look at this, sir!"

'It was that very photo you see there. And like you, I thought it was unquestionably Luxmoore! It stopped me dead, I can tell you. I felt rather queer and had to sit down! At first, of course, I thought it was a tasteless joke . . . but Mundy's demeanour convinced me that was not the case. I had to go to the meeting but I told Mundy I would investigate the matter thoroughly as soon as I could. Unfortunately, he talked to several people and the print was shown about, before I impounded it.

'Needless to say, Lombard and I went very thoroughly into the matter. All other prints taken from the glass plate showed the same unmistakable figure. Yet no-one claimed to have seen the spectre of M'Tutor at the event. I even got Heatherall, the science master, to investigate the negative; but there was no reason to suspect jiggery-pokery. When people have asked me about it, I've treated it lightly: made a joke of it: "Nice of the old boy to come along." It's a bit like my "Mezzotint" story after all; to say nothing of your friend Groves's "Man with the Roller". Come, now, Batchel—you're a bit of a scientist yourself: what do you think of it?'

Mr Batchel felt some concern. His old friend had become rather agitated, and clearly the matter had affected him far more than he cared to admit.

'Why', he said, 'we are only just beginning to understand the sympathy in photography. If one accepts the notion that this was an occasion in which Luxmoore—had he been alive—would have rejoiced and have been interested; what more "natural"—if one can use such a word—than that he should have been drawn in some fashion, however briefly, to the scene? The photographic plate is incredibly sensitive, and despite the bad publicity that fakers have caused, I believe it can record things that we are not yet aware of, just as some clever chemists can bring out the colours that are also locked into that emulsion.'

The Provost nodded thoughtfully. 'Well, that is one aspect. What I haven't told you, is that I feel his presence at times, in this building . . . and my papers are re-arranged or upset. Is he trying to tell me something?' He attempted a laugh. 'It's not poor Jane Shore*, I can tell you that! I have never seen her, despite living in these cloisters for the past 15 years!'

Mr Batchel laughed. 'You are not a person who sees ghosts, M. You are overtired and not a little dispirited, that's all.'

The Provost yawned and stretched his arms above his head.

'You may be right. It has been a bad year for me. Now I've lost Alington to Durham, Ramsay to Magdalen and with Walter Fletcher dead, I've no confidante at hand. Lombard does his best to jolly me along, but losing those four masters in the climbing accident, Dr Ley's illness and to cap it all, the struggle to raise funds for the Codex, have all been a bit much. The press have been anti-Codex from the start. The Americans are waving dollars at the Russians. To be only five hundred pounds short now is so frustrating; you can't imagine.' He hit the palm of his hand with the other fist. 'If only M'Tutor were still around, he'd have come up with something. Still, I'm an old moaner, Roly . . . don't heed me.'

'Luxmoore would have told you to stop worrying and go to bed, M. Man proposes, God disposes, and all that.'

'I daresay you are right,' the Provost smiled. 'You know, I have a notion that the old boy might make his presence known to you.'

'Why me? I hardly knew him!' said Mr Batchel curiously.

'You are like that clergyman of Le Fanu's: 'there seem to be ghosts about you.'

'Thanks,' said Mr Batchel. 'You mean the Rev. Jennings's father. The son cut his throat, remember?'

'So he did,' said the Provost. 'Well, don't do that; goodnight!'

The bell in Lupton's tower was striking one, and the cold north east wind was rattling the casements as Mr Batchel got speedily into bed, still a little peturbed about his old friend. However he fell asleep easily enough over the small press booklet.

* Jane Shore prevented her lover Edward IV from destroying the College. When she was out of favour, the grateful College authorities sheltered her in Lupton's tower.

He awoke from a dream of an International Detectives Congress, at which he was applauded for his acumen in unmasking several of the Napoleons of crime. Dr Fu Manchu was clearly none other than Charlie Chan, Carl Petersen had to be Hanaud; Raffles was certainly Lord Peter Wimsey and who could Professor Moriarty be but Holmes himself? The rosy feeling of success faded with the realisation that he was cold. Moonlight flooded the room and there was nothing but dead ash in the fire grate, stirred by the wind whistling in the chimney.

Despite the cold, he sat up, convinced that there was someone in the room. 'Is that you, M? This is no time for pranks. Be your age. Be visible, whoever you are!' As silence answered an obvious thought presented itself: 'Luxmoore, if it's you, show yourself, man! What do you want?'

Mr Batchel thought that he had never cared much for Luxmoore alive: found him rather supercilious, sharp-tongued and caustic—not unlike Arthur Benson had been. He found that he cared for him even less at that moment, when nothing stirred but the wind.

As he reached for the bedside switch there came a sudden howl of wind down the flue, blowing a cloud of ashes into the moonlight. Suspended there for an instant: as if the dust was blocking in like an artist, was the bulk of a tall, round-shouldered figure with a mop of hair. Then the impression faded as the dust particles drifted to the linoleum, eddying slightly in the draughts.

Mr Batchel watched spellbound. It seemed as if a stick or pencil or *finger* drew an outline in the dust on the floor. It was not a very good drawing that he craned his neck to see, but looked for all the world like a sundial: a pillar with a triangular blob on top.

He switched on the light . . . there was the dust; there was the tracing in it, and a sort of footprint as well.

Tutting to himself in prosaic concern for the housekeeper, Mr Batchel swept up the dust as best he could with the fire brush; then he went resolutely back to bed. If there were other visitants, he slept through them.

At breakfast in the parlour, his host—never a good riser—was rather tetchy over the eggs and marmalade and deprecated Mr Batchel's expressed wish to walk around the College environs, with a 'Suit yourself', before busying himself in the day's mail.

There were no letters for Mr Batchel, so he took up his stick and set out; not through the Cloisters, but into Weston's Yard and on to Lombard's villa.

That worthy young man was busy signing orders for boys departing that day. 'Be with you in a minute, R.B.'

At last he was free . . . 'Where will I find a sundial?' demanded Mr Batchel. 'Is there one in Luxmoore's garden?'

'Why, yes, there is,' said Lombard. 'The old boy built it himself from bits of Lower Chapel masonry, during repairs. He dedicated it to Monty, you know. The inscription is a queer one—not Greek or Latin, as you'd expect, but a concoction of psalms. Lemme think now; yes: "Thou my companion, my guide and mine own familiar friend" (Psalm 55, 14) and "The earth is full of thy riches" (Psalm 104, 24). Just the sort of quirky things old Lucky used to say: pointed, y'know.'

Mr Batchel beamed. 'Can we get in there?'

'What? Luxmoore's garden? At this hour? Well, yes, I suppose so; but hadn't you better tell me what this is all about?'

They crossed from Weston's by Gaffneys, in front of Upper School, the Chapel and churchyard, then through a passageway into Baldwin's Road and across the field to Tangier island. It was still bitterly cold and Mr Batchel was struggling to keep up with his athletic young friend, as he puffed out the salient points of his night-time adventure. Lombard had procured Dr Elliott's key and soon they had crossed Friendship bridge into the winter-time desolation of the garden.

The sundial stood where Luxmoore had been in the photograph. It was of plain stone and the edges of the table top held the incised inscriptions. Mr Batchel was happy to let Lombard grapple with it; trying to twist the pillar this way and that. Unexpectedly the table moved and it was lifted gingerly to the frosty ground. The pillar was hollow and Mr Lombard reached inside, drawing up a terra-cotta pot.

It was full of sovereigns: tarnished and dull, but indubitably modern coin of the realm.

After replacing the table top, the two men sat in the wooden shelter, counting the money . . . three hundred and six pounds.

'Well,' said Lombard. 'I guess there's no doubt it belongs to Monty: Luxmoore always said the sundial was his. Let's go and tell him about his windfall.'

'No,' said Mr Batchel. 'I've got a better idea. Let's go and knock up the Bank first; then I suggest we shamelessly importune some of the masters and Fellows and any parents we can grab too. Surely we can make it up to five hundred.'

'Hmm. Two hundred is a lot to winkle out, R.B.,' said Lombard, catching on. 'Here, I can manage twenty-five, myself. Look we'd better telegraph Millar at the Museum to get moving.'

'I'll do that,' said Mr Batchel, 'And if I put in twenty-five too, why, we're well on the way.'

Mr Batchel and the Provost were returning, surpliced and cassocked, across School Yard to the Cloisters, after Christmas morning Communion, and looking forward to their breakfast. They had just reached the Provost's door, when a forbidden bicycle swept in from Weston's Yard, carrying a uniformed telegraph boy.

'Telegram for Dr James,' he said, offering the orange envelope.

The Provost paused in the doorway, his face a study of anxiety.

'Oh, no,' he said. 'Not bad news today of all days.'

Mr Batchel took the envelope and pushed it at him. 'Better open it and see,' he said, feeling beneath his cassock for his money pocket to tip the lad.

The older man fumbled in distraught fashion at the envelope and looked up. 'Why, dash it! You're grinning, Batchel! What is it?'

Then his eyes focused on the message:

'Codex ours. Thanks Luxmoore. Millar. Museum.'

In the Provost's own words: if it had been a bad year, it was at least a miraculous Christmas!

Author's note: Fuller details of the mysterious Luxmoore photo can be found in Angus Macnaghton's *Haunted Berkshire* (1986) page 30. The Codex Sinaiticus did actually come into the Museum's possession on Christmas Day 1933. Refs: Pfaff, R.W.: *Montague Rhodes James*, (London, 1980) page 389; Metzger, B.M.: *The Text of the New Testament* (London, 1964), page 45.

PEACE ON EARTH, GOODWILL TO MOST MEN

by John Whitbourn

John Whitbourn (b. 1958) is an archaeology
graduate and works in local government. 'Peace
on Earth, Goodwill to Most Men', and several
other of his tales which have appeared in
anthologies, are part of a long series entitled *The
Binscombe Tales*, set in a present day suburban
community and all involving the enigmatic Mr
Disvan and his associate, Mr Oakley. These
stories construct a 'mythology' for modern
England. Whitbourn has also written several
'alternative history' science fiction novels.

'Same again, Mr Disvan?'
Disvan looked into his glass and gave the question more
thought than usual.
'Maybe not, Mr Oakley,' he said eventually. 'Given the season of the
year, perhaps we should consider an alternative.'
This sounded a bit ominous. Mr Disvan was a creature of habit, like
most old men, and not the sort to let the occasion of Christmas Eve
interfere with the orderly passage of Binscombe life.
'Alternative?' I asked cautiously. 'Like what?'
'Like going to Midnight Mass at St Joseph's, for instance.'
This really was a bolt out of the blue. Nothing could have been further

from my mind. I tried to express my 'stunned ox' status in a reasonable fashion.

'Church? But you're not a Christian, are you? I mean . . . well . . . and as for me . . .'

'As for you,' muttered Disvan, 'you're what's called a "yuppie", yes, I'm aware of that—and you're too Porsche and pound orientated for matters spiritual. It'd still do you some good to go. Me likewise. I realise I may be some distance from Christian orthodoxy . . .'

I intervened with an overdone 'you're not kidding' expression.

'. . . but it's a respectful distance, even so.'

Disvan was clutching at straws, I could tell—but he pressed gamely on.

'Anyhow,' he said, 'it's sort of traditional and . . . appropriate. There was no point in asking any of this lot.' Here he gestured to indicate the rest of our friends and acquaintances in the Argyll's public bar. 'They're neo-heathens for the most part. I thought you might be interested though.'

Not wishing to disappoint, I gave the notion a quick once-over. It wouldn't hurt, I concluded and, all things considered, my bachelor Christmas *could* do with an injection of festive jollity.

'Okay,' I said. 'I'm game for a laugh.'

Mr Disvan smiled but not, I suspected, at my little joke.

'Oh, there'll be laughs, Mr Oakley,' he said, 'I can assure you. That's half the reason for going. So come on then, off we go.'

He was already on his feet and labouring into his coat.

'Hang about,' I said, staying put in my seat. 'There's miles of time yet.'

Disvan looked very concerned.

'No, there isn't, Mr Oakley. We've got to be early and get a seat at the front.'

'But it's only 10:30!'

He shook his head and tutted.

'Don't you read the papers, Mr Oakley? It's all change in the C of E nowadays. Midnight Mass starts at eleven!'

It had sounded like a bit of peculiarly Disvan logic but proved to be true. *Midnight Mass—24/12/1990—11:00 p.m.* stated the noticeboard outside the church.

I accepted the anomaly, rode it and forgot it. Like the workings of the City of London, whence I commuted each day, life in Binscombe village was quite often a few degrees askew from normality. The secret was not to worry about it.

The bitter cold was less easy to sublimate. It was a brisk, frosty night and, with twenty minutes in hand before the service, I'd envisaged waiting inside the church. However, Mr Disvan restrained me from entering.

'Not yet,' he said, barring my way. 'There's a bit of a practice going on.'

I listened carefully. Sure enough, I could hear the sound of singing coming from somewhere within.

'Maybe they've started early,' I said. 'Let's go and see.'

Disvan was emphatic.

'No,' he said. 'We must wait for the practice to end.'

Okay, fair enough, I thought—but at the same time, I was now very cold, increasingly fed up and, truth be told, a bit sulky with it. First we didn't have to be late, now we had to hang around outside. What the hell was going on? Why was I being mucked about?

By now, other people were turning up and queuing patiently alongside us. To my surprise, and despite Disvan's opinion of them, some of the Argyll crowd, Mr Bretwalda, Mr Patel, Doctor Bani-Sadr et al arrived. They nodded politely to everyone and waited in silence.

I didn't feel so stoical and started to stamp my feet to restore life to them.

'It's the choir, is it?' I asked, addressing no one in particular.

Apparently I was speaking Albanian. The Binscomites exchanged blank looks and then ignored me.

'The singing,' I persisted, 'it's the choir, is it?'

'Um . . .' Disvan replied.

'They sound very cheerful.'

'Yes, Mr Oakley, they do, don't they?' He seemed pleased to have something he could agree to. 'And why shouldn't they at this time of year.'

'I don't recognize the tune though.'

Disvan raised his eyebrows as if shocked to the core.

'Don't you?'

Doctor Bani-Sadr disguised a snigger under the cover of a coughing fit. I was beginning to feel subtly got at.

'I mean, are they all little boys or something?' I asked. 'Because the voices are very high—shrill almost.'

And at that precise moment the singing rose to a crescendo and stopped. A deep silence followed. No one seemed inclined to break it.

Then the church door creaked open and a grinning face emerged from within.

'Good evening, Reverend Jagger,' said Mr Disvan. 'Merry Christmas to you!'

'And to you—to you all!' the vicar replied. 'Welcome to St Joseph's—please come in out of the cold.'

We did exactly that. It was nice and warm inside—and, apart from the Reverend Jagger, entirely empty.

'Where's the choir?' I asked Mr Disvan as we settled down in our pew. 'Where've they gone?'

'What choir?' he replied innocently.

I ground some enamel off my teeth and pretended to rise above it all. He was in one of his annoying moods.

Disvan had insisted on a seat near the front. This happened to place us in the shadow of the pulpit and under the vicar's eye. Happily, to start with, the holy man was safely occupied browsing a great bound Bible ('Looking for loopholes' whispered Mr Disvan) but soon enough he glanced up and caught our gaze. Vicars, like policemen, made me feel guilty without cause.

'Hello there, Mr Disvan,' he boomed. 'Glad you could make it. Good year?'

'Middling. And you?'

'Could be worse.'

'Looks like you'll have a fair crowd in tonight.'

They both surveyed the rapidly filling church. It was true, the front portion at least, was getting to be fully occupied.

'Oh yes,' Jagger agreed. 'And there'll be more before kick-off—you get all types at this service.'

This seemed to amuse them and they had a swift laugh-in from which I was excluded.

'Of course,' the vicar continued, 'I *hope* there's no trouble but there always is.'

'The times we live in,' said Disvan sadly—but he was still smiling.

'Yes, absolutely,' echoed Jagger—also beaming brightly. 'Still, it's an ill wind   eh?'

With that he returned to his reading.

'Trouble?' I hissed. 'What trouble?'

Mr Disvan didn't seem very alarmed.

'Well, you know how it is, Mr Oakley. Midnight Mass attracts these types, straight out of the pub.'

'Like us, you mean?'

[283]

'No. I mean drunks and yobbos and lager-louts, come to lark about and disrupt the service.'

'Oh.'

This didn't sound very promising. I don't like close physical contact (saving the sexual kind), particularly in the context of brawling with drunks.

People had continued to stream in, including, puzzlingly enough, the choir, who'd arrived in ones and twos and gone off to get changed. The front four or five pews were now jammed. The rest were much more thinly dotted with worshippers, anonymous latecomers, heavily wrapped up against the chill.

I was absorbed in staring at a crucifix and had calculated a 40:60 chance against God's existence when the service suddenly started.

The Reverend Jagger slammed his Bible shut and the organist abruptly piled into 'O little town of Bethlehem' as the clock in the tower above began to strike eleven.

Everyone bar me seemed prepared whereas I had to leap to my feet, grab a hymn book and desperately flick through it looking for the right page. I never did find it and had to hum along instead. Then we all sat down again.

'Dearly beloved . . .' said the Reverend Jagger—and so on.

It went along painlessly enough until the sermon. At that point the door crashed open and a rabble of riff-raff sauntered in. They came and sat uncomfortably close to us, only a couple of pews back, and started to make loud, inappropriate comments. One of them blew a raspberry (at least, I hope that's what it was) and their own incense of beer and Brut wafted before them. My back felt horribly vulnerable and I heard Mr Disvan sigh.

''Ere!' came an *EastEnders*-coached voice from their general direction, 'look at that poofteraaargh!'

Up to then I'd not dared to look round but instinct took over. The yobbos were being effortlessly hauled away by members of the congregation, their cries of protest (or worse) cut off by hands clamped over their mouths. It was a very neat, indeed, surgical, operation.

'I've never heard of a church with bouncers before,' I whispered to Disvan.

He smiled wisely.

'No? These came with the church.'

'But I don't recognize any of them.'

'You wouldn't, Mr Oakley; they're from before your time.'

'Pardon?'

'Nothing.'

'But why are they taking the yobs down into the crypt? Why not just chuck them out?'

Disvan smiled again but said nothing.

'And,' cried the Reverend Jagger, distracting me, 'there you see proof with your own eyes; the Lord *will* provide us with our daily bread, whoever we are, whatever we may be!'

The congregation tittered politely but I couldn't see the joke. It was all a bit puzzling. And was that someone pouring water down in the crypt or—sort of gobbling noises . . .?

The same process happened a few more times. Groups of undesirables fell in the church, misbehaved and were duly dragged away—not to be seen again. It must be getting awfully cramped in that crypt, I thought.

Naturally, I was full of admiration for the dark and silent bouncers. They appeared to be absolutely fearless and were doing a great job, overpowering the opposition and then keeping them out of the way. My only cavil was that some of them were taking too much interest in innocent little me. Every time I looked round it seemed that five or six pairs of eyes were fixed unflinchingly upon me. I found myself trying to act as respectable as possible, visibly joining in the prayers and shouting out the responses.

The final incident was when some tipsy adolescents chuntered in and started playing the fool. They too sat not far back from Mr Disvan and me, and their shrieks and cat-calls sounded much too close for comfort. Accordingly, when a powerful gust of wind raised the hair on the back of my head, I suspected a prank on their part and turned to protest. I was just in time to see some Levi 501s and a pair of trainers disappear through the trap door into the belfry.

It couldn't have been a bat carrying him, I insisted to myself; bats just don't grow that big.

The remaining youngsters were still in a state of shock, staring open-mouthed up at the roof.

''Kinnelll' said one but the rest were struck dumb.

It didn't save them. They too were manhandled (or possibly not manhandled—my suspicions were already alive and twitching) away down to the crypt.

'Right then,' said Jagger, 'let our voices, like our brother just now, rise up to the Lord—hymn number 30: 'While shepherds watched their flocks by night.'

I sang extra loud to drown out the eating noises I could hear coming from the crypt and directly above my head.

Absorbed in some pretty pressing thoughts, I still tried to pay at least outward attention to the service. We came to that point where everyone has to shake hands while trying not to look embarrassed. It was the chance I'd been waiting for.

The Reverend Jagger bowled down to us and muttered something about peace being with me. I felt far from at peace and held on to his proffered hand. Pointing discreetly in the direction of the crypt, I said, 'Um . . . vicar, what is . . . er, you know . . .'

'Oh, that,' he replied warmly. 'Don't worry about it, Mr Oakley, you're in no danger.'

'But . . .'

'Most old churches and graveyards have them, Mr Oakley—unquiet and unforgiven spirits. The problem is that they get terribly . . .'

'Hungry?' suggested Mr Disvan.

Jagger nodded.

'. . .or *empty* as the centuries go by. The way I see it, you can either exorcise them or—put 'em to some good use!'

A sense of humanist outrage made me open my mouth—but nothing came out.

'It's a good deal,' Disvan whispered to me and Jagger smiled modestly. 'In return for no trouble at other times, on Christmas Eve we let them have a little . . . feast.'

'I think of it as Christian charity,' said the vicar. 'They've got enough problems, poor things, without me imposing starvation as well. I mean, even the church mouse in Betjeman's poem got a slap-up meal *once* a year, at Harvest Festival. Binscombe's deceased black sheep have their party at Christmas, that's the only difference. You wouldn't begrudge them, Mr Oakley, if you knew how *much* they look forward to it!'

'We heard their celebration before we came in,' said Disvan.

'Yes,' said Jagger bashfully. 'They like to put on a little thank you concert for me—so sweet really. Woops! We're keeping everyone waiting—must be off.'

The service went on. As it did, Mr Disvan observed that I wasn't my usual happy self.

'Oh, come on, Mr Oakley!' he said. 'Don't be so po-faced; where's your Christmas spirit? Everything's got to live—even if it's not alive!'

I fought the temptation but couldn't resist glancing round. My gaze hit one of the shrouded figures at the rear. Before I could swivel back to safety, he or she or it noted my inattention and flashed a yellow, ravenous, smile.

'Now,' said the Reverend Jagger, 'we'll sing hymn number 390: 'Firmly I believe and truly!'

I sang along and sincerely hoped I was convincing.

CHRISTMAS ROSE

by Mary Williams

Mary Williams is one of Britain's most prolific
writers of ghost stories, and has also published
over 20 historical novels. The majority of these
are set in Cornwall where she has lived for over
40 years. Among her many interests are barge
life, mountain climbing, the theatre and Celtic
history.

S he stepped on to the bus hoping the conductor wouldn't notice
she was wearing bedroom slippers. But really! they had been so
difficult at the hospital, hiding her clothes away—even the full-
length cashmere coat that would have been welcome for the cold grey
afternoon. Still, her dressing gown could pass for a coat in the fading
light, and she'd been able to grab a headscarf from a peg when she
reached the long visitors' corridor. Luckily there'd been no one about.
Visiting hours were over, and nurses and orderlies were having a gossip
and cups of tea at the far end of the long ward. What a relief it had been
to reach the swing doors opening from the maze of dreary sterile
corridors, down the few steps to the street—to feel the sting of cold air
and thin snow against her cheeks and lips, and then the jarring groan of
the vehicle making its way from the town with her safely inside. Of
course, it should not have been like that. There should have been
friendly transport organized to convey her home; she was quite well
enough—completely recovered from the stupid accident that had landed
her for so long in that huge antiseptic-smelling place. There had been no
legitimate reason at all forcibly to retain her just as though she was at
death's door or some sort of criminal.

'Yes, dear!'—'No dear!'—'Just be patient now, and rest.' 'We don't want you to have a relapse, do we?' 'Now lie back and have your tablet, dear—'

Tablets! Pills, potions! God! What a travesty. And what right had they to be so *patronizing* and bossy? So *dumb*! Couldn't they have admitted she was well? Realized that the one thing essential to her regaining complete good health was a glimpse of her home and of Richard who was due back at Wildcroft the following day? She had told them and *told* them. He'd said so in his last letter. 'I've got leave, and will be with you on Christmas Eve. See you're waiting. Trust me, darling. I love you. Richard.'

She trusted him; oh, yes, she did—just as he trusted her. She'd be at the front window or gate watching for his tall uniformed figure appearing round the bend in the lane leading to their cottage. Nothing would deter her now—nothing in the world. She'd escaped officialdom, and stupid constricting rules that would have prevented the beloved meeting after so long apart. Richard! her young gallant husband and love. Darling Richard, she thought as the bus stopped briefly allowing a passenger to dismount. At last, at last they'd be together again.

At this point her thoughts were broken by the bus jerking on again. Glancing round she saw with surprise that she was the last remaining occupant. But then Wildcroft *was* rather off the beaten track—remote and apart from other dwellings and human beings. She'd have to get off at the corner of the lane and walk a short distance, leaving the vehicle to continue to Haymere, the terminus.

It would not be long now.

'Please stop at the crossroads,' she called to the conductor, repeating the request because her voice, even in her own ears, sounded thin and rather faint. That was normal of course, after such a wearying period in 'that place'.

The man merely half turned his head, and brushed his cheek, as though a fly had touched it.

A morose sort of character, she thought resignedly. But perhaps he'd been extra busy that day—the day before Christmas Eve. Or perhaps he was lonely, poor man.

She shivered slightly. The very idea of loneliness always oppressed her. She would have been unbearably lonely during Richard's long absence if her life had not been so completely filled with thoughts of him—of looking after their lovely cottage—planning constant improvements and surprises for the day when he returned, redecorating and painting—keeping the garden in order, seeing that old Harris, who spent one morning each week there, kept the ornamental shrubs and borders tidy—well-pruned in the Spring, but not *too* much—he could be a little too free with the secateurs unless a watchful eye was kept on him, that was the trouble. Still, so long as he'd remembered to place belljars over the budding Christmas roses during November she wouldn't complain. Richard had planted them the first year following their marriage and how profuse they'd been that winter. 'A symbol of love,' he'd said. If it hadn't been for the wretched war . . . But she must not remember the war now. It was the future that mattered—tomorrow and Richard's return. Oh, how she hoped the roses would be in bloom. So white, so pure—whiter than driven snow under leaden skies. White, white!—hospital wards were white too!—her mind wavered as the past and present became curiously intermingled. She forced her eyes to the window where spangled drops of sleet and snow blew wraith-like against the glass. The undulating rise of hills appeared steeper than she remembered in the feathery fading light—ethereal-looking tumps bordering a thread of winding lane taken intermittently into clouded swirls of rising wind. She'd forgotten how far from the town Wildcroft was; all other sights and sounds of human habitation were now far, far behind. There was no sound but the soughing of air and faint crunch of wheels as the slope steepened. The driver's form had become no more than a blurred, hunched shape at the wheel.

She tried to speak, to call—'Please don't pass my cottage. It's ahead there—on the right—somewhere.' But she couldn't see it, and no words left her lips.

Time died. Nothing registered, but the soundless motion of crawling forever upwards in a grey journey through a grey wilderness of haunted half-forgotten memories, and then suddenly the shrouding mist was pierced by a quivering flash of the day's last light. She lifted a hand to her eyes and the bus came to a halt. Somehow she got to her feet, although she felt no contact with the wooden floor—her legs were paper-frail, weightless as the soft brush of chill air on her face. For a moment, moving, almost floating to the entrance, she felt herself panic. Her bag! where was it? She hadn't paid. Would the conductor try to stop her getting off? But he couldn't, not now, because her cottage was silhouetted there against the snow, its path curling welcomingly from the door in a rosy muted glow from a window.

So Mrs Miggs, her daily, had been, thank God. And tomorrow Richard would be here.

Richard!

She pressed forward, eyes wide and staring, heart expectant, as the stinging wind tore the headscarf from her streaming hair, leaving it free and wild as the cobwebs blown from the leafless trees. The pink glow dimmed. All was a pearl-pale vista of light and shade not only from snow, but with the frosted clumps of blossoming flowers bordering paths and ice-glittering lawn. A little cry of joy—or was it only the wind's sigh?— stirred the air. He was *there*—the beloved uniformed figure leaning over the gate, with his face turned towards her—a day early, but in time to greet her after the long, long parting.

Seconds later two shadowed figures became one, and, arms round each other, drifted soundless up the garden path to be taken through the waiting door.

Next morning, early on Christmas Eve, a nearby farmer who happened to be passing that way paused at the gate of the cottage garden. Funny, he thought, that those Christmas roses should've come to bloom again after so long. But kind of right for that particular day, which was supposed to herald good things for the world. New birth. And how profuse they were, a whole garden of them. Well, it was good soil round there, but the cottage had come to be no more than a ruin, and ought to be pulled down properly or else rebuilt. Houses were needed these days.

He mentioned the matter later to a crony of his over a pint of ale in the Golden Cow.

'More'n forty year', he said, 'since young Luke Forest was killed. Flying he was, in the war. And Alice his young wife never got over it. So sick with grief you could say, she ran straight in front of a car and got crippled for good. Later they took her to the asylum—been there ever since.' He touched his head significantly. 'Mad as a coot. But you must've heard the story.'

'Ah, well, she's over it now,' his friend remarked almost fatuously.

'What d'you mean?'

'Found last night in a hospital corridor stone dead on the floor all dressed up in a headscarf and dressing gown, smiling too—just as though she was off on an outing, poor old thing. Postman told me. They were used to it, though. She was always trying to get away. Funny thing was, there was a flower on her chest. A Christmas rose. How it got there, God alone knows.'

A statement perhaps more profound than he knew.

ACKNOWLEDGEMENTS

The Publisher has made every effort to contact the Copyright holders, but wishes to apologize to those he has been unable to trace. Grateful acknowledgement is made for permission to reprint the following:

'Marwood's Ghost Story' by Marjorie Bowen. Reprinted by permission of Hilary Long.

'The Chinese Apple' by Joseph Shearing. Reprinted by permission of Hilary Long.

'Diary of a Poltergeist' by Ronald Duncan. Reprinted by permission of the Trustees of the Ronald Duncan Literary Foundation.

'The Leaf-Sweeper' by Muriel Spark. Reprinted from *The Stories of Muriel Spark* published by The Bodley Head.

The following stories are reproduced by permission of the authors:

'The Illuminated Office' © 1990 by Derek Stanford; 'The Case of the Seven Santas' © 1990 by H.R.F. Keating; 'Mage of the Monkeys' © 1990 by Sydney J. Bounds; 'Nostalgia' © 1990 by Maggie Ross; 'The Reluctant Murderer' © 1990 by Roger F. Dunkley; 'Cyanide for Christmas' © 1990 by John S. Glasby; 'The Cloak of deSouvre' © 1990 by Elizabeth Fancett; 'The Soldier' © 1990 by Roger Johnson; 'The Case of the Fiery Messengers' © 1990 by Ron Weighell; 'The Codex' © 1990 by David G. Rowlands; 'Peace on Earth, Goodwill to Most Men' © 1990 by John Whitbourn; 'Christmas Rose' © 1990 by Mary Williams.